Rachel Gillian North has a keen interest in Equine Podiatry and enjoys helping others to try and achieve healthy hooves, in addition to keeping her own two barefoot horses near Whiddon Down, Devon. Rachel also helps with the family business providing branding and website help to local entrepreneurs as well as having a part time job working for a large organisation. In her spare time she loves to write and be with her animals.

'A Horse Called Red' follows her debut novel, 'A Horse Called Ambition.' With both books, she wanted to tell stories which real horse lovers, with real overdrafts and fears, could relate to.

It's not all about riding; it's mainly about getting covered in mud, gruelling hard work, especially in the winter months, and the juggling act equestrians must perform to balance their horses with the rest of their lives – emotionally and practically!

A Horse Called Red

Rachel Gillian North

Indigo Dreams Publishing

First Edition: A Horse Called Red

First published in Great Britain in 2016 by:
Indigo Dreams Publishing Ltd
24 Forest Houses
Halwill
Beaworthy
EX21 5UU
www.indigodreams.co.uk

ISBN 978-1-910834-22-0

Designed and typeset in Minion Pro by Indigo Dreams.

Cover design by Indigo Dreams, artwork supplied by K Taran-Tula & R G North

Printed and bound in Great Britain by 4Edge Ltd
www.4edge.co.uk

For those too special to be grounded by this reality any longer.

Thank you to the horses, you make joy possible. In particular to Shiny, my red horse, for telling me everything; to my confident Squeak, for challenging me every day to be better; and to Lord Revel, a king amongst us, as stoic as any soldier, wise as any scribe.

To Liz, Sam, Spencer, Beccy, and my ever patient parents, thank you for your help in making this book become real.
To Ronnie and Dawn of Indigo Dreams, for your love of Soxx, and your faith in me. I am grateful beyond words.
To K, you are more perfect than you will ever know, thank you for being your you to my me.

A Horse Called Red

Dear Tina,

Thank you so much for
Sharing Lottie with us

Love
Rach xx

Without judgement,
I am measured
Without words,
Without complications,
I am known better than anyone could know me
My actions reflected in his shiny coat
My virtue sealed with each greeting
Amongst the contrived,
I have a baseline for my character
With rules simple as air,
He loves me only for the goodness in my soul

Chapter One

Regret is a burden.

Rosie Hall lay motionless on an unmade bed. Long chocolate brown hair fanned out over the bare mattress. Cold blue eyes fixed unseeing on the white textured ceiling. As usual, she felt numb. Any physical energy her body might have had was sapped by the dark cloud over her head.

It seemed like an eternity ago, but life had not always been like this. The spare bedroom had once been a place she bustled in and out of, merrily preparing for guests. Now, it was the only room she could rest in.

The baby had taken up what had once been the office. Since her husband, Matt, had been working away from home during the week, her own bedroom made her feel lonely. The sofa in their small but cosy lounge seemed too big when she had it to herself.

She didn't beg Matt not to take the promotion he had been offered, which came with the condition that he work out of the company's Oxford office. It was a three hour drive from their cottage, nestled in one of the many valleys which made up Devon's beautiful Flackdown Hills.

Despite the logic in the whole family moving closer to his new work, Matt hadn't even suggested that they relocate. He knew how much Rosie adored their home and that she was planning to return to her job in Exeter once her maternity leave had finished.

He had simply found himself a flat to rent in the city, no drama, to use during the week. He returned as soon as he could on a Friday evening to begin his precious weekend at home.

He was a good husband. The job was further away from the long held dream of starting a business of his own, but a step closer to the stability he felt he should offer his family. He had taken the position without hesitation because it meant a bigger salary, which meant a better quality of life for his wife and baby.

Only it didn't, because Rosie's quality of life had diminished more in the past six months than she could ever have made better with money.

She hated the nursery, with its expensive cot and designer wall paper. She hated the new fridge with its integral ice maker which gurgled periodically and made her jump. She even managed to frown whenever she turned on the hot tap and the brand new boiler remained silent as a network of shiny pipes brought forth consistent temperatures.

The spare bedroom was the only one in the house which had not been tarnished with the benefit of their new found affluence, so she didn't hate it.

She knew she wasn't allowed to hate the baby - that it meant you were unnatural if you hated your own child. She knew she wasn't allowed to hate Matt for taking hold of a brilliant opportunity.

The only thing she still loved with all her heart was Red.

She sat up so that she could look out of the window. Sure enough there he was, mid doze, resting a hind leg. The six year old American Quarter horse was handsome and sturdy, a rich red roan with four white socks and a refined almost Arabian head. She drank in his powerful quarters, his gentle half closed eye. He was stood in the bottom corner of the field closest to the house, even though his companion, a black Shetland pony called Peat, was grazing at the top. It was as though the horse knew it comforted his master to have him close by. She opened the window and leant on the sill.

'Hey, my darling...' She spoke softly to the animal, gently waking him in order to hear his dusky whicker and see his diamond shaped ears prick towards her.

She smiled at his sleepiness and for a second enjoyed the sun on her face.

But only for a second.

'Whaaaaaaaaaaaaaaaaaaaaaaaaaa!' Came the first of Eve's cries.

Red put his ears back, curling his nostrils into a sneer. He continued to scowl as he moved away to join Peat where the sound couldn't reach him.

'For fuck's sake.' Rosie wearily made her way towards Eve's room, deciding to pick her up to prepare the bottle, rather than enduring the sound while the milk heated.

The four month old baby stopped crying as soon as she saw her mother and a gurgling smile lit up her bright blue eyes. Rosie picked her daughter up, holding her where the child couldn't turn its head towards her breast, and made her way to the kitchen.

20 miles south in the village of Stoke Rewe, Juliette Rogers called her horse.

'Romeo!'

The big Irish bred hunter swished his chestnut tail and carried on grazing. He was trying to ignore his owner.

'Where for art thou Romeo...?' Jules called again, smiling at his hurried snatches of pasture. He lifted his head and blew a huffing sigh out of the generous nostrils which finished off his proud Roman nose. 'Come on Rome you know you want a ride really, we can't let you get fat!'

The horse ambled towards her, resigned to his fate. She giggled.

He was kept in a sparse and well grazed paddock to avoid him putting on weight, but the recent downpours, interlaced with bright spring sunshine, had made the grass taste a little sweeter.

'It will still be there when you get back, but you will have earned it!'

She had owned Romeo for nearly 5 years. Up until recently he had been stabled at a farm near her house in the village of Kysford, but, in a bold and slightly scary move for a pragmatic solicitor, whose decisions were usually calculated fastidiously, she had sold her home and invested in her friend's Arabian Race Horse training business.

She hadn't expected her life to turn out like this. She had expected the usual things. But that was perhaps the reason for her decision. In the absence of being able to bear a child and the absence of anyone even close to a husband, she needed something to be as big and important as those things.

After she and her long term partner had split up and Tristan had moved out, she had lived in the house she owned, alone, for over a year. There had been a few casual boyfriends along the way, but no one special enough for her to share her life and her space with had come along. So, she packed her things, her beloved Border Collie dog, Ziggy and Romeo, and started a new adventure. Jules had never been one to rest on her laurels; progress was her watchword, however unconventional it might turn out to be.

She wondered where her friend and business partner was. Gillian Newman had disappeared first thing that morning to 'run errands' which, knowing Gill, meant she was doing something Jules wouldn't approve of.

Already close friends, events just over a year ago had cemented their bond for life.

Romeo, Gill's Arabian mare Khaleb's Ambition and

prize stallion Monday's Eclipse had been stolen from Gill's yard in broad daylight. All of the horses had been recovered, but not without months of torture as they imagined the fate of their beloved animals at the hands of those cruel enough to rip a creature from it's home.

It was behind them now.

Gill had tried to persuade Jules that she should live in the house with her. The large square building sat half way up the drive which led to the horse barn, surrounded by the paddocks which were filled with horses in training, broodmares and liveries. Jules had declined, preferring instead to use part of the proceeds of sale from her cottage to commission the erection of a single story annexe. The build represented her own space, with the comfort of an integral door between her and the bustle of family life. As much as she loved Gill, and was fond of Gill's younger partner George, she did not want to play gooseberry. Especially as the unlikely couple could rarely keep their hands off one another.

No, Jules would be happy in her own little two bed extension with the stylish kitchen she had chosen and of course, with her Ziggy. The two year old dog was agile in both body and brain, entirely black apart from a jagged blaze of white running down over his head and between his intense amber eyes.

Ziggy sat patiently while Jules groomed Romeo on the yard next to the American style barn which housed what was now, at least partly, her livelihood. Precious Arabian racers bred for speed and stamina filled each of the looseboxes waiting, not always patiently, for their chance to run.

Kelly, Newmans full time groom, was out with two of the yard's racers, riding one and leading the other. She often exercised the horses two at a time on long hacks in the mornings and in the afternoons she and Gill, and sometimes Jules herself if

13

she finished work early enough, would take the horses in strings out to the new all-weather gallops and give them a pipe-opener around the two miles of dirt.

'Ms Rogers...um...I think you'd better come down to the house.' said Bert, who appeared behind Jules and made her jump. Bert was one of the builders involved in the project to erect Jules' new home. He nervously wrung his cap in his hands and eyed Romeo as a shrew might regard a badger.

'Tis the kitchen see, they delivered it and we was gonna start fitting it, but the dimensions is all wrong and the plumbing for the dishwasher ain't in yet.' Bert's Devonshire tones tailed off and he stepped back in horror as Romeo casually used his tail to dissuade the first of the spring flies from landing on his strong hind legs.

'Cant Keith deal with it?' Jules stood up from fastening a brushing boot to Romeo's foreleg and tried not to smirk at Bert's terror. 'I mean, Keith is in charge, if there are decisions to be made he can make them. I don't mind where the dishwasher goes as long as I have one.'

'Keith ain't ere Ms, called away to another job we're doing over Exeter way...' Bert set his cap back on his head, 'thing is we'll be behind schedule if we don't get it started today...'

'Right.' Jules tore the Velcro apart and pulled the boot back off. 'I only had an hour before I had to start work again and I really wanted a ride, but, down to the house I must go.'

'Sorry Ms....' Bert shuffled backwards away from Romeo and waddled down the drive towards the house.

Jules stood with her hands on her hips, looking at Romeo, who she could have sworn was grinning like a Cheshire cat.

By kind permission of the partner at her law firm, she was allowed to work from home two days a week and she loved a quick lunchtime ride to clear her head from whatever case she had spent the morning working on. She let Romeo into his paddock. He gleefully trotted back to same spot and resumed his rhythmic munching.

'There's always tonight Rome...'

Every time Rosie bent over to pick up another collection of droppings, she could smell the sick in her hair. As she pooh picked the horse field, she breathed in the pungent scent of one of Peat's offerings for the dung heap and relished the alternative to vomit.

Eve had thrown up nearly all of her mid-morning feed and promptly fallen back to sleep. Rosie knew it was her fault, she had encouraged the tiny baby to drink more formula than would have been comfortable in her stomach. Feeding Eve and the midwife's approval of her steady growth seemed to be the only thing she felt like she did right and today she had even messed that up.

She stood up straight and removed her gauntlets to fish the baby monitor out of her jeans. She held the device up to her ear and was relieved to hear Eve's soft breathing where she lay in her cot. Matt was always telling her to ask Mrs Mathers from the house up the lane to come in and sit with Eve while she did the horses, but Rosie felt the baby monitor was sufficient and she wasn't about to call the old lady every time she wanted to pop outside.

Mrs Mathers, with her steel grey hair and supreme knowledge of all things baby. She appreciated the on-call sitter but she didn't appreciate the constant criticism with its sugar coating of helping her become a better mother.

Peat, who had been grazing just behind Rosie, chose the moment she bent back over to stomp expectantly towards her.

"Hello you little monkey, it's not dinner time yet!" She spoke to the pony while she continued with her chore, which dissatisfied the tiny gelding and he demanded her full attention by sharply biting her bottom. Rosie fell forward and landed belly first on one of Red's elephant sized droppings, covering her sweatshirt in still warm excrement.

"Oh Jesus Christ, you bloody sod!" Rosie exclaimed, clutching her throbbing cheek with her gloved hand. Little monkey didn't seem appropriate any more. Rosie glared at the pony, who was marching towards the stables, expecting that she would now feed him.

"Not very likely!" Rosie called after the ample black rump and started to get up out of the crap. Red nuzzled the top of her head and she used his neck as an arm-hold to get herself upright.

Hobbling and fed up, Rosie made her way back towards the house to get out of her filthy clothes and wash her smelly hair.

She checked on Eve before running a bath. She knew the baby would wake again soon and decided to take the opportunity to briefly soak her aching behind before the next round of child and horse care duties began. Now that winter was almost at an end and the horses were once again turned out full time, things were decidedly easier. But, with every change in season came a new routine to dive into and Rosie resented all the little things she hadn't been able to do because Eve took up so much time. The fences needed a tidy up, a new section of rail here, an overhanging bush there. Red's winter rugs needed washing and re-proofing ready for the autumn. But, like so many other things she used to take being able to do for granted, Rosie was having to ignore these jobs and resign herself to Eve's constant needs.

Rosie stripped in the kitchen and put her soiled clothes

straight into the washing machine, along with the collection of baby grows she had been meaning to set going. Nothing got done unless she did it herself.

Naked, she headed towards the bathroom to check on the water. The phone rang as she passed its charging cradle in the hall. She snatched at it, hoping it would be Jules or Gill. She knew her friends had been busy with the build and looming racing season, but she still longed to talk about something other than which nappy rash cream worked best. Something the collection of new mum's she had befriended at baby-group seemed to want to discuss at unreasonable length.

'Rosiekins! Give me an excuse to leave early!'

Rosie was pleasantly surprised to hear Valerie's voice.

'Umm....do you want to visit?!'

'Do I ever. Need to escape. I will leave on the dot of 3:30 and be with you shortly thereafter! Do you need anything?'

Rosie pondered.

'Chocolate.'

'Done.'

Rosie replaced the handset and smiled. Val visited every few weeks despite having her own family and hectic schedule to contend with. It was great to have a connection with her office. She didn't feel remotely ready for work and still had another 6 months before she would have to go back, but talking with her favourite colleague and catching up on the office gossip was nearly as good as talking about horses with her favourite equine friends.

Rosie made a mental note to ask Val how one of the more chaotic clients she had been trying to house was getting on in supportive lodgings. Rosie had worked for almost 12 years at the City Council, Val had been there even longer. They both answered to "Relocation Officer" and their job consisted of finding accommodation for people who needed help and stability to get their lives back on track. Rosie loved her job and was good at it. She certainly preferred it to being at the beck and call of an infant, which she wasn't very good at.

Rosie ran to the bathroom, suddenly aware of her nakedness and possibly overflowing bath.

The water was just right. As she dipped her toe into the deep white panelled bathtub her hair fell forwards, reminding her of the sick. She didn't really want a rancid milk infusion. She withdrew her foot and stood in front of the mirror. It was too late to have a shower and she wanted to soak her bottom.

She didn't want sicky hair.

She didn't want to be alone all week. She didn't want to push a buggy around a supermarket. She didn't want her life to be a constant mire of never ending tasks.

Her heart pounded and the tiles swam at her feet. She felt a sinking certainty that she had no choices. There was no going back now.

With a set jaw and emotionless eyes, Rosie reached for the black handled scissors Matt used to trim his beard from the shelf beside the mirror.

Soft falls of two foot-long hair slid over her bare shoulders and drifted to the floor as she worked on autopilot to cut a straight line around the nape of her neck.

Only when she had finished did she meet her own eyes in the mirror.

Staring back at her was a severe, sad, naked woman. The short bob hairstyle was one she had not had since she was a girl. She recognised the twelve year old, the one who had been ecstatic with joy when she got her first horse. A horse she had never sold and shared the majority of her life to date with.

Now the tears fell, but not for own plight; they fell for

Harry.

The 15hh grey Welsh cob had died six months ago and she just didn't know who she was any more.

She didn't like her new life.

She was fond of Peat, even now with tooth marks on her bottom, but he had only been borrowed to keep Red company because Harry was gone. He was the wrong horse in the right field. Everything she had aimed for in life up until that day in November had been about Harry. She had only purchased Red as a four year old two years before, because Harry had been ready to retire from being ridden. She and Matt had worked so hard to be able to afford the cottage with its little orchard and paddock, so that Harry could live with them at last after years of renting space at livery yards and farms. They had toiled and slaved with limited funds to build stables on the land so that Harry would have a warm bed in winter.

Now she had a baby and a Shetland pony and an absent husband and none of the joy that came with achieving the impossible, because there was money enough to simply buy whatever she needed.

Rosie climbed into the bath and sat in tepid water. She looked over at the hair on the floor. She felt the regret that would probably last until it grew back.

She had made the ultimate step towards conformity. Now she had a sensible haircut to match her grown up life. She might as well get herself a people carrier and start collecting coupons.

'Oh Harry...' Rosie drew her up knees and wrapped her arms around herself, 'I miss you.'

Jules stood in the skeleton of her new home, surrounded by bare plasterboard and a mess of pipe work, while Bert and the rest of the crew looked expectantly at her waiting for an answer.

'Look...I don't care where the dishwasher goes, so shuffle all the units up that way and stick it over there.' Jules gesticulated vaguely, but it seemed to satisfy the men, who nodded and dispersed. The basic structure had come to life so quickly, but now it all seemed to be slowing down and she was dying to move in and get her things out of storage at last. She had been living out of boxes for three months and she'd had enough of never knowing where anything was.

She glanced out of the kitchen window, which overlooked the driveway leading up to the horse barn. She smiled to see Gill trotting towards her grinning. The slender but freakishly strong 44 year old was one of the most attractive women Jules knew. Shoulder length naturally blond hair danced around her regal jaw line and high cheek bones. The sparkle in her pale blue eyes softened her air of elegance.

Despite only hunting for clothes in charity shops and feeling most comfortable in her old jeans and a rugby shirt, Gill always seemed to look like a film star to Jules.

Jules had a vast and beautiful collection of suits for work and regularly had her thick ebony hair professionally cut. But, for all the attention she lavished on her appearance she never felt like she came close to the timeless style Gill achieved without trying.

Jules endured a battle with her appetite. She loved food but it didn't seem to love her and she fluctuated between sizes 12 and 14. She was incredibly sexy in a delicious curvaceous way, but always appeared ham faced and dumpy to herself. The only things she didn't hate about her body were her perfectly rounded and buoyant breasts, they were her saving grace.

'Come!' Gill popped her head through the plastic sheeted gap which would be replaced by a kitchen door if the glaziers ever brought the right size.

'Come where..?' Jules caught the excitement in Gill's voice and couldn't help but be intrigued, 'I haven't had my ride and I have to start work again soon. Bloody kitchen people cocked up.'

'Never mind that, this is worth it - come along now!' Gill skipped across the patch of mud which would eventually become a patio garden, and let herself through the small gateway onto the drive.

Jules sighed and ran after her friend. When she caught up with Gill, the older woman linked arms with her.

'Now then. You might be a bit annoyed with me because this wasn't a planned spend...'

Jules rolled her eyes.

'Oh dear.'

'But you will love it Jules, I promise!'

Jules bit back a retort. In addition to a well needed cash investment to improve the facilities at Newmans, her most valuable contribution to the business to date had been her attention to the jumbled finances. There were no more piles of feed merchant's bills or envelopes of cash from livery owners dotted about the office. Now they ran a tight ship where accounts were kept on a spreadsheet and every expense was documented to offset the tax bill.

Gill had been dissuaded from impulse purchases and the best price was found for each item the yard needed. Gill had been very good so far, but Jules was anxious now that her old habits had not quite died.

Gill let go of Jules' arm and gestured for her to stand behind the horsebox which was parked across the yard. Gleefully Gill flipped the catches and hauled on the ramp. She skipped up the rubber clad incline and stood before a large paper wrapped rectangle.

'Are you ready?!'

'I guess so.' Jules smiled in spite of herself.

Gill tore at the paper and it fell away to reveal a smoothly lacquered white sign with carefully carpentered edges and proud black letters. A herd of Arabian horses galloped across the bottom in silhouette.

Newman & Rogers
Barefoot Arabian Racing, Stud and Livery Yard
www.barefootarabians.co.uk

'It's to go beside the main gates; Bert said he would put it up for us tomorrow morning! I wanted to wait and let you come home from work and see it there, but I had to show you.' Gill grinned as Jules stepped into the box.

'I don't know what to say Gill!' Jules was incredibly touched. She had been happy to invest the money for the expected revenue and the opportunity to utilise some business acumen, she had not even thought about having her name above the door.

'Say – Whoooooo hooooooo!' Gill laughed and put her arms around the young woman she admired so much.

Jules enveloped Gill and squeezed.

'It's your business though, you do all the horse work and the planning and training – I didn't expect you to change the name of the yard!'

'I know you didn't and that's why it felt absolutely right to do it.' Gill held Jules' shoulders and looked straight into her wide hazelnut eyes. 'I don't know how I can ever thank you for what you have done for me. Even this sign seems too small a gesture, so don't even start to question it – it's the beginning of great partnership.'

Jules smiled.

'Now, get back down to the house and hurry up and finish your work so we can go up to the gallops later!'

'Yes Mum!' Jules turned to head back to the house, 'Thanks Gill.'

'Don't mention it. Oh – before I forget, the sign maker is sending a jpeg of the artwork so we can use it for the website and our headed paper and stuff.'

Jules nodded enthusiastically but then started to laugh.

'Did you just say jpeg?'

Gill put her hands on her hips.

'Don't mock me. I am much better at computers now!'

Jules raised her eyebrows.

'Yes, ok, I had to ask him what it meant...'

Jules cackled as she strolled down the drive. She gazed over at Romeo who had stuffed himself and fallen asleep in the shade cast by the Leylandii which bordered the paddock. The future seemed as bright as the afternoon sun and Jules could easily have burst with happiness.

'Oh my...'

Val had opened her mouth to compliment Rosie's new hairstyle but the former vision of girlish curls and dreamy smiles looked so harsh, she didn't know what to say.

'I know.' Rosie burst into tears and Val gently pulled her in for a comforting hug.

'Rash decision?'

'Mmmm.' Rosie mumbled into the larger woman's comforting shoulder.

'You know it will grow back.'

'Mmmm.'

'But in the meantime we need to tidy it up - you look like

Edward Scissorhands had a go before he got the hang of it.'

Rosie giggled through her tears but then cried harder.

'What is Matt going to say? He is back tomorrow and I don't know how I am going to face him. He loved my hair.' Rosie part-wailed in Val's ear.

'Why did you do it Rosie?'

'That would take a while.'

'Get me some scissors. You talk, I'll utilise my hairdressing prowess. Brought up three kids on a budget, got pretty good.'

'Thanks Val, I am so glad you are here. I'm so lonely.'

'Oh Rosie, you seemed fine last week?'

'It's an act Val, I have been pretending I am fine but I'm not. I am not cut out for motherhood and I miss Harry so much I can barely make myself get out of bed in the morning and Matt is never here...this wasn't what I wanted.' Rosie's voice trailed off as Val took her hand.

'Scissors, then you tell me everything.'

Rosie nodded and led Val to the kitchen.

By the time Val had finished shaping Rosie's hair into a style which at least looked like it was intentional, she was trying to form a plan. Part of the reason Val and Rosie got on and worked so well together was that despite their difference in years, when they saw a problem they didn't moan about it, they looked for a solution and they carried it off without masses of fuss. They were do-ers.

As Val combed through the chin length waves which were springing up into buoyant curls as the hair dried, she despaired for Rosie.

Rosie was the together one, Val knew, amongst her friends and the rest of their colleagues. She understood how hard it would be for her to talk to Jules and Gillian and even Matt.

How could you, as the one everyone went to with their problems, fall apart and not be able to cope? How could you, as the one who had laughed in the office as you talked about the new life growing inside you and your plans for its future, talk about the feelings of regret you now had?

Val put down the brush and patted Rosie's shoulders.

'Go and have a look – Toni & Guy couldn't have done a better job.'

Rosie stood up and smiled at Val and Val decided she looked rather beautiful despite her shorn appearance.

Val set about sweeping the kitchen floor and then hunted for a dustpan and brush. She opened one of the kitchen cupboards thinking that there must be one somewhere.

'God that looks loads better, thank you Val.' Rosie came back into the kitchen to find Val stooped over and staring into the cupboard she wished her friend hadn't opened.

'Rosie...what on earth?'

'Oh I just haven't got round to sorting it all out.'

Rosie tried to sound casual.

'But Rosie, these are all Eve's clothes - what are you dressing her in?'

'She's a little baby she doesn't care what she wears!'

Val continued to stare into the cupboard. Piles of adorable baby outfits, soft toys and presents, some not even unwrapped, filled the cupboard under the sink. The cupboard you would have expected to contain bleach, maybe a dustpan and brush, contained delicate baby things which should have been adorning the nursery and child.

'Rosie this is a bit...'

'A bit what?' Rosie folded her arms, staunch in her resolve that Val was overreacting.

'It's a bit...odd?'

'She doesn't know! She doesn't wake up and demand Prada! It's just easier to have her wear the baby-grows, it saves on washing.'

'Yes, but her toys – and don't you dress her when you go out?'

Rosie's arms dropped to her sides, she was going to have to admit defeat.

'She doesn't go out. Mrs Mathers watches her when I need to run errands.'

'Oh Rosie.' Val stopped looking in the cupboard and turned to face her. She put a hand on her friend's shoulder and addressed her with meaning, 'You do know this is wrong don't you?'

Rosie stirred Red's dinner. She gazed around the feed room. Harry's rugs and tack were still on their pegs. She didn't want to give them away, but it seemed silly to keep them. She sat down on the concrete floor, trying to think of something to do with them that wouldn't feel like a betrayal, but wouldn't be a shrine either.

Harry's empty feed bucket sat on the floor in the middle of the room. She had to walk round it all the time. It had no place. It had always either been in his stable with him, or full of the next feed ready for the next mealtime.

She didn't want to put it away, it would be like admitting he was gone, disrespectful. Sometimes she sat on the floor next to it, and imagined his soft muzzle eagerly lipping up fibre mash.

She thought about the times she had let him down. Like when he had dropped weight because he couldn't chew the haylage she was feeding him. She reprimanded herself for the months that had passed when she had tried to ignore the condition slowly dropping off the horse, thinking that it meant he was coming close to the end of his life. The equine dentist's report had clearly shown he didn't have many teeth left and he had gained weight nicely once her feeding regime changed.

Then there was the time he had started bucking and she had schooled him harder thinking it was bad behaviour, until she had realised his saddle no longer fit his ageing back.

She allowed such thoughts to plague her, tortured herself with the memories she had learned from, made up for, and let go of once already. Harry in his wisdom had forgiven her every time, she was only human after all, but she would not forgive herself so easily. She couldn't mourn him properly while she allowed those thoughts to eat at her, filling her head with regret. It suited her to beat herself up continuously, because she was not ready to celebrate his memory or give thanks for his long, predominantly happy life with her.

She leant over the feed bucket and placed her hands inside it. She loved the horse so much, she overflowed with emotion at the thought of him, but could not redirect it, was not prepared to allow herself to feel that much again.

Val had sent Rosie out to care for the horses. She would be in the house fussing over Eve and undoubtedly moving everything from the cupboard into the nursery. Rosie ought to have felt relief, she supposed. But she didn't. The anxiety was still there. The feeling that everything was wrong and that she couldn't find her way back to right, was as strong as usual.

The dreams she had contributed to her anxiousness, topping up her fear by re-infecting her almost every night. Because the dreams were so vivid, and so persistent, they consumed her and transferred into her waking life. The dreams varied in content, but the beginning and end were always the same. She would find herself trapped inside the Cottage, unable to get outside to Red, and Harry, who was always still alive in the dream. Then Eve would start to scream, and Rosie would dash from room to room trying to find the baby, but Eve would always vanish just before Rosie got to her, the pain in her ears visceral despite it being a dream. It seemed to have no end. It made her feel like her mental health was deteriorating.

So, until today, she had made all the right moves and done all the right things not to raise suspicion or alarm. But she was a consummate actress, with a secret cupboard, as a result.

Now Val knew, she would force Rosie to get help.

It just made her feel more trapped, even further away from the person she wanted to be.

After she lost Harry the pain had been acute, uncontrollably public. Tears in floods arrived without warning every time the memory of her horse touched one of her senses. Her hands in the morning expecting his soft fur, her eyes as they registered fading daylight in the evening, when an old horse needed nutrition. She physically felt like she should be using her body to look after him, even though he wasn't there.

Everyone had been so sympathetic, putting the extent of her grief down to the fact that she was heavily pregnant.

Unwittingly, those around her gave her pain a deadline.

She would feel better when the baby came, they said. It was expected that Eve would make everything right in her life to the extent that she had gone along with it.

Everything wasn't right though, she was merely playing a role. New mum was the title of her character, something she was instead of a person.

Inside, behind the mask, she was frightened of her own shadow. She retraced her steps to check her own tasks, almost to the point of being obsessed. Such was the lack of trust she now had in herself, she couldn't persuade herself that she was capable of shutting the field gate, of locking the tack shed, of sterilising the bottles, so these things were often done twice.

A loud and rhythmic banging started and Rosie realised the horses were still waiting. She picked up the buckets and made her way across the small concrete yard to the stables. Peat continued to bang an impetuous hoof against the wooden door until the tiny bucket of low calorie chaff was placed in front of him. She only gave him a small feed to keep him quiet while Red had his dinner. She had taken to shutting them in to feed them. Peat was so relentless in his pursuit of Red's feed that Red, who probably didn't really need the hard feed either, had started to give in and let the little gelding dive his little black head into the bucket. Once Peat got his head firmly inside, he would slide the bucket along the floor away from Red and gobble most of the fibre nuts before Rosie could stop him.

She let herself in with Red and left the half door open, Peat was safely shut in and Red would not walk away from his bucket. Deftly she smoothed a soft body brush over Red's already gleaming fur. He barely grew a winter coat, even during the harshest of winters, so his spring moult was quick and tidy. Peat on the other hand still looked like a giant black haystack and tufts of dead hair billowed from him every time the wind blew. She knew he needed grooming more than Red did, but being beside her horse, witnessing the health which radiated from him, and which she could attribute to herself, was hard to resist.

She smiled at the sheen which made the red and white horse almost reflective.

Red pricked his ears towards the house and Rosie followed his gaze to see Val walking up the field, Eve in her arms. She tried not to scowl.

'Deny she looks cute.' Val proffered the small baby, dressed in denim jeans, a pink, stripy top and matching booties.

'She looks daft.' Rosie laughed.

'Rosie, I was going to come up here and tell you that you need to get Eve out more, to bring her up here in her buggy and let her watch you do the horses. I was going to point out how sweet her smile is, how she is nearly old enough to make the amazing sound that a parent never forgets, her first laugh.'

Rosie felt involuntary tears roll down her cheeks, mourning the emotion she wished she could muster. 'But you and I both know that's not going to be enough. You are struggling on more levels than just Eve aren't you?'

Rosie nodded. She put the brush back on the ledge beside the manger.

She stepped out of the stable and took Eve from Val. The baby gurgled at her, grinning inanely.

'It's like I know what should be there, I know how I should feel when I look at her but there's a numbness instead, like there are too many things blocking it.'

'You need proper help, you need Matt to come home or someone to move in. You need to choose when you spend time with her so that you feel less trapped.'

'But how?'

Chapter Two

'Did I remember to say Amber is waxing up?!' Gill's excited voice rang out into the crisp evening air.

'Oh it's going to be soon!' Kelly squealed.

Kelly, Gill and Jules were riding towards the gallops. The 2 mile all-weather track with its white rails and gentle incline was Jules' idea. She was convinced of the value in on-site facilities, not just for their convenience, but also because potential customers would be impressed.

'How long do you reckon then Gill?' Jules asked, wondering what waxing up was.

'Could be any day now! If her milk is getting ready to come through it's a sure sign.'

Jules smiled at the thought of a tiny baby to gaze at from her new kitchen window.

Gill's mare Amber had been covered by an unknown stallion at the hands of the man who had purchased her from the horse thieves who had taken her. He had refused to give any information on the stallion, or when exactly she had been covered when he had been questioned him at the time. Gill was so delighted to have found Amber and so reluctant to put the mare through any stress, she had simply decided to keep the foal, whatever breed or size it was, despite the fact that with no known sire its breeding could not be proven, and therefore any racing potential it might have, mute.

Marilliums Immortal Mist, or Milly, walked calmly, leading the pack. As Jules turned in the mare's saddle to look back at Gill and Kelly, a pigeon flew up out of the longer grass near the hedge, but Milly scarcely flinched.

The mare had been as green as the grass they were riding on when she had first arrived at the yard. Now that she was into her third Arabian Racing season she took everything in her long stride. She no longer used up her energy fretting before the race, or fought with the jockey on the way to the start. She understood what was expected of her and the security of that knowledge was such that she was currently on a winning streak of five consecutive races.

There was a time when Jules would have felt nervous even at the prospect of hacking the mare, but now she was happy ride her to the gallops for her evening workout as one of the yard's best prospects.

Gill, on the other hand, was wrestling to keep her own mount going in a straight line. The youngster flirted from side to side, alert to every innocent noise around him. Gill sat secure but gentle, perched on top of the tiny racing saddle. She put both reins into one hand and smoothed the colt's slender neck to reassure him. Eclipsed by Hazinee was a five year old son of the beautiful black stallion Monday's Eclipse, who walked with a measured and effortless stride beside his offspring, with Kelly on board.

Gill would have backed Zinee to ride only, giving him a few years low pressure work with maybe a few shows or endurance events before race training him. But his owner Norah Ranger wanted the young horse on the track as soon as the new season started.

Norah owned Monty, Zinee and two other horses who were in training at Newmans, so Gill couldn't afford to argue too much with what the affluent businesswoman and racing enthusiast wanted. Her monthly direct debit was the biggest single source of income Newmans had. With some racing organisations permitting the running of horses much younger than Zinee, Gill had to be grateful Norah had allowed him to wait until he was five to begin his education and career, as she did with all of her horses.

When Monty had been stolen, Norah had been supportive and loyal, allowing the horse to go straight back into training with Gill when he had been recovered and sending three more horses to be trained with her shortly after. Gill couldn't help but like the commanding and blunt woman, even though she was the source of a fair amount of worry. Norah was as assertive as she was knowledgeable, and Norah's word was law.

'It's ok poppet, little run round, at your own pace, then back for a nice bucket of dinner.' Gill rubbed his neck again and thankfully, he started to relax.

'Well that sounds lovely, but I would prefer my dinner on a plate if that's all the same...' Kelly said quite seriously and made Jules giggle.

Jules admired Kelly. The 18 year old was incredibly mature, had a great sense of humour and was as dedicated to her job as it was possible to be. Part of Jules' decision to invest in Newmans had been because it came with such a valuable asset; Kelly would work tirelessly and hold things together if Gill went off on a whim. She was small and blonde and still had a traces of puppy fat around her face and middle. She had none of the glamour and traditional good looks that Gill's daughter Charlie had. Even though they were the same age, Charlie looked like a woman where Kelly was still very much a girl. She was clearly going to be a late bloomer though, with sharp eyes and a generous smile. Jules wondered how long it would be before a boyfriend came along and sincerely hoped it wouldn't distract the groom too much when it happened.

They picked their horses up into a working trot to warm

and supple their tendons as they approached the gallops.

'Right then, Monty up front, nice steady pace please Kelly. Then Zinee, and Milly can bring up the rear. At the half mile marker, Jules – bring Milly up alongside Zinee, get him used to having a horse running close by and we can see if he is inclined to hold pace.'

Jules nodded and Kelly saluted as she eased Monty into a canter, giving him a chance to stretch before rising up in her stirrups to balance over his neck. He responded by lengthening his stride and galloping just short of the terrific speed he was capable of.

'We'll show your lad the way, eh boy?' Kelly beamed down at the sleek black neck and thought, as she often did, how much she adored her job.

Jules held Milly with a light contact until Zinee was a little way in front, he had fought Gill and bucked a few times but was starting to look more balanced as he settled into galloping.

When they reached the half mile marker Jules gave the mare her head and in seconds they were alongside the younger horse. Zinee flattened his ears and Gill reminded him to hold his course as he meandered towards the rails.

'Nothing.' Gill shouted and shook her head.

'Nothing what?' Jules barked into the wind which rushed headlong at the rider's faces.

'He isn't trying to get ahead, ask Milly for a bit more.'

Jules pushed her mount forwards and as soon as they started to make a lead on Zinee, he suddenly fought back and pitched to keep up, not wanting to be left behind.

Gill smiled. He might never to be a natural like his Dad, but if he could hold pace with Milly and didn't like the thought of being overtaken, there was hope yet.

Rosie boiled the kettle.

Sue smiled at Eve's bouncer which was on the kitchen floor. The baby had fallen asleep and Rosie didn't want to move her into her cot and risk disturbing her.

It was Friday, the day that brought her husband home. She knew he would be tired after a week's work and long drive but dishevelled or not, she couldn't wait to see him or benefit from his enthusiasm for Eve, which would allow her some time for herself.

Sue stood up and leant on the kitchen counter. The stout, rugged faced woman drummed her fingers loudly on the work surface, but quickly stopped when Rosie's alarmed face reminded her she was in the presence of a sleeping baby.

'Rosie. You know I think you are competent, I wouldn't have loaned you Peat otherwise. But, I have to say he is a laminitis outbreak waiting to happen in that field.'

Rosie set a cup down in front of the neighbour who had kindly brought the little black pony over as company for Red after Harry had passed away.

Rosie's face fell and Sue smiled.

'We have had just enough sunshine to make it lush and he is definitely fatter than he was when he got here.'

'Oh...' Rosie fought hard not to cry in front of Sue. Sue's yard was only a couple of miles away, but they didn't know each other that well and Rosie hardly wanted to start blubbing in front of her.

'Look, let's section him off a little paddock, won't take us long and then we will have caught him early enough.'

Rosie nodded and smiled.

'I am sorry Sue, I just didn't think.'

'Well you have had other things on your mind,' Sue nodded towards the baby bouncer, 'don't dwell on it Rosie, let's just sort it, eh?'

'Ok, we will have this cuppa and then head on out.'

Sue had called in to see Rosie and say hello to Peat on her way back from a trip to see a stallion she was interested in buying and had caught Rosie in the middle of desperately trying to straighten the house up before Matt came home.

A bad fall coupled with advancing years and an increased sense of mortality had seen Sue give up riding ten years ago. Rosie loved to hear Sue's stories about the various characters she had ridden and loved throughout her life. Although she no longer rode, Sue still kept an equine herd. She carefully selected youngsters who needed a good start in life and some TLC and raised them at her yard, selling them on when she felt she had found a good match for them. She had an innate ability to recognise when the personality of a horse would complement the personality of a human and had a reputation for securing life-long partnerships for the animals she meticulously prepared to begin their ridden careers. When Rosie had needed company for Red, Sue had not hesitated to deliver Peat. The pony had the potential to be nervy, could shut down in the wrong hands, but with the right amount of love he bloomed into a spunky and opinionated little character and Sue had known before Rosie that he would be a good match for both her and Red.

Rosie smiled across at Sue, formerly married and mother to two grown up sons, she was now a self-proclaimed spinster by choice, whose animals were all the validation she needed in life. Rosie peered out of the kitchen window and was relieved to see the heavy grey clouds which had descended over the valley had not yet released their burden and in fact, looked like they were on the move.

'We might not get wet after all if we head out now."

'Aren't you forgetting something?' Sue smiled.

'Am I?'

'Little one there – who is going to watch her if we are building fences?'

'Oh no it's fine, I take the baby monitor when I am out in the field.'

'Oh, ok.' Sue shrugged and slurped her coffee to fill her mouth with something other than judgemental words.

Rosie sipped her own coffee and had to resist biting the rim of the mug in frustration, her admiration for Sue lost in the realisation that, despite her apparent earthiness, she was still just as over cautious as Mr Mathers when it came to a baby. Why couldn't everyone just butt out?

An hour later, fence built and Peat sulking within its confines, Rosie waved Sue off and headed back into the cottage. Eve had woken up and was gurgling.

'Right then kid, come on.' Rosie lifted the baby up and put her into the state of the art pushchair which had been a present from Matt's parents. Eve grizzled and threatened to cry, she had expected a cuddle not to be put straight down again.

'Oh there there, we are going outside for a bit!' Rosie smiled down at the baby and felt the smallest flutter in her heart when Eve's eyes lit up and she smiled back. Rosie wanted to make sure Peat wasn't too depressed about his new paddock and give him some hay, and thought she would let Eve enjoy the afternoon sunshine while she groomed the little pony. Maybe she could do it, maybe there was happiness to be had in the foreign land her life had become.

'Bugger!' Rosie announced to the baby as the phone started ringing.

As she reached for the phone she made a mental note

not to say bugger in front of the baby.

'Hello!'

'Darling.' Matt's voice came down the line and Rosie excitedly started to tell her husband she was about to take Eve out to spend some time with the horses but he quickly and gently cut her off.

'I am going to have to work this weekend. I am really sorry and I would have given you more notice but I thought I might be able to get out of it. There are two sites that still need to be migrated to the new server; it all just took longer than we had hoped. The fibre optic connection is running through old cabling so it's not straight forward...' Matt trailed off, he sensed from the silence at the other end that Rosie didn't care about the Leeds and Manchester offices or their IT needs.

'You can't.' Rosie's voice was small and scared.

'Darling I miss you both like mad but if I don't get this project signed off we can't move on to the next phase and that is what they promoted me to do...'

'Please come home.'

'Rosie don't!' Matt couldn't believe his practical, easy-going wife was being so needy. He despaired at the situation, but there was nothing he could do.

'I swear I will make it up to you.'

The anxiety grew in Rosie, her heart beating at double speed, panic drenching her limbs with adrenaline.

'Make it up to me? It will be too fucking late!'

Rosie waited.

15 minutes after she had put the phone down on Matt, he still hadn't tried to ring her back. She comforted herself with the notion that he might be getting into his car, making his way to where she needed him. But she knew in her heart he wouldn't

be, knew her reaction to his not coming home would be puzzling him, but because she had hidden her true desperation and sadness from him, he would not realise the magnitude of her words.

She started to wonder if she should ring him back. But she couldn't bring herself to call and tell him it was ok because it wasn't, she had only got through the last week in the knowledge he would be home at the weekend. Now he wouldn't be.

She opened the front door and pushed Eve out into the sunshine. She made her way through the garden with its blossoming apple trees and up the field towards the stables and Peat's enclosure. Sue had been right, the ground was firm and the grass was decidedly greener. Thank god she had popped in.

Red eyed the buggy with suspicion and kept his distance.

Rosie parked the baby just out of reach of Peat's prying teeth.

She picked up a curry comb and lifted the Shetland pony's thick black mane so that she could work the rubber teeth into the pony's crest. He leant into the wonderful scratching and half closed his little brown eyes. Clouds of the pony's shed winter coat flurried about in the gentle breeze as Rosie cleaned out the comb.

Rosie wished Matt had not phoned. Another night alone. Another 8 nights, filled only with sad microwave meals for one and the TV for company. More going through the motions. More time to chicken out of telling Matt the truth, because she knew it would break his heart and he would blame himself for leaving her.

As she worked the comb over Peat's withers and started to itch his thickly coated and ample rump she noticed Red walking towards Eve.

The horse stepped gingerly towards the buggy, his head

low, ears pricked. She put the comb down on Peat's back, poised to run towards the horse and intervene. She hesitated by the fence of Peat's enclosure. Red stretched out his head and blew sweet grassy breath onto the baby's face, his whiskers tickling her.

Eve squealed in delight, chuckling to herself and reaching her hands up to touch Red's soft muzzle.

Rosie smiled. In that single moment she felt like everything could be all right.

Red stamped his hoof to rid his leg of a horse fly. The noise and vibration frightened Eve and she let out a piercing cry. Red fled to the opposite end of the paddock. Even Peat hurtled around his enclosure, scared of the sudden sound.

'Right. Back to the house then.'

Eve's screams rang out across the valley as Rosie wheeled her down the field. Relentless noise forced tears of helplessness from her own eyes. She just couldn't win.

She let go of the buggy and walked away from the screaming child.

She opened her mouth to scream herself.

She shut her eyes and let the primal animal inside her howl for all she was worth.

In the carnival of noise she and her baby created between them, she found a blissful inner silence. Because her eyes were shut, she could not see her worried horse, running back and forth at the top of the field, too frightened to go to her.

Before she drew breath, strong arms were around her, pulling her in to hold her and rock her. She looked up and realised it was Jimmy.

'Oh Dad.....'

'Shh now Rosie, I'm here.'

Rosie's eyelids fluttered open from the deepest most restful night's sleep she'd had since Eve's birth. As she focused on Crystal's face she realised her step mother must have done all the night feeds. The sun appeared high in the sky through the spare bedroom window.

'It's midday. We wanted to leave you to sleep.'

Crystal placed a mug of coffee on the bedside table.

'Your Dad is out with the horses. Peat has broken out.'

Rosie managed a smile.

'I thought he might.'

'I will leave you to get up. Eve is fine.'

As Crystal stood up she noticed Rosie's smile fade at the mention of her daughter.

'Once you have sorted out the horse we can talk properly.'

Rosie's scowl deepened and Crystal's cheeks flushed. Rosie realised the awkwardness she had created and decided she didn't want to scare Crystal off.

'I am so glad you are here.'

Crystal smiled and nodded. She came back to the bed and kissed Rosie's forehead.

'We aren't going anywhere.'

As Rosie walked up the field towards the stables she couldn't help but grin.

The little pony was frantically snatching up mouthfuls of forbidden grass. Every time Jimmy, gingerly clutching the Shetland's head collar, got close, Peat would break into a canter. Once a safe distance away Peat resumed munching, until the man approached again.

'Come on little Peat!' Jimmy spoke softly to the pony who turned around to eye him with contempt before resolutely ignoring him again.

'Oh Dad.' Rosie giggled and Jimmy turned around.

He abandoned his pursuit of the pony and enveloped her in a hug.

The night before his only concern had been to get her into bed and let her sleep, but he could see now she might be ready to talk about the episode in the field and the dark rings under her eyes.

'I guess he is supposed to be in there?' Jimmy motioned towards the gap in the small paddock, the strands of electric tape snapped and hanging loosely on the plastic posts.

'Yeah he is. I didn't think the battery had enough charge in it. I will plug it in in the tack shed and put him in the stable until it's ready. His owner came over yesterday and said he needed to be on restricted grass.'

'Laminoptis?'

'Close, Laminitis! Well, the threat of.'

Rosie smiled. With all the time he had spent with her and Harry when she was a teenager it wasn't surprising he remembered a few things.

'Your friend's pony had it at the Ringwell stables didn't it? Alice was it..?'

'Mmmm - Poppy.' Rosie smiled as she thought about the bay pony she and Harry had often ridden out with, she always remembered horses.

'Are you still in touch with Alice?'

'Oh god no. There were so many kids with ponies at that stables, I was glad to leave to be honest.'

Jimmy nodded, taking her hand, encouraging her to go on.

'I never really liked kids.'

Jimmy shook his head, remaining silent.

'I don't really like being a mum.'

Jimmy nodded and stroked her hair. No recriminations, no disappointment, just love.

'It's ok. We are going to help you through this.'

'Thank god you are my Dad.'

Rosie held onto Jimmy, meaning her words with every part of herself. Jimmy wasn't her biological father, but he brought her up and loved her with every part of himself. Her real father, a man named Eddie, was someone she knew of, had even met a few times, but did not want in her life. Jimmy was all the father she needed.

Unlike Eddie, Jimmy was solvent and did not have a criminal record.

'Show me how it's done then.' Jimmy handed Rosie Peat's head collar.

'Well, if this was any other horse, you would get a natural horsemanship display right about now, but, as its Peat...' Rosie trailed off as she headed towards the feed room.

The moment she opened the feed room door and made her way inside, Jimmy heard Peat's thundering hooves. He moved back as the pony passed him and skidded to a halt on the concrete outside the feed room.

Rosie appeared at the door and casually slipped the head collar on his nose.

'Right.' Jimmy covered his eyes with his hand in shame.

Rosie led Peat to the stable and shut him in with a small net of soaked hay to keep him quiet.

'I'll just pooh-pick a minute.' Rosie said as she headed towards the wheelbarrow.

'No need. Done it.' Jimmy smiled wryly.

Rosie stopped walking and eyed Jimmy quizzically.

'I got bored. I have been trying to catch that bloody thing for hours!'

Rosie couldn't help but laugh, it felt good to laugh.

They walked in silence towards the cottage and joined Crystal, who was in the kitchen sterilising bottles.

Rosie and Jimmy sat at the kitchen table and Crystal placed mugs of coffee in front of them. She ruffled Jimmy's hair affectionately before she excused herself to check on Eve.

'She is great with Eve.' Jimmy smiled fondly after his wife. 'As you know she didn't have children but her siblings are much younger than she is, so she has had plenty of experience.'

'Did she want children?'

Jimmy nodded.

'Just one of those things. By the time we met it was too late and I don't work as you know. We did try though, we were going to adopt but the longer we waited for IVF to work the older we both got and in the end we decided be happy with what we had. Her nieces and nephews adore her. And now she has a grandchild too.'

Rosie sipped her coffee. She had no idea they had tried to have a baby together. She felt sad that she had never thought to ask. Jimmy had already been through the agony of fruitless attempts to have a second child with Rosie's mother, then he had found out Rosie wasn't his after bringing her up, then he had endured this with Crystal. She felt a pang of pure empathy in her heart, and it deepened her guilt about not being able to feel very much for Eve. If she had been Crystal's baby she would have had an abundance of love.

'Did Matt ring you?' Rosie suddenly realised since they had arrived, she hadn't asked what had made them come.

'No. It was your friend Val. But I did speak to Matt as well.'

Rosie looked ashamed.

'You went through a massive trauma losing Harry and

44

then gave birth, plus you are on your own five days a week. It's not surprising you are finding this hard and I am just sorry I didn't see it for myself last time I was here.'

'I was hiding it pretty well.'

'You don't have to anymore.' Jimmy caressed his mug and studied the knots in the wood of the table for a moment, 'Matt was pleased we were coming, but didn't sound as concerned as Val. I am assuming that is because Val knows more?'

Rosie nodded and tears pricked her eyes.

'Do you want me to talk to him?'

'No.' Rosie eyed Jimmy sharply, 'I know I need to talk to him, but I need him to be here first.'

Jimmy nodded and sipped his coffee.

Crystal had been standing in the doorway behind Rosie but at that moment moved forwards to sit beside her.

'We will stay as long as you need us.' She patted Rosie's hand and Rosie grabbed her fingers and held on, tears suddenly streaming in relief at the answer to the question she had been too frightened to ask.

'But what about your job?' she sobbed. She knew Crystal was a London Borough Trading Standards Officer and had expected them to leave again on Sunday.

'Tough times in local government. I took voluntary redundancy. Just finished my last week.'

'And I can oversee the businesses from here. I have brought my laptop, assuming your broadband still works, that's all I need.' Jimmy reached out and took Rosie's other hand.

She felt safe at last.

'Thank you both, so much.'

'Sorry to call you on a Saturday, Juliette.'

Jules smiled as she cradled the phone on her shoulder and reached towards the computer to copy a website link into an email.

'No worries. Sending it now.'

'I just want to get my head round this case before the client meeting on Monday.'

'James, would it surprise you to hear that the reason I answered the phone so quickly is because I am sat with the Appledown file in front of me as we speak?' Jules laughed.

'No, Jules. It wouldn't. We are fated to have our weekends ruined, it's the law of the Law.'

'Makes me wish I worked in a supermarket, once your shift ends you go home and that's that!'

'You would be terrible at working in a supermarket.'

'Yeah I know. I can barely find my way round the village shop.'

James was an associate solicitor at the firm which had recently moved in to the ground floor of the Hodges and Grath building. It suited the managing partner of Hodges, her boss David, to have a hot new business subletting some of the building his own firm had always been a little lost in.

Although some of the lawyers who had to move offices had grumbled, and some of the secretaries who had had extra desks squeezed into their work areas were still complaining, for Jules and James it was wonderful news.

Both originally from Gloucestershire, they found themselves sat next to one another in class on the first day of their Law degree at Exeter University. Realising they had grown up just towns apart, and then that their dorms were in adjacent campus buildings, their friendship had happened naturally. So, it was no surprise to either of them when, after a few years with limited contact, his firm had ended up in the same building as hers. They often joked that they couldn't avoid each other; life always seemed to throw them together.

He had an aptitude for property law and she specialised in finance and equestrian litigation but they had a similar regard for the fact that for their clients' livelihoods and reputations were often at stake, something which their lecturers had been keen to instil in them back in the early days when they were fresh faced and eager. Over the years since they had been estranged each had blossomed, James had got married and had children, and Jules was on a fast track to becoming a partner. On the very first day Law Skill had moved into the Hodges building, much like that first day at Uni, their matched sense of humour and comfortable closeness had seem them lunching together regularly, but this time it was to discuss their cases, instead of their course work.

'You will be fine on Monday James. You have prepared really well and that always sets you off on a good footing.'

'Thanks Jules. I had better go, Lisa and the kids are nagging me to take them to the beach!'

'See you Monday James.'

Jules put the phone down and looked at her case file, but she couldn't ignore the sunshine outside and her gaze was drawn to the paddock where Gill was brushing Amber. She was so pleased to have James back in her life. Many of the senior associates and partners at the firm were quite brilliant, but took their work so seriously they were not prepared to engage in even the tamest of office banter. She and James had a laugh as well as working hard. It was refreshing.

Jules loved the Newmans office. It had a great view of the paddocks and in contrast to Gill's tendency to avoid the room at all costs, Jules found she was productive when she was sat at the large oak desk. She wondered if Gill would mind her continuing to use the office for work once the annexe was

47

finished. It would allow her to separate home and work a bit and would also give her regular opportunities to check the Newmans accounts and update the website the yard now had.

Jules decided she had done enough work considering it was now Saturday afternoon and wandered out to see Gill, Ziggy trotting by her side.

'Not long then eh?' Jules smoothed Amber's forehead and let the mare lip at her palm. Gill was delicately brushing the tight round expanse of belly with a soft brush. The foal was sitting low and large and the mare looked exhausted.

'Poor lass. She has had enough now. I think she is starting to wish it would happen!'

Jules regarded Amber's tired eyes and slightly listless expression.

'I expect it's really heavy for her, it looks it.'

'I don't know whether to bring her in or not. They say horses prefer to foal outside and most of the mares we have had here did – but Amber loves her stable and she is so comfortable in the barn. What do you think?'

'Umm.' Jules didn't know what to say. She didn't really know anything about foaling but she was touched Gill had asked her opinion. 'You know her best Gill, if you think she would be happier in the barn you should take her in.'

At that moment Amber nosed Jules out of the way and walked slowly but resolutely to the gate of the paddock, where she stood waiting.

'There's my answer then!' Gill shook her head. She never failed to be amazed by Amber's aptitude for communication with humans.

Jules smiled and followed Gill to the gate.
Together they added two extra bales of straw to the largest stable

in the barn to make a deep bed for the mare while she calmly munched at a haynet and looked on approvingly.

Monty wuffled to her through the bars of the next stable and she met his muzzle with hers. They breathed each other in and Amber sighed. The black stallion's breathing quickened in excitement and he strutted up and down the divide between them. Amber let out a high pitched squeal of disgust and turned her head away from Monty, who stopped strutting and appeared rather deflated.

'Oh dear Monty. I don't think she is going to be interested in you for a while yet.' Gill laughed. 'Better move him to the other end of the barn I think.'

Jules chuckled as she finished squaring off the edges of the oversized straw bed.

Gill let herself out of the stable to fetch fresh water buckets. Ziggy padded in through the open half door. As he passed the mare's hind legs she squealed again and lifted a hoof, threatening the dog with a kick.

'Come on Zig,' Jules quickly ushered her collie back out into the walkway, 'Doesn't look like Amber wants any male attention at all today.'

Gill came back with the water to find Amber glowering with curled nostrils and pinned back ears.

'Best keep him out of her stable now, mares can get quite funny about dogs once they have a little one.'

Jules looked down at Ziggy and smiled, he cocked his head and gazed up at his master, his desire to be near her was more powerful than his fear of a hormonal horse.

'Afternoon Jules!'

George strode into the barn, blonde hair and green eyes lighting up the air around him. He winked at Jules as he passed Amber's stable and crept towards Gill, who was bent over a feed bin and hadn't heard her boyfriend arrive.

'Oooohh!' Gill squealed as George spanked her behind then wrapped his arms around her when she stood up in shock.

'You horrid man!' Gill reprimanded, but melted into his height and strength, laying her head on his chest.

'Sorry, couldn't resist. It is such a nice ass after all.'

'Get a room you two.' Jules chided as she left Amber's stall.

'We've got one. It's the one along the corridor from yours.' George smiled.

'Ahh well – not for long.' Jules smiled back.

'Oh?'

'According to Keith and his band of merry men, my place should be finished in two weeks!'

'Jules that is fab news!' Gill let go of George to hug her friend. She loved having Jules in the house but the annexe provided the perfect compromise between being close by and not on top of one another. 'Let's go for a ride to celebrate!'

'Ok.' George nodded, 'I don't have to be back at the restaurant until six.' George co-owned the recently renamed Bloomswell, a well-loved up-market restaurant which was just a few minutes from the yard, in the village of Hexham. The restaurant had originally been called the Barton Mill, which had been the name on the sign outside when they bought the tumbledown house. Flooding and gales earlier in the year had both blown down and submerged the sign, rendering it rotten, and the business partners had decided to re-open with a more personal name, which amalgamated Rob's surname, Brandswell, and George's Bloom.

George let himself into Monty's stable. Although Monty was a stallion and a racehorse he was the easiest horse to ride at Newmans and he carried George effortlessly. The two had struck up a close bond over the last year. It was another reason on a long list which saw Gill dreading the day when Norah retired him from racing and he would inevitably have to leave the yard.

'I will ride Zinee, he needs more roadwork.' Gill said; she had resumed her rummaging behind the feed bin.

'Actually I won't guys, if that's ok.' Jules picked up Romeo's head collar as she spoke. 'I really want to give Rome a bath while its warm and I am going out with a few girlfriends tonight.'

Gill stopped looking for the overreach boots, deciding Zinee could do without them, and called after Jules who was leaving the barn to fetch Romeo.

'Hang on madam! You aren't exactly the Saturday night boozing type. Is it really a date?!'" Gill's eyes twinkled as Jules turned to face her.

'No it isn't really a date. An old friend asked me along to her birthday and some of the others I used to know from our Legal Practice Course will be there so I thought – sod it – why not go on a girls night and get drunk, I work hard enough!'

'Go girl!' George punched the air and laughed.

Gill swatted at him and sent him to find his hard hat.

'You have fun, be nice for you to let your hair down!'

'Girl power!' Jules called as she continued out of the barn towards Romeo's paddock. Her voice sounded confident enough but she was glad they couldn't see her face because, in fact, she was nervous as hell. She couldn't remember the last time she had a night out on the town. She was only 31, by the standards of some of her similarly aged acquaintances she ought to have been pubbing and clubbing every weekend.

She much preferred to curl up in bed with Ziggy and a good book; perhaps a box of chocolates.

But, now she had a commitment to Abbey, a dearly

loved friend who she rarely made the effort to see, a wardrobe full of clothes which could be described as either work or horsey to muster an outfit from, and rising dread. The bustle of the city centre on a Saturday night, fighting drunks and overdressed girls spewing in the gutters - it wasn't exactly her scene.

Jules momentarily consoled herself she might meet a nice man, but then remembered she would be unlikely to find anyone of like mind out on a Saturday night.

'Well Rome, if I don't like it I just won't go again.' Jules said to her horse as she slipped his head collar on. She smiled and put her arm over his neck as they walked to the barn together. 'You, on the other hand my boy will be delighted to know there will be no going out for you – you can just stand still and have a nice bath.'

Jules collected buckets of warm water from the barn's kitchen, a sponge and horse shampoo. Ziggy sighed loudly and flopped himself down on the concrete in the sun. He knew the drill, this meant no ride. Jules liked to bath Rome once a month in spring and summer, believing the cleaner the horse was, the less likely he was to be bothered by the hordes of newly emerging flies which seemed to be unrelenting in their pursuit of the horses.

Gill led Zinee into the yard, followed by George and Monty. Ziggy saw tack on horses and hats on riders and stood up, tail wagging.

'Can he come with us?' Gill asked, noticing Ziggy's hopeful stance.

Jules laughed, it would be a boring evening for him and she couldn't deny the dog a chance to run alongside the horses. Ziggy stared up at Jules, waiting for permission.

'Go on then!' Jules made her dog's day and he skittered towards the driveway before running back towards the horses and dancing from side to side, unable to hide his impatience to get going.

'Ooh!' Remembered Gill, as she gently sprung onto Zinee's green back. 'Rosie called this morning, she is coming tomorrow afternoon for a catch up!'

'Brilliant!' A wide genuine smile lit up Jules' face. She hadn't seen Rosie for almost a month and it felt like far too long. 'I am glad you said afternoon and not morning though. I think I am going to be busy with a hangover until lunchtime!'

Gill and George chuckled as they rode down the drive. Ziggy settled into a steady trot alongside Monty's long legged stride, close enough that Gill wouldn't have to worry about him, but keeping enough distance to be safe.

Jules sighed happily as she watched them round the corner at the bottom of the drive. Unconventional though it may be, life certainly wasn't unpleasant.

'There's something wrong with Monty...' George interrupted Gill, who had been chattering away about a new racing client whose horse would be arriving the following weekend.

George had jumped from Monty's back before Gill had a chance to halt Zinee, let alone get off herself.

'Sounded like this foot.' George naturally looped the reins around the crook of his arm before bending over to pick up Monty's unshod fore hoof. Gill bit her lip as she watched him examining the sole. He was so good with the horses, so sensitive and instinctive.

'Ahhh. That's the culprit.' George pulled his Leatherman from the pocket of his jeans and deftly flicked out a stone which had been wedged against the large frog which dominated Monty's pebble hard sole. George allowed Monty to replace his hoof and the horse looked relieved when it felt normal again. George picked up the stone and held it up for Gill to see.

Gill studied the stone and nodded. She sat on Zinee, waiting for George to re mount Monty.

'What's that silly face for?' George looked at Gill as he gathered up his reins.

Gill was grinning inanely.

'I just love you.'

George smiled across at her.

'Come on you silly arse, wake your horse up.'

Gill gently nudged Zinee to walk on and was relieved when he didn't burst forwards. He was slowly getting better. He was starting to realise a small subtle aid only required a small subtle response instead of exploding when he felt pressure.

As they walked their horses through the village and towards the large National Trust Estate which sprawled for miles and held endless possibilities for riding routes, Gill was still grinning. George knew he had impressed her by being able to hear that there was something up with Monty before the stone had done any damage and he couldn't help feeling smug.

Praise from Gill was guaranteed to send his spirits soaring. They had been together properly for just over a year now and he felt he would always be in awe that she was his.

She had certainly made him work for it.

George had spent a few years admiring Gill before he had actually done anything about it. She had ridden past his restaurant aboard various horses on an almost daily basis. He knew who she was back then, as did most of the village.

When she had purchased Newmans and started building her training business, there had been some grumbling from Stoke Rewe's residents about horse poo on the lanes and increased traffic. George had admired her from day one. She worked tirelessly, especially in the early days before she had Kelly to help her, sometimes riding past on three different horses in one day.

As soon as the village shop keeper realised the livery owners were coming in regularly to pick up lunch, and the publican started to see Gill's owners calling in after a visit to the yard, everyone was ok with Gillian Newman. She brought business to the area and that was always received well.

George came from humble beginnings. His parents, having retired from farming and handed their home and livelihood back to the Church when they became too old to do the dairy herd justice, lived in the village in a small flat. They had no desire to leave the modest dwelling and even now that George was relatively successful, his father still refused offers of help. His father certainly wouldn't entertain the notion of George buying a nice home for them, what on earth would they want a bigger kitchen for?

George had scrimped and saved for his contribution towards the Barton Mill. His business partner Rob was fairly affluent and had no trouble finding his share of the capital. Rob had even offered to buy the whole thing. But George's determination to match his partner and have an equal share would not be weakened by an altruistic gesture.

George had been working for Rob as a sous-chef in a large country hotel near the south coast. When the hotel's owner had decided to sell to a large chain, the restaurant had been asked to cut costs and operate from a ruthlessly commercial business plan. The pair lost enthusiasm once they were no longer able to be creative or innovative with their food and concocted a plan to go it alone instead.

When they found the Barton Mill for sale on an estate agent's website, they knew instantly. A former pub, it had a great location and masses of potential, and it was a stone's throw from

George's home. A new thatched roof was needed immediately and plumbing and electricity had to be installed from scratch. Rob was always more content to relax with a bottle of wine while the contractors worked, but George involved himself in the project and managed every element meticulously.

It had cost George his relationship. When Daisy had finally had enough of trying to get his attention, he was relieved. She was an exquisitely pretty girl, but her motivations in life lay in having nice things and keeping up appearances, which did nothing for George. The less money he had to lavish on her, as he sunk everything into his new venture, the more sullen and demanding she became. George realised he wanted a partner who would muck in and get involved, or at least have a project of her own to work hard at.

He was happy when she found someone new, an accountant with the cash and connections to give her what she wanted. She still called into the restaurant sometimes and he was never sure why, they had little in common and she claimed to be happy. He was too polite to challenge her or tell her to leave when she dropped in on the odd Sunday, but it wasn't something he mentioned to Gill.

After three years of bachelorhood following Daisy's departure, it was the theft of Amber which finally saw George compelled to take some action in Gill's direction. Gill's passion and dedication for horses was so acutely apparent to him even from afar, he knew how much the loss of the horses would be affecting her and he was determined to help if he could.

When he had first visited Newmans and seen the hollow shells where vibrant eyes used to live, the desolation that surrounded her like a cloud, his heart had melted. He persisted, sometimes in the face of outright scorn, until she had finally allowed him into her life.

There was an eight year age gap between them. Gill joked that he had pulled her for a bet and laughingly proclaimed he would soon get bored. After Amber had finally been found and Gill had found her smile again, George had moved in to the cottage and they had developed a connection which went far deeper than the tangible physical attraction between them.

Because they were both so dedicated to their causes, the horses and the restaurant, they never questioned one another's busy times, nor felt jealous when a supplier muck up saw George dashing down the road on his day off, or a sick horse saw Gill's side of the bed empty.

George glanced over at Gill. She was talking to Zinee softly to reassure him as they passed a stray trail of bunting left over from the Shillerton Estate Fete.

He knew he should tell her about the problems he and Rob were having, but decided not to spoil the afternoon with his concerns about the older chef.

Chapter Three

Gill had found herself thinking about her child. She was rarely aware of it enough to act on it, but it was like there was some kind of kinetic bond between them, so that her daughter was usually on her mind before she came to visit.

As she listened to the sorry tale, she couldn't help but think that Charlie was so beautiful, even with puffy eyes and snotty nose. Blond hair cascaded around her, naturally straight, so long she could almost sit on it. Symmetrical green eyes, almost cat-like, were at the centre of her beauty; she was slim yet curvy, willowy yet real.

Charlie was almost 19. She had finished studying law at college the year before. She somehow managed to get A grades, despite giving the impression right up until the exams that she would barely scrape through. At the time she had already been living with her father for almost a year, so Gill didn't feel the same pang of loss when upon getting her results, Charlie had announced she was taking a gap year and got herself a job applying temporary tattoos at a tourist resort in Cornwall.

Charlie's big adventure to the neighbouring county had only lasted for as long as the good weather held out. She soon realised the bustling streets, endless surf shacks and even more endless free love came to an abrupt end as soon as the trees turned autumnal. She came home in November and went back to her Dads. George had moved in to Newmans by then and although Gill would dearly have loved to have her, Charlie had insisted her mother needed space.

Since then there had been various coffee shop jobs but

predominantly, she had filled her days and most of the nights with Darran. Darran was a musician, Darran was so funny, Darran was so intelligent. During many of Charlie's recent visits to Newmans, Gill had found herself a little bored of hearing about Darran. She thought it was sweet though, her daughter's first love.

She wasn't feeling sweet about it now. Darran was a sod and Darran needed gelding.

'He said I don't love him or I would be keeping it.' Charlie wailed.

'It's his fault too darling. He has no right to make you feel guilty.'

'I don't want a baby. It's as simple as that.' Charlie buried her face in Gill's lap. Gill stroked soft golden hair and wished she could take the anguish away.

Charlie had found out that she was pregnant a few days before. She told Darran immediately. And immediately, she realised his views on what to do next differed fatally from her own.

'It's not fair of him to guilt you in to keeping it. It should be your body and your choice.' Gill cradled Charlie's head and turned her daughter's face towards hers. 'Charlie, I am not proud of you for this, there is really no excuse for being careless about protection. But accidents do happen, and that is why choice exists. You have to be sure it is what you want though? You seem to have made up your mind very quickly?'

'I am totally and utterly not ready to have a baby. I can't believe this has happened. I want to start Uni' in September and I do love Darran, but he is so immature sometimes.'

'If you decide to keep it I will support you, and if you decide not to I will support you. But, from what you have said, you may well lose Darran over this. Although he can't stop you having a termination, if he wants you to keep the baby, your relationship may not survive.'

Charlie stared past her mother and fixed her gaze on the ceiling.

'That's the problem. It is my body yes, but it's his genes, I feel rotten that I have the power to make this choice and he has no power at all. I just wish he would stop romanticising this for long enough to see the bare facts.'

Gill sighed, Charlie would always be burdened by her own ability to see both sides of any argument, probably as a result of having parents with polar opposite personalities.

'Choosing whether or not you reproduce is one of the better things about modern life. If we still lived in caves and caught our meals you wouldn't have the option, but you wouldn't have the pressure of needing to have a career or to make something of your life either. Living in a world with modern conveniences comes with modern compromises. All the morality in the world won't pay the bills.'

'He lives in the smallest bedsit in Exeter and his band usually gets just enough gigs for his share to cover his rent. If he thinks we can raise a baby together he is deluded.'

'Has he said how he thinks you'll manage when he is telling you to keep it?'

'He thinks he can get a job in Dad's business by day and still be able to gig at night and that we will live in West Hill.'

'At your Dads?'

'Yeah.'

'Has he met your Dad?'

'Yes, but you know what Dad is like in company. He's all ultra-positive and gushes about everything, so Darran is under the deluded impression that he will be 'just spiffing' about it.'

The situation was not appropriate for being amused, but

Gill smirked at her daughter's impression of her ex-husband.

'Did you laugh then?' Charlie scowled. 'This is not fucking funny – I am fucking pregnant.'

'I know. And as much as I said I would support you if you kept it, the prospect of potentially being a grandmother is definitely not funny.'

It was Charlie's turn.

She smirked. When laughter erupted her tear swollen sinuses let out a snort.

'Oh god we can't laugh about this!' Gill clamped her hand over her mouth. She momentarily thought about how close she and Charlie had become in the last few years, and felt humbled by her own ability to make her girl feel better. Even in such dire circumstances.

'Have you told your Dad?'

'Hell no. Not going to either.'

'Charlotte.' Gill said the name she had chosen for a tiny baby of her own as a warning, challenging her to justify being dishonest.

'I am not having it. I have already made the appointment. Why would I put him through that instead of getting on with it, dealing with my mistake and moving on?'

Gill considered the logic. Charlie clearly hadn't realised that meant Gill was being asked to keep a secret, but Gill supposed it was a secret all round and Alex would just be another of the many people who would probably never know. Gill's concern was more about Charlie's emotional state than honesty for honesty's sake. She sounded confident, almost too logical about her decision, surely at some point during the trauma to come, her heart would catch up with her and she would need all the love she could get.

'Don't you want his support though?'

'He has barely dealt with the idea that I have sex at all, he couldn't handle this. If and when I do decide to have children, when I am ready, I can make him a happy little old man.' She glanced up at her mother and knitted her brows together, 'You on the other hand had to know because I need you to take me to the doctors.'

Gill nodded. Alex was being spared something she would rather not have to do herself. A common theme in their lives. Even if he did get the impression something was up, his self-preservation would prevent him from asking too many questions.

'I need you.'

'You don't even have to say it. No matter what you do in life, if you are honest with me I will be here for you.'

'Good.'

Charlie snuggled in to Gill's lap and sighed.

Gill sighed too, this was not going to be easy.

Jules ordered another vodka.

The club heaved. Synchronised flashes of coloured light and the heartbeat drone of dance music made the whole place seem alive, the people who flowed through it were part of the animal.

Except for Jules. She was the same age as the friends she had come with, but she felt old.

Abbey, fuelled by alcohol and a distinct comfort at being in a packed club, had pulled at Jules' arm and tried to persuade her to join the others on the dance floor, but she had felt sick at the thought of trying to move to the music in public.

Jules thought back to her college days. She had partied and drunk her fair share of cheap cider. But even then, she thought as she waved back at Abbey and the others, who were making beckoning gestures to her and laughing, she always preferred the conversations at the end of the night, and the quieter house parties where intellect and marijuana were shared and no one was put on display.

At the wine bar earlier in the evening she felt at home, sipping martini and catching up on everyone's news. She had enjoyed telling them about her investment in a racehorse training business and her forthcoming partnership at her firm. It made her able to be genuinely pleased about Abbey's engagement and the fact that Rachel was moving in with her boyfriend. Now she felt uncomfortable. She didn't like the gazes of the intoxicated men as they leered at her, hoping for someone to take home at the end of the night. She didn't see the point in one night stands. She knew that wasn't the point, most of the girls she had come with were happily in relationships and just looking to dance and enjoy each other's company, but it didn't stop Jules, as the single one, feeling like she was being assessed for her easiness.

Jules had been making a concerted effort not to scowl. She realised she must have failed as Abbey and the girls shrugged and gave up on her, turning their attention to shouting lyrics at each other and whooping.

'I'm such a misery guts.' Jules muttered to herself. She wondered if she should leave and stop dampening the evening. One of the bartenders passed her again and she shouted her order at him. More alcohol, she decided, was the only way.

She downed the double vodka in one gulp and headed towards the ladies to freshen up, then, she told herself, she would get into the spirit of this thing and damn well dance.

As she tried to find the ladies, she found herself going through double doors which led to what her intoxicated brain could only describe as paradise. Vines crept up the stone walls of the enclosed courtyard. Seated on wooden benches, illuminated by fairy lights which were wound around the poles holding a canopy over them, were relaxed people enjoying conversations, away from the deafening noise inside.

She floated towards an empty bench and sat. She wondered momentarily if she was going to throw up but that thought was quickly replaced by surprise as someone sat down next to her. She turned, expecting to have to fend off unwanted attention, but found herself gazing into familiar eyes.

'James!!' She exclaimed and immediately threw her arms around her friend.

'Juliette. Of all the clubs in all the towns...'

'I know I know – what on earth am I doing here?! What on earth are you doing here?' She stabbed him in the chest with her index finger to reprimand him and tried to focus on his face.

'Stag do. Terrible. Came out here for some peace.'

'Old work mates reuni...onion.'

'Reunion?'

'That's the one!'

'You are quite funny when you are drunk.'

'I'm going to be terribly embarrassed on Monday aren't I? They wanted me to dance and I just can't – not that kind of dancing anyway – and I thought if I got drunk it would give me some courage.'

'But now you are too drunk?'

'Probably...' Jules giggled again and belched loudly.

'Introducing Juliette Rogers, the newest and most pissed partner at Hodges and Grath!' James put his arm around Juliette as though welcoming her to the board, 'Speech!'

'Well, I, um, I just don't know what to say! Thank you, Thank you!' Jules flailed her arms dramatically and pretended to burst into tears like she was receiving an Oscar.

Jules glanced at James , he was laughing with her. He

was tall and slender, angular but giving the impression of strength. Delicious brown eyes which matched her own in colour moved quickly over her face, resting so briefly on her lips. His reddish brown hair spiked upwards from his forehead and she wondered what it would feel like if she ran her fingers through it.

She had never looked at him like this before. She was fond of him of course, but in all of their years of friendship, nothing beyond plutonic had ever been on the cards, for her anyway. Suddenly he seemed so attractive she didn't know what to do with her hands and shyly looked away. Silly Jules, must be the vodka. And the fact that he was like a familiar island in this foreign land. That must be it she decided, then had to stop thinking in order to concentrate on not throwing up. The ground seemed to be moving beneath her feet. She screwed her eyes shut and willed her surroundings to keep still.

'Right Miss, you stay here – I am going to fetch you a pint of water.'

James ruffled her hair as he got up. She opened her eyes and smiled up at him. She bit her lip as she watched him walk away, noticing how firm and bouncy his bottom looked in jeans. She shut her eyes again and told herself to sober the hell up.

Gill heard the sound of the alarm on her mobile phone and struggled to wake. Charlie stirred on her lap where they had dozed off on the sofa.

'Sweetheart....' Gill stroked her daughter's hair and gently shifted herself forward to reach her phone.

'What's that?' Charlie sounded groggy, small.

'It's my Amber alarm darling. She is going to foal any day so I am checking her every four hours at the moment. It's midnight. I'll make us a cuppa and then pop up to the barn, I won't be long.'

'No.' Charlie sat up and rubbed her red eyes. 'I'll come with you.'

'Are you sure you won't mind sleeping on the sofa?' Gill asked as they made their way by torchlight towards the dark horse barn. 'As soon as Jules' place is ready and she moves in you can have your bedroom back for when you stay– it's still full of George's stuff, we figured once Jules had vacated we would start sorting it.'

'Oh mother don't twitter on so, the sofa is fine!' Charlie linked arms with her mum and they fell in step, 'not like I get to sleep much at the moment anyway.'

They reached the barn and Gill undid the padlock. Without turning the main lights on, she slid the door back gently, not wanting to disturb the horses too much. Monty wuffled at Gill as she passed his stable, she caressed his cheek as she passed him.

Gill lifted the towel which was covering the feed she had made up for Amber earlier. Taking care not to make a sound she carried the bucket to the mare's stable.

Charlie held the torch for Gill as she undid the bolt. Amber would usually have been at the door, eager to start munching her sugar beet pulp, but the mare was unusually still.

'Put the main lights on.'

Charlie hurried away to do as instructed and Gill set the bucket down outside the stable and walked slowly towards Amber, feeling her way.

'Oh my darling...'

The lights illuminated the stable. Sweat patches covered Amber's sides, darkening her flank. The mare blew noisily through enlarged nostrils and sighed. Her tail lifted slightly, her chest beginning to heave as her quarters sunk.

'Charlie, grab me a tail bandage from the pink box on the rack over there.'

Charlie handed her mother the tail bandage and stroked Amber's neck, she was warm and sticky to the touch.

'Is she ok?'

'Yeah I reckon. But it's starting, isn't it my girl?'

'You mean she is going to have it now?' Charlie was horrified.

'Looks that way, based on the mares we have had foal here, I would say she is probably going to have it in the next few hours.'

Amber grunted and looked back at Gill who was winding the tail bandage around her long full flaxen tail.

'Just stops the hair getting in the way too much.' Gill explained to the mare.

'Should I call the vet?' Charlie had gone rather white.

'Oh good gracious no! There are complications sometimes of course but generally they just get on with it. With a bit of luck the vet won't need to see either of them until the foal needs to be ID'd for a passport.'

Amber shifted her weight, spreading her back legs apart like she was going to wee, but then stood back up again, showing the whites of her eyes.

'So what do we do? Shall I get some towels? Hot water?'

'Calm down!' Gill laughed, 'Best thing we can do is let her get on with it. Most mares prefer to be outside in the field to do this and they certainly don't like an audience. I just want to put an extra bale of straw down so that her bed is super comfy, her tail is out of the way, there is not much more to do. We might as well go back to the house and wait an hour or so then check her again.'

Charlie glared at her mother.

'I'm glad I am not having this bloody baby for a different reason now! Just leave me at the hospital I expect, go off for a quick ride would you?'

'Oh Charlie. You aren't a horse! They are much much better at this than we are!'

Charlie continued to stroke Amber sympathetically while Gill fluffed fresh golden straw over the top of an already thick bed.

'There we go darling.' Gill spoke to Amber and kissed her cheek, 'We'll be back soon.'

Gill took Charlie's hand and they left the stable.

'Right let's go and get something to eat, could be a long night, then we can come back and check on her.'

Charlie nodded and they walked towards the barn door.

Amber whickered so softly Gill almost didn't hear it. She stopped, listening.

Amber whickered again, deep and low.

'She doesn't want us to go.' Charlie looked accusingly at her mother and folded her arms.

Gill turned around. Amber was still stood in the same place in the stable, her ears pricked towards Gill. The mare gave one last pitiful whinny and Gill had to admit Charlie was right.

'There are sausage rolls in the fridge.' Gill gestured towards the barn's kitchen, resigned.

'I'll put the kettle on too.'

By the time Jules had emptied the pint glass, the water had started to do its job.

'Feel better?'

'I was very very drunk.' Jules slurred, 'But now I am only very drunk'.

James laughed.

'Why are you single, Jules?'

'Hideous wart like growths all over my body' Jules answered, deadpan.

'Seriously Juliette. I regularly marvel that someone as bright and beautiful as you hasn't been snapped up. I always thought you and Chris were going to be together forever, you were so helplessly in love with him.'

'You sound like my mother.' Jules laughed. She had fallen hard for one of the Engineering students whose classroom had been near the law block during her first year at Uni. Chris was complicated and emotionally reserved, often moody, and she had pandered to his every need, something which James had often commented on under the guise of concerned friend. 'It was never going to work. I was young and silly, I thought I could fix him, but of course that rarely happens, if ever. If it needs fixing, it probably isn't love.' Jules shook her head, realising she had done exactly the same with Tristan. Her relationship with both men had been incredibly hard work, and inevitably not stood the test of time. She mused that both would have been different with someone else, someone less demanding, less determined to achieve some higher level of closeness.

'You can't help who you love.' James smiled warmly, as though picking up on her sudden derogatory self-reflection. 'But then, Chris was never good enough for you anyway.'

'Now you really do sound like my Mother.'

'Oh good.'

Jules looked around her. The tables were filled with perfectly nice looking men. But none of them interested her.

'I guess it just took me so long to get over Tristan properly, I got used to dismissing the idea of being in a relationship and now I am not sure how to get the desire back.'

James nodded slowly, as though he really understood. It

made Jules feel comfortable enough to elaborate further.

'I did have a few casual flings after we split up, but it felt so wrong. I even started seeing a vet for a while, he was lovely, but when it came to getting physical, there was no spark. All I could think about was how different his hands felt to Tristan's. How strange it was to have sex with a man who wasn't him.'

James looked at her with a contradictory mixture of pity at her words and arousal at the thought of touching her himself.

'I am not in love with Tristan any more, I barely think about him. But he undoubtedly left a scar on my heart and I just haven't met anyone who felt right. No one seems worth the vulnerability.'

'It sounds like you have lost faith in love. That is a sad thing Jules.'

'I'm not in any rush, life isn't all about marriage and children you know!' Jules flashed him a sarcastic grin, 'Besides, you don't always need a man. I rather like pleasing myself!'

'I can't remember the last time I pleased myself.'

Jules sniggered and they both looked at the floor, the conversation was starting to border on flirting.

'I miss chatting like this. Lisa and I don't really talk any more.'

Jules raised her eyebrows, taken aback by the sudden mention of James' tiny and perfect wife. He glanced at Jules and ignored her reaction, continuing as though her own bearing of the soul had earned his in return.

'We used to talk and laugh and share everything. Now it's all about the kids and the house and whose turn it is to cook dinner. We don't have sex and we don't have fun, it's all functional.'

Jules struggled to think of something positive to say.

'Things will get better as the kids get older though won't they?'

'Don't know.'

Jules rubbed his shoulder gently, she felt genuine empathy for him. From the way he spoke about his home life in the office she had assumed he was living the dream in a perfect marriage with two perfect children. She had often felt sadder for her own situation purely by proximity to his.

'I am an employee. I do as I am told, I earn the money. But I feel like I could be anyone.'

'Maybe you could go on holiday together?'

'We tried that after Erin was born. She spent the whole time on her iphone texting her mum. I don't think we had an actual conversation the whole week.'

'I'm sorry.

'So am I, that was a bloody expensive holiday and I didn't even get laid!'

Jules sniggered.

James rolled his eyes.

'I bought lingerie and everything.'

'I am sure you looked lovely in it.'

'I really did. Stockings, a nice Basque, red like my hair...' James chuckled, but his smile faded as he continued, 'I felt like she was there out of duty, she didn't really see the point in me when there wasn't shopping to be carried or a car seat to be fitted.'

'Maybe you should talk to her?'

James nodded.

'Sorry, didn't mean to be such a downer.'

'It's ok – I was feeling like the downer before I bumped into you!'

James smiled.

71

Jules turned her head to look at him. When their eyes met she realised how close they were to one another. She could feel his breath on her nose, could count the freckles on his cheeks. She felt the intensity of his stare, clear as if he had used the words - I want you. Their friendship altered in that split second. Suddenly there was a new dimension to something she thought she knew the edges of. She was frightened and excited at the same time. They might have gone on learning the contours of one another's faces indefinitely had it not been for Abbey.

'There you are you little non-dancing stow-away!'

'Sorry Abbey – Abbey, James, James Abbey.' Jules gestured as she introduced them, squinting up at Abbey and smiling, acutely aware of the flush in her cheeks. Abbey was just intoxicated enough not to pick up on the moment she had interrupted.

'Come on, Becky is starving we are going for a kebab!'

'Oh god how awful. Right, ok...' Jules stood up as Abbey clasped her hand and started to drag her away.

'Night James...' She called, leaving him sat on the bench.

'Night Jules – see you Monday.'

Jules sat in the all night takeaway picking at the chips she had chosen as a safe option, while her friends tucked greedily into oozing garlic laced kebabs. She decided Abbey's interruption could not have been better timed.

It must surely have been that she was drunk. She had never looked at him as an attractive man before, he was always a friend, good old James, not someone she fancied.

Sat there, amidst the fairy lights and countless vulgarities, he had shone for her. The way he fetched her water, surely the reason she was still standing, his soft brown eyes searching hers, how his attention had allowed her to be funny and free. She tried to convince herself she hadn't done anything wrong because they hadn't actually touched one another, but as she imagined Lisa watching their encounter, she felt sure his wife would not have been happy if she had witnessed the long minutes they had stared into each other's eyes.

She resolved to put it out of her mind. She resolved to start paying attention to the conversation going on around her. She resolved to ignore the nagging realisation that James himself had been stone cold sober and his actions could not be placed in the hands of liquor.

'Right then ladies – cocktails?!'

Jules stood up abruptly and her entourage cheered their agreement and started to gather up their handbags. She knew, in the morning, she would regret the suggestion they drink more alcohol, but decided at that moment she didn't care.

'Charlie, are you sure you don't want to go to bed?'

Gill shifted her weight where her bottom rested on the plastic chair, trying to stave off the numbness. They had been in the barn for almost two hours.

'For the sixtieth time, no!'

'But, if she does actually foal and this isn't just wind,' Gill rolled her eyes at Amber who seemed to have dozed off, 'you are going to witness a birth – you don't know how that might make you feel?'

'No. I don't. But I have a pretty good idea and since you have sent George to bed I'm hardly going to leave you up here alone am I?'

'I could wake him?

'He looked shattered Mum. Besides, I kind of want to do this...' Charlie gazed over at Amber, who huffed and gingerly eased her weight from one hind leg to the other.

Gill nodded. Charlie was as strong willed as she was decisive. As much as she would have liked to have a daughter who occasionally took advice or did as she was told, she had to admit it was one of the things she loved about her.

When George had come home and realised there was no one at the house, he had joined them in the barn for a while. He had spoken kindly to Amber and rubbed her forehead gently, but had been persuaded to head back down to the house and put himself to bed. He was dead on his feet and it would all begin again tomorrow.

Gill had briefly thought something in addition to fatigue might have been troubling George, but with Charlie there and Amber seeming imminent, it hadn't been the right time to ask.

Gill stood up and stretched. Amber instantly lifted her head and locked her ears on Gill. Gill nodded at the mare, acknowledging that she still didn't want her master to leave, despite the fact that labour seemed to have subsided.

'Pop out the big horsebox and get a couple of sleeping bags from the Luton?' Charlie stood up and stiffly walked from the barn as Gill fetched two bales of straw. If it was going to be a long night, they may as well be comfortable.

'Taxi just dropped Jules off at the gates,' Charlie was laughing as she came back with the bags, 'she was having trouble walking in a straight line!'

Gill glanced at her watch, it was almost 3am.

'Someone had a good night then! Do her good to get out and let off some steam.'

'She is proper serious isn't she?'" Charlie chuckled as they spread a couple of the cleaner looking stable rugs over their straw bale bed.

'Yes. But she is about to be made partner in her firm, her hard work is paying off. That's what goes with being a solicitor Charlie – are you sure the law is for you?!'

Charlie swatted at her mother's arm.

'No one said all solicitors had to be boring workaholics!'

'No, but the successful ones are.'

'Maybe I should just have the baby, be much easier.'

Gill looked up from zipping the sleeping bags together to see if her daughter was serious. Her gaze was met with a wide grin.

'Don't underestimate me mother.'

Gill walked over to Amber's stable and decided to leave the door open so that Amber could see where Gill and Charlie would be laid without moving. She ran her hands over the large ungainly bulk of the foal within and Amber sneered, ears back, like she didn't want to be touched. The effort of turning her head to reprimand Gill made milk spurt from the mare's teats. Gill sighed and straightened the forelock of her beloved horse, hoping nature was simply taking its sweet time and that there wasn't in fact something wrong.

'Right, let's try and get some shut eye.'

Gill noticed that the barn was lighter as she stirred. Morning had come around. As she stretched on her straw bale and turned away from Charlie who was dribbling onto the rug-pillow next to her, she decided it was probably time to get the vet.

She stood up and walked towards Amber's stable. The mare was down. Sweat had once again darkened her flanks again in glistening patches and she breathed heavily. Gill knelt at her hind legs, it was clear the birth was already in progress. The pale birth sack covered two tiny feet which protruded from Amber.

'You kept that quiet didn't you sweetheart?'

Amber rolled a tired eye at Gill and collapsed her head into the straw, taking in a deep breath before straining noisily, as though she had been permitted not to suffer in silence.

Gill, who in hindsight would feel silly for the gesture, took the fetlock of Amber's foreleg and held it in both her hands, gripping tightly as though willing her to push.

Charlie stirred behind Gill, obviously waking up, but Gill's attention was focused entirely on her horse, willing her to find the strength to bring forth the new life which was finally ready to emerge.

Chapter Four

'You need to go to bed now!'

George implored Gill. She was gazing at her horse, and her new horse. He put his arms around her in an effort to drag her from the barn but she wriggled free and clamped her body to the stable door.

George had to leave for the restaurant soon and he was concerned that it was almost 11am and his partner still hadn't slept properly and looked exhausted.

'Rosie will be here soon and I want to see her, it's been over a month!'

'Then bed?'

'Yes.'

'Promise?'

Gill glanced at Jules who was nestled in the straw, despite her hangover she too could not take her eyes off the foal.

'Probably....not.'

'You bloody horsewomen are mad.' George despaired and made for the barn door while Jules and Gill cackled at his outburst.

'See you later darling!' Gill called and George smiled but shook his head disapprovingly as he headed down the drive.

Charlie had gone to bed soon after Jules had staggered into the barn. She was feeling nauseous but dying to see the new baby, after George had woken her and told her that Amber had given birth.

The tiny creature swayed and nodded his downy head. He had mastered getting up and standing on the long spindle legs which until a few hours ago had been curled beneath him and suspended in amniotic fluid. Walking, on the other hand, was taking a little longer to perfect. Every time he made his precarious way towards Amber's full and ready teats, the mare turned around to nuzzle his head, whickering to him.

'Oh Amber darling, stand still!' Gill laughed and let herself into the stable to stand at the mare's head. Once she was stood with Amber, holding the mares taught cheeks and asking her to stand, Jules laboriously got up from the straw and guided the foal towards the bounty his mother offered. His nose fumbled clumsily around Amber's belly until Jules gently took hold of his tiny head and steered him towards her teats. Once he was nosily slurping the essential colostrum Amber's milk would be rich with for the first few days of his life, Jules drew back. Amber turned her head and gazed in wonder at her baby, then shifted her weight as though she was going to turn and try to nuzzle his face again but Gill rubbed the mare's neck affectionately, encouraging her to remain still.

Gill joined Jules in the straw and they sat together, watching the spectacle before them.

'What are you going to call him?'

'I don't know. If it had been a filly I was going to call her Dorothy after my mum. But as it's a colt I really have no idea. I was convinced it was a girl. And I still can't get over the colour of him. He needs a special name.'

'He really does.'

The foal's head was a rich copper chestnut, the same shade as Amber, but half way down his perfectly crested neck the similarities ended. The lower half of his neck, chest and forelegs were a perfect gleaming white. Then came a second band of chestnut across his back and the top of his rump down his long hind legs. His tail was chestnut, with even white socks reaching just below his hocks, finishing the little horse off perfectly.

'I automatically assumed Amber had been covered by a gypsy cob when I saw his colour. But he is so fine, so Araby. It's such a shame he will always be part Arabian, part something...'

'Could you try and find the man who had her? Ask him?'

'He wouldn't tell the police before. I guess he is still in prison. Given that mine and Charlie's evidence put him there I would be surprised if he would even to talk to me.'

'A mystery...' Jules sighed and then had a light bulb moment and turned to Gill, raising her eyebrows and grinning.

'Nah, too corny...he is so regal and handsome, he needs a special name.'

'Special.'

'Special?'

'Enigma...Blessing...Miracle?'

'Are you still drunk?'

'A little bit... I will think of more names when I am less woolly...'

'Yeah...or don't.'

Jules shoved Gill gently.

'I am still wondering if I am going to be sick.'

'Well don't waste energy shoving me then.'

"Can you at least move the afterbirth?"

Gill laughed at Jules who was starting to turn green.

'Yes ok. You ridiculous excuse for a woman.'

Gill stood up to fetch rubber gloves and a muck bucket as Rosie walked into the barn.

'Hello Stranger! ' Gill rushed towards her friend and then stopped when she saw her hair, or lack of.

'Don't say anything. Completely regret it, don't want to talk about it.' Rosie put her hands up and spoke firmly. Gill accepted the plea and embraced her, ignoring how different she looked without her trademark locks. Gill was surprised when it felt awkward. There was something wrong with Rosie's eyes.

'What's up darling?'

'Oh, another time.' Rosie smiled genuinely and dismissively, 'Right now I want to see this foal and catch up on all your news and Not think about babies!'

'Apart from Amber's?' Jules once again hoisted herself upright and using the stable wall managed to get to her friend.

'Why is she green?' Rosie asked Gill, ignoring Jules.

'Hangover.'

'Ok if Jules has been out drinking I must have one hell of a lot to catch up on!'

'Shut up.' Jules snapped as she pulled Rosie in for a cuddle and leant on her friend a little too long.

'How am I am going to catch up on your news and hear about why you have a hangover if I am not allowed to talk?' Rosie asked as she helped Jules right herself.

'I don't mean don't talk,' Jules almost whispered, 'I mean do it quietly.'

'What was that Jules?' Gill barked and giggled.

'Seriously could everyone keep their voices down? My head is starting to pound.'

As if on cue, Monty whinnied loudly. He had noticed Gill stood next to the feed bins and was wondering if breakfast was ever going to come.

'And you can be quiet as well!' Jules laughed in spite of her queasiness.

'I can't believe I forgot to feed them!' Gill was aghast at her realisation, prompted by Monty's demanding call, 'I have just been watching the foal all morning.'

'Right, Jules go and sit back down you are clearly useless,

Gill – what needs doing? Let's get this done then we can all have a cuppa and catch up?'

'If you are sure Rosie.' Gill was already mixing feeds.

'I can't think of anything I would rather do! Horse pooh has become all the more appealing since I started dealing with nappies!'

By the time the morning rounds were done, Jules had staggered back to the house and fetched some paracetamol and Rosie was feeling altogether more like her old self.

Gill and Rosie sat on the usual plastic chairs which lived in the centre area of the barn, next to the array of feed bins and floor to ceiling racking where rugs were stored, while Jules took advantage of Gill and Charlie's straw bale bed from the night before and laid on her back with a sleeping bag over her legs.

'Urrrrghhhhh...' Jules wailed loudly and Gill threw a body brush at her.

'So, you have heard all about the build and the foal and the business...are we going to hear about you now?' Gill asked Rosie, conscious that for the two hours Rosie had been in their company, she hadn't really said anything about herself.

'I change nappies, I wash baby grows, my life is unbearably boring and really not worth the wear on my larynx or your eardrums.' Rosie shook her head as she spoke, as though she despaired of her own lack of life. 'How's your gorgeous daughter? Still enjoying her gap year?'

'Oh god. I wish you hadn't asked.' Gill put her head in her hands, remembering the conversations before Amber's foal had been born was like getting the news fresh all over again.

'She is back at the house asleep, she stayed here last night, came over with a rather disturbing announcement...'

'Oh what a shame, Eve has just gone back to sleep!' Crystal breezed into the kitchen, blooming from having a baby to care for, as Rosie was taking her wellies off at the back door.

'Oh that's ok.' Rosie just about concealed her relief.

'You can cuddle her when she wakes up for her feed later.' Crystal patted Rosie on the shoulder as she passed her.

'Yes...' Rosie smiled trying not to fill with dread at the prospect.

Her day at Newmans had reminded her too vividly of her old life.

There had been no guilty burden on her shoulders, no dread in her heart, just her friends and horses. She felt slightly bad that she had avoided talking about herself all day, but she hadn't wanted to be dragged back down during such a welcome respite. The noose around her neck had slackened knowing a baby couldn't suddenly cry and demand her attention. She could just be, with other people who could just be. The horse chores she had helped with didn't feel like work, the certainty of the equine's need to be looked after to almost the same degree as Eve did not feel like a burden. It was an honour to care for a horse. It was a retention which in itself brought freedom.

Now that she was back at the cottage she felt cold.

She smiled at Crystal who was making up formula to place in the fridge ready for Eve's next feed and headed to the spare room. She had insisted Jimmy and Crystal take her bedroom, saying as the guests and baby helpers they should have the ensuite and larger room, but in reality she had been unable to give up her spare room sanctuary. She sat on the floor beside the bed. Red and Peat were dozing in the late afternoon sunshine outside the stables, Peat in his paddock, Red close by, basking on the concrete yard.

Rosie thought about Amber's foal. She had spent hours

talking to the tiny creature. Laughing as his curly little whiskers tickled her cheek, gently stroking his perfect white shoulder, drinking in his impossibly cute miniature hooves as she chatted to her friends who were also spellbound by him. Beside her Amber had dozed, exhausted but content.

Rosie felt a welling up inside her heart when she looked at the animal, a desire to protect him, a wonder at the beauty of him. She felt disgust in herself that she could muster those feelings so easily for another creature's baby, but not for her own.

When she had heard about Charlie's pregnancy and her apparently imminent termination, she felt so stupid. She had got pregnant on purpose, how come a 19 year had more self-awareness than she did?

If only Eve was a foal. If only Eve was Crystals, Crystal had the Mum gene. The heaviness of the certainty that she could not go back in time weighed upon Rosie again and again until she felt both physically and mentally crushed by it. She crawled up onto the bed and let the exhaustion wash over her. As though her day at Newmans had not happened, she was right back where she started.

The kind of weariness which only comes from depression rendered her limbs so weak, it was an effort to haul the covers over her body. When she slept her sleep was clinical, no desires to colour her dreams, no hope to wake her.

What did wake her though, a few hours later when it must have been past the horse's dinner time, was the sound of Jimmy on the phone in the hall outside.

'...Matt look I can't go into details, Rosie wants to talk to you herself but she can't do that when you aren't here?

...I know Matt, I know, you can't lose your job.

...I do understand I just don't want this to escalate into

83

something Rosie can't come back from.

...Well yes I know.

...If you could. I know she will be over the moon.

...We will see you on Wednesday."

Rosie smiled and tucked her legs up to her chest, imagining Matt was lying behind her, arm wrapped around her legs holding her like he always did at night. Or used to always do. Wednesday. Just a few more days to go. She loved Jimmy and Crystal and their help with Eve was something she couldn't thank them enough for, but she needed her man. Together they could find a way out of this mess.

Rosie tossed back the covers and her feet hit the floor with an enthusiasm not felt for some months. She had horses to feed and not a lot of daylight to do it in.

Gill sighed happily as she strolled down the drive towards the house. Not even the incessant drizzle of April's half-hearted attempt at showers could dampen her mood. She had given Kelly a list of jobs for the day, and, confident in the groom's ability to run the yard, she was looking forward to having some time with George. Tuesday was his day off from the restaurant. It was the only day of the week when time together was not snatched in between shifts of horse care and cooking, and when he wouldn't have to leave just as other couples settled in for an evening together. She spent Mondays getting every horse ridden and every job done in advance while Kelly was at college doing her riding instructor's course, and now she had nothing but George to look forward to until the next day.

She had noticed he had been particularly stressed over the last few weeks and she resolved to insist upon counselling him through whatever it was. She had let him sleep in when she rose at 6 to feed the barn horses and await Kelly's arrival at 8.

Now it was 9am and she was looking forward to getting back into bed with him and waking him up by running her hands over his glorious body.

She poured coffee from the jug to take upstairs for them both, working quietly, excited, impish.

As she ascended the cottage's long straight, staircase she heard George's voice. He was clearly on a work related call because his tone had a serious quality and he sounded more assertive than home George. As she continued to climb, concentrating on the mugs in her hands, his words got clearer.

"Don't you understand how serious this is? We cannot afford to make things messier than they are. If the staff find out they are going to lose confidence in us."

Gill heard the sound of the covers being flung back and George stomped around the bedroom as he listened to the apparent delivery of bad news. She tried not to be too disappointed, something clearly more urgent than her need for him was going on.

"...Don't you dare throw that at me. If we were actually in this together I would have some support dealing with this instead of having to fix you as well."

Gill paused on the staircase. She didn't want to burst into the bedroom, didn't want to eavesdrop either. The increasingly harsh tone of George's voice made her stomach knot.

"....You need to get your head sorted out. The world doesn't revolve around you.

....yes of course I am coming. I don't want the staff to see you like this just go home."

She heard his pounding footsteps march into the en-suite, the shower was turned on.

"Hello my darling!" She said brightly as she walked into

their bathroom, expecting him to have a rant about the call he had just received.

"Hey gorgeous" George said, quite normally, sounding like George again. His back was to her and she couldn't help but watch the rivers of soapy water running down over his broad back, caressing his smooth bottom and smattering away to the tiled floor. She put the toilet seat down and set the mugs on the sink back. By the time she had seated herself he had turned round. His face looked normal. He smiled at her, with no trace of anguish.

Gill was phased, he had been almost shouting on the phone, clearly now had to go in to work, or somewhere, to deal with something, and yet he wasn't saying anything.

Gill felt a rush of paranoia, as though a tiny insect had scuttled through her brain, picking at memories of her marriage and all the deceit that she had endured, and linking them to the feeling she had now when George clearly had an issue he wasn't sharing. She decided to eradicate the feeling by encouraging conversation.

"That didn't sound like much of a fun phone call? Do you have to go somewhere?"

George turned around again, away from her, to rinse his hair, before speaking.

"I'm so sorry darling. I am going to have to go in, but I should only be a few hours, I just need to sort a few things out."

"Oh... Is it something I can help with?" Gill tried to sound supportive despite being gutted.

"No darling, its fine really. Another supplier cock up but it shouldn't take long then I will come home and we can chill together."

"Another supplier cock up? Maybe it's time to get a new supplier?"

"I think you are probably right."

Gill sipped her coffee, waiting for George to continue, but he didn't.

He turned the shower off and stood for a few seconds, hand on wall, as though composing himself. She stood up to pass him a towel and again when he turned to face her, his expression was a seemingly relaxed smile.

She decided in the absence of any real reason to mistrust him, she wouldn't push him, but resolved to encourage him to talk when he got home.

'You wretched, useless, pointless bloody monstrosity!'

Jules bellowed at the photocopier. The secretaries had gone home hours ago and she cursed her inability to make the machine work.

"Stand back, I am armed." James walked into the photocopier room, which their two firms shared, brandishing a fresh toner cartridge.

"Oh thank god you know what to do."

"The firm I trained with believed everyone should start at the bottom, so, not only can I fix photocopiers, I am also a dab hand with a letter opener!"

"I wish I was better at this sort of stuff, I feel like such a princess when I have to ask the secretaries to do everything for me."

'Well it is their job, but they do appreciate a fee earner who can copy their own documents from time to time.'

'Yes...although I think they appreciate you for a different reason.'

James looked up from his knelt position as he snapped the side door of the copier back into position.

'Oh right...how so?'

'You must have seen how the personal injury girls look at you! You are quite the heart throb on the fifth floor Mr Harkland.'

James blushed as he stood up and moved away to discard the old toner.

'Right, try it now.'

Jules re-inserted her documents and hit start. The copier whirred into life and started producing the paginated bundles she would need in the morning.

'My hero. I didn't even realise you were still here?'

'So I am a heart throb on the fifth floor then?'

'Absolutely, they giggle about you in the kitchen.'

'What about the photocopier room?'

'What about the photocopier room...what?'

'Am I a heart throb in there?'

It was Jules' turn to blush. She didn't know what to say. They had dabbled in flirtation since the night at the club. Her confidence swelled in the safety of a packed office where anyone might walk in. But now, here they were in a deserted building late at night, and all she could think about was how wonderful he smelled and how terrified she was.

Jules bit her lip and looked at the floor.

James laid his hand on hers where it rested on the edge of the copier. She flinched slightly and he immediately drew it away.

"So..."

"So."

"Are you all done now?" James asked.

"As soon as this has finished yep, all ready."

"Fancy going for a bite to eat?"

Jules looked at the floor again.

"Better not James, Gill is looking after the animals, I

88

should probably get home and get some sleep before tomorrow."

"Ah. Ok."

James appeared mortally wounded. He put both hands out and leaned on the photocopier and sighed. She wondered briefly whether his still being there so late had been engineered to get some time alone with her and she had just doused his plan.

"Another time though?" Jules said brightly.

"No you are probably right Jules, Lisa is already pretty irritated I didn't make it for Ben's bath time. I guess I had better get home."

Jules nodded. The tension was tangible. She felt like she had upset him but she shouldn't feel like that, he was married. It was his wife's job to go out for dinner with him.

The photocopier beeped to signify it had finished.

She leant over to fetch her papers and her arm brushed his hand.

The warmth between them lingered so forcefully she felt as though she had been burned.

'James...'

She couldn't move her arm. He leant forward so that his chin rested on her shoulder.

She ducked her head so that her temple brushed his forehead and they stood in a sort of awkward embrace, leaning against one another.

Neither of them noticed immediately, but the rising tone of the mobile phone in his pocket became incessant.

"Answer it then." Jules drew back and slumped against the copier, her body like jelly, her mind under control again.

She knew it was Lisa's ring.

Gill sat in the straw in the corner of Amber's stable. Since the foal had been born it had rained constantly.

It appeared the little skewbald was going to take after his mother.

Gill had tried to turn the pair out in the sand school, she wanted to let them run around and get some fresh air outside the barn. She had led Amber into the school and released her, the little foal tottering at her side to keep up. Amber had immediately turned towards the gate and stood glowering at the droplets which fell on her face, her foal all but tucking himself underneath his mother to avoid getting wet. She had so been looking forward to seeing them move, to witness the first footsteps into the open air, to watch Amber, relieved of her heavy belly, as she taught him to run.

But, timing was everything with horses, and just because she needed something to take her mind off the fact that George had gone, it did not mean Amber and her baby were going to deliver on the moment Gill had looked forward to.

She should have known better, Amber hated the rain with a vengeance and never appreciated being forced to leave the barn for anything less than blue skies.

Three hours after he left, George had phoned. She knew it wasn't going to be good news as soon as she reached for her flashing phone. It was going to take longer than he expected, he was sorry, she should go ahead and plan her day without him. She had been supportive, easy going, understanding. It was how their relationship was, if she was having a horse related emergency then she was the one apologising, so it worked both ways. His having to stay at work in itself wasn't what was bothering her.

It was Deja Vu.

Charlie's father had been working late in the months that led up to their divorce. At the time she had supported his need to concentrate on his developing company. She had not insisted on hearing about his day, nor questioned his need to work.

Then the truth which had ended their marriage had surfaced. His work had indeed been time consuming, but not as time consuming as having sex with his marketing executive had apparently been.

She didn't honestly believe George was having an affair, not really, but the familiarity of the situation was making her stomach churn involuntarily. Especially now it was almost 9pm and her partner still had not arrived home.

George knew all about Alex and Megan, maybe the answer was just to tell him how she was feeling and ask that he reassure her? Could she really admit that level of insecurity though? Neediness wasn't exactly sexy.

'Oh, I don't know.' She said to Amber's foal. The little horse had been standing over her and nuzzling her forehead with his nose. The foal folded his legs underneath him and collapsed into her hip.

Amber heard the barn door opening before Gill and turned and whickered to the foal to make him stand up so that he was prepared for any possible danger the intruder presented.

Amber heard Jules' familiar voice and turned back to her haynet, leaving the foal to shake his tiny head and stand precariously on sleepy legs beside her.

'Hey Jules, in here.' Gill called without getting up.

Jules, still dressed in suit and heels, leant over the stable door and smiled wearily at the foal.

'Long day?'

'Bloody prep for a case conference tomorrow. Romeo alright?'

'Yeah, fine. I guessed you were stuck at work so I checked on him and pooh picked his field.'

'Oh thanks Gill. You didn't need to do that on your day

off?'

'Change of plan, George got called in to the restaurant, so I have basically been wandering around doing little jobs in the hope he would get away all afternoon and evening. Zig is back at the house, but he came with me to check the fences in the summer paddock so he has had a good run.'

'Sorry your day got messed up.' Jules smiled at her friend, knowing how much of a culture shock it had been for Gill to actually give herself a regular day off from a job which had, until George, had planned all her time for her.

The pair watched the foal, who was literally falling asleep on his feet, swaying comically every time he started to drift off. Neither laughed properly. They each had things on their minds that they would rather not share. A jumble of feelings yet to be worked through.

'So, named him yet?' Jules asked.

'Oh god I don't know.' Gill shook her head. 'Kelly and I went through every name we could think of this afternoon and nothing would stick to him.'

Jules thought that James would be a nice name for a horse but quickly pushed the thought aside, embarrassed by herself.

"You said if it was a filly you were going to call her Dorothy after your Mum?'

'Yes, and Dotty would have been a great stable name considering his colour. But I think giving him a girl's name might be a knock to his confidence!'

Jules thought for a moment.

'What was your Dad called?'

'Theodore. But everyone called him Ted.'

'So...'

'Theodore's Ambition. Teddy for short.' Saying it out

loud Gill couldn't believe she hadn't thought of it herself.

Jules nodded.

'And Ted when he's older.'

'Teddy...' Gill called to the foal who opened his eyes and turned to face her with pricked ears, as though confirming it must be his name.

'Sorted.'

'I will register him tomorrow.' Gill stood up and went to Amber who was still at her haynet. 'That ok then girl, if we call your baby Ted?'

Amber carried on eating, as though confirming it mattered very little to her.

'Thanks Jules.'

'Think nothing of it.'

'Shall we go back to the house, you must be starving?'

'Suppose I must be, but I think I might just go straight to bed.'

Later that night, in the small hours long after she had drifted into sleep, Rosie stirred. She opened her eyes to the brightly lit room and squinted at Matt's face.

'What are you doing in here? I nearly got into bed with your bloody Dad!'

Rosie giggled, but then started to cry. She wrapped herself around Matt who was sat on the bed.

'I am so pleased to see you. I can't tell you how much.' She sobbed into his shoulder.

'I worked late so I could take tomorrow off, ended up driving back when I realised I couldn't sleep. I am worried about you Rosie.'

'I am ok now you are here.'

Rosie's heightened emotion increased the sensitivity of

her skin, her legs against the material of his suit tingled. Her pupils dilated and she pressed her mouth against his, her fingers found the knot in his tie and began to loosen it.

Matt pulled back. His eyes quizzed her, unsure whether sex was appropriate given the circumstances, and the fact that he still didn't really know what the circumstances were. He regarded her short hair with little interest, Jimmy had already told him about it and he had prepared himself not to react. Actually she looked sort of cute, with huge sad eyes and milky white shoulders, exposed without the cascade of curls.

'I need you.' Rosie met his eyes with longing. She reached up to push his jacket clear of his shoulder and as had always been the case, Matt was unable to resist his wife.

He allowed her to remove his shirt, felt himself swell as she kissed his chest.

Her eyes were dry as she straddled him, but her cry as he entered her was filled with emotion and desperation. He pushed the worry from his head, holding her on top of him. His part was more of duty than genuine lust, but he knew she would not talk to him about why he had been called home now, so he silenced his questions and focused on her orgasm, which came in trembles, and afforded her almost instant sleep.

Matt lay awake beside her for some time afterwards, before creeping to the nursery to check on his daughter.

Chapter Five

Secrets always lead to lies, Jules decided, as she watched her client.

A meeting about a matter which was due in the civil court next week had turned into a mediation. The defendant had turned up at the firm, tearful and desperate, and Jules' client, Jane, had agreed, as they were all there, to try and settle.

The case being brought was one of negligence. While Jane had been ill and in hospital, her business partner had made a series of bad decisions, leading to the collapse of the partnership and some quite serious breaches of trading law involving the sale of the horses they had bred.

As the half-truths which had led to a breakdown in communication unfolded, both women were starting to get emotional. Friends and partners for many years, the bringing of an action by Jane had led to them becoming adversaries. Now that they were face to face, the hatred they had formed via solicitors' letters and court papers didn't seem so justified.

Jules suggested a break out session once each side had laid down their version of the facts.

Jules nipped up to her office to collect a blank settlement agreement. The eye contact between Jane the defendant suggested things were not going to end in the court room after all.

Jules thought about her own secret as she waited for the document to print. She had not told anyone about James. There was nothing to tell really. Nothing had happened as such. It didn't stop her feeling like her entire world had been turned upside down.

Jules had sensed unease in Gill the night before in the barn. She had assumed Gill's tension of late was to do with the Charlie-baby situation and the looming racing season, but now wondered what her friend wasn't telling her.

When Jules returned to the conference room she found Jane and her ex-businesses partner together. Although Jules had left them in separate rooms, they had obviously not stayed put.

"Do you guys need a minute?" Jules smiled as the two women looked up at her. Usually she wouldn't have been happy for her client to converse with the other side without her present, but she sensed that the law would not come in to this discussion, and was indeed better left out of it.

As Jules sat waiting outside the conference room she eyed the defendant's solicitor, who had obviously had the same thought. They nodded politely to one another but didn't speak.

Jules wondered what Rosie was doing. She wished she could pick up the phone and talk to her friend about James. Something which would have been a certainty six months ago. Rosie was surely more likely to find closer friendships with those who also had babies and children now.

Jules thought about her friend's new hairstyle they weren't allowed to talk about, her insistence on focusing only on Jules and Gill and horses. She wondered what Rosie wasn't telling her. She wondered if they were even close enough that Jules could still ask.

Jules and Rosie had met through work, a client who had been cheated out of his share of a company and as a result found himself homeless, had needed the services of both women simultaneously. Their friendship had struck up upon Jules' mention of needing to get home to feed her horse. They had both been relatively fresh faced in their careers at the time and over the subsequent years they had grown together and grown fond of one another. Now, it seemed, they were destined to grow apart.

Jules suddenly felt very alone. Gill had George and Rosie had Matt. She only had her animals. She had other friends of course, but they could all be categorised into university friends, work friends and riding friends, none of whom she could talk to about James. The only other friend she would have considered confiding in was, rather irritatingly, James.

There was no way she could talk to her mother about having feelings for a married man. Marianne was supportive, loving and warm, but she was also a stickler for morals and she would undoubtedly convince Jules not to continue down such a dark path.

Her mother would be right of course.

"I think we might be ready to work this out." A tear stained but smiling Jane appeared at the door. Jules and the other solicitor followed her back into the room.

Rosie watched her husband and her daughter.

Matt had woken before her and brought Eve in on the bed with them.

As Rosie had stirred she had been instantly aware of the love in his voice. At first she thought he was talking to her.

He continued to tell the baby how precious and beautiful she was. Rosie stayed still, not wanting to embarrass Matt by letting him know she was awake.

Over the last few days, since Jimmy had told her that he and Crystal had wanted a baby, she had been concocting a plan in her head. She had convinced herself that she had found the perfect solution.

But now, with Matt right in front of her, she realised she hadn't.

As much as Crystal might want a baby, and as much as she knew Jimmy would do almost anything for her, there was no way Matt would allow the couple to bring Eve up.

As she watched him kiss the child's forehead she felt anxiety rise in her, how could her brain have deceived her, so that she had genuinely thought it might work?

Desperation. She concluded, resigned and numb again.

She was grateful she hadn't mentioned her ridiculous idea to Jimmy or Crystal, glad she hadn't raised their hopes. She was back at square one again.

Matt laid Eve on his chest and turned to Rosie. He smiled at her and mouthed 'morning' and she smiled back. If only this was life. If only having her husband next to her wasn't always so temporary.

As they continued to hold one another's gaze, Rosie wished she were telepathic. She wished she could convey all that she was feeling, without having to say the words. His eyes questioned her. Why had he been summoned home? Why were Jimmy and Crystal in his bed in Devon instead of their own in London?

Val had involved Jimmy, who had involved Matt.

Why did she have to go and cut all her hair off? At least her misery in silence hadn't hurt anyone else. Now everyone who knew was looking at her like she was a patient.

The daughter of an alcoholic, Rosie had endured those looks too often at school, until she had learned to keep her home life an absolute secret. Her mother, Selina, had placed a young Rosie and Jimmy in situations neither had wanted to deal with. Rosie had picked her mother up out of her own vomit, bathed her and put her to bed, when she should have been gossiping on the phone with a classmate or concentrating on a crush she had. The only solace she found, other than in Jimmy, who was too close to it all anyway, had been Harry.

His pricked ears greeting her when she arrived at the stable, his strong legs to carry her away from it all. Before she had been blessed with Harry she had felt so lonely. She had longed for the brother or sister whose absence had fuelled her mother's demise.

He might not have been able to answer her, but Harry was always there to listen and make her feel loved.
After Harry it seemed, the loneliness was destined to return.

She felt, as she often did, a longing to be with Red. She staved off the impulsion because Matt was there.

Eve's face crumpled into discomfort and she grizzled.

"What's wrong little girl?" Matt picked the baby back up and cradled her in his arms, concerned.

"Hungry." Rosie answered him, and as if on cue Eve started to cry.

"You are so good at this Rosie."

"Matt, I'm really not, that's what I..." Rosie stopped speaking as the bedroom door opened and Crystal appeared with a bottle.

"Do you want to do the honours Daddy?" Crystal smiled warmly as she handed the bottle to Matt and offered them both coffees before retreating again.

"She's amazing!"

"Yeah, a natural." Rosie smiled wryly, wondering when it was ever going to be the right time.

"I'm so sorry."

"You don't have to be sorry. It's all my bloody fault. I did this, I have to suffer the consequences."

"You didn't get pregnant on purpose."

"Contributory negligence. I had run out of the pill and the condom split. I should have got the morning after pill and I didn't." Charlie had studied Law at A Level at Exeter college and understood the legalities of risk. She knew the words anyway, in reality, she just hadn't thought she could be that unlucky. As they sat in the little purple vehicle, Gill in the driver's seat so that she could take them back to Newmans, Charlie's eyes were dry, but her energy was blackened. The hospital car park was filled with people with grim faces; the visitors who were there out of duty, the patients who received bad news. Of course it wasn't all bad, but Charlie saw only the misery around her.

The hospital appointment had not gone how she wanted it to. She had expected them to perform the termination there and then but it quickly became clear they would only be examining and scanning her in preparation, as well as ensuring she was under no duress and that the termination was planned, necessary and had been given adequate thought. She would receive another appointment for the actual procedure in a week or so.

"I thought I was invincible. But I am just a silly girl aren't I.."

"No. You are far from silly. You are trying to make the best of your life and you are making a difficult decision to be here instead of picking out pushchairs."

Gill leant across the handbrake and pulled her daughter in towards her, almost too tightly. She was so proud of, and so sad for her child in that moment she could have wept for all she was worth.

'Darran is away doing a gig in Leicester. I thought I could get it all over with by the time he came back and then tell him I lost it.'

Gill exhaled in a gust of despair.

'Oh Charlie. You never would have lived with the lie anyway.'

'I know. I have told him this is what I am doing. I just can't deal with any more discussions about it, it's all so depressing and I don't get a break from thinking about it as it is, because I feel so sick all the time, I can't forget. He is pretending to be all supportive now, but constantly trying to change my mind by coming up with more and more far-fetched solutions. He offered to be a stay at home Dad so I could still go to Uni. He even proposed. He just doesn't get it.'

'Those don't sound that far-fetched.'

"Yes. I can just picture it now, kid wearing bloody ear defenders parked in the corner of his guitarist's garage while they practice?"

'Oh, I see.'

'The worst thing is, he doesn't really want a baby either, he knows he would have to give up his dreams too, he just thinks if I go through with the termination it's inevitable we will split up.'

'Is it?'

'No. The thing that will make us split up is if he doesn't grow up a bit. Honestly he needs to get a grip, and a bloody job!! He is 20 now he is going to be unemployable soon. They don't exactly give jobs away do they?'

'What about some bar work?'

'Evenings are when his gigs are – he needs something more 9 – 5.'

Gill grasped the little steering wheel and sighed.

'One thing at a time Charlie. You don't have a deadline. You need to deal with this situation first.'

'Don't I bloody know it. Can we go now?'

As Gill ascended the drive she wondered where George was. It was 3pm so he usually would have been home napping ready for evening service, but the black Lexus was absent. She pulled Charlie's car around so she could drive straight out again, but she noticed her daughter was almost asleep in the passenger seat. Worn out from all the emotion, the disappointment, the hormones.

'Don't go back to West Hill now darling, come in and have a sleep in my bed.'

Charlie nodded wearily.

Gill pulled back the bedclothes and Charlie slid into the kingsize covers. Gill drew the curtains and sat at her daughter's back, stroking her forehead until her breathing got heavy and her eyelids closed.

Gill stood up and stretched. She should probably go up to the barn and see how Kelly was getting on with the afternoon rounds but she was worried that if George did now arrive home he might walk in to the bedroom and wake Charlie up. Gill sat on the edge of the bed and took her shoes off. Laying on top of the covers she curled her body around her daughter's back and rested her head on the pillow.

Rosie shivered as she waited for Matt to speak.

The warmth of the sun's height had descended with it and a cold breeze swept over Dartmoor.

The granite rock beneath her chilled her legs through her jeans, but she dare not complain. She had to let him process the information in his own time.

Many of the other walkers who had also decided to visit the Hay tor had long since gone home. Although she was glad they had the majestic outcrop of stone to themselves, she couldn't help but feel the bleakness of the open land. The rocks formed shadows around them, the darkness cast imposing and grim, like Matt's face.

"I love you." She said again, almost involuntarily.

"I know you do." He said, matter of fact.

She followed his gaze out over the expanse of moorland. There were usually tough little native ponies and collections of ragged sheep dotted around, but today the moor was empty. At that moment Rosie's dislike of herself was such that she could have believed the animals had moved to get away from her.

"I'm sorry." She murmured. He could only reflect her unhappiness back on himself and she knew, from past experience, he did not deal well with guilt.

"It's not your fault." She spoke again, almost desperate.

"Could you just be quiet. Please."

Rosie nodded. She dropped her head. He hated her.

When they had left Orchard cottage, on Jimmy's suggestion that they go somewhere alone to talk, Matt had started to gather up Eve's things. It was understandable, of course, his time with Eve was the opposite of Rosie's. It was not necessity, it was precious and short, but it had phased Rosie. Matt knew she needed to talk, that she had a serious problem she needed to share with him, why wasn't that enough to make him leave his baby for a few hours and concentrate on his wife?

It had taken her too long to start telling him. As they had driven around Devon and eventually stopped at Hay tor because it was a place they visited when they first started going out, it seemed natural to walk the slope from the road to the rocks and inappropriate to talk then. By the time they were finally sat together and Rosie had regained her breath, she could see Matt was irritated. Frustrated by hours in the car, by her silence or, worse, her casual observations about the things they passed. He had not demanded she speak, had been patient in that sense, but his clear annoyance with her made the pressure worse and she had explained herself badly, chosen all the wrong words, and then had to say it all again.

'It's just post-natal depression isn't it? I mean, isn't this common? Can't you go to your doctors?'

'I guess I could.' Rosie nodded.

'Well there is no guess about it. There must be something going on with your hormones.'

'I just don't like my life Matt.'

She lifted her head to meet his gaze. She felt like she had been stabbed. He was controlling his voice, using practical words, but his eyes had a fire behind them, they bore into her, branding her.

'And now you don't like me.'

'I don't dislike you Rosie, you are my wife. But I don't get it. I can't pretend to understand it.'

He shook his head and lifted his palms in frustration.

'When I look at Eve I am overcome with love, I feel..god I can't even describe it. I feel like my life led up to her, like everything I was meant to be is realising itself now. Being her Dad is my life.'

Matt paused and looked at his wife again, unmoved by her tears.

'I don't understand how you don't feel it too. She is so special, so precious, and all along you have been pretending. She deserves love Rosie. She didn't do anything wrong.'

'I know she didn't. I don't not love her, I just know I don't feel the way I should.'

'That's why this has to be medical. You need some anti-depressants or something. I want to take you to the doctor tomorrow.'

'Ok.' Rosie sniffed and nodded.

'You can't let this happen. You had a crap childhood, doesn't that make you determined not to give one to her?'

'I'm not cruel to her Matt.' Rosie couldn't bear the disappointment in his voice. He was talking about her like she was being as bad as her own mother, 'She wants for nothing. She is clean and fed and cared for and throughout all of this, no matter how hard I have found it, I have not once left her needing anything.'

'Except love.'

'You love her. Dad and Crystal love her.'

'Oh well that's ok then.'

'If you were home...' Rosie's voiced trailed off and Matt's anger got the better of him.

'Yeah I knew that was coming.' As he spoke he slid down off the rock and walked away from her in the direction of the car.

With a deep breath she fought the instinct to stay on the rock and return his anger. Instead she slid after him, to fall in step behind him, respectfully following her man. If there was one thing worse than how she felt about Eve, about her despair at her situation, it was the thought of losing Matt. Even if it meant becoming a better actress and convincing everyone she was ok, she would do it. She had to.

George got home at 5pm with an hour before he had to go back to the restaurant. He had found Charlie in the living room. Puffy eyed and forlorn, the girl was watching telly under a duvet. Beyond exchanging pleasantries he didn't engage her. He knew what was going on of course, but he didn't feel it was appropriate to ask her how the appointment had gone.

"Gill?" George called as he walked into the barn.

He saw the empty boxes and realised they must be at the gallops.

He had so wanted to see her. To hold her and hear about her day. Something to break the cycle and give him a rest from worrying. He also wanted to ask her about Charlie, so he didn't put his foot in it.

He walked around the side of the barn and capped his eyes with his hand so that he could peer towards the horizon. No sign of the returning horses.

He had had another row with Rob. His business partner was burying his head in the sand. There was no doubt now that they were in trouble. The customers kept eating, the money was coming in all right, but as full as the till was at the end of each evening, it wasn't going to be enough.

He decided in the absence of Gill, he might as well get an hour's sleep before another evening of pretending all was well began. Every effort he made felt pointless.

He laid on the bed and closed his eyes but his mind reeled in spite of his tired body.

He thought about his house in the village. He had let the property when he had moved in with Gill. The rental allowed him to increase his mortgage repayments. He thought of it as their retirement nest egg, an asset he could sell when he and Gill wanted to slow down, use the proceeds for an easier life one day. He wondered exactly how much equity he now had in the house and what it was currently worth. He would dig out his latest mortgage statement later.

His heart felt heavy as he rolled over, trying to get more comfortable.

It didn't really matter what the figures were, the inevitability was that he was going to need a whole lot of cash to avoid losing his business and any available resource would need to be liquidated. He thought about his car. He loved the black Lexus.

His mind jumped back to conversation he had with his parents about the little flat they rented, just around the corner. He worried about what would happen if their landlord sold and it comforted him to know he had a property they could move into without too much upheaval. He would take away the contingency plan if he sold the house. He decided to get the car valued.

He desperately didn't want to sell either, but he was running rapidly out of options.

Rosie woke early, rose and saw to the horses.
Matt had barely spoken to her after they had arrived back at the cottage the evening before. He had been friendly as usual with Crystal and Jimmy at dinner and when they had gone to bed he had cuddled in to Rosie out of habit and perhaps not to instigate a row if he hadn't, but he had not even motioned towards wanting to have sex with her.

She had ran back to the house after the horse jobs were done, hoping to get back in to bed with him and regain some intimacy, show him she was still his girl despite what he had learned the day before. But, he was already up and hunched over the laptop at the desk in the spare room, deep in conversation via a video conference with the office and totally engrossed in work, trying to make up for his premature departure remotely.

Rosie laid on the bed, hoping he would finish the call and join her but after half an hour of waiting she tiptoed back out of the room.

She wandered into the living room.

Crystal had left the television on.

Rosie stared blankly at the news, not really taking it in,

her brain, as usual, busy with too many thoughts.

Rosie comforted herself with the promise of better times to come with Eve. When she was talking, when she came home with her first school problem, first love, first dilemma – Rosie knew when Eve was older she could be a great mum. Knew it as though it were as definite as the tide. It was the years in between then and now which made Rosie want to go to bed, stopped her feeling excitement, stopped her riding. How to get there intact, without losing Matt in the meantime?

Rosie got up to make herself a cup of coffee and noticed the kitchen door was open. She saw Jimmy on the bench in the Orchard, Eve in the pushchair beside him. Both appeared to be asleep.

She walked quietly towards her Dad and as she sat next to him his eyes flickered open.

He reached for her hand. They watched the horses in the field beyond. Red swished his tail at the flies and Peat dozed in his little paddock next to his pile of hay, the grass eaten down to all but nothing, the pony had created a patchwork square of paler green amidst the lushness.

'How did it go?'

'Don't know really. He still hasn't said much. He wants me to go to the doctor later.'

'I think that is probably a really good idea. Don't beat yourself up Rosie, you can't always be strong and how you deal with the weaknesses, that's what really counts.'

'It all feels so certain. So...choice-less.'

'There are always choices Rosie, but when you try to ignore yourself and what you need for too long, and depression sets in, you stop seeing the choices.'

Rosie stopped watching Red and turned to look at Jimmy's face. There was a knowing in his eyes.

'You sound like you have been there.'

'We have all be down at some point Rosie. Show me a man who says he has never felt despair, and I will be looking at a liar.'

Rosie nodded. Maybe she wasn't as alone as she thought she was. She flinched as she thought about how much more alone she could be, especially if Matt couldn't or wouldn't support her.

Red drew his head up and pricked his ears. He shook his head like a stallion and Peat woke up, as though he felt the sudden electricity in his companion. Red cantered to the edge of Peat's paddock and together they raced up and down its length, bucking, challenging one another. Faster they went, running for the joy of running until they reached the corner again. Peat snorted, head high, while Red slid to a stop and they stood panting together.

'They make me jealous when they do that.'

'You could always run up and down with them.' Jimmy teased.

'It's their freedom, to suddenly run like hell just for the hell of it. I don't feel like there is anything I do which is just for the hell of it.'

Jimmy considered for a moment. Eve stirred in her buggy, eyes opening briefly, she yawned before falling back to sleep.

'Isn't that why you ride?'

Rosie nodded. She knew it would probably make her feel better, but she just couldn't bring herself to do it, something so sacred and joyful, when she felt so rotten and low. The desolation inside was no longer a rational or controllable thing. It spread into her limbs and rendered them sluggish, so that she could have dragged her feet when she walked without a considered effort not to.

Feelings used to be ancillary to Rosie's day. Now she was consumed by her own turmoil, it seemed her mind would not permit her body the strength to do the things she loved.

'Why don't you go and see Jules and Gillian again this afternoon?' Jimmy patted her knee, smiling encouragingly at her.

'What about Matt?' Rosie felt the bud of panic open in the centre of her, she had got so used to never planning anything during Matt's time at home in order to make the most of him. Even when he cared for Eve, she was only ever out in the field with the horses, or asleep.

'I think he will be working most of the day, and then I thought I would suggest he Eve and I go for a walk.'

'Right.'

Rosie eyed her father and scowled against his unchanged bright smile, not liking the thought of being discussed.

'He needs some time to get his head around this. Maybe the opportunity to talk about it would do him good?'

Rosie nodded, half returning the smile. She chided herself for her own pride. Pride was not something she could afford at the moment.

Chapter Six

Jules decided to work the rest of the day from home.

She had seen James briefly in the corridor. Their chat had been functional and work related, because an endless stream of colleagues kept coming out of the lift. The halls of Hodges & Grath had never seemed so busy, it was typical of course. Jules mused as she fled the office, trying to get home with enough lunch break left to take Ziggy for a head clearing run, that it was probably best. What was the point of talking about their feelings anyway? If-onlys plagued Jules as she drove away from the city, all the ways it could have been different, and that the prospect of falling in love could have been wonderful instead of doomed.

Of course, she didn't know for sure that he loved her beyond the fondness of their friendship, but at the same time, if she was honest, she knew him well enough to know it. Jules shook her head as she pulled into the drive and popped her car into the space next to her developing new home. She had so much to look forward to, so much to do and so much of herself to give to the annexe, the racing business, her career and her animals. Why-oh-why then must she insist on ruining her own potential joy by longing for someone unobtainable?

'Silly girl.' She said out loud as she got out of the car and was pleased to see the new kitchen door finally being fixed into place.

'It came then?' She called to Keith.

'At last eh – not long now Juliette, the plastering has started!'

'Wooohooo!' Jules laughed and beamed at Keith, who

blushed slightly before carrying on with his job.

'Now why can't I fall for a nice bloke like Keith eh Zig?' She said as she opened the kitchen door of Newmans cottage and the black dog wagged his tail so hard his whole body weaved in delight to see her.

'Oh got 'yer eye on the builder have you?!'

Jules nearly jumped out of her skin when she realised Charlie was sat at the kitchen counter.

'No.' Jules sighed and grinned at Charlie, 'that is part of the problem.'

'You could do a lot worse, something a bit spunky about him, and his big leather tool belt.' Charlie emphasised the word tool and her eyes twinkled at Jules who shook her head in mock disgust.

'Charlie! What would Darran say?'

Charlie rolled her eyes and scowled at her phone where it sat on the counter beside her. She picked the shiny pink device up and held it towards Jules so she could see the screen, filled with unread texts from 'My Beau'.

'Darran would say quite a lot. But I am not listening.'

'Oh.' Jules reached down and ruffled Ziggy's ears, averting her gaze from her friend's daughter and feeling awkward. She wasn't sure how much she was supposed to know, much less what to say.

'It's ok Jules.' Charlie said quietly.

'I'm just so sorry you are having to go through this Charlie.' Jules looked up and smiled sympathetically.

'Me too mate. Me too.'

Ziggy growled as the kitchen door opened and Jules had to spring out of the way to avoid being hit by it.

'Darling!' Jules threw her arms around Rosie before her friend had a chance to fully cross the threshold.

'Hello guys.' Rosie said warmly, smiling at Charlie when Jules finally let her inside.

'I had just come home to work here for the afternoon, how long are you staying?'

'All afternoon, Jimmy and Crystal have the baby so I'm a free agent!' Rosie didn't lie, but didn't offer the truth either.

'Fantastic. Give me five mins, I'll phone work and say I am taking leave instead!'

'Great.' Rosie smiled as Jules danced away to the office to make the call.

How weird, Jules thought as she dialled, that she had spent the morning thinking about Rosie, and now her friend was here. She felt totally justified in blowing off work – deciding it was fate.

While she was waiting to be put through to her secretary, she noticed the letter head of her firm peeking out from underneath a pile of post addressed to George on the desk. Chiding herself, she snatched at the letter, thinking she must have left some of her papers out. Tutting, Jules scanned the letter to see which case file she needed to return it to. Her eyes widened as she realised the letter was addressed to the Bloomswell.

Without thinking she read the subject line, but didn't have time to read any further because she heard footsteps coming down the hall. She scrabbled to stuff the letter back under the post pile.

Her secretary answered just as George walked into the office.

Jules felt the flush in her cheeks as she smiled briefly at George who stood at the door, gesturing he wanted to come in. Jules invited him with her free hand, mouthing that she wouldn't be long.

George walked over to the large grey filing cabinet where he kept his paperwork.

Jules quickly explained to her secretary that she was taking leave and would see her tomorrow and stood up. George clutched an Orange folder. Jules noticed it had the address of his house in the village handwritten on the front.

'I'm just leaving George, it's all yours.'

'Thanks Jules,' George said and waited for her to move out from behind the desk so that he could sit down. As he did he pulled the pile of post containing the letter towards him. 'Accounts eh, the ruin of many an otherwise productive man!'

Jules flushed again and mumbled bye as she left the room. She would not have made a very good spy. She felt intensely guilty at having looked at George's private mail, despite the innocence of her initial mistake, because if she had not heard him approaching she would have carried on reading.

What on earth was George hiding? He must be hiding something, why else would he have received a Letter Before Action from her firm's personal injury department, and not mentioned it to her?

'So, she doesn't want to go home until the deed is done.' Gill finished updating her friends about Charlie and tipped the last of her coffee into her mouth.

'Isn't Alex wondering why she isn't there?' Rosie asked.

'She's told him she has lots of shifts at the bar and it's easier to stay here for a few weeks.' Gill sighed, 'I love having her of course, I just wish it was for any other reason. She doesn't want to have to lie to her Dad. George is being very sweet with her, he's easier company than Alex too.'

At the mention of George, Jules' adrenaline peaked again. She looked past Gill and focused on Zinee who was nodding over his stable door hoping for some attention. She wanted to mention the letter to Gill, but she had no idea whether she knew about it.

Gill didn't notice Jules' silent anguish, but she did notice the haunted look in Rosie, it was the same look she had seen in her friend the other day.

'So Rosiekins, must be nice having live in babysitters for a bit?' Gill smiled at Rosie, hoping to encourage her to talk a bit more about herself.

'Yeah they just love Eve. It's nice to have company while Matt is away during the week too.' Rosie picked up a leadrope which had been strewn on the floor next to her chair and began coiling it, giving her hands something to do while her lips weren't saying that Matt was in fact with Jimmy right now, discussing her precarious emotional state.

'What made them come and stay? Will they be down for long?' Jules asked, wondering how much freedom Rosie might have and whether she could utilise it to spend more time with her.

'Crystal has taken voluntary redundancy so they are in no rush to head back.' Rosie said, honest but keeping it vague.

'Sounds ideal, especially now the weather is better and you can get out riding more.' Jules beamed.

'Mmm..' Rosie smiled politely. 'So Gill, how is your lovely man?'

'Yeah he is great.' Gill smiled, attempting to look normal, but burdened by her own private concerns about the increasingly long hours her partner was spending at work and the telephone conversation she had recently overheard.

The awkwardness of all they were not saying to each other hung in the air, like fog between them, blocking their usual openness. Each was trying so hard to behave normally, they barely noticed the changes in one another.

'Shall I go and get Rome?' Jules jumped to her feet, not wanting the conversation to be about George either.

'Yeah ok it would be nice to see him!' Rosie latched on to doing something other than talking about her home life.

'You can ride him if you like?' Jules said, 'I don't mind riding Milly!'

'Oh, sorry I thought you meant just to see him, I am not really dressed for riding.' Rosie tried to sound natural, not wanting to have a conversation about why she didn't want to ride. 'I just came to cuddle this little guy really!' Rosie stood up and walked away from her friends, leaning over the half door to watch the little skewbald foal suckling his mother, so that they couldn't see her face.

Gill eyed Jules quizzically, wondering since when not having the right jeans on meant Rosie would pass up a chance to ride?

Jules started to say Rosie could borrow her spare jodhpur boots but Gill cut her off, deciding it was best not to push it, for whatever reason Rosie didn't want to ride today and it seemed a waste of a precious afternoon together to back their friend into a corner.

'Speaking of little Teddy, it's finally not raining so I think it might be time he and Amber went out for a bit!'

'Ooh I will get my camera!' Jules squealed and she trotted out of the barn.

Gill stood up. When she was sure Jules was out of earshot, she put her arm around Rosie.

'You know I am always here if you need to talk don't you?'

'Yep.' Rosie drew back from her vacant stare and turned her head to smile as she felt Gill behind her, 'Of course.'

Gill kissed Rosie's shoulder before drawing away to fetch Amber's headcollar.

For a single second Rosie wanted to turn and collapse into Gill's arms, to tell her everything, but she carried on standing, frozen by pride. Val, Jimmy and Matt knowing seemed like too many people already and the more people who knew, the more people she would have to lie to about her progress.

'Got it!' Jules called breathlessly, bending over to allow her lungs to recover. She positioned herself outside the barn. Gill led Amber out of her stable and Jules poised her camera to start snapping the foals first footsteps in the sunshine.

'Oh tripe!' Gill shouted and halted Amber just as the mare was about to step outside.

'What's up?' Rosie called from behind them.

'I forgot Monty is out.' Called Gill, 'Amber is going to come into season any day..'

Jules and Rosie waited while Gill continued to stand, unsure how much it would bother Amber if the stallion was amorously pursuing her, albeit over a fence.

Amber delicately pawed the ground with a slender foreleg, reminding Gill she would quite like to get her baby into the field.

'Sorry darling,' Gill rubbed her neck, 'Rosie, could you bring Monty in quickly now?'

Rosie ran to the stallion paddock, where Monty was already stood by the gate. She slipped the headcollar on to his sleek black head.

'Take him in the back door, he is in the end stable at the moment anyway,' Gill called. She had moved the stallion from his usual stable because Amber had been disgusted by his attention. Now however, as Rosie led him across in front of them, Gill realised the mare's viewpoint had changed rather significantly.

Amber grunted and pulled Gill forwards before straddling her back legs and weeing on the concrete. The smell hit Monty's keen nostrils and the shining Arabian arched his neck and whickered deeply, confirming his interest.

'Keep him walking Rosie!' Gill called, slightly concerned about how Rosie was going to get him past the mare now that she had given him the ultimate come on.

Luckily, Monty allowed himself to be led away and Gill turned to Amber and laughed at the mare's disgruntled expression.

'So you want another one do you?'

Rosie re-appeared having successfully confined Monty to his stall. She had shut the top of his half door as well for good measure and left him to pace, whinnying desperately.

'Blimey, you wouldn't think she would be interested already!' Rosie looked in horror at Amber, 'I didn't want Matt anywhere near me when Eve was only a week old!'

'Well,' Gill laughed at Rosie's expression, 'they usually come back into season within a few weeks of foaling, so I am not really surprised. I should have been more mindful.'

The foal stepped out in front of his mother to sniff at Jules and the camera. Gill noticed his boldness and grinned.

'Look at him! What a brave little thing you are!' Gill spoke to the foal but his attention was firmly on the camera which he was trying to gum with his tiny toothless mouth. Jules laughed and almost fell over backwards where she crouched when the foal leaned on her, sniffing at Ziggy who was stood behind her. The dog licked tentatively at the foal's muzzle. Teddy shook his head and snorted through his miniature nostrils.

'Let's get them into the paddock.' Gill led Amber

forward, when the three of them had stopped laughing.

Rosie closed the gate and they waited for the magic.

But instead of the long anticipated celebratory run around, Amber began snatching frantically at the grass. Monty, and apparently her foal, forgotten, the mare ate the succulent spring crop as though her life depended on it.

Teddy marched up to Jules and tried to get his mouth around the camera again.

'Well,' Gill couldn't help but laugh, 'not quite what I expected.'

'Highly unexciting!' Jules agreed as she stood up, bringing the expensive piece of equipment up and out of the foals reach.

'Give the girl time, she has milk to make!' Rosie chided them both for their disappointment in Amber.

Jules walked back to the fence to stand with her friends, Teddy tossed his tiny head up and down and then trotted back to his mother to investigate what on earth she was doing with her teeth and the green stuff beneath his feet.

Gill folded her legs beneath her and sat on the grass. Jules and Rosie followed suit either side of her.

They sat in silence, watching Amber as she continued to graze, and Teddy gazed, captivated, at the world around him.

Amber lifted her head and pricked her ears. Teddy sensed her sudden alertness. They stood together watching a buzzard which had taken off from its camouflaged perch on the top rail of the fence, and was using the air currents produced by the warming ground to gain height in wide arcs.

Jules snapped a few pictures of the pair as they posed.

Once Amber was satisfied the bird posed no threat to her baby, she finally gave the friends the performance they had been waiting for.

The mare cantered forward and Teddy raced at her side.

Jules stood up and followed them, camera working overtime.

'You are so lucky Gill.' Rosie sighed, wishing she never had to go home.

'Yes and no.' Gill sighed, unable to truly feel the joy of watching the foal learning to run, leaping the tussocks of longer grass and celebrating his freedom with his first attempted bucks, because she knew her daughter's life was in turmoil and there was nothing she could do to protect her from what she was about to go through.

'I had a termination once.' Rosie said, so that Gill took her eyes off Amber and turned to face her friend, 'It was when Matt and I first got together, we barely knew each other and we decided it just wasn't the right time.'

Gill continued to look at Rosie, moved by her friend's willingness to share something so private.

'I could talk to Charlie if you like?'

Gill nodded gratefully.

'Thanks Rosie.'

'You know me Gill, always help if I can.'

'Yes. I hope when you need it you let others help you.'

Rosie smiled grimly and patted Gill's leg.

'No time like the present.' Rosie stood up and started to make her way down to the house.

Gill watched her friend leave, wishing she could do something for Rosie in return, anything that might dissolve the worry which Gill was convinced was in her eyes, but which Rosie seemed to be determined to deny.

'Why is it Romeo, that the world looks so much more beautiful from your back?'

The week had been a hectic one and Jules had arrived home with barely enough daylight to ride, but it was Friday evening and she needed the solace of her horse and the freedom his bare hooves allowed her.

As Romeo marched eagerly for home on a loose rein, she gazed over the top of the hedgerow that bordered the lane at the beautiful view across rolling hills and towards the horizon. The low haze of setting sunlight gave everything an orangey sheen and Jules beamed openly at how fulfilling a simple short bareback ride on her horse could be.

She liked to think it was his affinity with the surroundings that made the wild flowers in the banks more radiant, the green buds more striking in their colour, because she viewed in from his back and his perspective. In truth it was her own joy that made everything appear so much more vibrant. Astride her horse, with her dog trotting alongside them, she had no need for big words, no cause to exercise her intellect, she could just be.

Rarely was she afforded the time to appreciate the world around her. Romeo provided a vantage point she couldn't imagine being without.

When she had first purchased the 16hh chestnut hunter she had been focused on competition. Her aim in having a horse was to excel at cross country jumping and she kept Romeo at peak fitness and had regular lessons, competing whenever she could. She was always nervous at events and it had affected their progress. In the formal setting of a well attended hunter trial, fear, which did not normally plague her when riding the steady and willing horse at home, often took over. At best she was wooden in her aids, at worst she had been a hindrance to Romeo who was incredibly generous and would jump almost anything without a lot of direction.

She had been obsessed with having the latest saddle, rugs were discarded for being too muddy and Romeo was kept spotless at all times.

After Romeo had been stolen though, things had changed. The sheer and utter delight at having her horse safely returned had made everything else seem trivial. She no longer felt scared at the prospect of competing, a promise she had made to herself during the long months she had been without him. The enjoyment she gleaned even now, over a year after he had been returned, at just being able to touch Romeo, to put her arms around his neck and breathe in the earthy and unique scent of him was enough for her. Perhaps once the racing season was over and the winter hunter trials began she would compete properly again. It was all possible now.

Despite her formerly traditional approach, she had removed Romeo's shoes after he had been recovered. During the time when he had been stolen, no attention had been paid to his feet. His long unkempt hooves had failed to hold onto the old shoes and he had suffered an injury when one had twisted off. At that point she had decided not to have them replaced. Gill had been delighted, believing for some time that Jules could successfully keep him barefoot with just a few tweaks to her horse care routine.

She knew that to shoe or not to shoe was a question that had all but divided the horse world. She didn't have any strong views either way; she believed it was your horse and your decision. Some of the liveries were shod and Jules never made any comment. It was personal choice. She knew it suited the racehorses in Gill's care to be shoeless, because of the way she fed and worked them. She knew it seemed to suit Romeo, who had become more flowing in his stride and after an initial period while he feet transitioned when he had needed the protection of hoof boots, he had been consistently sound. She loved the sound of his hard and well developed feet as they confidently hit the tarmac beneath them, there was something so natural and free about it.

Jules' phoned beeped in her pocket but she decided to leave reading the text until she got back home.

She steered Romeo onto the bridle path which provided a short cut back to Newmans and urged the horse to canter, revelling in the feel of his muscles bunching beneath her, looking down to watch the strength released in his shoulder as his legs stretched forward. She glanced back to see Ziggy loping behind them and grinned.

By the time she had settled Rome back in his paddock and the horse had yawned fittingly, she was yawning herself.

As she kicked off her boots by the Newmans kitchen door, she heard Charlie and Gill talking in the living room. Deciding not to interrupt she headed straight to her room, only pausing to grab a family sized bag of Maltesers from her cupboard and a few dog biscuits for Ziggy.

As she sat up in bed, happily munching chocolate and watching a film on her laptop, she remembered her phoned had beeped and she fished it from her pocket.

The text was from James.

Lisa is taking the Children to see her sister tomorrow, I have a free day, would you like to meet up for coffee?

Her first thought was that it would be lovely to have coffee with James. Her second, was guilt. Their friendship and its longevity should have allowed them to spend time together, but somehow it felt different now, like there was pressure for the growing feelings between them to end in action.

123

Jules shook her head. She wasn't going to allow it to happen, of course they were friends, and would be friends. She cared too much about James to lose him in a flurry of misguided lust.

She tapped out a reply.

Yes, ok. Where and when?

As she was setting her phone down and about to un-pause her movie, Jules heard a knock at her door.

'Only me darling.' Gill called.

'Come in.'

Jules couldn't help but laugh at the sight of Gill, hair wrapped in towel and face masked in a covering of a green gloop.

'Charlie's idea, a pampering session to cheer us up. I don't feel very cheerful, I can't smile or my face will crack. Will you be around tomorrow?'

'Popping out for a bit in the afternoon but otherwise yes.'

'Fernhay Arabians are having an open day. I had the invitation weeks ago but I only just noticed it's tomorrow. I should probably go along, might be an opportunity to drum up some business. Charlie wants to come with me and Kelly is going to be at home studying for her exam on Monday. The liveries will be coming up to ride anyway but I always feel happier knowing the Arabs are checked at lunchtime?'

'No problem Gill.' Jules said, nodding. If the racers were having a day off, they would all be out in the paddocks anyway.

'Great, thanks Jules.' Gill turned to leave the room but something about the tense expression on Jules' face made her stop. 'You ok?'

'Yeah.' Jules smiled at her friend wearily, 'Work stuff.'

Gill rolled her eyes.

'I need to go wash this off, it's tightened my face up so much it's starting to hurt!!' Gill remained expressionless.

'That means it's working!' Jules called after her friend and chuckled.

'Come down and have a glass of wine with us?' Gill shouted from the hallway.

Jules pondered for a second and then decided she had gone off her film anyway and would be destined to sit thinking about James for the rest of the evening if she stayed in her room.

'Ok, be down in a sec.'

Chapter Seven

Gill sat in the high backed chair and as usual, racked her brains for things to say.

Her mother sat upright in her bed, staring blankly out of the window. The gardens that surrounded the medium sized nursing home were breathtaking. Tulips that bloomed in vibrant red, purple and yellow bordered the green lawns and the water in the large fish pond was crystal clear. Gill wondered if Dorothy was able to appreciate the view she had. In truth she didn't really know how much her mother was aware of any more.

Dementia had rendered the once fun loving woman mute many years ago and the total lack of recognition when Gill visited, meant visiting was a rare occurrence. She knew her brother Mike visited at least weekly but Gill couldn't really see the point. Theodore had died when Gill was in her 20s. Dorothy had lost the love of her life. They got through it together, taking one day at a time and Dorothy had some good years where she was able to celebrate his life and have one of her own without him. Unfortunately, once the early onset vascular dementia had taken hold she had regressed. Every day she relived losing him. It was almost a relief when her memory had finally faded altogether because at least she appeared at peace.

Fernhay Arabians was only a few minutes' drive from Glencoe nursing home and guilt had seen Gill resigning herself, and Charlie, to calling in on their way. She couldn't have consciously driven past the Victorian building without visiting her mother. Unusually, Charlie had not complained.

"I called Amber's foal Theodore, after Dad.' Gill

suddenly began talking again, 'He is chestnut and white and he is so bold. I think he is going to be like Prince, he isn't scared of anything.'

Dorothy suddenly turned her head and looked sharply at Gill.

Almost as soon as Dorothy had focused her eyes on Gill, they unfocused again and the blankness was back.

'Did Grandma like Prince?'

Gill frowned, unsure of the ethics. Was it ok to talk about her mother while she was in the same room?

'It's ok Mum, as Gran isn't in a very chatty mood I am sure she won't mind if you answer for her.'

Gill smiled at Charlie with immense pride. Rather typically, Charlie scowled.

'Yes. She was never tempted to ride him, even though I used to beg her to sit on him, but I often caught her chatting away to him when she was in the garden and she was devastated when he died.'

Charlie moved over towards her Gran and sat on the bed beside the white haired woman. She picked up a wrinkled hand, criss-crossed with purple veins, and held it while she spoke.

'I made a mistake Grandma, but I am putting it right and then I am going to University. Do you think I will make a good lawyer?'

Gill turned away and looked out of the window again. In the early days she had sat like Charlie was now, imploring her mother to respond, so many times.

Charlie continued to talk to the grandmother she had never really known until Gill decided they had been there long enough and ought to get to the open day.

'Right then Mum, we had better be off.'

'So Rosemary, tell me what has brought you here?'

'Rosie – Rosie is fine really.' Rosie smiled shyly as the counsellor nodded and made a note on her file.

She sat on a comfy chair in the small room. Fresh flowers sat on the table between her and the petite lady who had introduced herself as Maria.

It had all happened so quickly. Yesterday she had allowed Matt to escort her to the local doctor's surgery, today she was here, on a Saturday no less, having counselling.

'Your GP asked me to meet you today for an initial session to see if I could help you. I specialise in helping people to find ways to cope with the kind of depression you are experiencing now.'

'What kind of depression is that?' Rosie looked up sharply. She had refused the anti-depressant medication the doctor had offered her, why was she being labelled as depressed?

'Post-natal depression, Rosie.' Maria leant forward and engaged Rosie in eye contact, 'The feelings you are experiencing now are common. Everyone's lives are different, everyone's circumstances unique, but if you feel, as the referral notes I have here suggest, that you aren't connecting with your baby and you are finding it hard, you are not alone, and I can help you. If you will let me.'

'I haven't hurt her. I wouldn't.'

'Rosie, if your GP had thought your baby was at risk you probably wouldn't be here.' Maria opened her palms towards Rosie, expressing her patience, 'I specialise in cognitive behavioural therapy, in helping you to help yourself. No one is suggesting you are doing a bad job, and it's a really positive thing that you have recognised things aren't quite right and want to try and make things better.'

But I don't, thought Rosie. She looked at the painting

which dwarfed the room. The canvas was too big for the wall and depicted a golden sandy cove with azure blue sea beyond. Rosie wished she could be on the fictitious beach instead of trapped inside the counselling room. The room of shame. The minutes ticked by.

'Rosie, this always works better if you talk to me. Ultimately, I can't force you to talk, but without knowing what your problems are I can't really help you.'

'You sound like me.' Rosie laughed bitterly.

'Like you?'

'I am a housing support officer, I help people out of difficult situations.'

'And do you think that's why this is hard, that you are the one who might now benefit from some help?'

'Probably.'

'You aren't a bad mother Rosie. You don't need to feel ashamed about this. It is a common problem and a solvable one too.'

'I need a break.'

'Ok, well maybe that is something you could try and arrange, maybe a holiday would allow you a fresh start?'

'My Dad and his wife have moved in. They are already looking after my baby anyway.'

'Do you feel better for having that support?'

'Yes.'

Marie stood up and walked over to the window sill to pour herself a glass of water from the decanter which sat on a tray beside a stack of glasses.

Rosie could sense the woman's frustration, knew how awkward she was being.

Rosie did not want to get to the inevitable question. What do you want to achieve? How would you like things to be in future? Because the answer was that Rosie wanted to go back in time and that was neither possible nor rational.

But, as much as she wanted to remain silent, she couldn't risk the situation escalating from a few counselling sessions to something more formal. She had to convince Matt everything was going to be ok. She had to come out of the session and get into his car and be bright and positive. She knew as soon as she had told him, that she should not have told him, that it was too much for him to process and deal with on top of an already stressful job and tiring life.

She took a deep breath. For Matt's sake, she would have to go through the motions.

Jules walked through the fields in the sunshine wishing she wasn't ruining her day with nerves.

Ziggy pelted at top speed towards her and skidded to a halt before gobbing his ball out onto her feet.

She picked up the slimy tennis and hurled it for him. He bounded after it and leapt into the air to catch it between his teeth.

'Nice one Zig.' She called.

She paused when she reached the paddock which contained Milly and the other geldings. She put her arms over the fence and stood watching the horses, who were grazing avidly, enjoying their rest day.

In two hours she would meet James.

She had agreed to a garden centre café in Crediton, it seemed to fit the bill of being completely unromantic, the sort of place two friends would get together. She also wanted to have a look at plants for her new patio.

Jules had already spent some time with Teddy and Amber who were adjusting to life outside nicely, topped up the water in the stallion paddock and brought Monty in so that Zinee could have the rest of the day out. She had tidied up the barn after the liveries had descended first thing to have their Saturday morning ride on the animals they owned, but paid Gill for the care of.

They were all lovely women, most had full time jobs which took up most of their time during the week, some had children and husbands at home as well. For all of them, their horses were their escape from the mundanities and stresses of life, their happy time. They all got on well and often rode out together at the weekends, hacking across the Shillerton estate and catching up on each other's news.

Jules had been at larger livery yards and seen how badly disagreements between owners could diminish the joy of having a horse at all. Gill was very lucky that all her liveries were so easy going, but she had also been shrewd in her decision making. She had also only agreed to take a horse once she had got to know the person and was satisfied that they would fit in with the existing owners, some of whom had been keeping their horses at Newmans since Gill had purchased the property. The livery pasture at Newmans was large and could cope with 5 horses or ponies at a time, it was just enough extra income to provide the business with a healthy cushion, but not so much work for Kelly and Gill that it detracted from the main aim of the yard.

Ziggy, who had been repeatedly picking up his ball and trying to give it to her, started to whine to show his impatience.

She laughed as she picked up the ball and the dog's excitement peaked.

Having ridden her horse, completed her rounds and then killed another half an hour cleaning Romeo's saddle, Jules stood in front of her wardrobe. It really didn't matter what she wore. It was ridiculous to spend time deciding on an outfit that really had no function, other than to be comfortable. She pulled a low cut black top with an a-symmetric hem over her head. The rounded tops of her large breasts sat proudly above the square neckline, the angled hemline accentuated the curve of her hip. She turned to face the full length mirror which hung on the wall opposite the wardrobe. She looked sexy even to her own critical eye. She tutted at herself and decided instead on a loose fitting checked shirt over boot cut jeans and flat sandals.

Ziggy looked up from his bed and cocked his head, one ear lifted slightly, he knew what the donning of shoes meant, and his expression posed the question. Jules looked at her dog and considered the answer. She flipped her laptop open to check the website of the garden centre. Well behaved dogs on leads welcome.

'Ok then boy.'

Ziggy stood and stretched, his tail wagging.

Jules looked at her watch. She was still way too early.

'Oh sod it, let's go and look at some plants for our new garden!'

As Jules walked along the rows of potted plants, shrubs and trees. She concentrated on trying to look like she was shopping. Because in truth, despite the intention of getting some ideas for how she might arrange her patio garden, she wasn't really concentrating on landscaping at all.

She looked over at the tiered outside seating of the centre's café. It was getting busy, many of the seats filled with couples and families who had been unable to resist the lure of an afternoon cream tea. She wondered if she ought to go and find a table now. It was still 20 minutes until she and James were due to meet.

She noticed a man on his own, away from the throng he

was seated at a small table in the shade.

It took her a minute to realise it was James. In sunglasses, a fawn t-shirt and jeans he looked so different to the suited James she had got used to seeing at the office.

He looked at his watch and then checked his phone. He scratched his ear and glanced furtively at the entrance. He was as nervous as she was. How ridiculous. They had known each other for ten years.

She decided to put them both out of their misery.

'Juliette!'

James almost knocked the table over in his eagerness to get up. He said hello to Ziggy then reached for Jules. He put his arms around her and held her, tucking his chin over her shoulder, breathing her in.

'It's so good to see you.' He said as he let her go.

Jules blushed. 'You only saw me yesterday!'

James signalled to the waitress.

'So, had a good day?' He clasped his hands together and leant on the table, giving her his full attention.

'Yeah, not bad. Gill is out for the day so I looked over all the horses for her.'

'Ahh, doing your bit for the business eh?'

'Yeah,' Jules smiled, and inevitably started to relax, because James was after all someone she got on incredibly well with. 'It was funny, it's not very often I am the one left "in charge", it felt quite nice. I kept looking across the land and thinking, this is mine – in part at least.'

'God you are so lucky.' James shook his head and smiled at her. He still had his sunglasses on even though they were sat in the shade and it was strange not being able to see his eyes. 'I wish I had something as exciting going on in my life.'

'Well, you are responsible for making decent adults out of your children, that must be pretty exciting!'

'Oh yeah, of course, but Lisa is kind of in charge of Erin and Ben. And the house and our schedules. Sometimes I wish I had more going on that I felt like was mine.'

'What would you like to do?'

'Oh I don't know really. It's just, well, like today. I had an actual free day – it is such a rarity to be able to do what I want. I was even worried I might get bored because I am so used to being told where to be and what to do.'

'And?'

'It was magical Juliette!'

Jules laughed. She tried to ignore the stir deep within her when he said her name.

'Well it stands to reason. Maybe you could try to talk to Lisa? Tell her you would like to do more with the kids, more by yourself? Regain a little control over your life?'

'You know that night I saw you out in Exeter?'

'Hardly forget it – or the two days I spent a rather attractive shade of green after it.'

'You told me to speak to Lisa then.'

'And did you?'

James dropped his head. He sighed and started to speak but the waitress interrupted them.

'What can I get you?'

'Cream tea?' Jules' eyes twinkled as she made the suggestion.

'Two cream teas please.'

After the waitress had scrawled on her pad and moved on to the next table, James stood up and walked away.

Jules watched him fetch the dog water dish from the door of the cafe and carefully carry it back, setting it in front of

134

Ziggy.

Ziggy lapped a few times at the water. Jules recognised it as politeness in Ziggy but James was delighted and ruffled Ziggy's head telling him he was a good boy, before returning the dish.

He sat back down. Jules folded her arms and shook her head.

'Nice try. Did you talk to Lisa?'

'Yes and no.'

Jules rolled her eyes.

'Yes I talked to her...but I am not sure if it isn't a bit weird to be talking to you about it?'

'Right.' Jules wasn't sure where to look. She had assumed they would just continue having a chat, talking like they always had, to cement that they were friends.

'It just feels bizarre talking about my relationship with the woman I am married to with the woman I wish I was with.'

'It can't be coincidence that you suddenly feel something more than friendship for me at the same time as things are going wrong in your marriage?'

'How do you know it's sudden?'

'Don't re-write the past James. I was there remember, how many times did we sleep on the same floor and not even come close to having sex?'

'Because you were with someone.'

'James stop it. Don't ruin us.'

James turned away from Jules, she flinched when she saw his lip involuntarily quiver. She had not expected to be the voice of reason, but she supposed it must have been within her all along for the words to flow so easily when the question of their feelings was raised.

'Do you have any other female friends?'

'None I feel as comfortable with as you.'

135

'And do you ever talk to any of your male friends about being unhappy at home?'

James' eyebrows lifted above his sunglasses.

'So talk to me.'

And James talked. In between mouthfuls of fresh scone, clotted cream and blueberry jam, he talked about how emasculated he felt. He talked about the ridiculous situation he found himself in, being a successful and respected litigator, but being treated almost like a child at home. He talked about the lack of intimacy with Lisa. He talked about his children, his wonderful beautiful 6 year old Erin, and his playful innocent 3 year old Ben, who he wished he could be a better man for, but didn't feel he had a say over.

As Jules listened and sympathised, made helpful suggestions about how he could try to improve things, she couldn't help but feel better about her own part in his dissatisfaction.

But, of course that was silly. She cared about him and she needed to help him, not make things worse.

He had everything to lose, she had nothing, but it didn't stop her revisiting the question.

'Do you think maybe the feelings you think you have for me are more to do with the fact that you aren't happy at home, than actually being about me?'

'I have been unhappy for a long time. Yes I suppose it's possible you might be escapism, but I just feel so happy when I am with you.'

'I think maybe you owe it to yourself, and your family, to at least have a go at saving your marriage. Work at it, maybe go for counselling together. See if you can be happy in the life you have?'

James took off his sunglasses and rubbed his eyes. He

slid his empty plate to one side and reached for Jules' hand. She let him take it and smiled at him.

'I will have a go Jules.' James paused as they both exhaled. 'I appreciate your sanity and I will try.'

Jules smiled. When James listened to her, he pondered and savoured her words and then found sense in them. It made her feel so worthwhile, so validated. Ironically, those were the same feelings she brought forth in him.

'Come on!' Jules picked up Ziggy's lead and stood up from the table.

'Come on where?'

'I need to pick some plants for my new garden!'

James laughed and stood up too.

They found a member of unsuspecting garden centre staff, and asked, through giggles, which shrubs would be suitable for a person who routinely killed house plants and would inevitably forget to water their garden.

Gill watched Charlie drive away and marvelled, as she did so often, at the level of her child's bravery.

Charlie had received a text from her Dad to say there was an important looking letter waiting for her at West Hill. Knowing her father would be away all weekend, so she wouldn't have to see him, she had insisted she would drive there to collect it herself, even though Gill offered to get it for her. It was likely to be her hospital appointment.

After collecting the letter Charlie was planning to visit Darran and end the silence on her part. She seemed determined to be honest with him, maybe she felt guilty for shutting him out. Gill wondered if the visit to see her grandmother that morning had an effect on Charlie. It could of course be that she was just sick of Darran's constant texts and voice-mails and recognised that she had to speak to him sooner or later. Like the baby, Darran was not just going to go away by magic and her guilt was not justification for punishing him, which would only lead to more guilt anyway.

Gill was pleased to see George's car parked in its usual spot.

She noticed an unfamiliar car pulling up next to Jules' on the drive. She didn't recognise the man who stepped out of the Audi, but couldn't fail to notice Jules beaming as she stepped out of her own car and they started to unload a tree from his boot together. Jules' laughter rang out across the still evening air and Gill smiled involuntarily before ducking her head underneath the paddock fence and making her way towards Amber and Teddy.

Jules thanked James profusely for following her back with the garden centre purchases that wouldn't fit in her own car. She had admittedly gone a little over the top and the potted plants and miniature bay trees looked somewhat cramped once they had put them in her little garden area. She would worry about that later.

James stood by his car; he opened the door and paused. He was going home to his wife with a clear conscience.

James' eyes darkened and he didn't get in.

'It is going to be so hard to try. It feels so pointless.'

'It is a good thing you are trying, you owe it to Ben and Erin.' Jules smiled dropped and she almost felt annoyed with him for breaking the spell the lovely time they had together had cast.

'What kind of example is it to set to know something in your heart and yet continue live a lie?'

Jules looked at her feet. He had a point, but this wasn't a discussion they could have with their resolve so recently set, and him about to get into his car.

'Where will you tell her you were this afternoon?'

'With you. She won't care anyway, she couldn't give a damn what I do as long as it's not at the expense of my chores.'

'James.' Jules softened and took his hand, about to pull him in for a hug.

As she did, Gill appeared from the driveway, on her way to the house.

She smiled curtly as she passed them, immediately picking up on the tangent emotion between them.

'Get in. Go home and be a good husband.'

James acquiesced and got into his car, a grimace spreading over his face.

'Be a good man for someone who doesn't appreciate it. Great.'

He eyed her as he spoke but she couldn't hold his gaze. She shut the door and walked away.

As she turned at the fence of Romeo's paddock to watch his car rounding the corner and disappearing out of sight, she tried to process all he had told her. She felt so sad for him, but also conflicted, because as much as she had to discard her feelings for him, she could not deny that they were there, regardless of her scorn at his motivation.

She decided to do the only thing that would clear her mind of him and ride.

She clucked softly at the gate and her strong honest horse rewarded her by walking towards her, head low, ears pricked softly. She slid his headcollar on gently and fastened the buckle.

As she led her horse out of his paddock, she acknowledged the feeling of being watched.

'Hey.'

Gill folded her arms.

'Don't you hey me. Where have you been? Why was that man here?'

Jules' irritation over being questioned when she was innocent mingled with the sadness which had shrouded her because James was gone, and created a combination of angry words and wet eyes.

'He helped me bring the stuff I bought for my new garden home.'

'Don't be coy with me. I overhead your conversation. He is married.'

'Yep and that is why he has just gone home to his wife. It's James, my old friend from Uni. He is having some troubles at home and he talked to me about it, like a Friend.' Jules said the word again, emphasising it.

'Good.'

Gill regretted her harshness, but she couldn't bear the thought of any woman being betrayed as she had once been. Of course if her own situation had been different, her attitude towards Jules would likely have been different. Anxiety over George created a monster in Gill, the monster wanted everyone she knew to stay in the relationships they were in, was not intelligent enough in its wrath to see past the crudeness of an 'affair' to the possible reasons behind one. The monster was not interested in truth.

Jules and Rosie had already been friends for over a year when they met Gill. Jules remembered the extreme discomfort she had felt in Gill's presence on their first meeting, it was the same feeling she had now, with a wrathful Gill standing over her and questioning her.

During the interval at a demonstration of natural horsemanship, she and Rosie had popped to the ladies. They couldn't fail to hear Gill sobbing inside a cubicle. Rosie, moved by empathy as always, had investigated, while Jules stood back, knowing if she had been the one sobbing, she would not have wanted any witnesses. Gill had just learned that her husband was cheating on her and was facing the end of her marriage.

Shock had bound a wounded Gill into a mixture of tears and fury. And much like then, when Jules had not wanted to get involved in someone else's problems, Gill was clearly not interested in Jules' problem now, beyond satisfying herself that her friend was not involved in cheating.

It was Rosie who had befriended Gill, embraced the woman having made an instant judgement of her character, and it wasn't until many months later that Gill had invited Jules to hers for dinner with Rosie, probably at Rosie's request, and a friendship had started to grow between them.

'He is having problems with Lisa but he is trying to work them out. He doesn't have anyone else to talk to.'

Jules felt obliged to explain the embrace and intensity Gill had witnessed between them.

Her explanation seemed to satisfy Gill who offered to fetch Monty in order to accompany Jules and Romeo on their ride. Unable to admit she needed time alone, because the inevitable 'why' might poke the monster again, Jules smiled brightly and falsely in agreement before turning her back to concentrate on Romeo.

An hour later Gill left Jules in the barn to finish up the evening rounds and let herself in through the Newmans kitchen door. She expected George to be getting ready to leave for the evening shift but the house was silent.

She noticed a small white box and a note on the island in the middle of the kitchen.

Hello darling, hope the open day was good.
I have decided to take tonight off, wake me when you get home.
G xx
PS. We have come up with a new range of petit fours, thought you and Charlie might like to try them..

Gill peaked into the box and the sweet smell of chocolate wafted up from a delightful array of hand crafted sweets. She could almost have cried. Bringing her home things he thought she would like, taking the night off to spend with her; she had thought they were things of the past but here he was, her George. Maybe the problems at the restaurant were at last over.

Gill decided to go back to the barn and help Jules finish up before she woke him, he had looked so tired lately. She put her own need to see him second to her desire to care for him and donned her boots.

Gill found Jules sat on a feed bin sobbing.

'I am sorry for being such a bitch earlier.' Gill embraced Jules, knowing George was napping in their bed, with the promise of their evening together filling her heart, the green eyed monster was silenced in favour of helping her friend.

'I know why.' Jules looked up at Gill, meeting her gaze to show she was truthful, 'but this is not like it was with Alex and Megan. He wants to leave her, but I persuaded him not to. Sent him back to her to make an effort and go to counselling.' Jules' shoulders shuddered with the force of her sobs. Gill was, after all, a person she could trust and confide in, she had sharp edges, demons, but who didn't?

'We are friends. There is nothing more going on, we haven't done anything and we won't. But I can't lie to you Gill, I wish things were different.'

'You don't have to explain yourself to me darling. I should have known better than to judge you so harshly, you are such a good person.' Gill fondled Jules' shoulder.

'Right man, wrong time.'

'Maybe things will change?'

'To wish for that is to wish for the end of a marriage. I have to hope that he can make it work with her, don't I?'

Gill considered the question.

'Actually, Charlie would have coped far better with mine and Alex's break up if there hadn't been deceit involved and I hadn't hated her father so much. Relationships end, it's how you handle it together that counts. You might stop being together, but being parents is something you have to share for life. If James is really unhappy, that unhappiness will seep into their lives and the children might be better off with divorced but happy parents ultimately.'

'Hmmm...You could be right, but it's not right for me to be involved either way.'

At the mention of parents, Jules suddenly felt the urge to be with her mother. Over-bearing, over-enthusiastic Marianne, who never failed, often to Jules' disgust and irritation, to be right.

'Might head up to Gloucester for the evening.'

'Mum time?'

'She's going to flip.'

In spite of her predicament, Jules had to laugh.

'I will finish up here, you pop Romeo back in his field and get off?'

Jules nodded. As she stood up from the bin and they momentarily caught hands, squeezing tightly.

'Come on Milly, let's get you away from these horrid

little pests.' Gill put her arm over the grey mare's mane as she walked her towards the barn, trying to waft the midges away from her sensitive skin. Milly had always suffered with sweet itch and Gill knew once she had started to rub her mane and tail where the gnats landed and elevated her histamine levels, the itch-scratch cycle would begin. Best, she had decided when she saw the mare, irritably swishing her tail and breaking into a trot to get away from the early evening swarms, to bring her in for the night.

She never liked to bring a horse in alone. She decided Zinee could have a barn night when she saw Amber dozing contentedly in the middle of her paddock against the backdrop of a cloudless blue sky.

Once she had squared their stables, tied up their haynets and left Zinee peering adoringly at Milly through the bars which separated their stables, she picked up the knapsack she always carried when walking the paddocks and secured the barn for the night.

She checked on the liveries in their pasture, a cursory look over to make sure they were all ok, knowing they would have had a pampering from their riders that morning. Then she checked the racing mares and geldings, taking the hoof pick from her bag to clean out their feet where they stood in the field.

The racing paddocks were equipped with areas of hardcore to allow the horses to get off the inevitable mud when it was wet. The horses often chose to stand with their toes embedded in the finer areas of gravel when they slept. Her farrier, who had moved almost entirely towards barefoot trimming and rarely shod horses any more, had suggested the tracks a few years ago and although the ground preparation and tons of stone had been expensive, she was delighted Jules had agreed to the spend last summer, in the run up to their official collaboration.

Gill groomed Monty for a while, knowing the stallion missed out on mutual grooming sessions with other horses due to the confines of the stallion paddock. Finally, saving the best till last, she walked in to Amber's paddock and emptied a carrier bag of stud feed onto the ground for her mare. Amber wuffled at her master as she walked eagerly towards the feed. Gill scanned the field for Teddy and saw him trotting away from Kelly to follow his mum.

Kelly didn't get up from where she was sitting, back against a fence post in the corner of the paddock.

'What you doing here Kel? You are supposed to be studying!' Gill called to the groom, concerned about her exam which was less than 48 hours away.

Gill was so used to the groom's infallible good nature, it took her a minute to realise there was something wrong. Kelly wasn't the sort to make a drama out of nothing, or indeed anything small or rectifiable, so Gill took the fact that the groom was slumped, teary eyed and silent, very seriously.

Gill reached her and gently took the girl's hand, not speaking or demanding, just comforting.

'Hi boss...' Kelly sniffed.

'Hey you.'

'Oh Darling don't cook!' Gill shed her boots whilst simultaneously shouting at her beloved man, whom she had walked in to find pre-heating the oven.

'I don't mind.' Laughed George as he came towards her for a hug.

'Seriously, let's just get takeaway, it's hardly a night off for you if you cook more is it?'

'But I like cooking for you. I have to cook for people I

145

don't love every bloody day, cooking for you is more important than cooking for them!' George steered his tired looking partner towards a stool and helped her onto it before planting a kiss on her forehead.

'Sit there. Tell me about your day?' George moved to the other side of the island and started making pastry.

'What are we having?'

'Gruyere and pear tarts, with...?'

'Chips!!' Gill gave the answer she always gave and George retorted as predicted.

'You will look like a bloody chip.'

Their eyes met as they laughed, each finding comfort in the familiarity of their banter.

Gill's father had often cooked for the family, as a girl Gill had often sat with him in the kitchen, chatting to the fascinating and highly intelligent man she had loved so much, Dorothy flouncing in and twittering about the mess he had better not be making, causing them to giggle after she had left the room.

George just appreciated the rarity that was Gill sitting still. It was worth the busman's holiday to have her undivided attention.

'Well,' Gill began, smiling as George switched the fryer on and selected potatoes from the sack in the larder, 'today brought mixed blessings. I got a new racing client from the open day. Chap with a few Arabs, thinks he has a gelding who might be worth a season or two's try outs. Wrong time of year of course but he is delivering him next week so we might get him fit enough to have his first time on the track in August.'

'Brilliant. Well done love.'

George deftly sliced potatoes and tried not to frown. He had been planning to tell Gill about what was happening at the restaurant, to be honest with her about having to sell his car, but hearing about her success in securing a new client, his resolved weakened as his pride tried to take over.

'But. That was the good news.' Gill continued.

'Oh?' George looked up and the knife worked without the supervision of his eyes.

'Found Kelly crying in Amber's field.'

'Kelly?'

'I know.' Gill rolled her eyes as the weight of Kelly's news descended on her, flattening her shoulders and causing her to sigh, 'Her mother, who she lives with, has a sister in Australia. She told Kelly this morning she plans to emigrate and she wants Kelly to go with her.'

'Oh shit.' George put the knife down.

Kelly and her mother had lived in the village together ever since Kelly's father had left when the girl was small. They had very little family in the UK and Kelly's mother had moved to Devon for a job at the large hospital in Exeter.

'She doesn't want to go. But she is only 19 and apart from the friends she has made at college and here she doesn't really have anyone. If her mother goes she won't be able to afford to take over the rent at the cottage and she doesn't know what to do.'

'Could she move in here?' George suggested the first thing he thought Gill would have been considering.

'Her mother desperately wants her to go with her, she's really putting the pressure on. Apparently there are lots of horsey jobs over there and being a nurse her mother is one of the approved professionals for getting an automatic working visa. Kelly didn't ask if she could live here. I don't know whether she would want to and you know how things are with Charlie.'

George nodded. Charlie's jealousy over the relationship her mother and the groom enjoyed had lost its venom in recent years, as Charlie had matured, but George understood she may react badly, especially given her current state of mind and the fact that she was currently there herself.

'I guess we will just have to wait and see how things pan out. Her mother hasn't actually done anything yet, just told Kelly it was her plan this morning.'

'So it's not set in stone?'

'Sounds like she will be going at some point, just a matter of how soon. It's such bad timing. I am surprised at her mother, knowing Kelly has her final exam on Monday. Maybe she didn't realise Kelly would be so upset.'

'Maybe. It's a new life, better climate, an exciting prospect for some?'

'Kelly has been talking for months about teaching though. She had already asked me countless times if it was ok to use the school for giving private lessons. She has been so excited about finally being a riding instructress and she will be so good at it. She already has a few customers lined up and she has drafted a whole page for our website on lessons, wanted it to be a new service we could offer.'

'She could find a yard over there though?'

'Yes, but you know how much she loves it here, how she loves the horses, Monty. And what on earth am I going to do without her? I can only do as much training as I do because she is such a hard worker.'

George caught the despair in Gill's voice and walked around the island to hold her.

'I guess all you can do is be there for her. Wait and see what happens and deal with the outcome once it is known.'

Gill nodded, comforted by his voice of reason.

He wished, as he cradled her head in his hands, that he could apply the same logic to his own work situation. They stood in silence for a few minutes, not wanting to break their embrace, until George decided to do what he did best and cheer his woman up.

'Right, off you go to the shower, it will be ready in about 20 minutes.'

'Oh I can't be bothered.' Gill groaned.

'Go on. And while you are there, trim that lady garden.' George smiled devilishly as Gill blushed.

'It's not that hairy!' Gill cried, outraged but grinning.

'After we have eaten, I might want to eat you.'

Gill smiled with a flush, feeling silly but at the same time aroused. She slid from the stool and paused to allow him to slap her behind as she passed.

As she rummaged in the bathroom cabinet, looking for a new razor, her troubles were far from her mind.

Later that night, after they had eaten in slow seductive silence, broken only by Charlie ringing to say she would be staying over at Darren's, and convincing her mother it was a good idea, George had ordered Gill to their bedroom.

So lost in their own private world, they had not heard Jules come home. They had existed for a few hours only for each other.

In the small hours as Gill lay wrapped in the arms of her spent man, it suddenly dawned on her she had not asked about his day.

'Are things getting better at the restaurant now George? You know I am always here to talk if you have a problem?'

'Not really darling. It's all a bit of shit storm at the moment.' George muttered into her back.

Gill turned around to face him, his eyes dark in lamp light.

'Tell me, maybe I can help?'

'You, spending time with you and having an evening like this evening, is all the help I need.' George meant his words. Despite the urge to come clean, he couldn't bear to say anything that might take away the remnants of pleasure in her eyes and replace them with worry. Gill caught his sincerity and rewarded him with no further questions.

'I love you, so much.' Gill murmured as she turned back onto her side, allowing him to cuddle into her again.

'I love you too.'

Chapter Eight

'How has this week been Rosie?'

Maria set a mug of coffee in front of Rosie and sat down, ready to begin.

'Not a bad one. Me and Dad took Eve to the supermarket and then to the park in Honiton yesterday.'

The counsellor nodded enthusiastically. It was the third session and Maria was excited by Rosie's apparent progress. Rosie had moved her appointment to a Friday morning, because this meant it did not encroach on Matt's time at home. Although things were strained between them, she still wanted him at home, and Fridays held the hope of things being better when he arrived. If her sessions had been on a Monday morning she might have found it much harder to hold it together.

It wasn't that she was lying to Maria, who seemed a genuine and caring person. She only mentioned during their sessions the things she felt comfortable talking about. She did not feel comfortable talking about the fact that she still felt like something was missing when she held her child, she didn't feel comfortable talking about Matt's averted eyes and awkward body language. Instead she talked about how much easier things were now that Jimmy and Crystal had moved in, and how much she looked forward to the weekends and the hope she felt that her husband would be normal with her again. Both of these things were true.

'Did Eve enjoy the park?'

'Well, it was quite funny – I think she enjoyed shopping more! She was so fascinated by all the shelves and the colours, by the time we got to the park she was almost asleep in her buggy.'

'And how did you feel being out with your baby?'

Rosie thought about the child seat and the buggy which had to be collapsed and stowed in the boot, it hadn't actually been as much hassle as she thought it would be. She still couldn't have imagined doing it alone though.

'I was glad Dad was there, but a couple of people stopped to smile at her and say how cute she was, which was nice.'

'Tell me about your horse Rosie, are you getting more time to spend with him now, I know you said caring for him was one of the things you found hard when you were on your own.'

'Oh he is beautiful.' Rosie's smile lit up the room as she pictured Red's welcoming face. 'And yes, I have been able to do all my fence mending so I feel a bit more on top of everything.'

Rosie thought about Red and Peat, the sanctuary that was her field.

Everyone assumed she was riding. The hours she spent with the horses, the assumption that she was doing the thing she had always done. She had even got away with finding an excuse not to ride out at Newmans every time she had visited. Maybe that was something the counsellor could know.

'I haven't ridden him, my horse, for a long time.'

Maria was not a rider herself but had a vague understanding of why that might be a problem.

'You don't have to put pressure on yourself though do you Rosie? If spending time with him makes you feel happy?'

'He is getting quite fat and he is only a young horse, he should be getting out and doing things.'

'So what is stopping you, now that you have help with Eve?'

'I just don't feel right. I can't bring myself to do something so self-gratifying.'

'When was the last time you rode?'
'The day before Harry died.'

By the time Rosie left her session she felt worse. She admitted she hadn't been able to ride. It was nothing to do with the end of her pregnancy, giving birth, her physical capability. Eve's birth had been relatively easy, physically she would have been ready after just weeks. But, every time she thought about getting on her horse, even now she had the extended daylight and good weather to go out, something stopped her. Riding Red would not be a betrayal to Harry, the time for that would have been after she had retired the old horse.

She knew she was causing herself another problem.

Red was young, had only been properly backed and ridden for a year, and had now had over six months sat in the field. When she did come to get on him, she would have to go back to basics, take it steady, possibly to an extent have to start again and she wasn't sure she could do it.

Rosie sat in her car and sobbed. She didn't deserve Red. She didn't deserve to ride. Her sixth sense kicked in and told her that if she tried to ride her lovely willing horse, her lack of confidence in herself would transfer to him. It was so much easier to remain in blissful ignorance of at least one of her current shortcomings, rather than to tackle it head on and risk having to admit to herself that her darkness was affecting her connection to the horse. He was the one thing that could still make her smile.

But what were the alternatives? Just give up and waste his youth, waste hers?

She sat until she cried herself out.

She felt clearer the other side of the tear storm.

She decided amongst all of her faked improvement, she

owed it to Red to make some genuine progress too. So, instead of going home to mope, she decided to take action. Selling Red simply wasn't an option, and if her riding problem could be partitioned aside from her baby problem, maybe she could find the courage to fix it.

She started her car and went to the one person who could help.

'When's her appointment?'

'Monday.'

Gill smiled grimly at Rosie. Ever since Charlie's appointment letter had come, Gill had been torn between wishing the time away so that it was all over for her child, and dreading the day actually arriving.

The friends sat at the kitchen table sipping coffee. Gill was busy, but she was pleased to see Rosie and she didn't want to ruin it by having to insist they head straight for the barn.

Darran was now, to Gill's surprise and relief, genuinely behind Charlie's decision. Charlie had spent most of her time with him over the past few weeks and their relationship seemed have reinstated its usual intensity. In preparation for a possible meltdown after the event, Gill had insisted that she should still be the one to take Charlie to her appointment and that her recovery should be at Newmans.

'She lost her job.' Gill paused to top up their coffees from the jug on the hot plate. 'I mean, it was only casual waitressing, but I was proud she was working while she waited to start Uni, especially when Alex is so keen to support her financially. They kept calling to find out why she wasn't turning up for her shifts and she kept ignoring them, I can't blame them for firing her. I made her write a letter of apology.'

'Well that's something, at least she drew a line under it.'

'She said she wants to do some volunteering work over the summer. Not sure if that's guilt and hormones talking, but it would be nice if she did do something altruistic.'

'How does Alex feel about it all?'

'Oblivious. She doesn't want to put him through it when he doesn't need to know.'

'Hasn't he wondered why she has been here?'

'Not really. You know what Alex is like.'

Rosie considered and nodded. Alex was just self-obsessed enough not to realise anything was wrong.

Gill glanced out of the kitchen window, aware she had a mountain of preparation to do before the first race of the season, which was coming upon her at an alarming speed. She turned back to Rosie who looked lost in her own anxiety again.

'Rosie. Tell me about you? How's Red?'

'He's why I am here. Gill, this is hard to admit but I need to do something about it.'

'Tell me.' Gill watched her friend intently, so relieved she was finally going to explain whatever it was she had been denying.

'I haven't ridden since Harry died.'

Gill opened her mouth to ask why, to quiz Rosie, but decided she probably knew. She remembered the feeling from when she had lost Prince. The death of her childhood pony had led to her giving up horses altogether. It wasn't until Alex had bought Amber for her in her 30s that she had started riding again. She looked into her friend's worried eyes and decided action was the best medicine, they could leave words for later.

'Come on.'

Rosie took Gill's hand and slid off the stool. Together they donned their riding boots and headed for the barn.

155

"Great, see you next week!"

Kelly waved off her latest pupil and beamed at Rosie and Gill as they approached the barn. She was holding Badger, who looked rather tired but content, having been round and round the school for the last hour.

"Wow, look at you!" Rosie broke into a little run to reach Kelly and embrace her. Kelly was dressed in cream jodhpurs and a white shirt, topped with a brand new riding hat. Rosie felt, as Gill had been feeling since Kelly had passed her final exams, immense pride.

"It's going so well Rosie! I have four clients already!"

Gill smiled at Badger. He had come to Newmans as a racing prospect for training, but after a slow and placeless first season, she had been worried about the prospect of racing him for a second. His owner was at University and had wanted the horse to do something while she was away, but she didn't mind too much what that something was, as long as he was worked and cared for. Kelly had needed a calm average sized horse for giving lessons and Badger had fit the bill. In fact his owner had been delighted because in addition to not having to pay a race training fee, Kelly had offered to cover his feed and livery costs in return for using him.

Gill had been mildly disappointed initially, but if Kelly's clients kept coming, she was likely to make a similar amount back in the percentage Kelly was insisting on giving her for use of the school and time out from her day job. Gill was quietly concerned about what would happen if Kelly and her mother emigrated, she didn't like the idea of Badger's owner being messed about. Since the day in the field when Kelly had been mortified about the prospect of having to leave, she hadn't mentioned it and seemed fully committed to building up her little business. Gill wondered if her mother had gone quiet on the subject of moving. Hoped anyway.

"Who would you like to ride Rosie?" Gill found a window in her friend's conversation with Kelly to pose the question.

Rosie eyed Badger, fully tacked up, dozing off quietly in the sunshine. The horse looked inviting and the prospect of riding quietly around a school seemed more appealing than embarking on a long hack with a potentially hot Arabian. Gill smiled wryly as she followed Rosie's gaze to badger's saddle. She wasn't going to get help riding out after all.

"Do you want another pupil Kelly?" Rosie asked nervously.

Kelly glanced at Gill, confused.

"I need to get on, I will leave you two to it." Gill winked at Kelly and headed into the barn.

"That's it, lovely seat, you are such a natural." Kelly enthused, complimenting the way Rosie was walking Badger at a sedate pace around the ring as though she had just executed a perfect dressage test.

"Oh Kelly, stop it!! You are supposed to be giving me a lesson!" Rosie giggled. She had almost bottled even getting on the stocky Arab, but now she was on board, she felt surprisingly fine.

After Rosie had explained she hadn't ridden for six months, and briefly mentioned Harry and her emotional barrier to being aboard Red, Kelly had dismissed her concerns about Badger being too tired for a second lesson on the basis Rosie only wanted to walk, and was determined to help.

At Kelly's instruction, Rosie walked Badger in small circles on both reins, feeling his delicate mouth with a gentle contact, her body naturally encouraging fluidity in the close coupled horse. As she rode, she felt the safety of being inside the school, of Kelly watching her and directing her. She hoped she would feel as relaxed when she came to get on Red.

After 20 minutes, Badger halted abruptly in the middle of the centre line, the place he was used to having his rider dismount. Rosie and Kelly looked at each other and laughed.

"Ok Badger, we get it." Rosie patted the mottled steel grey neck of the gelding, who had set his feet foursquare in a rigid stance, making his intention to do no more work clear.

Rosie dismounted and together they un-tacked him. Kelly let him rub his head on her shoulder before he marched to the top end of the school to eat the grass which was creeping under the fence from the paddock.

"If Gill can bring him over some time, can I have a lesson with you on Red?"

Kelly looked flustered for a second, before protesting.

"I can't teach you anything Rosie, you ride better than I do!"

"Oh you flatterer, and liar – no seriously, having your voice guiding me makes me feel safe. I am worried after all this time, Red is going to need a lot of encouragement."

Kelly nodded, she understood. Even in her short week long career as an instructress, she was already learning that making better riders was not really about physical ability, it was about how the rider and the horse felt and what was blocking their connection.

"Tell you what, I will come to you?"

"That would be brilliant."

"Save bothering Gill – she is starting to get that manic look in her eye she always has before the season starts."

"Perfect – thanks so much Kelly."

"Let's make it an evening, that way I can work usual

hours for Gill and we can take our time?"

"You are such a little star aren't you? Gill is so lucky to have you Kelly."

Kelly smiled, but turned away to take Badger's saddle to the barn, so that Rosie wouldn't see the worry in her eyes. Kelly didn't want to voice her concerns so close to race season, but exactly how much longer Gill would remain lucky was causing daily arguments between Kelly and her resolute mother.

By the time Rosie got home she was ready for a nap. She found counselling draining and although her ride on Badger had been short, the muscles in her thighs were complaining.

She wished she could feel more proud of herself, more entitled to a nice sleep, snuggled into the duvet. Instead her brain nagged at her, yes she had ridden, but the problem was riding Red, and she hadn't done that. It was easy to sit astride badger and ask him to go through the motions he knew and understood, the horse had confidence in abundance and didn't need Rosie to be reassuring or genuine in order to perform simple tasks.

Kelly was coming over in a few week's time. She intended to do some groundwork before then to start to get Red prepared for being ridden, but even the thought of doing any more than cuddling, pampering and feeding Red was making her heart beat faster. The crux of the matter, she decided, as she let herself in to the cottage and was relieved to see a note from Jimmy and Crystal saying they had taken Eve out for the day, was she didn't t believe in herself.

She'd had no inkling that she would find it hard to connect with Eve, no internal warning that she would become so miserable so quickly. Your brain was supposed to be on your side wasn't it?

Rosie headed to the desk in the dining room. She fired up her computer and poured herself a glass of milk while she waited for the slightly antiquated machine to fire up. She intended to look up post-natal depression online. There was a blockage between her current self and the self she knew she should want to be. Maybe, if she could start to take steps to understand how, hypothetically, she could get past her own resistance, the message would sink in and her brain would start being nice to her again.

Rosie's email account popped up when the computer had finally reached the desktop screen and she screwed her face up when she saw the amount of unread messages. She had just wanted to do some light reading and then head for the spare room but now she felt obliged to go through the hundreds of communications that had arrived since she had last logged in.

After ten minutes of trawling through mostly junk, Rosie's eyes focused on a familiar and completely unexpected name.

Surely her mother wasn't online? She had ditched her laptop almost as soon as she had stopped working all those years ago.

Rosie hesitated before she opened the email, which was titled "Hello".

Did she really want to be upset by whatever her mother had to say? To give her brain something else to pour over?

'Oh sod it.' Rosie muttered and clicked Read.

Dear Rosie,
I wonder if you could send me a picture of Eve?
I can understand that a long car journey would be difficult with a small baby, but I would like to see what she looks like.
Mum

No kisses, no how are you. Rosie's brain started automatically to list the reasons her mother's email was negative.

She read it again. Selina had expressed understanding for why Rosie hadn't brought Eve to see her, had made no recriminations about the fact that everything she knew about Eve was from Jimmy as Rosie herself had not contacted her at all.

Rosie pondered. She navigated to Matt's pictures folder and selected April. She found a recent picture of Eve smiling in Matt's arms and attached it to a reply.

> Mum,
> This is Eve.
> How come you are on email?

Rosie shook her head after she had clicked send. Wonders would never cease. She carried on ploughing through the endless messages about must-have clothing and Viagra.

The computer dinged at her. She could hardly believe the speed of Selina's reply.

> What a lovely looking baby. My Granddaughter.
> Wow. I have a job, of sorts. Jeanne who I used to
> work at the magazine with is running her own fiction
> house. She is publishing some new author work with
> real potential. She asked me to do some copy
> editing. Suits me because I can do it from home, she
> even sent me a laptop and set me up this email
> address.
> Before you ask I haven't stopped drinking. But I have
> to concentrate when I am working so I guess you
> might say I have cut down a bit.

Rosie was flabbergasted. The fact that Jeanne had contacted her, and was now paying her for editing services was beyond Rosie's comprehension. Everything she believed about her mother was in question, based on a short email.

The computer dinged again.

Ps. I am really sorry about Harry, you must miss him.

Rosie felt the prick of tears smart in her eyes. It was probably the nicest thing her mother had ever said to her.

She drained her glass of milk and started to type a reply.

I do miss him, a lot.
Great about your job, I hope it works out well for you.

Rosie paused. She had been so used to being clipped with her mother. So many years of functional conversation, of expecting and receiving only coldness and snide remarks. She felt like she wanted to say something more personal. She added a line, dropping her guard everso slightly.

It's nice to hear from you.

Rosie hit send. She suddenly felt overdue for her nap. The rest of the emails, and her own search for personal development, could wait. She logged off and headed for bed.

Jules glanced at George's filing cabinet. She wasn't really working. Her mind kept wandering.

She had come in to the Newmans office to draft a letter, even though it was Sunday. She sighed. She didn't really need to work, she was already completely prepared for the busy week ahead. She was tired but also fractious, impatience plagued her. She wished it was Monday.

She used to long for the weekends, but lately she found

herself longing for them to be over, because from Friday evening to Monday morning seemed like an eternity.

Her new home only needed bedroom carpets now, and they would be fitted next week. Romeo could have done with being ridden more, Gill could have done with all the riding help she could get. There were so many reasons to be at Newmans, but none of them seemed to have the gravitational pull required to keep her there. Instead, she found herself at Hodges and Grath, even on the days she would normally had worked from home.

Since she had persuaded, or perhaps more accurately instructed James to try again with Lisa, they had both been very disciplined and platonic with one another, but that didn't stop her from orchestrating her life to ensure she spent as much time in his company as possible. She represented her need to spend time with him as being supportive, being there for him while his life was such a mess. She didn't admit to herself that every minute she spent at the office with him close by, was a minute when the incredible yearning for her forbidden colleague was slightly more bearable.

Her gaze wandered again to George's filing cabinet. She wondered if it was locked. She wondered if the letter was inside it.

After a brief period of everything seeming normal with Gill and George, things seemed to be slipping into disarray again. Gill was so busy with the horse's fitness, she looked tired and tense. Jules wasn't sure how much of the tension that knitted her brow and saw her up at 5am every morning was yard related. How much, Jules wondered, was actually down to the absent and increasingly dark eyed George?

What on earth was going on? Gill still hadn't mentioned any solicitor's action against George and she felt sure her friend would have come to her for advice if she knew George was potentially in trouble.

If only Jules could find out, without breaking into filing cabinets or potentially creating a conflict of interest within her firm.

Jules rested her elbows on the desk and decided she needed to take herself out of temptation's way. She would go to the barn and see if Gill wanted a hand, at least there was one way of helping her friend.

Rosie tried to concentrate on what Kev was telling her.

She could see Matt, stood at the gate, holding Eve. Even with the distance afforded between the stables and the garden she could tell her husband was annoyed.

She was worried about Red. She had noticed with alarm that his feet had grown much longer than she had seen them before and that he had splits forming in the bottoms of the hoof walls where they had splayed. She felt instantly guilty for not having noticed sooner.

Worried that she might make the cracks worse, she had stopped trying to lead him out in preparation for riding him and called her trimmer. She tried not to arrange anything for the weekends when Matt was at home, but Kev had said he could fit her in on the Sunday morning and she had accepted. Unfortunately Kev had been held up and now horse time was encroaching on the plans they had made to take Eve out for the afternoon.

As Matt slammed the gate behind him and carried Eve back through the orchard, Rosie knew that he had decided she was trying to avoid the family outing. Every weekend was becoming a battle, with Matt desperate to spend time with Eve and Rosie desperate to have him to herself, having missed him during the week. She wanted to do the things they had always done together, to feel like their relationship was still whole and sufficient in its own right. Jimmy and Crystal encouraged them to make the most of having live-in babysitters, but Matt always declined. Since the day on the moor when he had been so angry with Rosie, he had avoided being completely alone with her. She felt rejected by his desire to spend every second of his weekend with the baby, but wondered how much of his enthusiasm for Eve was to make up for her lack of it.

He asked her how her counselling had gone every Friday evening, and instead of eeking the details out of her to make sure she was progressing and allowing her to talk, as would once have been normal, he seemed completely satisfied with her brave smiles and one word answers of "fine" or "ok".

'Woman, are you listening to me?'

Kev allowed Red to set his hoof back on the ground and patted the horse as he stood up and addressed the owner. Kev was a well regarded hoof care professional. The health of a horse's foot was more than a job to him, it was a passion. He was always ready to learn more, to understand better how the hoof could be supported to maximise it's potential. He was also a fantastic listener and his clients joked that they should pay him not just for equine podiatry, but also for counselling.

With slight build and hippy values, he was not arrogant or sexually aggressive, but in a quiet unconventional way managed to be completely gorgeous, perhaps because his soul was so radiant. He resolved that happiness was the only real thing in life and he genuinely believed everyone deserved at least some of it. The way the horses he trimmed reacted to him also increased the trust the owners had in him. Because the animals they loved were so comfortable and calm in his presence, he had the ultimate character witness.

Even Rosie had found herself having deeper

conversations with Kev than she would comfortably have had with her close friends. She could completely understand why many of his clients found themselves a little bit in love with him.

'Rosemary Hall – would you please at least pretend you are listening to me?'

Rosie finally came back from her thoughts, eyes refocusing on her horse.

'No.' Rosie said honestly, smiling with half a mouth.

Kev sighed and put his arm over Red's withers, shaking his head as though sympathising with the horse who, with ears pricked pointedly in her direction, was also trying to get Rosie's attention.

'Why have you not been riding your horse?'

Rosie looked sharply at Kev who continued to stare at her from Red's shoulder. How did he know?

'Look at him. He is desperate for something to do and he is wondering what he is for. Why you don't take him out? He is fat.'

'Is there something wrong with him?' She asked the question that had been plaguing her, the one she didn't want a yes to, knowing it would be her fault.

'You usually keep his feet in good nick because you ride him regularly. We might not be able to go so long between trims if he is going to be a field ornament. Even if it wasn't apparent he needs to be working from this,' Kev stepped back and patted Red's overly large belly, 'I know you haven't been working him because I know what his feet should look like. Can I suggest you try and get him out at least once a day and walk him in hand. As long as he is comfortable, get him moving, once he is a little fitter and firmer, get on.'

'Ok.' Rosie failed to hide how mortified she was and Kev softened.

166

"His feet are not dreadful and as usual you are being a horse-o-chondriac. He just needs more work and less fat to carry around now, before it becomes a more serious problem. You have recognised things aren't quite right nice and early. You need to stop beating yourself up.'

'Someone else said that to me recently.'

'Well maybe, as that's two against one, you should stop beating yourself up and give me and this other person the benefit of the doubt?'

'Ok.' Rosie blushed.

'Trust your trimmer, woman. And stop giving him a huge feed every day.'

'How do you know what I feed him?

'Are you giving him a huge feed?'

'Yes.'

'Good guess. Stop.'

'But what about his minerals?'

'Mix them with no more than a handful of plain chaff, and section off some of that lush grass, way too much for one tubby horse.'

'Ok.' Rosie glanced over at Peat who was glowering at her from within the confines of his paddock, now she was going to have buy even more electric fencing. Her lip started quivering again and she bit it hard, telling herself to man up.

Kev stepped forward and caught Rosie completely by surprise when he put his arms around her. He held her and patted her back.

'I don't usually preach to you about diet and exercise because I didn't think I needed to. But things are clearly not right in Rosie land? I promise you that whatever is making you unhappy can be made better, or at least more bearable, by doing what you love. Ride. Not least because he needs it.'

Rosie nodded into his chest and burst into tears.

'Come on silly woman, enough with the water works.' Kev released Rosie and reached into the back of his estate car, which was parked across the yard. He pulled out a business card and handed it to Rosie.

'My mate Dan,' Kev explained as she read the card with a puzzled expression, 'He runs a horsemanship centre in Wiltshire. He has similar views on horse training to you, I think you would get on. Give him a call, get your horse using those feet properly and then go and see Dan.'

Rosie nodded politely and stuffed the card into the back pocket of her jeans. Even though she had already asked Kelly for a lesson, she felt slightly offended by the suggestion from someone else that she needed help with Red. The confidence issues she had were her own, there was nothing wrong with Red, he was an easy and naturally well mannered horse.

'Not because he has issues,' Kev seemed to pick up on her thought pattern, 'because you do. Your well being affects his.'

Rosie didn't really want to hear it. She turned away, running to the tack room to fetch Kev's money while he completed his paperwork.

'Call me if he isn't right in a few weeks, lead him out as much as you can, start riding for half an hour a day, increase it when you are both ready. Remind yourself, you do actually know exactly what to do. If he doesn't come right quickly, we can think about fitting him for hoof boots but I really don't think it's too bad, now that the excess length is gone, he just needs to be back in work.'

Rosie nodded and smiled.

'Thanks for coming Kev.'

'Pleasure is all mine Mrs Hall.'

Rosie waved Kev off up the lane and shut the field gates after him. She walked back to the cottage, feeling happy that Red's feet at least looked normal again after their maintenance trim, the cracks were not anything serious, and that she had a plan of action to get him right.

She called out as she let herself in through the kitchen door, but the house remained silent.

She glanced out of the window at the empty car port and realised, heart sinking, that Matt had taken Eve and gone without her.

Her momentary positivity over Red left her, replaced by the familiar drowsiness which saw her heading for the bedroom.

'So, what time is the first race on Saturday?' Jules asked Gill, once they had settled their mounts from a mile of working trot back into a long striding walk.

Gill smoothed Zinee's arched neck. The horse was in peak condition and the contours of his rock solid muscles comforted her momentarily. At least she would have prepared his body. There was nothing she could do to prepare his mind. Gill had tried to convince herself she wasn't worried about his first experience on the track, but when Jules asked about the race and she pictured him there, her heart quickened.

He was a sensitive and loyal young animal. He watched for her, called to her. She was the only one who rode him, because he was so much calmer with her on board. He fought his natural urge to flee from things that frightened him because Gill told him it was ok, that nothing would hurt him. Now in just 6 days he would be on a racecourse. The deafening announcements and sound of an excited crowd would fill Zinee's ears, the smell of the sweat of unfamiliar horses would entice his heart to speed up, making it still harder for him to stay relaxed.

'One' Gill finally answered Jules.

Gill glanced over at Milly, who was walking long and loose. Jules looked relaxed too, they were harmonised. At one time Milly had spooked and worried at every rustle in the hedge row. It could happen, they could chill out as they matured, in spite of the heightening of senses that a racing fit horse would experience.

'It will be Ok my darling.' Gill ran her fingers through a mane so soft and silky, just touching it made her smile.

Gill made the decision before her brain had finished listing the pros and cons.

She would ride him herself. She still had her jockeys licence from the early days of racing Amber, before she could afford to use professionals. The anchor in a sea of strangeness around the horse would be her hands through the reins, her voice in his ears. She would have to clear it with Norah out of courtesy, but she felt sure her client wouldn't concern herself with such details, as long as the horse was fit enough to race.

'And which race is Milly in?'

'Second, and Monty is in the 4th, Norah's other gelding Pop is in the third.' Gill answered Jules but carried on thinking about Zinee. If she was going to be jockey she would need more help.

'Actually Jules, could you come?'

'To Taunton?'

'Yeah, I am going to be a bit short handed. Four runners in the first four races, it's going to be tight.'

'Yeah, of course.'

'I am going to ride Zinee, so I will be weighing out when Milly will need to be in the ring.'

Jules patted Milly's neck and smiled, she usually felt like a spare part at races and preferred to help out at the yard rather than attend meets, but if she had Milly to organise on Gill's behalf she would feel quite important.

'No worries.' Jules paused, wondering how to put her concern without sounding too Mumsy, 'You haven't jockeyed for a while Gill, how do you feel about it?'

'Cacking myself. But I can't let this one down. John is a great, really gentle with the nervy ones but you know what Zinee is like, I just think he will be much less freaked out if he hasn't got the added stress factor of having a man he has never met on his back.'

'You will be careful wont you?'

'No. I thought I would ride hatless, naked and one armed.'

'Lowest form of wit.' Jules shook her head and wished she hadn't bothered, Gill never took concerns over her safety seriously, blinkered to the plight of the horses in her care, she rarely considered herself.

But Gill wasn't listening already. Her mind took her to the racecourse again, then it took her to the hospital with Charlie, then it took her to her bedroom, which was empty, because George was always at the restaurant. Scenes played out like television broadcasts, desperate to be vivid enough to stop her channel hopping to the next. She had always had trouble dealing with too many things happening at once, not because she wasn't motivated and capable, but because her imagination was too vivid.

Rosie's exposed face popped into her head. Charlie had seemed braver since Rosie had confided in her about her own experience with unwanted pregnancy. Hearing someone else's story - guilt and fear slowly becoming acceptance and survival - had comforted the teenager so much. Rosie was so selfless. Clearly she was suffering, even after her brave step back towards riding, the fear behind her eyes remained. As Gill studied her friend's face with her mind's eye she could see her friend, familiar and illuminated by the light of who she was, but behind the familiar, deeply concealed by the strength of her taut features, was a snared rabbit, desperate and terrified.

Jules was riding one handed and looking at her phone.

'I am worried about Rosie.'

'Do you know something?' Jules stuffed her phone back into her pocket and looked expectantly across.

Gill was about to explain it was the lack of knowing anything that was bothering her when the peaceful rural environment changed. They were riding past a tall hedge which enclosed the garden of a private house, beyond the hedge someone started a petrol strimmer, just a few metres from them. Milly skirted forwards, unsettling Jules. Zinee's legs went to jelly under him and his sharply raised head meant his neck was in Gill's face. As they struggled to soothe and control their mounts, the unknowing gardener moved the strimmer along the hedge beside them, further adding to the horse's conviction that they should run.

'Go left.' Gill barked as they reached a cross-roads, which allowed them to ride away from the noise.

Once the horses were a little distance away from the incessant buzz, Milly settled. Zinee remained tense but held his composure and walked.

'Which way will this take us?' Jules asked, not familiar with the lane.

'We can get back around to the Shillerton estate from here, it's a slightly longer ride with a bit of a main road but it should be fine.'

Jules gazed about her, excited by the prospect of learning a new ride which she could do with Ziggy and Romeo later in the week. Romeo loved new places; he would march eagerly along taking in every detail of his new territory.

'So tell me about Rosie, I thought she seemed in good spirits when she last came?'

'Notice she didn't mention Eve once though. And that she was avoiding riding.'

As Gill posed a question Jules had considered, as well as one she hadn't, the lane before them widened. A large grass verge opened out to the left of them, beyond which was a dual carriageway.

Milly was unfazed, having encountered fast roads before, the mare was satisfied that it was far enough away not to let the deafening sound of tons of vehicle whizzing along at unnatural speeds beyond the fence bother her.

'This is why I don't do this ride very often, there's about half a mile of this.' Gill had to raise her voice over the noise. Zinee winced with every passing car, his blood pumped faster, filling the veins in his legs, making them bulge. Gill remained relaxed. She comforted him with her legs gently resting on his sides giving just enough pressure to keep him moving steadily forward, despite his desire to stop, stand stock still and listen.

'You are such a good boy.' She spoke loudly enough to demand the horse's attention over the drone of the road, whilst keeping her tone soothing. He flicked an ear back and listened to her, seeking the reassurance. So she continued. Jules remained silent while Gill told him over and over again how special and good he was, her voice a steady stream of comfort.

By the time they were half way along the lane, Zinee was walking with a more measured stride, Gill had promised him it was ok, and nothing bad had happened, so slowly he relaxed.

'That's a poppet.' Gill patted Zinee's neck and beamed.

'You are right. You should ride him on Saturday. He

trusts you completely.'

'It's the hardest thing about training. He is not my horse so the decisions are not mine, but I feel so protective. And of course there is the little issue of their inevitable departure once they retire or if the owner moves them on.'

Jules nodded she reached forward and affectionately pulled Milly's ear, allowing the soft grey fur to slide through her fingers. She saw the horses in training in terms of the monthly figure they added to the account, but she had to admit she was now at a point with Milly where she would be incredibly sad if the mare were to leave.

'Right. Back to Rosie.' Jules laughed, attempting to start the conversation for a third time.

But they didn't get the chance.

*

Chapter Nine

As the horses walked beneath their riders, Jules tried to listen to Gill.

Instead, her ear was drawn to a sound behind them.

Above the noise of the dual carriageway, Jules could hear a higher pitched and more insistent whir. Milly heard it too and the mare's slender ears flicked back to enable her to focus on the sound.

A large green transit van rocketed up the lane. Zinee pitched forward as he heard the approaching engine noise and Gill turned in her saddle. She glimpsed the driver's face, set jaw and wild eye, whatever mission the man was on he clearly had no intention of slowing his progress.

'Get them on the verge.' Gill shouted above the din and urged Zinee onto the grass between the lane and the dual carriageway. Jules didn't have time to protest about taking the horses on to the grass, sandwiching them between two evils, the van was bearing down on them and from the protest of the struggling engine, appeared to be speeding up towards the horses and riders.

The footing of the verge was squelchy and soft. The strip of grass had poor drainage and as the horses sank fetlock deep into the mire, the stench of stagnant water rose up around them.

The van driver drew level with them and for some reason, a reason they would ponder over for months to come, saw fit to sound his horn, despite the fact that he had already forced them off the road and out of his way.

The scream of the engine changing pitch as it passed

them, the sudden incessant whine of the horn, coupled with the proximity to the main road – it was all too much for Milly. The mare weighed up the situation for a fraction of a second, before employing her most primitive instinct, flight.

Her powerful haunches bunched beneath her before Jules had time to attempt to reason with the mare and she was off. Plunging into the soft waterlogged ground, Milly raced almost level with the object of her torment, before the van drew away from her and she ran alone.

Jules fought the urge to panic. She knew she had to get the mare under control.

Jules wanted to scream stop, even considered bailing out to save herself, to get off the rollercoaster and hit the squelchy ground and savour its stillness.

'Whoa Milly, whoa my girl, it's ok, it's all ok..' Jules murmured between gasped breaths, trying to mimic the steady flow of comforting noise Gill had used on Zinee not minutes before. She gently squeezed the reins, taking care not to jab Milly's mouth and increase her panic further, but struggling to retain balance while the mare plunged and pitched.

To Jules' relief Milly slowed at last before stopping abruptly and trumpeting out a loud and desperate whinny. The mare whipped around, almost unseating Jules, and to their joint dismay, they realised Zinee and Gill were not behind them.

'Steady angel, steady boy.' Gill watched Jules and Milly disappearing around the bend and struggled to make a decision. Zinee trembled. He had been terrorised by the van and the still imminent threat of the road next to them, and worse, his companion had left him. Abandoned and frightened, the horse plunged on the spot, throwing muddy water up around him, the frantic breaths rasping through his nostrils louder than the sound of his rider's words. They were close to the ridge of pavement between the verge and the road, where the mud was deepest.

Worried for Jules and Milly, Gill decided the only course of action was to follow them, as much as she baulked at the idea of asking the scared youngster to run, she gathered him up and attempted to urge him forward and out of the mud.

As she squeezed him tentatively, asking him to move, the fear in her limbs made her contact feel alien and the horse reared, seeing no other option than to lift himself into the air. Gill remained in the saddle, but her balance was thrown off by the sudden vertical explosion. As his hooves touched down, Gill expected his desire to be with Milly would force him to take the decision to comply with her request.

But it didn't.

In the face of his worst fear, and the fact that he could no longer see or hear Milly, the horse decided to go home.

As he swung himself at lightning speed in the opposite direction, Gill fell.

Had her head not been spinning from the rear, she might have stayed on, but with her impulsion directed towards Milly, she didn't stand a chance when Zinee's front legs disappeared from under her.

Gill was aware of the ground coming towards her at breakneck speed, aware that her face and head were about to meet the ground, then silence as the impact assaulted her body. She heard Zinee's hooves as he veered back onto the tarmac, opened her mouth to call to him, to beg him not to run off alone to the danger of approaching cars, with flailing reins dangling amongst flailing hooves, asking for an injury. But no sound emitted from her winded lungs.

Gill did not remember blacking out as such, but when she heard

Jules' voice calling anxiously to her, she realised she had no idea how much time had passed. She struggled to lift herself from the pooling muddied water, which suctioned itself to her body and made her limbs ache in protest. Her head rested on the edge of the pavement. She had managed to hit the hard part of the ground with the most delicate part of herself, which explained the throbbing coming from beneath her hard hat.

'Zinee..' Gill wailed, her speech slurred and less audible than she intended.

Jules ran to her, having dismounted, trailing a spent Milly behind her. She helped Gill up.

'Zin....' Gill wailed again, unable to finish the word, the sky seemed darker than it should have been and she clung to Jules to stay upright.

'It's ok Gill, he is still here.'

Jules sat on the sofa in the Newmans living room, the cordless phone one side of her, Charlie on the other.

She wished George would ring.

She glanced at Charlie who looked twitchy, and wondered if she was going to have to convince her not to go to the hospital, again. There was no point until they knew more.

Gill had insisted on walking home with the horses that afternoon. Jules had desperately wanted to call an ambulance but Gill had been resolute in her insistence that she needed to get the horse home herself. Zinee had heard Milly's hooves as Jules had ridden the mare at a fast trot back along the lane to find Gill, lying in the mud. The horse had waited at a distance, further back along the lane before it joined paths with the main road, wanting to be near his companion and Gill, but not brave enough to return to the scene of the accident. After Jules had pointed the horse out to a panicking Gill, she walked towards the horse, desperate to feel his soft black coat and whisper into his worried ears. Gill had felt too dizzy to remount, and instead led the horse, her arm over his saddle she used him as a prop. The drama over, the horse had walked sedately, as though he knew Gill was not right.

The closer they got to home, the more Gill's walk resembled that of a drunk person. From her position behind them on Milly, Jules could see that Gill kept shaking her head, as though trying to clear it, and that she frequently tripped over her own feet. As they approached the Bloomswell, Jules shouted at Gill to stop and wait. To her relief, Gill followed the instruction and buried her face in Zinee's mane as the horse stood and began to pull at the young beech leaves growing from the hedge.

Jules dropped to the ground and led Milly over to the kitchen door of the restaurant. She knocked and almost instantly, George opened the door. Jules had barely finished explaining what had happened before George was running back inside to fetch his car keys. He re-appeared less than a minute later from the front of the restaurant, driving the Lexus towards Gill and Zinee.

Clearly confused, Gill allowed her hand to be prized from the horse's reins. Jules quickly remounted and took Zinee from George. She called to Gill that she would get them home safely, after all there was only quarter of a mile to go, but Gill didn't respond. George had helped her into the car and sped away.

George had called twice since. Once to say they had been seen almost immediately in the accident and emergency department, then later to say Gill was waiting for a CT scan, was conscious and intermittently lucid.

That was three hours ago. Jules was torn between not wanting Charlie to rush to the hospital unnecessarily, especially when she had to go there herself first thing in the morning, and wondering if they should in fact both be there in case it was something more serious.

Not wanting to tie up the landline, Jules decided to use her mobile to call Rosie. The call failed, the mobile signal in the Newmans living room was often poor through thick cottage walls. She excused herself and left Charlie on the sofa to step outside the kitchen door where she would be able to make the call.

Jules poured the story out.

She felt exhausted by the time she had finished telling Rosie what had happened, in relaying it, she re-lived it. Until then Jules had only thought about Gill and the horses, but Rosie offered gentle reassurance that Jules had done the right thing and questions about whether Jules was ok. Jules felt tears slip from her eyes.

'It's over now darling.' Rosie said gently.

'I know.' Jules gasped as her tears became fatter and her lungs contracted.

'Let it out. I would be crying too.'

'I love you Rosie.' Jules said honestly. It was perhaps a little over the top, but Jules' intention was not to dramatise the situation, just to express gratitude for Rosie's level headed empathy in a way which was more encompassing than a mere thank you.

'I love you too, very much.'

Jules had no idea that Rosie was also in tears, because at the other end of the phone she could hide it. It was not the time for Rosie to start explaining why hearing that she was loved was such a welcome and emotional assault.

'I can't help but think if they were really worried, or she was seriously ill, they would have got her in for a scan already and we would know something. They treat the most serious first, yes?'

'Yes.' Jules allowed herself some comfort in the rationale.

'What time is Charlie's appointment tomorrow?'

'She has to report to the ward for 9am. I have to be in court first thing.'

'Right. Well on the basis that even if they let Gill home tonight she is not going to be up for driving first thing in the morning, why don't we agree now that I will take her?'

'Can you?'

'Jimmy and Crystal were planning to go out for the day and I was going to be with Eve, but we can do that Tuesday instead – nothing was set in stone.' Rosie momentarily despised herself for the relief she felt that her first day in weeks alone with Eve would be delayed. Given the circumstances, relief was hardly appropriate.

'Charlie hasn't mentioned it.' Jules said, wondering whether Charlie would agree to the idea.

'Go and grab her and I will have a word?'

Jules opened the fridge. She couldn't hear what Charlie was saying outside and hoped the assumption that her mother wouldn't be taking her in as planned the next day wasn't freaking her out.

She hadn't eaten since that morning, it was almost 11pm. Charlie had been told she must be nil by mouth after midnight and Jules contemplated making them both a sandwich while there was still time. Her stomach was knotted, worry rendering her appetite mute.

The landline started to ring from the living room. Without closing the fridge door, Jules ran to answer it.

'Jules, its George.'

'How is she?'

'Ok. She has a severe concussion and some bruising to the brain, they have said she has to do literally nothing for the next week, total bed rest and no reading or TV. Her CT scan was hours ago, but we have been waiting until just now for an x-ray – looks like she has a broken rib. The pain in her head was so bad she didn't realise there was anything else wrong. They have given her some really strong painkillers and she is much happier - totally doolally!'

George's relief spread through Jules like a warm current and she suddenly felt famished.

'They should be letting us go within the next half an hour.'

'Thank fuck.'

'Thank fuck indeed.' George laughed, 'you frightened the crap out of me when you arrived at the restaurant.'

'Sorry George, was it a problem you had to leave?'

'This was more important. Besides it was about time Rob picked up some slack.'

Jules detected a hint of resentment and saw her opportunity to try and initiate a conversation about what was going on at the restaurant.

'Problems?' she tried to sound friendly.

'Yeah. Not the right time now, but I might need to pick your legal brains soon.'

'Of course George, if I can help I will.'

They said goodbye and Jules returned to the kitchen to give Charlie and Rosie the good news.

The sound of the front door opening was soon followed by the sound of Gill giggling.

Jules and Charlie were sat at the counter in the kitchen,

eating cheese and ham toasted sandwiches. Jules wiped her mouth and stood up to greet Gill. George looked tired.

'My girls!' Gill cried and reached across Jules to simultaneously embrace Charlie, who only just managed to save her sandwich from being crushed against her.

'Good painkillers then Mum? Charlie rolled her eyes but was unable to hide her smile at seeing her mother in one piece.

'Oh yeah...' Gill nodded and started giggling again.

George pulled out a chair for Gill to sit down, but Gill lumbered towards the back door. George moved swiftly after her and pulled her gently away from her wellies.

'No horses. Bed.' George said firmly.

'Yes Daaaaaad.' Gill moaned and put her hand on her hip.

'All done.' Jules said, 'They have been fed watered and loved, so you can go straight to bed.'

Gill looked confused, then resolute.

'But my lovely Charlie is here!'

'And I still will be tomorrow.' Charlie said firmly.

'Come on.' George led Gill away.

Gill's giggles and repeated announcements that she wanted candy floss continued as they listened to George trying to organise her up the staircase.

A while later George returned. He relayed the strict instructions he had been given by the hospital about the care of Gill's head injury, which included doing absolutely nothing. Jules decided it wasn't the right time to bring up the issue of Saturday's race and turned her attention instead to Charlie, who piped up as soon as George had finished talking.

'Rosie is picking me up at half eight and there is no need to bother Mum with it until I get back.'

George, like Gill, had clearly forgotten about Charlie's

183

appointment.

'Thanks Charlie. ' George patted his partner's daughter on the arm tentatively, wanting to show his gratitude, but not feeling that they were yet close enough to hug. 'I am going to take a few days off, I don't think Gill should be on her own, so I will be here when you get back tomorrow – is there anything you would like or need?'

Charlie shook her head and smiled bravely.

It wasn't until later when she was nestled under a duvet on the sofa that she allowed herself to sob. Rosie was lovely, but how on earth was she going to get through this without her mum?

Rosie took her trusty Vauxhall Vectra up through its clunky but reliable gears. The old vehicle sailed along the dual carriageway, leaving Exeter behind them. Rosie had expected to feel drained after the day she had endured. She had expected to be tearful, knocked further into the abyss.

But to her surprise, she felt calm and more centred than she had for a long time.

The altruistic gesture in taking Charlie to her appointment had felt like a burden prior to the event, but now that it was over Rosie realised just how much of her general wellbeing was dependant on helping others. When she had been at work and looking after her two animals, she had been completed, her craving to validate herself by her deeds satisfied.

Today, when she had been a rock for Charlie, waited with her and kept her upbeat, then taken her home and settled her into her old room, she had been valuable.

As she drove, her smile faded. The unwelcome sounds of her thoughts turning sour, overpowered the good feeling she had, told her how sick it was to feel good as a result of something so bad.

She wished the part of her that hated her would shut up. But the negative voice within her refused to quiet as always, it created tenuous and unfounded links between the things she thought were right and the things she thought were wrong, so that no matter what she did she always came out wrong.

Maybe recognition of this was a good first step.

Maybe it just meant she was mad.

She had always imagined there would be peace in madness, a point beyond which you stopped caring and so you just existed. How naive. Her state of mind gave her a unique insight into the lives of the mentally unwell clients she tried to find homes for. The loneliness and desperation borne of no longer being able to trust your own mind to be on your side, was unparalleled by anything Rosie had ever felt before.

For the first time in her life she had a glimpse into the oblivion that had seen her mother succumb to alcoholism.

Charlie pulled the duvet over her, glad to be within the walls of the safest place on earth. She was so grateful to George for thoughtfully clearing her room out and making up her bed. Newmans had not always been a happy place for her, overcome by angst in her early teens, but she would always think of it as home, no matter where life took her.

At the hospital with Rosie she had been brave, even when she had first come round, the nurse who had tended to her had been so nice and sweet. No one had made her feel judged, everything had gone as planned.

They had warned her she could bleed heavily for the first twenty-four hours after the procedure, but being prepared didn't stop her feeling undignified and uncomfortable.

The sickness which had taken over her body was gone. As soon as she had woken up from the anaesthetic she had known with no doubt that she was no longer pregnant.

In all her weeks of resolve, winning over Darran to her way of thinking, not once had she felt regret over the decision she was making.

Now, with the deed done, she allowed herself to mourn. She allowed herself to feel the emptiness within her and she said a silent apology to the life that could have been. One day, she promised, we will do it right and you will get your chance to be real.

'Oh my darling.' Gill all but swooned as she walked through the door into her daughter's childhood bedroom to see her, colourless and breaking her heart. Gill wobbled awkwardly towards the bed.

'No no Mum, it isn't how it looks. I am ok I promise. Just having a little moment.'

Gill sat in close beside Charlie. They didn't embrace, Charlie for fear of hurting her mother's broken rib, Gill through inability to reach her arms out forwards.

'What a pair we are.' Charlie laughed through her tears.

'How do you feel?' Gill's eyes were not focusing properly but her voice was as warm as the woodburner.

'Better for seeing you.'

Later that evening Gill insisted on venturing downstairs to eat the soup George had prepared. Clean sheeted and smiling again, Charlie had taken hers to her bedroom, accompanied by Darran, who had arrived at Newmans looking a mixture of sheepish and concerned.

Gill had not helped his nerves by asking whether it was sensible for him to accompany Charlie to her bedroom, then audibly concluding that ship had sailed.

George had chided her for her blunt behaviour, but she excused herself by virtue of a bump on the head.

'I think I had better start thinking about what to do on Saturday. There is so much to sort out,' Gill spoke suddenly, breaking the silence as the couple ate.

'I am so glad you are not still planning to ride.' George exhaled heavily, letting the worry he had felt since Jules had told him go.

'To be honest, I know I am not up to it.' Gill smiled grimly before helping herself to some French bread. 'I know I can't ride any of them between now and Saturday, let alone ride in a race. I just wish my head wasn't so fuzzy, I can't think clearly about what to do.'

'Then that is a sure sign you shouldn't be thinking at all.'

'Hmmm..' Gill murmured as she dipped her bread into the chunky vegetable soup. She should be planning her contingency, calling the owners of the entered horses, sorting out the entries themselves. The fog around her brain would not allow her to hold on to any one thought for long enough to act on it.

'Let's take it a day at a time.' George put down his spoon and squeezed her hand.

'Are you going back to work tomorrow?'

'Nope.'

Rosie stretched and sighed. Eve was asleep, so were Jimmy and Crystal. She uncurled her legs from beneath her and sat on the edge of the sofa.

She thought about calling Matt. Where once she would have shared an emotional experience like today with him, she now felt a hesitation at the thought of picking up the phone. She missed him. Not just during the week when he was away, but all the time. The distance between them yawned into a cavernous void with every missed opportunity to talk and reconnect. Was she supposed to be doing more? What could she do while he was so cold with her?

With the void had started to come indifference, she internalised her anguish and became harder as a result.

She switched off the telly and paused as she passed the computer. She had been intending to try and go to bed but it seemed pointless, given that she wasn't remotely tired. She wondered whether her mother had emailed.

She decided to have a wee while the computer fired up.

As she passed the door to the nursery she heard the baby stir. She crept towards the cot to see Eve's little arms shoot up above her head. The baby yawned and stretched before lolling her head and dozing off again. Rosie smiled. The night light illuminated the infant's peaceful face in a soft haze. She reached out to smooth the backs of her fingers over the soft forehead of her child.

'I wish I could be better for you.' Rosie spoke softly, meaning her words but as always, feeling a detachment from the situation, similar to the distance between her and Matt.

Rosie fixed herself a hot chocolate to take back to the computer, hoping it would help to make her feel sleepy.

She was undeniably pleased when she saw there were two emails from Selina. The first was asking for more pictures of Eve, the second gave her skype account name and suggested they instant message rather than emailing if Rosie was ever online in the evening.

Rosie opened the Skype account Matt had installed for her. He had done it so that they could chat while he was away during the week, back when they had expected to spend every evening they were apart talking to one another. He worked such long hours though, they barely spoke.

Rosie struggled to remember her password and guessed at Harry, she was right.

She searched for her mother's screen name and sent her a request. Almost immediately her mother instant messaged her.

SHarding2013: You are up late child.
HorseyHall80: So are you.
SHarding2013: I do most of my work in the evening. Not a morning person.
HorseyHall80: Neither am I.
SHarding2013: Ahh but you have to be, you have a baby.

Rosie wondered how open she should be with her mother. She wasn't sure she wanted to let the woman, who basically felt like a stranger, in. There was an anonymity of sorts, in typing to her mother. Because she couldn't hear her voice she felt less irritable.

HorseyHall80: I don't do much of the early morning stuff since Jimmy and Crystal have been here.
SHarding2013: Why is your Dad there?
HorseyHall80: They have moved in to help with the baby. Matt works away during the week now I only see him at weekends.
SHarding2013: Oh right.
HorseyHall80: Crystal dotes on Eve, loves feeding her. Dad is pretty hands on too.

Selina stopped typing. Rosie wondered whether her mother had gone. She felt stupid for sharing so much with her, she usually preferred to keep her mother firmly out of her life.

HorseyHall80: Are you still there?

SHarding2013: Yes. Just processing. Bit jealous if I am honest, your Dad is getting to be a hands on Grandad and I haven't even met my Granddaughter.
Horseyhall80: They didn't move in to spite you. They moved in because I wasn't coping.
SHarding2013: You are the strongest person I know, what do you mean you were not coping?

Rosie's fingers slid from the keyboard and she slumped in her chair. How could she be the strongest person her mother knew, she knew next to nothing about her?

SHarding2013: I know we haven't exactly been close since you were small, but I still know who you are, you are my daughter.

Rosie scowled. Of course she did, it was what made her so infuriating.

Sharding2013: Tell me what you mean, what weren't you coping with?
Horseyhall80: I don't know where to start.
SHarding2013: At the beginning.
Horseyhall80: Well you know I lost Harry. I guess it started there.
SHarding2013: I know that must have been very difficult, but it doesn't explain why you can't feed your own baby in the morning?
Horseyhall80: I don't know. I don't know why I can't find whatever it is mothers are supposed to have.

Selina's icon remained inactive, which only served to make Rosie more frustrated.

Horseyhall80: Of course I wouldn't expect you to understand. Mother of the year that you are.
SHarding2013: Yep, I deserved that. If it makes you feel

better to lash out at me, you go right ahead. It's the least I can do.
Horseyhall80:   Oh fuck off.

Selina would usually have scorned Rosie, dismissing her as over-emotional, cleverly making Rosie feel that it was her own flaws which made her weak enough to blame her upbringing. Rosie wasn't sure whether she preferred the self-deprecating acceptance or not. She was ready to log off, to end the conversation in a flail of insults as would always have been the case.

SHarding2013: You can blame me if you want.   But I think you should know that when you were a baby was the happiest time of my life. I simply could not have loved you any more than I did. You were my world. It was when I realised that I couldn't have another baby, and when you started to think for yourself and judge me, that it started to go wrong. You were so close to your Dad, you adored him and the two of you made it very clear your bond with each other was stronger than either of you wanted with me.
Horseyhall80:   Oh there's the Mummy I know, that's right, blame me.
SHarding2013: I am not trying to apportion blame. I know it lies firmly with me. What I am trying to explain to you if you would try to drag yourself into the present, is that I did not have post natal depression. I was completely in love with you. Just stop hating me for a second and hear me. What you are experiencing is not something you got from me.

Rosie gave the finger to the screen. But then started to cry.

So typical of her mother to absolve herself of blame rather than trying to help her.

Horseyhall80:   Ok point taken. Not your fault as always.
SHarding2013: I am not trying to pinpoint fault, Rosie for fuck's sake, I am trying to reassure you that this is not something you are pre-disposed to, and not something that is

likely to have stemmed from your own experiences. You are only going to work this out if you understand it.

Horseyhall80:   But I don't understand it. Part of me doesn't want to. I just wish I hadn't had a baby.

SHarding2013: If there is one thing you should have learned from me, it is that burying your head in the sand never resolves anything. But, that being said, if you are not ready to deal with it, maybe you should stop trying to

Horseyhall80:   And do what?

SHarding2013: Get some distance. Maybe you need to miss her in order to realise how much you feel for her. I am sure it's in there. Convinced. There are just other things in the way in your head.

Horseyhall80:   But that is why Jimmy and Crystal are here. They are doing everything for Eve so that I can choose to spend time with her and not feel so alone when Matt is away.

SHarding2013: Maybe that is not enough distance. It's your birthday on Saturday, why don't you and Matthew go away together?

Horseyhall80:   You remembered it was my Birthday?

SHarding2013: Don't change the subject child.

Horseyhall80:   I am almost touched.

SHarding2013: Focus.

Horseyhall80:   Matt won't do it. We have hardly spoken since I told him how I feel about Eve. He is overcompensating so he only wants to spend time with her when he is here. There is no way he will give up a weekend with her to spend with just me.

SHarding2013: Do you realise you picked a man who is almost an exact carbon copy of your father?

Horseyhall80:   Now who isn't focusing

SHarding2013: It just goes to show though doesn't it. Blood means nothing. Jimmy is not your biological father, and yet you have modelled your life on his influence.

Horseyhall80:   Well I could hardly have chosen a man like Eddie, I don't know him well enough to know if   someone was like him.

SHarding2013: Eddie didn't bring you up.

Horseyhall80:   And now I am not bringing Eve up.

SHarding2013: You are not neglecting her either, you didn't break her before Jimmy arrived did you? Stop beating yourself up. If going away with Matt isn't an option, maybe you need to get some distance by yourself.

Horseyhall80:   And go where? What about Red?

SHarding2013: I am not claiming to have all the answers am I? I just think maybe if you took some time now, and sorted this out before Eve is old enough to understand what is going on, you could fix this and avoid screwing her up like I screwed you up.

Horseyhall80:   I am having counselling.

SHarding2013: You know your own mind better than anyone. If you want to get to a point where you can have the life you want, it's going to have to come from you.

Horseyhall80:   You can't tell me to stop having counselling!

SHarding2013: It's bunkum.

Horseyhall80:   You do talk rubbish. I have seen it work, seen my client's bloom from talking through their issues.

SHarding2013: For people who need guidance to help them work things out for themselves yes. But you know how to work things out.

Horseyhall80:   So why haven't I worked things out.

SHarding2013: Go up the page and read what you wrote. You don't want to work it out. You just want it to go away.

Horseyhall80:   And you think the answer is for me to go away?

SHarding2013: I am just suggesting you remove yourself from the situation so that you can clear your head and look at it with perspective.

Horseyhall80:   Makes sense. But I am not leaving Red, he is the only thing keeping me going. The only thing I have.

SHarding2013: You have me as well.

Rosie sat back from the computer and laughed. Who would have imagined. In the absence of being able to relate to the people in her life she held dearest for fear of alienating them, she was having a positive discussion with her mother. Rosie smiled and shook her head. Working was obviously agreeing with Selina, this was the most human she had appeared in years.

Horseyhall80:   I had better go to bed.
SHarding2013: Ok, I had better finish going through this chapter. The author has gone a bit off topic, I'm not sure it works.
Horseyhall80:   Night Mum.
SHarding2013: Goodnight child. I am online most evenings.
Horseyhall80:   Ok.

Rosie shut down the computer and shut her eyes. What a day. She wondered how Charlie was doing. She must call to ask after her and Gill in the morning.

'But now to bed.'

As she eased herself between cool inviting sheets, she was surprised to find her head unusually clear.

Instead of the anxiety which plagued her in silence and darkness, preventing sleep, her brain was quiet.

She shut her eyes and waited.

But still the voices that tormented her remained without words.

Rosie nestled her head deeper into the pillow and enjoyed the serenity of drifting off to sleep.

'Thanks Mum...'

Chapter Ten

'The only thing we haven't done is told Norah about Zinee.' Kelly added nervously, 'We weren't sure what you wanted to do.'

'You are not riding.' George eyed Gill before excusing himself to the office to make a call.

Jules and Kelly sat in the kitchen waiting expectantly for Gill's reaction.

Gill looked at her employee and her business partner and couldn't help but smile.

They had come in to Newmans and announced they had been work riding all the horses except Zinee and delivered an obviously pre-prepared speech about how they were going to take the runners on Saturday and ensure the yard was still able to compete in the first race of the season.

'You are right about Zinee. My ribs are not going to let me get on a horse any time soon and my head is still woolly as hell. But I think I will at least be able to come on Saturday.'

'Are you sure you should, it's only Wednesday you don't have to decide now?'

'As long as Maurice is driving the box, I can't see why not.'

'I have been to enough races to know what to do Gill, you honestly don't need to be there.' Kelly said firmly, but then seeing Gill's face softened slightly, 'Unless you want to be, of course.'

'Maurice has said he will hang around, and help if we need it.' Jules smiled encouragingly. Maurice owned the farm up the road from Jules' old Cottage in Kysford. Stabling Romeo in his yard for four years, she had become close to the older gentleman, and had utilised his lorry licence to take Romeo to events on numerous occasions. He was more comfortable with cattle, and mostly refused to wear anything but a scruffy old tweed suit, usually adorned with mucus, manure and other delightful substances, but he could hold a horse if needed. When Jules had called him to ask for his help, he had been more than happy to oblige, saying a day at the races was just what he needed. Jules knew he ran his farm largely on his own and apart from the odd Sunday lunch with his sons, he rarely had the opportunity or the inclination to go anywhere else.

Gill nodded. The movement made her head spin. She tried to think of anything else the girls might not have remembered, anything else she should be doing, but her brain still wasn't playing ball.

'So you just need to have a think about Zinee?' Kelly reminded her, noticing her boss appeared to be drifting off.

'Could we get the jockey to come and ride him here?' Jules suggested, thinking that if the horse had an opportunity to meet the man before the race he might be more relaxed.

'Trouble is, he hasn't been ridden since Sunday, we usually make sure they have exercise every day up to a race to keep them fit and supple.' Kelly frowned. Gill was the only one who rode Zinee, she hadn't wanted to bother her by asking permission.

'John wouldn't have had the time anyway.' Gill confirmed, alleviating Kelly's guilt. 'He jockeys for the National Hunt Races as well as the Arabs. It's because he is good, he is in demand. Thank you both. I really appreciate this.' Gill smiled.

'Least we can do boss.' Kelly winked. 'Speaking of which, we had better go and get these horses out?'

'Yep!' Jules nodded.

'Don't you have to get back to work?' Gill was confused.

'Took today off.' Jules explained, 'In Court on Friday so will have to go in tomorrow and then, but today I am all Kelly's.'

Gill patted Jules' arm in thanks.

'Right, I had better go and phone Norah. Wish me luck.'

Jules and Kelly called encouragement as they left to head to the horse barn, leaving Gill to make her way to the office, to deliver the bad news to Norah. How she reacted could have major consequences for the yard, and Gill's heart quickened, which made her head pound.

As she reached the office door she could hear George on the phone.

She hovered in the hallway.

'Can I see you?' came George's voice from behind the door. He sounded almost desperate.

'It won't take long, but I really need you.'

Gill slumped onto the floor, thinking the closer she was to the ground the less frightening her dizziness would be, praying her head would stop thundering so that she could process what she was hearing.

'Ok Thursday, I will come to yours after lunchtime service.'

Gill's side started to throb in time with her head, where blood pumped around her slowly healing ribs, exacerbated by her awkward position leant against the wall.

'What are you doing?' George almost fell over Gill as he went to leave the office.

'I need to call Norah.'

'I think you need to go to bed?'

George tried to help Gill up but she waved him away.

'Jules and Kelly are going to take all the horses except

197

Zinee on Saturday. They think they can do it.'

George sighed so heavily he ended up sat on the floor next to Gill.

'I am so relieved.' George held Gill's hand, 'I really thought you might have to compensate the owners.'

Gill squeezed his hand. She had no idea he had even been thinking about the race, he had been so intent on caring for her.

'There is still Norah to deal with. Zinee can't run now either way.'

'Later. You must rest - you look dreadful.'

Gill allowed herself to be ushered to bed. As she laid flat on the bedclothes and listened to George retreating down the stairs to pop to the restaurant for a few hours while she slept, a niggling memory of the call she had overheard tried to get her attention.

'Later,' she murmured to herself, as the painkillers she had taken, took hold and she started to lose consciousness, 'think about it later.'

George returned that evening to find her still asleep and decided not to wake her. He ate alone, reluctant to go back to the restaurant again for the evening shift in case she did wake and wondered where he was. He spoke to Jules about the plans for Saturday and learned of Gill's plan to persuade him to drive her to the races. He smiled and shook his head, but decided if she was well enough he would take her.

Jules went to bed early, exhausted after the day's yard work and riding. He decided to turn in early himself. The various sources of worry were starting to have a cumulative effect. The pending legal action at the restaurant made it hard to switch off, his brain constantly nagging at him, how would he afford it, how would he keep it from Gill, should he? Now he was concerned about Gill too. His heart had not slowed down properly since Jules had arrived at the restaurant after the fall and he had his biggest fear about his partner's vocation realised.

As he carefully slid under the covers beside the woman he loved, he could have wept with guilt. He knew it was time to confide in her, to tell her about Daisy, about it all, but he also knew that while she was recovering from a head injury was hardly the time to burden her.

'I love you. I'm sorry.' He whispered to the sleeping blond head he was helpless to protect.

'What on earth is all that noise?!' Rosie called from the spare room, where she had been planning to change out of her horsey clothes in order to take Eve for a mid-morning stroll in the sunshine. She ran through the house, worrying it was going to collapse around her, such was the vibration and rumbling coming from outside. She didn't stop running until she had laid her eyes on Eve through the kitchen window. Crystal was with her in the Orchard, having pushed the baby's stroller away from the din. The horses were grazing at the top of their field untroubled by the noise below.

Satisfied everyone was safe and the noise which had woken her was not in fact Armageddon, Rosie slid her flip-flops on and made her way outside.

She found Jimmy, talking to the driver of an incredibly large lorry, which appeared to have wedged itself between the banks of the narrow lane which led to Orchard Cottage. Assuming the lorry driver had taken a wrong turn, and content that Jimmy was going to see him backwards and out of his predicament, Rosie had been about to head back inside and have a cup of coffee.

'Wait darling.' Jimmy called as he climbed up the bank to get behind the lorry.

Rosie stood in the lane, impatient, she could only see the cab's front, which bore no logos to give away its cargo, what did it have to do with her?

Once Jimmy had seen the driver back to the large layby just before the turning to the cottage, the driver finally killed the deafening engine and dismounted from the cab looking stiff.

Jimmy clapped the driver on the back and congratulated him. Rosie decided it was a delivery which was meant for him, maybe something to do with one of his businesses.

'Would you like a cup of tea?' Rosie called to the driver, desperate for caffeine herself. The driver nodded eagerly and Jimmy asked for a coffee.

She trotted back to the kitchen and boiled the kettle, stifling a yawn. She had been up late every night since she and Selina had started instant messaging. Sleeping late was a habit that she really shouldn't get into. If Jimmy and Crystal left any time soon, she was going to have a serious shock to her system.

Rosie set the mugs onto a tray and headed back to the lane.

As she walked towards the lorry, she saw the driver manoeuvring a van off the lorry's ramp. As he swung the vehicle around in the layby, she realised it was not a van. Not a normal one anyway.

Jimmy all but danced towards her, beaming.

The driver finished parking. As he took his tea he nudged Jimmy with his free elbow and chuckled.

'She doesn't look very happy?!'

Rosie slurped her coffee and continued to stare at the vehicle, not believing it could actually be for her.

'Am I actually seeing this?' Rosie turned to Jimmy.

'Birthday present from your hubby. Two horse converted Mercedes Sprinter, with side opening ramp and jokey door, rear facing travel, custom built by HorseForce,' Jimmy read from the brochure the driver had given him.

'Matt bought me a horsebox?' Rosie said and started to cry. Not because she had in front of her the thing she had dreamed for years of being able to afford, but because it must surely mean that Matt still loved her. 'I have to go and phone him.'

She handed to the tray to Jimmy.

'Don't you want to look inside it?!' Jimmy laughed.

'Yes!' Rosie called as she dashed away from him, 'but I need to ring Matt first!'

To Rosie's disappointment Matt's phone went straight to voicemail. Still walking on air, she left him a garbled and enthusiastic message, gushing with the swell in her heart, thanking him profusely, not just for the box itself, but for the thought.

She skipped back outside, her brain repeating the words "he still loves me" over and over again like a mantra for joy.

Jimmy encouraged her to get inside the box and the driver started to show her all the high-tech features, which included a CCTV system. From a small screen set in the dashboard, she could see into the back of the box, meaning she would be able to check that Red was travelling happily just by glancing down.

'I do like this job,' the lorry driver laughed when Jimmy thanked him, 'makes me feel like I am delivering happiness!'

'And indeed you are, chap!' Jimmy laughed, nodding his head towards Rosie who had jumped from the cab and was undoing the catches to open up the back.

The horse area impressed her even more. The ramp was low and stable, with a non-slip surface for extra grip, so even the most travel weary legs would find traction. The centre partition, as well as the breast bars, were covered with wipe clean padding, ensuring comfort even in the event of having to brake hard. In the very rear of the box was a tack area, which was equipped with its own tiny sink and a streamlined wardrobe for rider's clothes sat above the double saddle rack.

She had never had a brand new vehicle. Not even a car. Now she had something she had always dreamed of and it came with the freedom to take Red wherever they wanted to go. It was as fresh and sparkly as it was practical.

Beaming through her tears she embraced Jimmy, then she cuddled the driver who giggled like a schoolboy.

Jimmy and the driver continued to talk about the many virtues of the box, and Rosie half listened, eyes fixed firmly on the metallic grey bodywork, while the words in her head repeated themselves to the exclusion of any other thought. Matt loves me.

'Hello...?'

Gill answered the phoned and mumbled groggily into the receiver. At first it appeared to be part of her dream, just a background noise. But the ringing had gone on for such a long time Gill had eventually been roused enough to make it stop. She had gone back to bed after spending the morning convincing George to go to the restaurant. She had insisted she was fine, when, in fact, she was quite woozy and in need of still more sleep.

'Gill, it's Mike.'

Gill smiled at the lovely sound of her brother's Devonshire tones.

'Hey Mikey...'

'It's Mum Gill. Just had a call from Glencoe. They said

she has had a stroke, she is being taken to Exeter hospital. Ginny and I are just leaving to go in, but I wanted to call you first.'

Gill tried to process the information. Mike sounded strained. She wanted to comfort him but she wasn't sure what to say. In that moment, with an already cloudy head, she wondered what the point was. Of course she should be feeling as upset as Mike clearly was, should be praying for recovery. But recover for what? To go on sitting in a chair, staring blankly ahead for god knows how many more years? To be fed mashed up food whilst wearing a bib, being prompted to swallow? To be bathed by strangers whilst thinking nothing, doing nothing and having no aspiration.

Later of course, Gill would come to repent over the thoughts, but in that short moment, she hoped for the end of many years of suffering on all sides. She hoped for a release for Mike, who surely must have a small part of himself eroded away every time he sat in the chair, talking to someone who couldn't hear him and would never respond.

'Do you want me to come?' She asked, her offer to go in support of him, rather than a genuine belief she could help her mother in any way.

'I think it would be sensible.' Mike was tight lipped.

'I will have to wait for George to get home, I can't drive at the moment.'

'Why?' Mike sounded concerned but distant.

'Bumped my head, long story, will tell you when I see you. I am fine I am just not quite up to being on the road.'

'Well I could ring you from the hospital once I know more?'

'It's ok, I will get George and see you there. Text me where you are and I will find you.'

Gill found it hard to balance as she pulled her jeans on.

She held the bannister to steady herself as she walked down the stairs. She passed the phone in the hall, paused, but instead headed to the front door, deciding it would be easier to walk to the restaurant where the Lexus was parked anyway.

She shuffled along the lane, fought not to allow the tarmac to swim beneath her. Looking resolutely ahead she drove her feet forward, determined.

Before she reached the Barton, she saw the distinguishable black car, heading across the junction ahead her, towards the centre of the village. She rounded the corner and looked in the direction she had seen him go, expecting to have missed him entirely.

But he had parked up outside of one of the larger houses.

She watched him get out of the car and walk up the drive. A newly painted bright red door opened before he reached it, and a red haired young woman dashed onto the porch to kiss his cheek and invite him inside.

Gill continued to stand at the junction, cars passing her, the world carrying on around her.

She struggled to remain upright. She made herself turn around. She took the few steps needed to enter the village shop. Maisy was behind the counter.

An extreme headache negated pleasantries. Without greeting Maisy, she asked her a direct question.

'Who lives at the big house with the red front door?'

Maisy eyed Gill, who was uncharacteristically stony faced, and appeared to be having trouble seeing.

'Not sure Gill. Hang on.' Maisy walked to the door of the store room behind her, 'Bob,' she shouted, 'What's the name of that couple who just bought Sunningdale?'

Maisy told Gill to hang on and went into the store room. A few seconds later she reappeared.

'Hunt, chap's called Roy, and we think the girl is a Daisy. Seem like a nice young pair, must be quite successful to have...'

Maisy trailed off when she saw the colour had drained from Gill's face.

The redhead from George's old photos. Daisy, the name of his ex.

It all made sense, and, it made no sense at all. Gill's head pounded violently, pain searing through both temples, numbing her hands and feet and making her want to vomit. She clutched at the counter in front her to stop herself from going down.

'I don't feel very good,' Gill whispered through dry lips, 'could you take me home.'

'Oh give me a break!' Jules slammed her palms against her desk, making her coffee cup jump, splattering the cold liquid across her face.

'Steady on girl,' James had walked into her office mid her outburst. He handed her a tissue.

'I needed to leave ten minutes ago, Kelly and I have to get the runners up to the gallops before sunset and I just lost the document I was working on. It needs to go out tonight.' Jules screwed up her face in frustration. 'Bloody useless sodding computer.'

James knew about Jules' endeavour to ensure the yard still ran at the weekend, and how much the pressure of trying to be Gill was getting to her. She had confided in him over lunch, after he had updated her on the progress he, Lisa and their new marriage guidance counsellor, were not making.

'Is it the Alloway file?'

'Yeah. Client keeps changing her mind. If I don't get this out the court will rule in summary.'

'Give me the file.'

205

Jules looked up from her frantic mouse clicking.

'It's just an extension application right?'

'Yes.'

'I think I can handle that. Go.'

'James...what about your Court case tomorrow?' Jules was already mentally putting her coat on, but guilt made her hesitate.

'All my prep is done. I was even going to leave early myself, but I don't have any horses that need me, so get gone.'

'I will,' Jules paused as she hit the shut down button on her computer and simultaneously slid her feet back into her shoes, 'make this up to you – any time you need a favour, it's me – ok?'

'No need. But ok.' James laughed as she handed him the case file.

Jules threw her arms around him in a hurried gesture of genuine appreciation, but he held her so tightly the embrace ended up warmer than she had intended.

Footsteps outside her office caused them to break away. They stood awkwardly while they waited for the secretary to pass.

'Go!' James pointed to the door.

'Thank you...' Jules fled.

'Hellooooo!' Jules called as she opened the front door of Newmans. Ziggy bounded to her and she caressed his head, promising him a full cuddle once she had changed out of her suit. 'Hello?' Jules called again but again no one answered. Jules' phone beeped in her pocket and she smiled, thinking that it must be James telling her not to worry about the Alloway file, but it was from Rosie.

Can't make it Sat, long story, sorry. Hope it's a good day and good luck xx

Jules frowned at her phone. Rosie's help would have been useful and it wasn't like her to let, well, anyone down. Before she allowed herself to curse her friend, she thought back to the conversation she and Gill had almost had before Gill's fall. She resolved to call her later that evening and dashed up the stairs to change.

Kelly smiled and slapped Monty's sleek muscular neck. The black horse's forward ears framed the viewed across the fields towards Newmans and Kelly wished the sight of the yard could still make her smile, instead of filling her with fear. She didn't mention the fear to Jules, who was playing with Pop's mane as the spent gelding ambled home after their 2 mile workout on the all-weather track.

Popping Merriment was a chestnut gelding who Norah had bred and sold as a foal. The owner had given the horse a great start, not backing him until he was four, then showing, some endurance, some jumping.

A car accident had put an end to their partnership. As much as the woman had apparently loved Pop, she couldn't bring herself to allow him to be a field ornament, after the doctors confirmed the injuries to her knee would only heal well enough to allow her to walk if she avoided strenuous activity or the possibility of further injury at all costs. It was a sad story, one which had forced Jules to think about what she would do with Romeo if something like that happened to her. She had concluded she would learn to drive him, or take up horse agility, anything not to have to part with her own chestnut gelding. She admired the woman though, for making a brave decision.

Norah had taken him straight to Gill's, deciding that as she had to keep her promise to buy back any horse she had bred if the owner needed to sell, she would give him the same job as the others she owned.

Jules knew Gill was quietly excited about the ripe conker coloured horse. He was seasoned, sensible, and very eager to please, if what you wanted was to run like the wind, he would do his best to give it to you. His first race could be a good indicator of the rest of his career. Jules wondered if his old owner would have him back when he retired. She hoped so.

'He kept up with Monty and doesn't seem too puffed.' Jules mused out loud.

Kelly smiled over at the ordinary looking gelding. 'No previous form so he will have rubbish odds but I am convinced he will win it. It's only a mile and he can do double that without breaking a sweat. He beat Milly last time Gill and I rode them up here too.'

'And the happier Norah is with Monty and Pop's progress, the less she will mind about Zinee not running.'

'I wonder if Gill has remembered to call Norah yet?'

Jules and Kelly were still chatting away about the race, and Kelly's plan to give all the runners a short pipe opener the next day while Jules was at work, when they arrived back at the barn.

In the fading daylight it was hard to see George's face, but his anxious pacing said it all.

'Where is Gill?' He demanded as they rode towards him, uncharacteristically abrupt.

'Down at the house isn't she?' Kelly was confused.

'No! I thought she was up here with you? I came back to check on her and I can't find her.'

Jules quickly dismounted. Gill was pretty much either at the house, at the horse barn, at all times. The horsebox was in the drive. The Landover where it always was behind the barn.

'Have you checked the paddocks? Amber and Teddy's field?' Kelly suggested helpfully.

'I have checked everywhere.' George's voice did not lift. A cold dread spread over him the moment he realised Gill was not in bed, where he had expected to find her.

'Call Mike? Charlie? Charlie could have come and taken her out somewhere?' Jules suggested.

George nodded but stood still, his eyes raking over the dimpsy paddocks, for any sign of her he might have missed.

'Kelly, if you don't mind untacking Pop for me, and finishing up here, I will go and help George look?'

'Of course – text me when you find her?' Kelly took Pop's reins.

Jules nodded and started to walk back to the house, pausing to stare at George, who then followed her.

Ten minutes later George and Jules stood in the Newmans kitchen, still none the wiser.

Mike had confirmed he had been expecting Gill at the hospital. Charlie had confirmed she had not seen her mother, or heard from her, all day. Jules told her about her Grandmother, thinking it was the right thing to do. Charlie said she would join Mike, in case Gill had simply caught the bus into town, and forgotten to tell anyone.

'Go and have a drive round the village, see if anyone has seen her.' Jules suggested to George who was pacing again. 'I'll wait here in case she comes back or Charlie finds her at the hospital.'

George nodded and fished his car keys out of the bowl on the kitchen counter. He squeezed them in his hand while Jules called Rosie's number.

'This is my fault,' He mouthed, 'shouldn't have left her.'

Jules curled her lips inwards in sympathy.

'We don't even know anything is wrong yet, go on and have a hunt round, keep your mobile on.'

George turned to head for the front door. He noticed Gill's door keys on the shelf in the hallway. He tried not to panic.

Jules listened to Rosie's voicemail greeting for the second time and thought how unlike her friend it was not to answer.

'Where are you?' Jules muttered to Ziggy, who was laid on the cool stone of the kitchen floor, licking his paws, apparently unconcerned about the absence of Gill and the ignorance of Rosie.

George jogged along the lane towards the village, unaware he was taking the same steps as Gill had done hours before. He checked at the restaurant in case Gill had arrived or called since he left. He ran past Daisy's house and felt a shudder of guilt. He asked in the pub. He doubled back around the housing estate and noticed with passing indifference that the shop was in darkness, a "Sorry – closed early due to emergency" sign on the door. He slowed to a walk. He checked his phone again. He had no idea where to look next.

Chapter Eleven

Rosie usually used the stables to avoid being in the house. When she needed space from Eve, from Crystal's doting, from Jimmy's ever patient and concerned eye.

This evening though, she had quickly done the jobs, the evening feeds, the end of day pooh pick, and retreated away from her horse.

She had taken him out for a walk as per Kev's suggestion earlier that afternoon. Such was his soundness, she had been tempted to get astride him, but resisted, wanting to get his feet as tough as possible before she asked him to bear her weight as well as his own.

Her mood had been high, the glowing presence of the brand new horsebox on the driveway inspiring her to get riding again. She had chatted to Red as she led him through the lanes, about a trip to the beach to run over the sand, about all the events they might now train for.

She smiled wryly as she reflected on the afternoon's joyful daydreams.

It had changed with the force of a smack in the mouth.

Her mobile had been ringing when she got back to the spare room, where she had accidentally left it on the bed instead of carrying it with her. She beamed when she saw it was Matt, returning her numerous calls.

From the moment she answered the phone, her joy was disbanded. Her frivolous planning, her pride in having been concerned about Eve when she had heard the initial thunderous noise of the box arriving, proving her maternal instinct was there

– it all felt so foolish in the short seconds it took her brain to process the dull irritation in her husband's clipped voice.

He explained that he had ordered and paid for the horsebox back in January, so that it could be built and delivered in time for her birthday, and had subsequently forgotten about it.

Back in January. Back before she had given birth, when she was still heartbroken over losing Harry, her loving husband had arranged an expensive surprise for his lovely wife.

She wasn't his lovely wife any more. She represented a thorn in his side. His idea of family and the life he had worked towards had been tainted by her failure to play her part properly.

When she had allowed herself to be persuaded to confide him about her problems, she had no idea of the rift it would create between them. She wished, as she had done so many times since, that she had persuaded Jimmy it was best kept between them.

After she had ended the call, prompted by his silence having finished his explanation of what now felt like a giant white elephant instead of her dream present, she had made for the field to take comfort in Red.

But the horse, like Matt, had refused to connect with her.

Such was the change in her demeanour from the carefree happy Rosie of the afternoon, the horse had simply walked away from her, ears back, not wishing to be infected by her gloom. Self-pity, she concluded, was not a fool Red would suffer gladly.

Not wanting to go back to the house, Rosie let herself in to the covered car port beside the cottage. She flipped the light switch and waited for the energy saving bulb to grow in luminosity. The horsebox, she and Jimmy had discovered when trying to park it, was too tall to fit under the steel roof and would have to live outside. Rosie was grateful now, because it meant she didn't have to look at it.

Her fingers slid along the canvas cover shrouding Matt's former pride and joy. The Vauxhall which he had painstakingly restored in order to attend local drag and drift races, had remained inside the car port, covered over and forgotten, since Eve was born. Although she used to worry for his safety when he was racing, she missed the Matt who was passionate about his engine, the one who would stay up until the small hours working on the car. Now every minute of his time at home belonged to Eve.

Rosie's empathy for the car ran deep.

She turned away, but found herself facing an equally depressing forgotten project.

The canvas on which she had half painted a vase of hedge row daffodils sat propped against the work bench. Her counsellor's suggestion that she try to be creative in order to use her brain for something uncomplicated and positive had prompted her to begin the acrylic study, but she had forgotten about it the very next day. Perhaps more depressing than the unfinished canvass was the muse itself. The once brilliant yellow daffodils had browned and atrophied, a decaying sludge grew mould around their stems where life prolonging water should have been.

Rosie pleaded with her brain not to make the connection.

But it was too late, the dead flowers became a physical representation of her dying marriage.

She would have wept, had the numbness not set in. In one day she had experienced ecstatic joy, followed by deep despair. It was too much. Her emotions shut down, unwilling to receive any more stimulation. She headed for the spare room and the lonely oblivion of sleep.

As Rosie pulled the covers back to slump into her cocoon she knocked her phone onto the floor. The screen lit up as she retrieved the apparently unharmed appliance. The notification warning flashed - 7 missed calls.

They were all from Jules.

'How long before we call the police?' George demanded as he strode back into the cottage.

'Hang on...' Jules was on the phone to Charlie.

George mouthed sorry and let himself out of the kitchen door, to stand in the darkness and listen to the silence for footsteps coming across the paddocks.

'Right. Charlie has found Mike, Gill isn't there. It doesn't look like Gill's mum has long left, Charlie wanted to stay there. Think Mike is finding it pretty hard and Ginny had to go to work, so she hasn't told him Gill is missing.'

George shook his head. Everything always seemed to happen at once.

'She has only been gone a few hours George, and let's face it, if she wasn't ill we wouldn't be this worried.'

George nodded. Jules seemed to want to play it down and be the voice of reason so he wasn't about to argue with her. Something inside him felt cold, it wasn't just fear, it was more somehow.

'Cup of tea?' Jules rubbed George's back through his thin shirt and he shuddered. He followed Jules back inside.

The phone began to chime as they waited for the kettle to boil, making them both jump. Jules snatched it up and answered within the first ring.

'Hello?' Jules waited and her expectant face crumpled into a frown as she listened. 'Yes, please could you hold on for just a moment?' Jules put her hand over the mouth piece and turned to George. 'It's Norah, she wants to speak to Gill to make sure everything is ok for Saturday.'

'Right.'

'Gill obviously hadn't got around to calling her, I think I had better tell her what has happened and about Zinee?'

George shrugged, not really caring.

'So sorry to keep you Ms Ranger, I am afraid we have had a bit of a mishap here this week...' Jules' voice trailed off as she head along the corridor to the office to finish the call.

George leant on the kitchen counter, using his elbows to create a prop for his forehead.

Gill was never gone for long, she never went far. The feed merchant delivered now, as did most of the other equine suppliers, since Jules had enforced a strict purchasing policy. She attended all the race meets where the yard had runners, but these were events planned months in advance.

Mostly, she was either with a horse, or in the house. To some it would seem a narrow existence. To Gill it was perfect, in fact, the things which took her away from the paddocks and peace of home were an annoyance. George realised, as he lifted his head and stood up straight again, that he was very similar. He was either at the restaurant or at home with Gill. Their businesses consumed their lives, but they had something many envied and few achieved – a love for their endeavours which was so powerful it occasionally made it seem wrong that they could earn money from them.

George noticed a pile of post addressed to him stacked beside the fridge. He wandered over to it and decided he might as well open it in the absence of anything better to do.

The first envelope contained a not to be missed opportunity to save on buildings insurance. He could almost have laughed, too late mate he thought. The second he recognised as being from the solicitor of the person who was attempting to take his business from him. The envelope was like a car crash. He didn't want to look, but he couldn't not. Plus he reasoned, he was already about as anxious as a person could be.

He tore the envelope and scanned the page. The letter was short.

The heading read "Final Offer" and the wording suggested that as settlement had not been reached due to the Bloomswell's reluctance to adopt a reasonable approach, they now had 14 days in which to settle in the amount of £10,000 including costs or civil court proceedings would be instigated.

George was on one hand relieved, he had built the figure up in his head to be more. On the other hand, he was angry. The allegation that was made about their restaurant had no way of being evidenced. If only they had made more effort to protect themselves.

They had had a bad year so far, one way or another. Flooding during the storms February had brought, instead of the usual wintry frosts that would have brought customers in for a hearty meal, had made the lane adjacent to the restaurant impassable and the road had been closed for some weeks. The incessant gales had found their way in through sections of roof that had previously been waterproof. Then they had realised their buildings insurance had lapsed, and had to pay for all of the repairs out of the business account. It had all only lasted a total of a month or so, but it had put the business into the red. George had been resilient, stopped taking his own salary and worked extra shifts to save on staff costs. Rob on the other hand, used to being able to afford the good life and bound to his own sense of pride, had struggled to maintain enthusiasm or direction. He loved the front of house work, talking to customers, creating a sumptuous dinning atmosphere. He loved the rave reviews their food would get on a regular basis, the returning customers who drove for miles just to have another helping of the local beef wellington they were becoming famous for. During the enforced closure he was despondent. The upstairs rooms he lived in had been made waterproof again, but the water damage had remained un-repaired and he was confined to the one remaining good room.

Then, once they re-opened, under their new name and with renewed enthusiasm, the income slowly started filling the void and both men found their smiles again. It seemed that they would survive, and perhaps even flourish.

Then had come the complaint. The woman who had barely touched her food, who had refused to pay her bill, and had then, a week later, had instructed a solicitor.

George felt a sinking sense of inevitability. For Rob's sake, for the sake of the business and his sanity, they needed this woman to go away, as much as it would pain him to hand over the cash. A court case could mean publicity. The woman was already threatening to approach the local presses. They were trapped by the "no smoke without fire" principle. He couldn't afford for anyone to doubt their quality and safety of the restaurant's food. Such was the price the small business paid for the sue first, ask questions later, culture. A culture that had changed the world from a place where two men with a love of food could share it with others to make a living, into one where you had to cover your back first, and do your job second.

George stuffed the letter back into the envelope and managed to conceal it in his trouser pocket before Jules came back into the kitchen.

Jules opened her mouth to start telling him about the conversation with Norah when the front doorbell rang.

They almost fell over each other to get to the door, knowing Gill had no keys.

It was Kelly.

'No news.' Jules immediately dashed Kelly's hopes.

'Horses are done for the night. I have locked the barn but should I leave the front gates?'

Jules and George remained silent. Kelly felt silly for asking the question.

'Gill's mum is in hospital, Charlie and Mike are with her.'

'Oh no.' Kelly bit her lip and wasn't sure what to say, the darkness from George made the brightly lit hallway seem gloomy.

'What's that?' Kelly stepped forward to peer at the letter box where the front door had been opened inwards. She pinched at the corner of a scrap of paper which was barely visible. She pulled the paper from the box and almost ripped it where it had become wedged between the draft excluder and the front flap.

She read the handwritten scrawl and her face whitened. She handed the note to Jules and George leaned forward to read it.

'I'll drive.' George ran to the kitchen to fetch his car keys while Jules continued to stare at the piece of paper. If only she had seen it when she had come home earlier.

Gill has had a funny turn, taken her to hospital
Maisey (from the shop)

Rosie awoke to the call of an owl. The bird sounded nearby, perhaps on the oak tree which towered over the gateway to the field. She felt drained, sad and un-rested, but knew she wouldn't be able to get back to sleep while the eerie calling persisted. She flicked on the bedside light and reached for the phone. There were 4 texts from Jules. She sighed and decided she had better read them. She hadn't returned her friend's calls earlier, desperate for sleep and closed off to anything but the spare room.

Rosie, we can't find Gill, she hasn't left a note and her phone is off, worried as her head is still bad, have you heard from her?

Rosie did you get my last message? I keep trying to ring you?

I am starting to worry about you now as well as Gill can you get in touch? I have lost your home number.

We have found her, she is in hospital. Her head injury is being investigated further. Rosehip ward, Exeter main. I hope you are ok.

"Oh fuck." Rosie cursed and heaved herself out of bed. She was still fully clothed. She headed for the kitchen and fired up the computer on her way. It was 2am. Too late to call Jules back. Too late even to text her for fear of waking her.

Rosie so often gave more of her time and attention to others than she afforded herself. But on this occasion she had failed. Reading between the short lines of her texts, she knew Jules had been frustrated with her. And she didn't even have a valid excuse. I am so sorry, I was busy being a really miserable cow. Didn't quite cut it.

Why was Gill back in hospital? Was she ok?

Too late to call the hospital or George either. She had excluded herself from a situation where she could have been useful, by ignoring her phone. Being self-obsessed led to guilt, which inevitably led to more self-obsession and more guilt.

"Why can't things go back to normal?" Rosie spoke softly to no one as she sat in front of the computer, hoping her mum was still up and online.

She wasn't. But Selina had left messages. It was almost as though every time something had popped into her mother's head, she had written a little more. She had sent her links to useful articles she had found on post-natal depression, and words of encouragement, repeating her suggestion that Rosie should try and go away for a break from everything. She had also messaged a rather lengthy rant about how difficult the author of the manuscript she was working on had been about the changes she had made. She messaged about how she had seen a girl out riding her pony from the train after a meeting with her new boss, and how it reminded her of Rosie and Harry and mentioned how sorry she was, again, for Rosie's loss. Her last message was rather abrupt, as though she felt silly for the preceding six which had not had replies.

Rosie shook her head.

She had messages from her mother. Just the concept was weird. Theirs had always been such a cold relationship, their interactions sharp, their irritation levels high. Rosie's mother was one of the only people she had ever properly argued with. The woman made her backbone go rigid. Until now.

Rosie consoled herself that she would call Jules first thing in the morning and set about typing a deserving reply to Selina, including the promise that she would try to log on more.

When Rosie had finished she turned off the computer, and headed to Eve's room.

She sat on the chair beside the cot and looked in at the sleeping baby.

"Why do you bring out the worst in me Eve? I don't seem to be able to do anything right since you came along." She spoke softly, her tone searching. "I wish I was better for you."

Eve continued to sleep. She smelled of fresh laundry and baby wipes. Crystal saw to her every need, she was contented, healthy and wanted for nothing.

Maybe, Rosie decided, the break away from home wasn't such a bad idea. Maybe if she could miss Eve, wonder about her instead of knowing, she could get enough perspective to try and put herself back together.

Her marriage on the other hand, she sighed as she gazed at her daughter, might not be fixable at all.

Rosie awoke on the morning of her birthday, not to the usual sound of Matt bringing her breakfast in bed, but to the sound of Eve crying.

Rosie swore as she donned her jeans and stomped from the bedroom. The noise was not coming from the nursery. As Rosie opened the door to the lounge she was met with a wall of sound. Eve expelled wails with the full force of her tiny lungs, whilst Crystal tried to rock and sooth her. The baby was red faced, balled fists gesticulating wildly in frustration.

'Not sure what's wrong.' Jimmy shouted over the din from where he stood sheepishly, trying to back away, in the doorway of the kitchen.

Eve was five months old. Rosie cast her mind back to the baby books she had painstakingly read in early pregnancy. She headed to the nursery and burrowed in the back of the ornate and dwarf sized closet. She found a tube of teething gel and checked the expiry date before going to the bathroom to wash her hands and returning to the living room.

As Crystal held her, Rosie peered into Eve's mouth. She gently applied the soothing gel to the reddest looking areas of the baby's gums. Eve dribbled and soaked Crystal's blouse.

Rosie hesitated when Crystal tried to give Eve to her, but acknowledged Crystal wanted to change her top and took Eve.

With the gel already anaesthetising her throbbing gums,

and the warm if reluctant arms of her mother, Eve's crying subsided. The baby looked up at her with wide blue eyes.

'I am completely impressed!' Jimmy laughed as he re-entered the room. 'Happy Birthday Darling.' He kissed Rosie's forehead.

'How did you know?!' A freshly clothed Crystal leaned in to kiss her step daughter's cheek.

'Remembered something I read about them teething.' Rosie shrugged off her seemingly effortless triumph.

'Well..' Crystal patted Rosie on the back and laughed, 'not sure what you need us for!'

Rosie's face fell and she tried to give Eve to Jimmy.

'No no, we can't cope with that much noise again just yet.' Jimmy backed away from her shaking his head.

'Bring her into the living room, we want to talk to you.'

Rosie could have dropped Eve for the sudden lead weight in her arms. Somehow she made it to the sofa. The adrenaline started to pump as she waited for them to fetch refreshments. Worry spread through her body like a virus, she shivered. At the mere mention of needing to have a chat, her brain automatically went to all the negative places. Even before the thoughts of them declaring some plan which would take them away from her had played out in her imagination, the physical response to a perceived danger had started.

She held Eve closer to her for warmth and tried not to squeeze the baby too hard. Eve gazed up at her, as though fascinated by her face, oblivious to the turmoil running through her.

'Nice pot of real coffee and some homemade waffles with blueberries – thought I would go a bit American for your birthday!' Crystal beamed as she brought in the tray and Jimmy followed with maple syrup.

Rosie's colourless face and open mouth almost made Crystal jump.

'Because of Red – he is an American horse isn't he?' Crystal mistook Rosie's expression for confusion.

'I know. I'm sorry. Thank you so much. Can we get the talk done?'

Jimmy sat down opposite his daughter and started to pour himself a coffee.

'This is good news Rosie.' He turned and squeezed Crystal's hand and she smiled warmly at him, 'at least, we hope it is!'

Crystal couldn't contain herself any longer and blurted out their plan, which, to Rosie's immense relief, involved selling their house in London and buying a property near Monkeswell.

As Rosie listened to them talk about the thatched cottage just over a mile away that they were going to view on Monday, how much they had grown to love the area, and how they wanted to be part of Eve's childhood, she couldn't quite quell her pounding heart. Despite their words the worry inside her persisted.

What is wrong with me, her mind screamed while her face was smiling and nodding.

Then she remembered Jules' texts.

Jules hadn't answered her phone, but had text Rosie 10 minutes later to say she was in Court and that Gill was still in hospital. Rosie had tried to call George but his mobile went straight to answerphone. A breathless Kelly had answered her phone but announced she was riding Milly and leading Pop and couldn't hold her phone and had to go.

Jimmy had offered to drive Rosie to Exeter, anxious to spend the day with her, given that Matt wouldn't be home until

223

the evening as usual. Matt had always taken Rosie's birthday off work to spend with her, but not this year.

Rosie insisted she was ok, and that looking after Eve was already favour enough.

Jimmy had watched her open the gifts he and Crystal had bought for her. Some stretchy riding jeans and a new numnah as requested, the things she would have asked for as a teenager. She was graciously grateful, but he had not been able to ignore the deflation in her eyes. No call from Matt, no card on the doormat. She had the usual ones from Auntie Sally and Val, and Nicola from across the valley, and an unusual one from Selina, which Rosie had opened with surprise. Crystal had made her a "For my Mummy" card from Eve bought some small but pretty silver earrings and written "love from Eve" on the tag. Rosie had hugged Crystal and worn the earrings after she had finished seeing to the horses, which had made Crystal happy.

Jimmy walked out to the car with Rosie.

'Are you going to meet Val?'

'No, she is off camping with her boys this week – Easter Holidays.'

'Ah. Seeing anyone else?'

'I doubt it. Just want to make sure Gill is ok, then I will come home.'

Jimmy nodded and pulled Rosie in for a hug.

As he watched her walk away he decided to call Matt and book a table for them tonight at the local restaurant. Perhaps an evening out together would put the twinkle back in his daughter's eye, even though he suspected it wasn't something Matt would have planned himself.

'My Mum is here too.' Gill said suddenly.

Rosie looked back at her friend, drawing her gaze from

the concrete view out of the hospital ward window.

'Is she ok?'

'Had a little stroke, panicked everyone for a bit. She can probably go back to the home today.'

'That's a relief. When can you go home?'

Gill bit her lip and stared down at her hands were they rested on the white bed sheet.

'Tomorrow.'

Rosie was about to say how good that was when she noticed tears dripping onto the bed sheet from Gill's down turned face.

'Darling what is it?' Rosie shook her head, the anxiety rising in her, but she felt determined to hold it together for Gill, whatever the answer. She braced herself to hear of complications to Gill's head injury.

'I don't want to go home.' Gill sobbed, her voice small, childlike, emotions weakening her already traumatised body. 'They said I probably tried to do too much, I shouldn't have been up and out of the house yesterday.'

'And that was how you ended up here?'

'Mike called about Mum. I was trying to find George. I found him. But then I came over all weird and my eyes wouldn't focus and the shop keeper from the village brought me here.'

Rosie shook her head, trying to work out if Gill's fuzzy head was the cause of her not making sense.

'But if you found George, why did the shop keeper bring you here?'

Gill sighed and looked up, the rivers of tears made glistening tracks down her face.

'I don't want to say it.'

'Say what?' Rosie's anxiety welled up again, the lump in her throat tried to strangle her as she tried not to demand the full story from a wobbly Gill. She didn't need to demand it. Despite Rosie's lack of confidence in herself, Gill still felt safer with Rosie than anyone else. Gill told her how she had seen George going into his ex-girlfriend's new house and that it all seemed to be happening again.

'I refuse to believe that Gill.' Rosie took her friend's hand and rubbed it. 'George is not Alex, far from him. There has to be another explanation.'

Gill shook her head and reached for a tissue.

'He has been acting strangely for months. Telling me he has been having trouble at the restaurant but not what, long hours, looking stressed. I had this niggling feeling but I told myself I was paranoid because of Alex and I ignored it. But here I am again, just like the day you found me sobbing in the loo.'

Rosie ignored polite hospital visiting decorum and sat beside Gill on the bed, with her feet on the chair she had been sat on. She encased her friend in her arms and let the full force of her sobs expel before she spoke again.

'You need to talk to him. There will be an explanation.' Rosie nodded firmly as Gill started to shake her head. 'I have seen the way that man looks at you, I can't believe he has room in his schedule or his heart for anyone else.'

'Either way he lied to me. When he left he said he was going to the restaurant.'

'What did you say to him when he got here last night?'

'Just said I was drowsy and had a headache, which was true enough.' Gill blew her nose again and caught sight of Charlie reporting to the ward sister's desk through the glass wall opposite her bed. 'I rang him this morning and said not to come today. Said I would ring him tomorrow when they discharge me. I don't want to do it here. Charlie is coming. Please don't mention this.'

'Do what??' Rosie's panicked voice made Gill hiss.

'End it. Do not mention this to Jules either, she has the race tomorrow to worry about. Smile now she is here.'

Gill sat herself up straight and painted on a smile to greet her daughter. Rosie slid from the bed and back onto her chair.

'There's the patient!' Charlie reached across the bed to kiss her mother before greeting Rosie. 'Just seen Mike off with Grandma, he is driving her back to Glencoe now.'

As Gill talked to Charlie about being discharged and asked how Darran was, Rosie marvelled at her friend's ability to be strong for her child.

Rosie walked out of the hospital 20 minutes later. Charlie, who was still between jobs and planning again with renewed vigour to start her law degree in the autumn, had nowhere else to be and had settled in to the easy chair next to her mother's bed. Realising she was not going to get another chance to speak to Gill alone about George, Rosie had left. She hadn't expected Gill to remember it was her birthday given everything that had gone on, but still felt strangely empty as she walked across the green in front of the large hospital building towards her car.

Her phone had been on silent during the visit and she reached into her handbag to activate it. She noticed a text from Jules had come in just a few moments before.

Court is finished at last - I can take lunch now if you fancy a birthday bite?!

Bless you Jules, Rosie thought and quickened her step. She tapped out a reply and suggested they meet at the pub close to Jules' office. Rosie felt warmed that Jules was clearly no longer upset about Rosie's lack of reply the night before. It was going to be hard not to mention the conversation she had just had with Gill.

'I think your Mum is right,' Jules nodded encouragingly as Rosie picked at her baked potato, 'you do need to get away. You need to clear your head and have some space.'

'I was going to try and talk to Matt. That's why I couldn't come to the races tomorrow. I really need to sit down properly with him before I lose him.'

Jules snorted through her diet lemonade and shook her head vigorously.

'You lose Matt? That's never going to happen.'

Rosie smiled politely at Jules' scorn. It was the same scorn that she herself had used when Gill had told her George was having an affair. If a couple who appeared so together and committed, like her and Matt, could be falling apart, maybe Gill was right about George. Only the two people who made the relationship could truly know what was going on inside it.

Rosie had confided in Jules about her home situation, her feelings about Eve and her distance from Matt almost as soon as they had sat down together. Although she hated to appear so weak, she gave a toned down, potted version of the last 5 months. Jules seemed genuinely relieved to have been allowed into Rosie's world again, having thought that the distance between them was because their friendship was decaying. Rosie felt a pang of guilt, the real reason she had started talking about herself was to avoid talking about Gill.

'It just goes to show. When you think something is aimed at you, it's usually nothing to do with you. If people seem different, the difference is usually with everyone else as well.'

Rosie smiled at Jules and could have cried.

If anyone could understand how the rest of the world felt when your self-esteem ran low, it was Jules. She had struggled through her break up from Tristan and it had taken her almost all of the last year to get over him.

'It was never you, you know I love you to bits. I have just been lost in this. Trying so hard to make things seem normal, to be normal, I haven't had room for anyone else.'

Jules sighed. 'I should have been there for you more though. I should have known how much losing Harry would affect you and seen through the act.'

'I wouldn't have let you in. I possibly still won't. But I am glad I told you. My anxiety gets so bad sometimes it's hard just to make a cup of tea or go to the toilet.'

Jules bit her lip. For a split second Rosie saw in her eyes what she dreaded, fear and pity.

'I am always here for you,' Jules' face changed again to serious, stronger, as though she had seen the effect her reaction was going to have. 'No matter what. You have always been there for me.'

'I am sorry I won't be there tomorrow.'

'Oh don't worry, you have more important stuff to do. Besides – how hard can taking three Arabians to a racecourse be?!'

Jules said the words confidently but then pretended to hide behind her menu and made a squealing noise.

Rosie started to laugh and Jules giggled nervously.

'I hope I don't let Gill down.'

'How could you, you are amazing! You are organised and intuitive and I don't think Gill could have chosen a better business partner.' Rosie said without thinking, warm and faithful. She listened to her words play back in her mind and thought how much like her they sounded, a far cry from the unfamiliar fear filled voices which had occupied her head of late.

Chapter Twelve

Jules couldn't believe how quickly the week had passed. But, based on how exhausted she was, it would have to be true.

When they had finally finished for the evening, she hadn't made it to the plastic chairs in the middle of the barn. Instead she had collapsed on the floor, resting her back against the wall of Monty's stable. Kelly, who had ridden or led all of the horses for a short workout that morning, and then spent the afternoon cleaning their racing bridles and headcollars and pressure washing the horsebox, had collapsed beside Jules.

As they sat in companionable silence they heard the unmistakable sound of Monty dumping a giant pooh onto his straw bed. Kelly went to get up but Jules stopped her.

'Leave it.'

'But if he lays in it I will have to strap him again in the morning...' Kelly groaned, but didn't get up.

'Let's just sit here a minute.' Jules closed her eyes and wished she felt more prepared. She had copies of the entry forms, a copy of Gill's training documentation and all of the horse's passports in a folder which she had stowed in the glove box. All the bridles, brushes, skips, buckets, sponges and saddle cloths were loaded. The horses were ready, Kelly had made sure of that – but surely she must be missing something. Even though Gill had sounded quite lucid on the phone that morning, Jules had picked up on the flatness in her voice and was determined not to bother her again.

The racehorses were unusually quiet.

Monty would normally have been whickering for extra

dinner, Pop would have been yanking on his small holed slow feeder haynet and getting frustrated. She looked at her watch. It was 11pm – maybe they just wanted the humans to go away and switch the lights off.

'Better get home and get some shut eye?' Jules patted her knees in an effort to spur her legs back into life.

'Can I sleep on the sofa?' Kelly asked, frowning heavily, her sudden dejection obvious.

'Of course.' Jules answered affirmative, but her tone was questioning.

'Can't cope with my Mum at the moment.'

'Oh dear,' Jules smiled wryly thinking of all the teenage quarrels she'd had, and still occasionally had now, with her overbearing but infuriatingly loveable mother, 'you two not getting on?'

'She is still banging on about Australia.'

'I thought that was all over?'

Kelly shook her head and pushed closed fists into her eye sockets, trying to fend off tears.

'I haven't mentioned it to Gill because of her being poorly. Mum goes on about it every night. She keeps printing things off the internet about the riding over there and how there is a big equestrian centre I could teach at near my auntie's place. I can't get away from her, she is like a dog with a bone.'

Jules sat up straight. She didn't want to encourage Kelly to go against her mother.

'I guess if she really wants to go...?'

'Yeah but I don't. Ever. I like the UK, I like working here, I am building up my lesson customers and I do not want to trek half way across the world so that Mum can live with her sister – who she fights with all the time by the way.'

Jules could scarcely hide her relief at Kelly's resolve.

Kelly noticed.

'Oh don't you worry. I won't be going anywhere.'

Jules patted Kelly's folded arm and said the thing she didn't want to say for her own sake, but felt she had to for Kellys'.

'But aren't you going to feel guilty if you stop her doing something she clearly has her heart set on?'

'I am not stopping her! It's her who keeps saying she can't go without me, can't leave me here on my own. I'm nearly nineteen, I am hardly going to stop eating or being able to do my own washing!'

Jules sighed, wishing she knew what to say. Rosie would know. What would Rosie say?

'Maybe it's not about your survival?' Jules had a momentary brainwave, 'maybe it is because she is worried about coping without you? It's just been you and her since you were small, right?'

'Yeah.' Kelly pondered, she had just been angry that mother was treating her like a child.

'It's quite a big thing to do on your own – emigrate – maybe she is scared?'

'Could be.' Kelly nodded, thoughtful, and Jules decided to collect Monty's dump before he could stand in it.

Together they checked each of the horse's water buckets and latched the bolts on their stable doors before plunging the barn into darkness and heading for the house. As they walked down the drive Kelly shone her torch into Amber and Teddy's field to check on the mare and foal. They were grazing, side by side, content.

'I might go home after all.' Kelly announced when they reached the bottom of the driveway and Jules turned towards the house.

'Do you want a lift – it's dark?'

'Nah, it's only round the corner and I have my torch.'

'Text me when you get there?' Jules didn't really want to leave her to walk home in the dark, but didn't want to treat her like a child and so let her stroll off down the lane.

Jules stood in Newmans kitchen, knowing she had to be up at 4am should have stopped her reaching for the chocolate cake, but she reasoned she would have it with a mug of warm milk in bed. As she climbed the stairs clutching her bowl she heard the front door opening.

'Night George!' she called and quickened her pace, not wanting to be caught with a massive slice of cake.

She got to her room and set her snack down on the bedside table, deciding to set out her clothes for the morning before she settled in. She had already packed some smarter clothes for the parade ring, but needed something comfortable and warm for the morning's mucking out, grooming and loading.

Just as she was about to don her pyjamas there was a knock at her bedroom door.

She opened it to a worried looking George.

'Hi.' She said when he didn't speak.

'All set for the morning?'

'Yep – ready as we will ever be!' Jules thought George looked grey. 'Are you ok George?'

'Just worried about Gill. She said she was fine but she didn't want to see me today.'

'Maybe she just needs her rest – after all they did say she hadn't rested enough and that was why she ended up in there?' Jules nodded encouragingly and George perked up a little.

'I can do the mucking out after you have gone tomorrow if you like, save you having to do the stables before you leave?'

'If you have time George, that would be fab.'

'Gill doesn't think she will be discharged until lunchtime so I have all morning, might as well be useful.'

'Yeah and we both know Gill will only do it when she gets home otherwise!' Jules giggled, and George raised a smile.

They said goodnight.

As Jules settled herself in her bed and positioned her book on her bent knees, so that she could read while she ate, she couldn't help wondering about Gill's instruction. Although she had apparently convinced George it was nothing to worry about, it was pretty strange that her friend did not want to see the man she so adored, especially whilst lying alone in a hospital bed.

Jules wasn't the only one who was worried about Gill.

Rosie excused herself and left the table to check her phone, which she had felt vibrate in her pocket during her appetiser. She let herself into the plush ladies facilities at the Par Gardens restaurant and read the text message.

Worried about Mum – did she seem odd to you today?

Rosie stared at Charlie's message and almost wished Gill had not confided in her about George. She didn't need more secrets, she had enough of her own.

Despite her frustration, Rosie couldn't betray her friend. She tapped out a breezy reply, putting Gill's mood down to not being within 20 feet of a horse.

Charlie replied immediately with a LOL.

Rosie looked at herself in the mirror. None of her hippy clothes suited her without long hair. The flowing dress with flared sleeves and beads which had previously been her favourite was incomplete.

She ran cold water over her hands, trying to freshen

herself.

Matt had embraced her briefly in a functional hug when he had arrived home, then presented her with a card. Loving printed verse written by some card company wordsmith filled the otherwise blank space inside, it was simply signed Matt with a scrawled single kiss. He reminded her she had the horsebox as an explanation for the lack of wrapped gift, as if that was needed, which it wasn't, and then asked Jimmy what time the table was booked before heading to Eve's room.

Rosie had decided then that a romantic dinner for two was going to be unbearable. She had tried to persuade Jimmy to let Matt off the hook, saying she would prefer to have a nice dinner at home with her lovely parents.

Jimmy had insisted she must go out for her birthday and arranged for Mrs Mathers to sit with Eve so that they could all go together.

Crystal had driven so Matt and Rosie could have a drink. In the car Jimmy and Crystal had chatted about what they fancied, proclaiming their hunger and trying to remember when they had last been to a really nice restaurant. Matt and Rosie had remained silent, sat as far away from each other as possible in the back seat. Rosie longed to reach for her husband, to have him pull her in for a snuggle and maybe a sly grope.

But, as much as she missed him, his coldness crushed her desire to make an effort.

It was unfortunate that what she mistook as disappointment and anger, was in fact guilt.

In his mind he had caused this, whatever he did he would only make things worse, surely. However much he had missed her while he was away, when he looked into her eyes he felt only distance. Her actions were so unfamiliar, uncharacteristically measured. He wasn't sure who she was any more.

When they had arrived at the restaurant Rosie had tried to rebel against the awkwardness by drinking too much too quickly. Not used to wine, she had always been a lager girl previously, and a coffee only drinker of late, she had made her own head spin and had struggled with her knife and fork, flicking the cranberries which adorned her baked Camembert across the white table cloth. Matt's unveiled disapproval had been sobering, Charlie's text and having to lie more so.

She returned to the table inwardly glum.

'Ah just in time!' Jimmy smiled, welcoming his daughter as the entrées were being served.

Rosie noticed Matt eyeing up her trio of beef as he started eating his own pork dish.

'Do you want some?' She proffered her fork towards him, smiling.

He shook his head, scowled, and carried on eating. He always wanted whatever she had ordered when it arrived. Sometimes they had even swapped plates half way through a meal. That wasn't going to happen tonight.

The alcohol in Rosie's belly needed to be absorbed and she ate her meal greedily, trying to ignore her husband's black mood and get through the evening.

'Lovely to see you tucking in Rosie! It's very good isn't it?' Crystal chirruped as she savoured her beef.

'She doesn't eat nearly enough you know Matt.' Jimmy addressed his son in law, shaking his head and rolling his eyes, trying to bring him in to the conversation.

Seeing that Matt was clearly not going to reply, and apparently didn't care whether she ate or not, Rosie finished her mouthful and piped up.

'Oh Dad that's an overreaction. Anyway, I needed to shed the baby weight.'

'Just a shame you can't shed the baby.' Matt muttered.

'What was that Matthew?' Jimmy's smile had faded and he set down his cutlery. He was sick of Matt's attitude. Whatever the problems they were having, it was Rosie's birthday and Matt's obvious desire to ruin the evening was as puzzling as it was disappointing.

Matt ignored Jimmy and continued to eat. Jimmy glared at him for a few seconds longer.

Rosie lifted her steak knife high and swiped it sharply through the air.

'What are you doing?' Jimmy laughed.

'Cutting the tension with a knife.'

Matt couldn't help but smile and as soon as he did, the atmosphere improved.

'So,' he said, finally letting go of his resolve that having an evening out when his life was falling apart was ridiculous, 'tell me about the horsebox.'

The hospital bed would not yield to Gill's body. She turned over onto her side. According to the clock she could see clearly, illuminated by the incessant strip lighting above the ward sister's desk, it was almost time for Jules and Kelly to be up and heading to the barn to give the racehorses a meagre pre-journey breakfast. She wished she was with them, leading the gallant adventure to the racecourse, where champions might be made and new clients might be found. Instead she was unable to sleep despite having been told she must rest, and unable to smile because there would soon be no George.

She loved him more than she had ever loved Alex. The strength of feeling she had for the younger man was such that she could almost convince herself to forgive him. She had been more reliant on Alex, more subservient in their relationship, but it hadn't stopped her immediately ending it when she had found out about Megan.

Pride would not allow her to stop this time. She had been so reluctant to get into the relationship with George, so fearful that the 12 years between them would eventually be their downfall.

Daisy was his age. She had been proven right she supposed.

For all her rightness, she could not have felt more wretched.

How was she going to live without him? How, when your bond was so tight, could this happen?

She felt sure she would never make love again. What would be the point? The sex she had with George was poles apart from any she had ever had in her life before. Before George, she would readily have admitted she didn't really like sex that much, after him, she finally understood what all the fuss was about. They were so playful, and yet so serious. Each act was an art form, perfection and abandon entwined.

When she used her mouth on him, far from the chore it had been with Alex, she found herself revelling in his pleasure, bringing him to the brink before coyly gazing up at him, her own confidence turning her on still more.

When she waited for him in the bathroom, striding out in nothing but high heels, watched his eyes darken and allowed him to position and dominate her, she felt she was all that existed. The intensity of their union, trust laced with just the right amount of uncertainty – surely he couldn't have been with anyone else?

Surely?

Gill longed to howl. She wanted to scream and cry and rock herself back and forth until the pain lessened.

But the lady in the bed beside her was fast asleep, and the nurses that padded softly in and out to care for the others in the ward did not need extra work.

So she lay still. She tried not to think about Daisy's house, where she was sure George was. Where he would be using the same hands, the same expressions, the things she thought were hers.

Her head started to pound again.

She slid from the bed and crept to the nurse's station to ask for a sleeping pill.

Rosie's t-shirt flapped in the breeze. The sun was warm enough, but she shivered.

Matt regarded her discomfort without pity. She would have liked his jacket. He suggested she went back to the house and fetched her own.

She scowled and folded her arms around herself.

They had walked to the top corner of the horse's field to talk. The fence which bordered their land was a thick solid post and rail. Perched upon it, they faced the valley which contained their home. After Dartmoor Rosie couldn't face driving anywhere, so she had chosen somewhere she was comfortable. Red had followed them as they climbed the steep hill, but had wandered a little way off to graze when he realised Rosie's pockets were empty.

The night before at dinner, when Matt had finally warmed up and joined in to the conversation, she had dared hoped things were getting back to normal between them. On the way home in the car she had reached for his hand and he had given it. Although they had not made love, he had folded his leg over hers, and she had fallen asleep in a familiar position for once.

She did not want a repeat of the moor so she started to speak without being prompted.

'I am not coping very well. As you know. I keep feeling worked up and frightened when there is nothing to be frightened of. But then, when it comes to dealing with something real, like the fact that our marriage seems to be falling apart, I just feel numb and I don't seem to be able to do anything, like I am watching it happen to someone else.'

'What about Eve?'

'What *about* Eve?'

'Well you are going on about yourself and how you feel and what you are going through, again. What about how Eve feels and how I feel?'

'Eve feels warm, fed and loved. Dad and Crystal being here is helping me to start to bond with her.' Rosie wanted a conversation about her marriage, but her thoughts turned to Eve as she waited for Matt to speak. It was true, she had a slow dawning of realisation that things would not stay the same forever, they would evolve, as would her relationship with Eve. What troubled her more of late, she decided, was not feeling in control of her thoughts or herself.

She realised she hadn't had the awful dream about Eve for almost a month. She smiled.

Then she looked at Matt's scowl and stopped.

'I have been talking to Mum on Skype, just typing to each other. Remarkably she has been really helpful lately.'

'Advice from an estranged, alcoholic mother. Very clever. I suppose you plan to make it up to Eve when she is in her thirties too?'

'Bloody hell Matt could you hate me just a little bit less please??'

'I don't hate you. I hate this.' He paused and then opted for honesty, 'I hate you being like this.'

'Yeah and I just love it, obviously.'

Matt sighed, looking down at his wellingtons.

'Go on.'

'She has been really understanding, quite unlike her really, it's weird but we do seem to be getting a little bit close at last.'

Matt rolled his eyes.

'Anyway, so as not to bore you, I will cut to the chase,' Rosie rolled her eyes back at her husband pointedly, 'she has suggested maybe I need some time away. Away from Eve and this place and everything. To give me a chance to work on my anxiety and miss her.'

'No.'

'Sorry?' Since when was he so pig headed?

'No. You are not running away. You have to deal with this. You are not abandoning our baby.'

'And your word is law now is it?' Rosie was outraged – since when did he instruct her like this?

'Rosie, it is not going to happen. It is bad enough I have to creep around my own house because my in-laws are apparently living with us. Bad enough you let Crystal look after Eve. You are not just going to fuck off completely and find your fucking self. End of.'

Rosie jumped down off the fence, anger surged through her as she walked away from Matt towards her horse. She didn't reach him though. Red swished his tail and trotted away.

She turned back to Matt, resigned. She hadn't thought about how he felt about Jimmy and Crystal being there all the

241

time.

'They are buying a house, possibly the thatch at the top of the lane towards Muddiford.'

'Why? Don't they have lives to get back to in London?'

'No. Crystal took voluntary redundancy, Dad can oversee the business investments from here. They want to be part of Eve's childhood.'

'Have they sold their house yet?'

'I don't think it's gone through why?'

'Well then there is still time.'

'Still time for what?' Rosie spat, what on earth was he going on about, how could he want to stop his daughter from growing up with hands on grandparents?

'I think we should move to Oxford. You, me and Eve. It's close enough to London for them to visit, and my Brother is in Marlow.'

'Are you joking?' Rosie looked desperately at her horse, longing to climb astride him and ride away, if only he was more inclined to come to her.

'No. We decided I would commute because you were happy here and our life in Devon meant a lot to you. If you are going to be this miserable, you might as well be miserable where I can see Eve every day and keep an eye on her.'

'Oh you have got it all planned out then?' Rosie's voice bordered on hysteria. How could he suggest they leave the place where Red lived, where Harry's soul was? They loved this house, it was as much a part of their relationship as Eve was.

'And my horse?'

'Already checked it out. There is a livery yard ten minutes from the flat. It's got an indoor school, lots of nice hacking apparently. They offer a full package so you wouldn't even need to muck out. A bit pricey, but we can afford it.'

Rosie leant over the fence, the ground fluid beneath her, she clutched, the grass a sea, the fence her buoy. She wretched involuntarily.

'So you want me to leave my home, my job, my friends and my life, to live in a flat without my horse?'

'Yes.' Matt got off the fence and stood beside her. 'I have made sacrifices for you. Now it's your turn. You need to do what is right for our child. You said yourself you need to get away.'

'For a few weeks, not a permanent relocation!' Rosie shouted at the floor in front of her. She couldn't leave her home. This was not happening. The need to defend all that she loved overtook the weakness she felt. She pushed herself up and away from the fence. She turned to Matt and looked straight at him.

'What sacrifices have you made then?' She spat.

'Oh let me see. Well, for a start we are stood in it.' Matt opened his arm and gestured across the paddock sharply, 'I don't need a field. I don't need a fixer upper cottage in the ass hole of nowhere. I didn't need to have to take this stressful job just to afford to make it habitable for our baby. And I don't need to drive for 600 miles a week.' His words got louder as he rose to his full height, spitting the words down at her so that she crumpled, landing on her knees.

His speech over, he started to walk away.

'Matt please,' Rosie cried, desperate, basal, 'don't do this. You love this house.'

He carried on walking. As he walked away from her, she felt the last of herself slipping away, the voice she held onto to stop the anxiety taking over completely seemed to be leaving her, along with Matt.

'You love this house!' she screamed after him again, praying it was all some kind of bad dream.

Matt stopped. He turned back to face her and spoke

243

slowly and deliberately.

'No. YOU love this house. I love my daughter. You clearly aren't going to step up, so I am going to have to start making the decisions.'

'Don't you love me?' she wailed, tears running freely, her hands stretched out towards him.

'Don't know.' As he turned away again and carried on walking, he felt tears smart in his eyes. He knew he was being cruel, hated himself for breaking her like this, but his desire to do the right thing was stronger than his empathy. This was the only way he could protect his family.

As she watched him leave the field she wished Red would come. But he had joined Peat beside the pony's paddock and was bickering with his companion over the electric fence.

She sobbed until her face ached. It was too awful, too black to comprehend. All her unnecessary fears and convoluted over thinking. Now she had something real to worry about.

There had to be another way.

Persuade him to quit his job? Persuade him she was ok?

It wouldn't change the facts - he didn't need a cottage in Devon. He only needed Eve.

She thought briefly that she could give him exactly what he wanted. He could take Eve to Oxford and she could stay at Orchard Cottage. See how he coped looking after her completely on his own. See how he liked being abandoned.

But then she would surely lose him. And Eve. And eventually her home.

If only their bond was as strong as it used to be, then he wouldn't even have suggested this hideous life.

It all led back to Eve. Surely her having post-natal depression was not the cause of his sudden and apparently complete lack of love or regard for Rosie?

It all started when she was pregnant. He had started to view the house so critically, constantly trying to fix it up on a budget. Then had come the job offer.

His love and nurture had changed direction. No longer was Rosie the centre of his universe. Even when she had lost Harry and been so desolate, his care of her had been to protect the baby inside her. It all made sense now.

Maybe her feelings about Eve had been made by his? Had she subconsciously realised Eve was now a priority over her? Was jealousy the fuel?

Rosie picked herself up from the grass and resolutely brushed the dirt from her jeans.

If all he wanted was his daughter, what was the point in trying to fight for him.

A strange calm came over her. There was no longer a dichotomy inside her. She didn't have to try any more. She might as well give up and resign herself to life without him. There was no way she was moving to Oxford to be with someone who wasn't sure whether he loved her any more. She already knew she would be miserable there. The cottage was everything she had ever wanted. How could she be happy in a flat with a part-time horse who was cared for by strangers instead of her, knowing but for Matt she could have kept her dream home?

There was no way she could afford to buy him out of the cottage, she would lose it now regardless, but she certainly wasn't going to go where the man who was taking it from her told her to, providing free childcare while he had a career and she abandoned her own. Yeah ok, Local Government was never going to make her rich like his job had the potential to make him, but since when was money the beginning and the end of everything? It had never mattered to either of them before?

Why as people who had worked hard for a frugal existence, must they suddenly become yuppies because they had a baby? Surely Eve would grow up more grounded and have a better understanding of the value of money if her parents had an average house and an average income?

Now, apparently, she was going to grow up with divorced parents instead.

Red stopped trying to bite Peat's ear and stared at her as she walked towards the stables. He pricked his ears hopefully. She had been leading him out every day and his hooves were so strong and sure, it was time to ride him again.

'Why not horse. It's just you and me now.'

She opened the tack room door, picked up a rag and started to the wipe the dust from her saddle.

Chapter Thirteen

'You are supposed to be resting?'

George shouted after Gill, but she continued to march in the direction of Amber's field.

She had been so bright at the hospital, convincing the doctor she was well enough to leave. She said she knew she wasn't right yet and promised to rest, but had been adamant she could do that at home.

On the way back to Newmans she had not spoken. Now she had left her overnight bag on the floor by the car and was walking towards the paddocks. Was she ok? Was her head injury more debilitating than he thought?

'Gill...' George called after her again.

Without looking back she shouted that she wanted to see Amber.

George picked up her bag but stood, watching her progress. One of the liveries whinnied at the sight of her, but she carried on walking until she reached the mare and her spindle legged brown and white foal.

Gill dropped her head and reached out the back of her hand. Amber sniffed it before nuzzling her hair, as though inspecting the location of her injury. Teddy blew over her face, smelling her, copying his mother.

Gill sat on the ground in front of the horses, giving her ultimate trust to them by rendering herself immobile. Amber stood in close and rested one of her hind legs, suggesting that they doze together. Gill laid her head back onto the ground, George drew in breath, worried that the foal would stand on her.

But Teddy folded his legs beneath him and flopped to the ground a few feet away.

The warm May sunshine bathed the trio in golden light.

Resigned, George let himself into the house to make her a sandwich.

'Weighed Out, Weighed Out.' Came the announcement.

Jules now understood, hearing the words over the tannoy for the third time that day, this meant the jockey would be on his way to the paddock to mount. She stood on the green in the middle of the parade ring and watched Monty walking calmly around whilst Kelly chatted to him. Monty was so professional. This was his domain.

Some of the other horses looked like they were harder to handle. A large grey, not unlike Milly, danced on the end of a short lead rope, stressing the handler's arm, unable to walk for the adrenaline which surged through tree branch arteries.

She thought how lucky they had been. Milly and Pop had both been cool and collected before their races.

Pop had only managed 4th place. Watching the race and talking to John afterwards, she was fairly certain she knew why. As soon as they had left the parade ring and Pop had entered the track, he thought the race had started. The jockeys had to canter their horses to the start, in order to race back towards the finish line. John had wrestled to keep the horse from running flat out and failed. Pop had reached the start way ahead of the rest of the field and then thought his job was over. By the time the starter had given the order, Pop was disgruntled and confused by the jockey's sudden change of heart and direction.

It was their fault she supposed, they had always started the horses workouts as soon as they reached the practice track at home, so naturally Pop thought that was when he needed to give his all.

John had said he probably could have stopped him on the way to start, but given it was the horse's first race and he clearly wasn't used to a heavy handed approach from his reaction to pressure on his bit, John had decided to let him have an easy first time out.

Jules hoped Norah was ok about it.

She glanced over at the owner, who was hobnobbing with the well-dressed by the side of the ring. A charcoal suit covered her commanding frame, orange lipstick matched the sash around her hat.

She really looked the part, she talked the talk too. Surrounded by her kin, those who followed her breeding programme with awe, and who had come specifically to see her horses race and be in her presence.

Norah had made sure she was there when John rode Pop back to the stands, quizzing him before he weighed in. She had laughed and appeared jovial, saying she hadn't even expected a finish from the horse so he had already surpassed her expectations. Jules hoped she was being sincere and her apparent indifference was not part of her race day bravado.

Milly had won. Norah had smiled over at Jules and nodded as she stood with the sweaty horse in the winner's enclosure. Norah didn't own Milly so the win was not one she would benefit from. Was it a rookie mistake not to have prepared Pop for a sensible amble to the start followed by a flat out gallop the other way? Would Gill have been doing that in the week leading up to the race if she had been there?

Kelly didn't seem phased and said she thought Pop had done really well for his first time out.

Perhaps it was only Jules in her ignorance that took it as a personal failure, having listened to Gill talk about the secret weapon the horse would be. You win some you lose some, she supposed.

John appeared behind her and she smiled, signalling Kelly to bring Monty across to them.

She legged John up for the third and final time that day, impressed again by the amount of spring the small man possessed, despite her feeble hold on his shin.

'Hello old friend,' John beamed as he slapped Monty's hard black neck affectionately, 'let's show them how it's done.'

Red picked up on Rosie's urgency to get away from the house.

The horse strode out confidently, mirroring the impulsion in Rosie's hips.

She tried not to think about the fact she hadn't ridden him for so many months, determined not to ruin their union by over analysing it. She had plenty to fill her head anyway.

She gave the horse a loose rein and allowed him to pick his way over the large stones at the entrance to the bridleway, concerned in case he was foot sore. She needn't have worried, he carried her effortlessly and as soon as his hooves hit the peaty track, she gathered him up and asked him to run.

He lifted into a steady canter but she scrubbed her heels against his sides.

'Go!' The red ears flicked back towards her, as though the horse was asking for confirmation.

'Go! Go go!' Rosie shouted at the top of her voice. Her ruthlessness flooded through her horse, who brought his head up high, before bursting.

His compact muscles bunched beneath him and he ran like a terrier after a rabbit. Ears flat back, satisfying his instinct to charge headlong away from danger. Once they reached the top of the track Rosie sat deeply in the saddle, catching her breath from the effort of balancing above his erratic gait. Red walked awkwardly, exhausted, his breaths sharp and heavy, and Rosie felt the heat intensify and rise up around her before he broke into a sweat. He wasn't fit enough to go flat out and she felt rotten for putting her own needs above his comfort.

Once they were back on the tarmac she hopped to the ground and loosened his girth, walking beside him while he cooled off.

His breathing, thankfully, returned to normal quite quickly and he walked with a loose stride.

He nibbled at her shoulder, companionably nuzzling her.

'Oh Red...' She burst into tears at the affection the horse was showing her, despite the fact she had just endangered his health and panicked him by shouting.

She stopped the horse and put her arms around his hot sticky neck, saturating her face where she pressed it against his skin. She was so rarely reckless, and never with a horse. What on earth was she becoming?

Without warning, Red almost pulled her arm off by making an unexpected swoop for some lush looking grass sprouting from the high bank which encased the country lane. She caught his head and eased it back to the middle of the lane just before his reaching lips closed around the tasty morsel.

'You are too hot for a snack. We can have a pit stop in a bit.'

She rested her elbow on the neck of her horse and straightened his forelock through his ears where the wind had kicked it up over the headstall of his bridle. As they walked she felt better, more centred and calm, her guilt ebbed away with his easy forgiveness.

'I love you.' she whispered to him, rubbing his belly.

The birds sang merry above them, as though their stomping ground was welcoming them after the leave of absence which Rosie could only blame herself for.

Now, facing the prospect of losing her home, she felt so stupid for having wasted so much time when she could have been enjoying her horse and her territory. But how could she have predicted that having a time limit on her life there was even a possibility?

'What am I going to do Red?'

'What are you doing there?'

Rosie was surprised to see her husband leaning against the wall which bordered their garden.

'Waiting for you.'

'Why?' Rosie asked indignantly, he hadn't cared where she was when he had left her breaking her heart in the field.

Matt shrugged and turned to walk back through the side gate and into the house. Now that he had seen Rosie safely returned, he could go.

'Where is Eve?' Rosie called after him, thinking it was unusual for him not to have the baby in his arms.

'Crystal is changing her. I need to post a birthday card to my Mum so I thought I would take her with me into Honiton.'

'I posted that last week.'

'Oh. Well she won't mind getting two.'

'But I always send her card, and your Dad's, why would you think I wouldn't?'

Matt shrugged again, the conversation apparently over.

Tears pricked Rosie's eyes as she led Red towards his stable. Since when did having an emotional problem render you useless? She might have been struggling with her feelings, but she hadn't stopped operating, in the main.

Frustration saw her letting go of the horse when they reached the yard, marching forwards and kicking at bucket which she had left on the floor.

Red shied away from the noise as plastic skidded across the concrete and collided with the timber of the stable wall. He stood a little way away from her, wondering if she was still safe.

'Sorry boy.' She gently removed his saddle and put her arms around his neck, apologising to the horse yet again.

She couldn't carry on like this. Something had to give.

Deciding to take action while she felt determined, she quickly brushed the dried sweat from his coat and let him go, so that she could return to the house and address her husband.

But his car was already gone.

Not wanting to speak to Jimmy or Crystal, she let herself in through the rarely used front door of the cottage and quietly slipped to the spare room.

She sat on the bed.

Matt's work laptop was on the desk which he had moved into the corner of the room, still open. She glanced uninterestedly at the screen which displayed a network diagram for the new system he was working on for the company's Bristol office. That was a point she could make, she mused as she lay back on the bed, intending to give her brain a rest and sleep while she waited for him. Even though he was based in Oxford he travelled all over the country regularly, his was a job which required constant mobility, she would still probably be alone for part of the week regardless of where she was stationed.

She closed her eyes but opened them again when she heard a mobile ringing. Following the sound she located Matt's work blackberry in the pocket of his suit jacket. The screen flashed the word Oxford at her.

She hit the green answer button and the caller started speaking before she had a chance to say hello.

'Hello Mattie – sorry to hassle ya – Manchester is down again and I need the server password. Hope your weekend isn't going too badly mate – have you spoken to her yet?'

Her?

Me, thought Rosie. Who the hell was this woman who apparently knew she was going to be told she was moving to Oxford before she did?

'Hello?' The woman demanded.

'Matt is out with this his daughter at the moment can I take a message?' Rosie snapped.

'Oh. Right. Can he call Joanne back when he has a minute please?' The woman's tone changed from bright and familiar, to curt as Rosie's own. Not bothering to say goodbye, Rosie hung up.

No "oh you must be Rosie". She didn't even know this Joanne and already appeared to have been judged by her. Furious that Matt could have been so disloyal, discussing her problems with a stranger, Rosie threw the Blackberry at the floor.

It bounced on the carpet, frustratingly unharmed.

Too wound up to sleep, she decided to groom Peat while she waited for Matt's return and the day's inevitable second argument.

'E's a right champion that Black 'orse!' Maurice cackled, tweed jacket crumpling in the driver's seat of the lorry, lapels around his neck.

Jules laughed and patted the old farmer's arm.

'Thanks so much for driving Maurice.'

They had cooled Monty off after the winner's enclosure, then packed and loaded the horses, only to find they were missing their driver. Kelly eventually spotted him stuffing wedges of cash into his pocket, having cleaned out an on-course bookie. He had clearly made far in excess of the amount Jules had offered to pay him for driving the lorry.

'Thas' alright Julie!' Maurice beamed and took his eye off the road for a split second to twinkle it at her.

The worst thing about leaving Kysford to move to Newmans had been saying goodbye to the farm and Maurice. She missed their early morning chats, his comfortingly unchanging demeanour, even the way he got her name wrong.

'Norah obviously planned that outfit for the press!' Kelly laughed from beside Jules, thinking of the picture which would probably make the racing post, of Monty receiving his certificate. The owner's black suit and orange sash had matched Monty's black coat and the jockey's orange and yellow colours, making for a perfect image.

'Bit rude, how she made us get out of the way?' Jules folded her arms around herself, conscious of being sandwiched between Kelly and Maurice, who despite having an apparently clean jacket and brown cords on, still managed to smell like cow.

'Oh she always does that, "can't have grooms in my picture"!' Kelly impersonated Norah's booming voice and shuffled over towards the cab door so that Jules could inch away from Maurice, who was elbowing her every time he changed gear.

Monty had sailed effortlessly into first place, as Norah had clearly expected. Instead of being on a high at the yard's success, as Kelly and even Maurice clearly were, Jules just felt relieved that Norah had been happy and all of the runners came home safely. Jules decided she did not have the stomach for racing, despite being part of a winning team. She much preferred organising the finances, paying for the equipment and helping out with the horses at home. Kelly and Gill could do the exciting bit.

She would be glad when Gill was better.

Maurice drove with a life's worth of experience transporting animals. Whether they were cows, sheep, or even horses, he drove with the same slow considerate concentration. He had empathy with the animals in the back, knowing innately how a corner taken at the wrong angle, or failing to judge the traffic and having to slow too sharply, could affect their balance.

In no time the box had eaten up the miles of motorway between Taunton and Exeter and Maurice was pulling it gently into Newmans.

Jules was disappointed that Gill did not appear from the house to greet them but guessed she must be sleeping.

Once they had unloaded the horses and Kelly started to walk each of them around the sandschool in turn to ease their muscles, Jules turned to Maurice and enveloped him in a hug. Maurice laughed off her embrace and stepped backwards, pretending to straighten his jacket.

'This is me best one - bloody woman! Go mucking it up with your daftness.'

'It was lovely to see you today Maurice, thanks again.' Jules meant her words. She reached into her pocket to give him the envelope she had prepared for him.

'No tis alright.' Maurice started to walk away from her towards his Land Rover.

She trotted after him.

'Hang on I must pay you!' Jules tried to thrust the envelope at him but he waved her away.

'Nah. Tis alright' Maurice waved her away dismissively

and started to get into his truck.

Jules couldn't help but laugh.

'Ok Maurice, if you are sure.'

'Oh 'ang on a minute. Where's the dog?'

Jules trotted into the barn to let Ziggy out of the stable where the animal had been patiently waiting.

The collie span in delight to see his master and skittered across the concrete after her. He threw himself at Maurice who hugged the dog and then told him to sit before fishing a biscuit out of his pocket and allowing Ziggy to take it gently from his calloused hand.

'What you doin' with un while you'm at work?' Maurice asked, unusually sheepish.

'Oh he stays here with Gill.'

'Ah right.'

'I could drop him out to you before work sometimes if you like though?'

Maurice stopped caressing Ziggy's ear and stood up.

'Only if you like maid. Cows is all out now so I gotta walk the fields every day to check on 'um. Be nice for Zig?'

'Yes it would.' Jules beamed.

It was only inconvenience, she would have to leave the house a bit earlier drive across to Kysford before heading to the office, but if it meant seeing Maurice a few times a week, and that Ziggy got to spend the day on the farm instead of mooching around the horse barn, it was worth it.

'See you Monday then.' Maurice nodded and hoisted himself back into his driver's seat. Jules noticed the interior light shining in the foot well, illuminating a thick layer of still moist cow dung covering the pedals, which explained the smell.

'Bye Maurice.'

'Bye bye Julie.'

Jules walked back in to the yard to see Kelly had returned Monty to his stable and was walking Milly and Pop, one in each hand, around the school.

'Shall I start unpacking the lorry?' Jules called, thinking while there were still remnants of daylight she might as well save herself a job in the morning.

'Better had!'

'Queue at the post office?' Rosie made Matt jump as he was getting out of the car. She had seen his car descending the lane into the valley from the stables.

'I took Eve for a walk round the park and then we went out for dinner.' Matt answered, flat toned. 'Here.' He offered her a paper bag. She took it and looked inside, it was fresh fudge from her favourite bakery. She was taken aback by the gesture.

'Thank you.' She reached forward and caught his arm, intending to kiss him on the cheek but he was already opening the back door to get Eve from the car seat and he elbowed her in the chest.

'Sorry.'

'Fudge makes up for it.'

He reached into the back seat, but noticed Eve was fast asleep and withdrew from the car, not wanting to wake her.

'Leave her there a minute?' Rosie moved towards the back of the car port and sat on the work bench. Matt followed and leant against his shrouded race car.

'You ever going to drive that again?'

'Maybe when Eve is a bit older. Shame she wasn't a boy.'

'Being a girl doesn't mean she won't like driving fast.' Rosie smiled.

Matt smiled back. They were both thinking of all the times Matt had clutched at his seat belt while Rosie rocketed through the lanes.

Rosie opened her mouth to start laying into Matt about the call from Joanne but couldn't bring herself to ruin the most civilised conversation they'd had in weeks.

'I don't really want to move Rosie. I just don't know what else to do. Neither of us are happy with the situation as it is and I can't afford to quit.'

Rosie dropped her head and tried to steady her breathing, although his voice was warmer, it was almost worse because his words were reasonable, and the only argument she really had for saying no to his suggestion was her own selfishness.

'I think it would break my heart.' She said honestly, all the rationales and arguments she had spent the afternoon rehearsing in her head seemed petty, the truth it boiled down to was that she didn't want to leave Devon.

'You broke mine that day on the moor.'

'I didn't choose to have this problem.'

'What are we going to do then?'

'Can we just see how things go? Could you go back to your old job?'

Matt shook his head, trying not to get angry again but frustrated by her lack of understanding about what he considered to be the only option.

'Only if you don't mind giving that horsebox back.'

'No of course I don't.'

'I don't think I could go back to earning less. I want to give Eve everything she deserves.'

It was Rosie's turn to be frustrated.

'Surely happy parents is more important than being rich? What about the business you always talked about running? Doing things your way instead of lining someone else's pockets?'

Matt shrugged and started to walk towards the car.

'For heaven's sake would you stop walking away?' Rosie snapped.

Matt's shoulders dropped and he turned back towards her.

'The job is stressful, but I can't just jack it all in to follow a pipedream which might not pay the mortgage. And I do like the people.'

'Couldn't bear to say goodbye to Joanne?'

Matt looked up sharply.

'She called for you earlier, asked if "Mattie" could call her back.' Rosie explained.

'Ok.' Matt turned away again and started to unbuckle Eve's child seat.

'Are you fucking her?' Rosie's hands shook as the question escaped her lips.

Matt sighed heavily and stood up again.

'No.'

'But she knows we are having problems?'

'Yes.'

'Since when did you start sharing your feelings?'

'Since you stopped caring about them.'

'Oh come on...', Rosie threw her hands in the air in frustration, 'I never stopped listening to you, I counted down the hours until you came home every week.'

'Yeah, so you could offload Eve.'

'None of this is any excuse for telling a stranger about our problems, if you had a problem with me you should have told me. I felt judged by her on the phone!'

'You are paranoid then, she's the one who has been reminding me you can't help this.'

'So you have been slating me so badly to these people, they feel sorry for me?'

'Come to Oxford and meet them, defend yourself.'

'Defend myself?'

'You are the one who thinks it's like that.'

'Evidence based. You are turning into an asshole you know that?' Rosie hissed, scorned.

'You throw your toys out of the pram more than Eve does.'

'Since when?' Rosie was generally the most laid back person she knew. Admittedly she had had her moments lately but it was hardly a measure of her entire character.

'Like when I couldn't come home that weekend so you got all shitty with me even though I couldn't help it and then summonsed Jimmy to give up his life and come and look after you. '

'I didn't call Jimmy.' Rosie spat through gritted teeth, 'Val did.'

'Oh, so now who is talking about their problems with anyone but me?'

'Touché Matt. Hope victory keeps you warm on the sofa mate.'

'Not a problem.' Matt scoffed and narrowed his eyes at his wife, 'Like mother like daughter.'

'What the fuck is that supposed to mean?' Rosie's voice became low, her heels lifted off the ground in an involuntary fight reaction to the argument, not that she would have acted on her desire to punch him, but it was there.

'Can't cope with life, so you turn Jimmy into your personal slave. Just like she used to. What about his life?'

It was Rosie's turn to walk away. She threw the fudge at the floor as she marched past the car and left him to retrieve his daughter. How much more could he possibly punish her for something she was not in control of and couldn't help?

If his aim was for her to dislike him, he was hitting the target.

George knocked on his own bedroom door.

When Gill didn't answer he slowly crept in, struggling with the door handle and the sandwich which he had wrapped in cling film hours ago.

He need not have worried about waking her. She was sat up in bed.

'Hey you, what are you doing?' He spoke softly, she appeared to be in a daze, staring straight ahead.

'Nothing.' She answered him, but her gaze did not leave its fixed position.

'Are you feeling ok?'

'Yeah fine. Well, physically.'

'Would you like your sandwich now?'

'No.'

George made space on the bedside table and set the plate down. He sat on the bed next to Gill and tried to take her hand. She inched away from him, under the pretence of re-arranging her pillow. After she had come back from the field earlier she had refused to eat anything and said she wanted to go to bed. Trying to be useful George had walked Ziggy and swept the horse barn.

'They have just come back.'

'I know.' Gill had seen the lorry trundling up the drive through the window.

'What's wrong Gill? I know you are not well, obviously, but I can't help feeling like you don't like me?'

'I don't.' She said, quietly, still not ready to say the thing she had been preparing to say all day.

'What have I done?' George looked genuinely perplexed, which threw Gill, Alex had known the game was up as soon as he had arrived home and seen her face after his dirty weekend away with Megan.

'You tell me George.'

George started to say he really didn't know.

But Jules burst through the bedroom door.

'Horses all done and settled, Kelly dropped home, thought I would come and give the boss the good news!'

'How did it go?!' Gill moved further from George and reached her arms out to Jules who skirted the edge of the bed to hug her friend.

'Monty won, of course, and Milly won too!' Jules grinned.

'Brilliant! First race taken by storm! And Pop?'

'Pop came fourth... Not brilliant, but the jockey did have an explanation...' Jules trailed off when she finally registered the atmosphere in the room and George's anguish ridden face, 'but I can tell you about that later if I have interrupted something?'

Gill's gaze fixed forward again, George remained silent.

'Ok I can fill you in in the morning.' Jules slid from the bed, feeling foolish for bursting in and wanting to retreat as quickly as possible.

'No wait Jules.' George looked up, stopping her just as she reached the door. He felt Gill's eyes turn sharply on him. The game was up, she had obviously, somehow, discovered his secret it was time to bare all.

'I have something I need to tell Gill and I would prefer it if you were here.'

'What's it got to do with Jules?' Gill snapped, not wanting an audience.

'I should go, really.' Jules hesitated by the door, not wanting to be the audience.

'I might need your advice Jules.' George looked her in

the eye. She walked back to the bed, where she perched uncomfortably.

Tears started to fall from Gill's eyes. This was it, he was going to announce his relationship with Daisy and leave her and he needed a solicitor to extract himself.

'Right,' George took a deep breath and held his cheeks with his palms, struggling with where to start. 'Just after we re-opened the restaurant, back in April...'

'This has been going on since April??' Gill exclaimed, her voice strained by her tight throat, the words came out at almost a screech.

Jules, who had put two and two together and realised what George was going to say must have something to do with the letter she had accidentally seen, waved her hand at Gill, indicating she should let him finish.

'We had our first busy night, about 15 covers, but we were fully staffed and on form. One of the tables was a couple and the woman didn't look very well. She sent her appetiser back, said it tasted funny, then she ate half her entree and ran to the ladies. She said there was something off about her risotto and refused to pay her bill. Her husband tried to pay, said he had enjoyed the meal. Rob was up for a fight with her but I just let it go, she was looking pretty green and I didn't want a scene in front of the other customers.'

George paused, as though the worst was still to come. Gill wished he would hurry up.

'That was the Friday. On the Monday afternoon an environmental health officer turned up. Said they had a complaint.' George stopped speaking and raised his face towards the ceiling. 'And that's where we fell down. We usually date sticker everything we prep so we know when it needs to be used by and we can usually evidence our systems. It's food safety 101.

But none of the prepped dishes were stickered, and there was a load of raw beef in the back of the main larder which hadn't been covered up. It all would have been sorted by evening service. I wasn't there and Rob was quite rude to the bloke by the sounds of it. Even though the sous-chef could tell him exactly when all the prepped food needed to go out and explained that we were over cautious, we weren't evidencing that we were managing critical control points so we weren't following our own system. The kitchen was a bit of a mess too, again something which would have been sorted before the evening but at that moment in time, it can't have looked good. The bloke didn't find anything really badly wrong, but because it wasn't perfect it cast a doubt over us.'

'What's a critical control point?' Jules had gone into lawyer mode, wishing she had a pad and pen.

'It's just a term we use for our procedures to manage food safety – it's the point at which something should be done to minimise risk – like date stickering, or chilling food, or heating it to the right temperature for the right amount of time to make it safe.'

'So like, to stop bacteria?'

'Yes. The status of a foodstuff and how high risk it is changes depending on what you do to it or how long it's been ready to consume.'

'I see.' Jules nodded.

Gill thwacked the duvet with her fists in frustration. George became less animated again and carried on.

'Then a week later we get this letter from the woman accusing us of giving her food poisoning. Rob was all for ignoring it; we could all see the woman was already unwell when she arrived that night.'

'And did you ignore it?' Jules tried not to let the worry sound in her voice, knowing how fatal failing to respond could be

265

to a case.

'No. I wrote back to her and said she seemed ill when she arrived, that if her meal had been bad it would have taken until at least the next day for her to become ill from it, and said we had no other reports of the same risotto from the same batch causing any other problems that night.

'About a month went by and we had a few shitty emails from the woman, which I didn't reply to. Then we get a letter from the woman's solicitor. It included exerts of this woman's medical records showing that she had been treated for stomach problems which could have been caused by food poisoning. They were asking for us to make an offer to settle the case before she went public about her experience. There were tables of expenses for loss of earnings she had suffered, taxis to the hospital. It all seemed so ridiculous because she was clearly ill before she even ate our food but because of the environmental health inspection not being perfect, I felt like we looked guilty.

'Rob, at this point, went slightly nuts. We just had the bill through for repairs to the roof and the flood damage to the cellar. He was all for counter suing her for libel.'

'But she hadn't actually written anything anywhere?'

'No, but she sent us an email listing all the websites she would be reviewing the restaurant on. She was going to go to the press too.'

'Why in god's name didn't you talk to me about this?' Jules shook her head at George, almost angry.

'The solicitor she's using is from your firm.'

'Well I appreciate you trying to avoid putting me in an awkward position but this is your life George – I could have at least given you some advice early on, referred you to another firm, someone I know and trust?'

'We couldn't have afforded the bill. I have been trying to

tuck away every spare penny I can. I listed my car on a load of auto sales sites last night. I am trying to scrape together the figure this woman wants to make her go away behind Rob's back because he is still insisting we shouldn't give her a penny.'

George glanced at Gill who looked like her blood was boiling.

'Gill, I'm sorry, I...'

'Get on with it George, I am assuming the best bit is still to come.' Gill snapped.

'She wants £10,000. Full settlement, she won't be able to take us to Court and she will promise not to go public about it.'

'And?' Gill demanded.

'And that's it. That's what I have been dealing with. I didn't want to tell you Gill, because I didn't want to worry you. I kept going to but I was ashamed. I want to be your rock, not a leaky boat.'

'That's not it at all. What about Daisy?' Gill's tear moist eyes narrowed in anger.

'Who is Daisy?' Jules was understandably confused.

George sighed and his head fell into his hands.

'Daisy is George's ex. But apparently not so ex – hey George?' Gill flung the covers away from her body and stood up. The blood rushed from her head and she quickly had to sit again.

'What are you going on about?' George, emotionally expired from finally getting all off his chest was genuinely perplexed, but Gill had her back to him and couldn't see his face.

'You know perfectly well what I am going on about.'

'Well I don't!' Jules turned herself around towards Gill.

'On Thursday, I went to find George because I had just had a call to say my mother was in hospital. He told me he was going to the restaurant, but he wasn't there.'

'Where was he?' Jules was too tired for verbal ping pong.

'Come on, George where were you?'

'I was at Daisy's.' George said quietly.

'I saw him going into her new house, which conveniently for George, is just around the corner. I went into the village shop and Maisy ended up taking me to hospital.'

'Oh god. Oh god Gill I am so sorry.' George realised the impact of seeing him go into his ex's house, realised the trouble he had caused by keeping his problem from her. He clambered across the bed and tried to wrap his arms around her but she wriggled her shoulders free of his hands and shoved him backwards.

'Why were you at Daisy's?' Jules asked, un-baited, because it genuinely didn't cross her mind that George would have cheated.

'To ask for a loan. It was embarrassing and I wish I hadn't gone and she loved every minute of it.'

'What's the interest then? Got to pop round and give her a good seeing to every week?' Gill turned and faced George, the whites of her eyes showing to a primitive degree.

'I had to find a way to make up the settlement without taking too much from the business. Rob still insists we shouldn't pay. We have rowed almost to the point of selling up altogether and I couldn't let that happen. I just wanted to quietly make it go away before anyone else had to deal with it.'

'So you went to your ex instead of me?' Gill found a way to justify the anger that still pumped through her, but the light was back on inside, she wanted to hug and hit him at the same time. The nightmare over, the unpleasant dream of the restaurant being sued in its place entirely more palatable. They didn't have to split up. He was still her George.

George opened his mouth to try and explain but wasn't sure if anything could make up for hiding it all from her. He should have gone to her. She was right to be angry, could he even, in hindsight, justify it to himself?

Gill saw it in his eyes.

She made towards him. He flinched, expecting assault, but found himself in her arms.

'Stupid man.' She muttered into his neck.

'I'm sorry. I don't expect you to forgive me but I promise I was trying to protect you, nothing more.'

'What will you do if you have a problem in future?'

'Talk to you.'

'And you will remember I am not a china doll and that we are a partnership?'

'Yes.'

'And what will you do if you have a legal problem?' Jules chimed in, elated that the hostility was gone from the room.

'Talk to the in-house solicitor.'

'And with that in mind,' Gill let go of George, so that she could reposition herself to face Jules, but stayed very close to him and reached for his clammy hand, 'what's the plan Jules, how can we get rid of this Bitch?'

Chapter Fourteen

'Try to keep his trot balanced, don't let him speed up and run ragged. When you ask for canter, use your seat and – that's it! Nice!' Kelly beamed as Red struck off on the right leading leg and cantered comfortably round the outer edge of the sand school. 'Keep him going, now you have it, keep the impulsion up.'

'Ha ha! Good Boy!' Rosie called, breathless from the effort, she had forgotten how exhausting a lesson could be, 'It's been so long since we have been in a school, cantering up straight bridle paths it doesn't matter!'

'You are doing really well.' Kelly smiled at Rosie and her stunning red horse.

'Stop saying that!! I want criticism and stuff to work on!'

Kelly laughed. She found it hard to teach Rosie, she had so much respect for her, because of the way Gill talked about her, but also because she had backed her own horse herself.

Sometimes it was a foolhardy endeavour, especially for someone who lacked experience, and it didn't work for everyone, but in Rosie's case she had created a happy and willing partner. So they were a little rough around the edges. They probably wouldn't win any dressage competitions at present, but it was honest, and it was kind. She had spent a lot of time trying to communicate with him on his level, so that even when she didn't ask a question in quite the right way, the horse met her in the middle and tried his best without getting stressed or frustrated.

Rosie had arrived at Newmans earlier that day with Red and Peat in her brand new horsebox. She didn't seem as proud of it as she should have been, parking it behind the barn and not wanting to show them the inside, brushing it off as functional.

Gill had laughed and mocked her affluence, asking her what it was like having a rich husband, but Rosie had changed the subject.

'Think he has had enough now?' Rosie called to Kelly, posing it as a question but allowing the horse to slow to a walk. He was quite fit now, she had spent the last month dedicatedly riding him every day, but school work was more tiring than hacking for them both, due to the focus on precision and outline.

'Think you have had enough more like!' Kelly laughed. 'I won't charge you for the hour.'

'Don't be daft.' Rosie chided as she allowed the horse to walk on a long loose rein, 'I want to support Devon's hottest new instructress!'

'I guess I should enjoy it while it lasts.'

Rosie's smile faded when she saw Kelly's face drop. Gill had confided in Rosie the week before about her groom's imminent emigration, and how miserable she was about it, so Rosie should have known better.

'I don't know what they are going to do without you Kel.' Rosie drew Red up beside the suddenly lost girl, coming to a halt in the middle of the school. Kelly reached out to Red and caressed his cheek and he leant in for a scratch, rubbing his face up and down on her shoulder.

'Sorry.' Rosie asked him to back up before he knocked Kelly over.

'I don't know what I am going to do without them.' Kelly looked up at Rosie with mournful eyes and shook her head, 'I still can't believe it's happening.'

Rosie nodded, empathising in a deeper way than Kelly could have understood.

'Right then. Gossip.' Jules folded her legs underneath her on the sofa and leant forward expectantly. 'What do we need to catch up on?'

'Well, George isn't having an affair!' Gill announced and then blushed, she was sat the other end of the sofa from Jules. Rosie laid on the floor in front of them, Ziggy on his back beside her, luxuriating in having his tummy rubbed.

'Yeah, we knew that.' Rosie tutted, Gill had texted her a few days after the revelation about the visit to Daisy's, much to Rosie's relief, but not surprise, 'everyone except you, knew that.'

'You are a bit of a tit head Gill.' Jules cackled and poked at Gill with her toe. Gill grabbed at the assaulting foot but Jules retracted it and almost spilled her wine over her lap.

'Yes. Alright. Moving on.'

Rosie had brought Red over for a lesson with Kelly, and ended up deciding to stay over. Red and Peat were enjoying a night of luxury in the barn with the racehorses, and Rosie was glad of the opportunity to get away from Matt. He would be departing for his week in Oxford first thing in the morning and she was relieved she wouldn't have to see him again until Friday, more so that tonight she would sleep in Charlie's room and be alone on purpose, instead of in the spare room at home, knowing Matt was in the next room. In the month that had passed since she had ordered to him to sleep on the sofa, he had made no attempt to get back into bed beside her.

In an unspoken tryst, they waited until Jimmy and Crystal had gone to bed, before going their separate ways, to avoid any questions about why Matt chose to sleep in the lounge.

'Speaking of tit heads,' Rosie remembered to ask, 'has that ridiculous woman stopped hassling the restaurant?'

'Yes and no.' Jules answered for Gill, ' Yes because we haven't heard from her since we wrote and rejected her settlement offer on the basis there was no liability, but no because the fact that she has gone quiet doesn't mean it's over.'

'George is scouring the doormat every day. He is convinced she will start court proceedings.' Gill added, sympathy for her partner clear in her voice.

'Is that likely then?' Rosie asked.

'Well...who knows? I doubt she would win, but if she does start we will have to find George a solicitor. I can't represent the restaurant because of the conflict of interest – my firm is representing the woman, ' Jules reminded Rosie, who nodded her understanding of the situation, 'but I am advising George on the QT for now, and I helped him word the letter.'

'Could you get into trouble for that?' Rosie looked concerned, but toned her fears down for Gill's sake.

'Potentially.' Jules nodded, 'but I have made my managing partner aware of the situation and agreed if formal representation is necessary George will use someone else. To be honest I am surprised our personal injury department took the case on at all, based on the evidence, but you don't know what the woman said to make them think it was winnable and I daren't look at the file – then I really could be in trouble.'

Rosie nodded, satisfied Jules was protected.

'Anyway,' Gill leaned forwards, smiling mischievously, 'moving on..has Jules told you she is in love?!'

'No!' Rosie screeched and made Ziggy wag his tail excitedly.

Jules shook her head at Gill.

'Sorry should I not have said?' Gill feigned innocence and smirked.

'Too bloody late now.' Jules turned back to Rosie, who looked slightly miffed at being out of the loop, 'He is married. Nothing is going to happen. So I pine for him, and that's it.'

'More information.' Rosie demanded, folding her arms.

'Well that's rich coming from Mrs Change the Subject – you never talk about your life!' Gill felt bad about spilling the beans and turned the focus on Rosie.

'That's because its shit.' Rosie looked down at Ziggy and held his paw gently to stop him jabbing her in the side, demanding more tummy attention.

When she looked up at her friends again, Gill's mouth hung open in disbelief and Jules face fell at the confirmation that since their last discussion on the subject, things had not improved.

'It's so shit, I don't know where to start.'

'Talk to us.' Gill spoke gently, using the voice that was usually reserved for Charlie.

'I'm sorry I didn't tell you before. Jules knows some of it, but not about Matt.'

Rosie described her postnatal depression after Eve was born briefly, to set the scene for the rest, rather than to share the feelings she still didn't understand. Then she talked about Matt. How her husband had become a stranger.

As she talked, she started to see clearly how their communication had broken down, even as she described the anger between them she found new understanding for each little misunderstanding, which had led to the situation they were in now. They only talked if it was necessary to put on a show for Jimmy and Crystal, not wanting to drag the couple in to their miserable world. Matt still wanted her to move to Oxford, she still didn't want to, and the stale mate showed no sign of coming to an end.

'The worst thing is, I don't even care anymore. I was already pretty numb and every time he is cold to me, I get colder back. I really honestly feel like my marriage is over.'

Rosie finished her story and finally looked up from Ziggy, who she had focused on throughout. She had remained dry eyed despite the sadness of her tale, but realised Jules was crying for her.

'I'm sorry. It's just so sad.' Jules sniffed and tried to compose herself. 'You guys are too good together to throw it all away. Especially if the thing that caused it all is resolving?'

'Yes, it is resolving. I feel much better about Eve. I am still not a natural, but I know I do love her, and the older and less baby-like she gets, the better it gets. I just wasn't cut out for the whole tiny helpless thing in my arms bit. If she had been delivered as a 5 year old, it would have been fine.'

'So if the way you feel about Eve is better, why are you and Matt still arguing?' Gill asked.

'He still thinks I should move up there so he doesn't have to miss her during the week. I still think that is something I am never going to want to do. It was never on the cards. I feel like he is using the fact that I had a breakdown to get what he wants, which is not to have to commute.'

'Surely not Rosie, isn't it more likely that he wants you close so he can look after you both, more so if you are having a hard time?' Jules' genuine faith in Matt was touching, if misguided.

'Part of the reason we are still not talking is because of how he handled it. He didn't look after me, or support me, he just rejected me and became over-protective with Eve, which just made things worse. He let me down.'

'What are you going to do?' Gill almost didn't want to hear the answer.

'I'm not moving to Oxford.'

'Oh that's like music – someone not moving away - I think if I lost you *and* Kelly *and* Charlie I would need a

275

therapist!' Gill laughed sarcastically at her own comment. 'Sorry is that selfish?'

'No. It's nice. And given that I am probably going to be single and homeless fairly soon, reassuring to be wanted at least by someone.'

'Why homeless?' Jules wiped her eyes and pulled herself together.

'Well obviously we are not talking so I don't know for sure – but he wants to buy a place in Oxford, and if he has custody of Eve I will have to help fund it, so we will have to sell the cottage.'

'You and the horses are welcome here.' Gill got off the sofa and sat on the floor beside her dear friend, wishing she could make what she was going through better.

Jules couldn't help but think about James. He was locked in an unhappy marriage too, and at least of late, it had been partly her fault. She couldn't get her head around the concept of Matt and Rosie splitting up. They were the couple she modelled her own idea of happiness on. Her parents' relationship had always been based on the acceptance of her mother being in charge. Rosie and Matt had always seemed so balanced.

'You are welcome at mine too!' Jules suddenly remembered the good news she had on Friday, her annexe was ready, all bar the finishing touches to the interior decorating.

'Thanks guys.' Rosie smiled at her friends, glad that, at last, she had found the courage to be honest with them. Selina would be proud she mused, as she sipped her wine and encouraged Jules to talk about her new house. After some reluctance, given the sombre nature of the conversation and her concern for Rosie, Jules had talked about the house warming party was planning the following Saturday.

'I almost forgot!' Rosie exclaimed after agreeing she

would bring Red and Peat for the weekend so that she could attend the party and stay over, thinking as a bonus she would be able to avoid Matt again, 'How did yesterday go?'

'Pop won!' Gill's eyes lit up and she described the yard's day at Shropshire racecourse where, third time lucky, Pop had given the sort of performance he gave at home.

Rosie listened eagerly to Gill's run down of the day, feeling more content than she had for some months. She thought that, if she did have to leave the place that had claimed ownership of her heart, there was immense comfort in knowing she and Red had somewhere to go.

She wished she had confided in her friends long ago, if only she'd had faith in them. Faith that was deserved, unlike the trust she had placed in Matt.

Two small birds perched on the edge of a water bucket. They ducked their tiny beaks into the refreshing liquid and ruffled their feathers. Kelly sat in the shade cast by the barn, watching Monty roam loose around the sandschool. When he approached the water bucket the birds flew away.

She wondered if there would be horses in Australia.

Of course there would be, she tutted at herself. She got up to stand by the fence, needing to feel the horse, despite her plan to create some distance between them. Monty strolled over to his groom, pushing his muzzle along her cheek affectionately.

The tears welled behind her eyes.

'I love you.' She murmured.

She heard Gill approach behind her and felt hands on her back.

'Ok darling?'

'Not really.'

Gill grimaced and continued to stand with her groom. Neither spoke. Gill's warm hands became sweaty, stinging Kelly's sunburnt shoulders, but the discomfort was worth the gesture.

Their connection was borne of their shared enthusiasm for the horses. Kelly had learned to anticipate Gill, enabling her to assist her boss without a great deal of instruction. They had never had an overly verbal relationship, they were more a well-oiled machine.

Now in Gill's hands, grasped around and holding tightly, Kelly could feel the emotion. There was no need to speak.

It was July. In two short months Kelly would be gone.

After Kelly's mother had admitted she didn't feel she could move to Australia without her, the dynamic had changed. Instead of rebelling against what she had perceived as over protection, Kelly felt a duty. Emigrating was something the woman wanted so much, and Kelly was all that was standing in her way. So Kelly had moved her own dreams aside.

'I don't know how I will say goodbye to him.'

'He will miss you.'

Gill gave Kelly's shoulder's a final squeeze before moving to stand beside the groom, putting her arms over the rail.

'You got any lessons today?'

'No. I'm only teaching people who had already started a block with me, seems stupid to advertise when I will be going soon.'

'There's a summer show on at Folklands. The ridden Arabian class starts at 2pm, and there's open dressage all afternoon. Want to take Monty?'

Kelly turned to Gill, her eyes lighting up.

Gill put her hands up, not wanting to over excite her employee, 'Norah said no jumping, but you can do the ridden classes – he's your horse for the day. We need to be back for Jules' party later but we can be fashionably late if necessary.'

Kelly threw her arms around Monty and Gill in turn.

'I don't have a showing jacket?' Kelly panicked, she had never been the competitor, always the groom.

'Mine will fit you. Get him in before he rolls in the sand. I've cleaned his tack it's already in the van.' Gill smiled.

'Thank you!' Kelly squealed and ran to the barn to fetch a headcollar.

'It's less than you deserve.' Gill said quietly, glancing up at Monty who was watching for Kelly, ears pricked towards the human who had earned his precious affection, simply by loving him, more than anything else, every day.

'It's not straight.' Rosie stood back and eyed the banner she and Marianne had pinned across the fireplace in Jules' new lounge.

'No. Alright.' Jules' mother eyed their handy work critically and then bellowed for her husband, deafening Rosie, 'Martin! Come and deal with this silly banner!'

Jules had popped into town to fetch the crate load of alcohol she had ordered, and was stopping at the Bloomswell to collect the party food George had prepared on her way back.

As soon as her daughter had left, Marianne had put Rosie to work assisting with the decorations. It was sweet Rosie thought, the banner read Welcome to your New Home Juliette. Not particularly imaginative, but nice none the less.

'Can you fetch me my handbag, it's in the second bedroom.' Marianne ordered without looking away, her eyes fixed on her husband who wobbled precariously on a plush leather dinning chair, trying to get the banner straight.

As Rosie walked through the newly built extension she

marvelled at how quickly Jules had made her home her own. Wooden flooring covered every square inch of the spacious ground floor property, clean white walls adorned with the tasteful fruits of Jules' previous travels around the world. In addition to the art and ornaments she had collected, least one picture of Romeo was subtly placed in every room. Even the bathroom a lacquered canvas print of Jules brandishing a hose, her clothes saturated, beside her freshly bathed horse, spread across the wall opposite the walk in shower.

'Come along dear!' Marianne's booming voice carried through the hall and Rosie stopped admiring the wooden carving of a collie dog, which sat on an oak book case.

As Rosie carried the handbag back through to living room, she thought about her own home. Mismatched furniture, which was worn with the scars of real life, co-habited uncomfortably with the new items they had ordered online since Matt's promotion. A pristine house with an array carefully placed things was very Jules, but it wasn't Rosie. She would have traded each new unnecessary purchase, including the beautiful horsebox she had driven to Newmans that morning, to have her old life and the old Matt back.

'Can I be excused now please Mrs Rogers?' Rosie said in a cockney accent, curtseyed and tugged an imaginary forelock at Marianne after handing her the handbag.

Martin giggled at Rosie's insolence and Marianne batted him across the shoulder.

'Silly girl. Yes be off with you. I quite fancy a cup of tea.'

'Come on then Gorgeous!' Rosie trotted towards the gate of the small, well grazed paddock Red and Peat had been given for the weekend. He roared a reply at her through thundering nostrils, as though telling her off for the sparseness of the grass.

'Sorry boy, not quite what you are used to?' She laughed as she slid his headcollar up over his nose and he turned his head to the side accommodatingly, to allow her to fasten the buckle. Rosie felt bad Red had to suffer starvation paddock for the sake of his companion, 'But it is not like you are starving is it Mr Porky?'

Red let out a long and huffing sigh, as though bored of her excuses. She laughed and led her horse towards the barn. He had lived at Newmans for five months while Rosie and Matt had been looking after the yard and house for Gill, so he was not remotely excited by being surrounded by other horses or the goings around the barn, even though it was so different to his quiet home life. They passed the paddock he and Harry had shared while she had been running Newmans, now occupied by Amber and Teddy. The foal was squaring up to his mother, tossing his head and trying to be bigger than he was.

She thought about that long winter at Newmans. At the time it had all seemed so dreadful, Gill and Jules desperately searching the country for Romeo, Amber and Monty. The theft of the horses had cast a black shadow over all of their lives, from the moment they had been taken, to the last minute before Amber had eventually been found, long after the others, Newmans had felt wrong.

But now, looking back on her own situation during those long and gruelling months of working, as well as trying to keep things ticking over for Gill, she realised how lucky she had been. Matt had moved into Newmans with her and helped her without question, rarely moaning about the inconvenience, the miserable Christmas or the amount of time Rosie had to dedicate to helping her friends. She had Harry there with her, the stoic and elderly horse a grounding point amidst the chaos. Now she had neither of those anchors, she had lost Harry and she was losing Matt.

It was during their time living at Newmans that Rosie, spurred by curiosity rather than any need, had located her biological father and met him for the first time. She had only found out Jimmy was not her Dad by blood some six months prior, and the whole thing, coupled with the theft of the horses, had been enough for one person to handle alone.

Then, when she met her real father for the first time, he had behaved suspiciously when she mentioned the details of the stolen horses. She had followed him and overheard a conversation which had led to the discovery of Romeo and Monty at a sale, just miles from the cafe where she had found a short lived fondness for her new father.

He had only housed the horses for a short time he said, and was not involved in the actual theft. But he knew they were hot merchandise and rather than coming clean to Rosie that day, he had tried to cover his tracks. It had severed any ties they might have made, any bond they might have formed was lost before it had a chance. She made it clear he should not contact her again.

Rosie had retained her usual composure through the whole ordeal. Her strength saw her keeping everything together. She would not though, she mused as she led Red into the horse barn, have been able to deal with any of it if it had not been for Matt. Although she had not leaned on him, just having his presence and support had been enough. He saw her through all of that, why now could her husband not deal with her anxiety and depression? Why had his attitude to this situation been so different?

She guessed the difference had been her. Not once had she been weak. Where Eve was concerned, where life continued without Harry, she was weak. She had changed the dynamic of their relationship, and he had responded by changing it more.

Why couldn't he just love her through this, like he had loved her through that? Why was he being such a massive arsehole?

Red stopped abruptly. The horse rarely picked up the slack in his lead rope but he stood rigid in the walkway of the barn, refusing to pass the feed bins and raising his head up out of her reach.

'Come on boy?' Rosie spoke gently. It seemed every time she started to get wound up about Matt the horse disconnected from her.

She led him into a free stable and the horse moved away from her as soon as she released him, walking to the bars which divided him from Milly to sniff at the mare, who was eagerly waiting to meet the gelding.

She decided to fetch Peat as well and give the pony some time out of the sun in the cool barn, allowing herself time to calm down before she attempted a ride.

'Speeeeech!" called George.

The rest of the party guests joined in and before Jules could evade her entourage and make for the door, she found herself being ushered onto a chair to address them.

Tipsy, she struggled to clamber onto the furniture. She handed her wine glass to Rosie and took the offered hand of one of George's kitchen staff in order to balance.

She looked around. Her open plan living and dining room was filled with people. In the hours before the party had started, the heavens had opened and the rain still lashed against her brand new double glazing, rendering her painstakingly completed patio useless. She was touched by the turn out. Some of her things still smelled musty from the spell in storage but an overpowering smell of fresh paint was enough to mask it. Ziggy was still getting used to walking on the wooden floor, skidding about on the smooth surface when he got excited. She planned to buy rugs to cover the wood panelling in places for warmth, but decided to put this off until after the party, predicting a new rug would be just begging for a red wine spill.

'Thank you all for coming!' Jules cried and beamed, before trying to get back down.

'No no no!' Gill and George, who were stood arm in arm, both unusually hammered, heckled her until she stood back up on the chair. It was nice to see the couple enjoying themselves after the stresses of the last few months, their partnership stronger for the trauma, they needed to let their hair down.

'Well...' Jules looked around at the expectant faces staring up at her. 'I had not expected to have to say anything, so I am at a loss!'

'Thank people...' Hissed Marianne, thinking she was being subtle, but her whisper was loud enough to be heard by all.

'Yes!' Jules laughed, 'Thanks for that Mummy darling – just when you thought you were old enough to be buying a share in a racehorse training business and building your own house, your mother reminds you of your manners!'

Laughter erupted back at her from the room and increased her confidence.

'Thank you firstly, as she asked, to my mother and father for coming, and for the lovely banner...' Jules paused and squinted at the red and white lettering, 'which is slightly crooked...' Rosie howled with laughter at the joke no one else got, 'but is lovely. And thank you to Bloomswell for providing the amazing food – three cheers for the best restaurant in Stoke Rewe!'

'Hey – we are the only restaurant in Stoke Rewe!' The

sous-chef shouted, putting his hand on his hips and inciting a jeer from his colleagues. After the restaurant had closed, most of the staff, invited by George at Jules' request, had trekked along the lane to join the party.

'Thank you to the builders – Keith and his gang, without whom we would all be getting wet right now!' Jules saluted to Keith, who had surprised her by accepting her invitation, and brought three of his staff along with him. Keith raised his can at her and smiled, winking at her and making her blush.

'And as for the rest of you...well you didn't really do anything did you, but here you are eating and drinking at my expense!' Jules laughed and the room laughed along with her.

She glanced over to the corner of the room where she knew James was standing, wondering if he had been as impressed as she was by her ability to make her audience giggle.

'Please can I get down now?' Jules shrieked and didn't wait for the answer.

She took a deep breath and decided that before she could get embroiled in any other conversations, she should really go and speak to James and the handful of colleagues from Hodges who had come. They were huddled somewhat awkwardly together; she had only invited them so that she could invite James. She had been disappointed when he had arrived with Lisa, but supposed it was for the best.

As she made her way towards the group she could already hear the harsh upper class tones of Lisa's voice.

'Well, of course, James is bloody useless at DIY so we always have to get a man in to do anything.' Lisa rolled her eyes at James, who pursed his lips and nodded, shielding his own embarrassment by not arguing with his wife. 'We couldn't have a house this nice, two children and a useless husband, I could do with a man in full time!'

The others chuckled politely.

'Good evening!' Jules addressed James directly and reached forward to give him a hug, it would have seemed more weird not to.

'Hi Lisa, thanks for coming.' Jules placed a kiss on the taut cheek of the slight angular woman. She was tiny, making Jules feel even more wobbly and cumbersome than usual.

She made small talk with the others but couldn't help being aware of Lisa twittering at James, hissing at him that she was bored and wanted to go.

'Juliette darling, introduce me to these first class looking folk!' Marianne appeared behind her daughter, interrupting the conversation.

Jules dutifully introduced her colleagues, wincing as her mother made pointed eye contact with James, momentarily protective and fierce with one glance, before beaming and pointedly making conversation with Lisa, who revelled in a new audience to moan about the state of her house to.

'Are you going to give me the tour then?' James spoke softly to Jules, realising his wife was completely engaged in describing the hideousness of her kitchen, which by her own admission had been completely replaced not two years ago, but wasn't a patch on Jules'.

Jules nodded and headed back through the throng. She turned around when she reached the hallway and was gutted to see that it had been taken as an open invitation and her secretary and his partner had joined them.

'That's an impressive shower!' James opened the door of the walk in shower enthusiastically, 'Get two people in there no problem.' James' eyes twinkled and she blushed.

'It's lovely Jules.' Greg, her secretary, nodded and headed back out of the bathroom.

James momentarily blocked Jules' way and whispered in her ear.

'You look....edible.'

'James stop it!' Jules tried to shove him out the way, it was highly inappropriate, Gregg and Terry were just outside the door waiting to be shown the bedrooms - Lisa was but a room away.

She caught a whiff of James' breath and realised how drunk he was.

'You are plastered?' Jules furrowed her brow, he had seemed so normal stood with Lisa, as though moving away from her had animated him and allowed the alcohol to take effect.

'Only way to cope with the ice queen out there.' James' eyes lost their sparkle momentarily. 'On to the bedroom then!' he cried and put his hands on Jules' hips to steer her back into the hall, completely unnecessary, but it was at least a way to touch her, albeit for a few seconds.

By the time Jules had shown off her bedrooms and they made their way back to where Lisa and Marianne were still stood, James had composed himself somewhat, but only after staring longingly at Jules' new bed and almost falling over Ziggy.

Marianne's eyes had glazed over. She rushed forward towards her daughter in an attempt to escape Lisa, who was describing in detail how utterly dreadful it was that they had not had a family holiday since January.

'Darling, Rob has said we can go back with him to Bloomswell and sleep in his guest room. Apparently it's only just been re-decorated so he is delighted to have it tried out!'

'Oh no, you can't leave? You were going to sleep in the spare room here?' Jules pouted slightly.

'Your father looks shattered and this is going to go on for hours yet, Rob is ready to leave so we are going to walk back with

287

him.'

'Oh ok, if you guys want to go to bed now that makes sense.' Jules nodded and leaned in for an enveloping hug from her Mum. Marianne whispered, this time, thankfully, more successfully, into Jules ear as they embraced. 'That woman is dreadful, I can see why he wants to leave her.'

Jules drew back sharply. Since her conversation with her mother about James, where she had been told in no uncertain terms to back off and get over him, Jules had tried very hard to do just that. Why would her mother make a comment that was so laced?

Marianne drew her daughter in again. 'You still can't though Jules.'

That was more like it. Marianne resumed her usual volume.

'Right then! We must away! We will be back in the morning to help you clean up and then we can go out for breakfast?'

Jules nodded and thanked her parents, kissing her dear patient Dad's cheek and seeing his eyes shine with pride at her.

Jules turned back to Lisa and James, about to resume small talk again, but Abbey and Rachel accosted and kidnapped her, saying it was tequila time.

Jules waved an apology but allowed herself to be dragged away, seeing that already Lisa had started twittering at James about leaving again anyway.

Chapter Fifteen

'So, how was the show?!' Rosie squeezed herself onto the sofa next to Kelly, topping up their cider glasses. She felt strangely ok about being at the party without Matt, she had been able to mingle without worrying about whether her husband was bored.

'3rd in the dressage, he was a little star, considering we hadn't really done any schooling for it.' Kelly's eyes shone at the memory of the floating Arabian stallion beneath her. 'And he won the ridden Arab class! I didn't bother with the in hand Arab class..'

'She couldn't bring herself to get off him for that long!' Gill chimed in, leaving George to a conversation with his sous-chef about a new cheesecake which involved a crème brulee style topping, and joining her friends.

Kelly giggled. 'I couldn't. He looked so stunning, no one could keep their eyes off him. Winning his class was the icing on the cake, just riding him around the show ground was magic enough!' Kelly bit her lip to stop her inane grin, 'Cor that cider has gone right through me! Off to try out the new loo!'

'How is she holding up?' Rosie asked Gill once Kelly was out of earshot.

'She really enjoyed today...' Gill's face fell, 'She doesn't want to go, and I don't want her to go. I am trying not to make it worse for her, I understand she feels she has to do this for her Mum, but I honestly don't know what I will do without her. I can't even try and get her replacement sorted and trained up now because I don't want to upset her.'

'What are you going to do?'

'Well she doesn't leave until September, I guess Jules and I will have to advertise nearer the time.'

'It's crap isn't it.'

'Yes. Very. Speaking of crap, how has your week been?'

'Not too crap actually.' Rosie smiled at Gill to show her sincerity, 'Matt and I haven't spoken, and I only saw him briefly last night. But I had a good week, rode lots, and Dad and I took Eve to the Country Living Park near Darmouth on Wednesday and had a lovely time.'

'Really?'

'Yeah – she was so sweet. She squealed when she saw the deer, really mesmerised by them and not a bit frightened, even though they were massive!'

'Well that sounds positive!'

'She's really starting to get animated now, and she laughs like an old fishwife, cackles from her belly, you can't help but laugh with her.'

Gill watched Rosie's face and eyes, her friend seemed genuinely taken with her baby at last. There would be a long way to go still of course, but she hoped her friend would eventually find the delight she had found in Charlie as a little girl.

'They look happy.' Rosie caught Gill's gaze and followed it to where Charlie was stood with Darran. The couple had their arms around one another and were talking with their faces almost touching. Charlie tipped her head back and laughed and Darran took the opportunity to burrow his face into her neck, his beard tickling her and making her laugh even harder.

'They seem to have come through it ok.' Gill nodded. 'Still not sure what is going to happen when Charlie goes off to Bristol in September. But for now at least, she seems to have got over her ordeal and is happy enough. I just hope she doesn't change her mind about university.'

'Oh I don't think she will Gill, 'she worked hard enough to get accepted and she is driven by her head.'

'I hope so.' Gill sighed as she continued to watch her daughter, who appeared to Gill to be so in love it would have taken a crow bar to prize her away.

'So, Kelly off to Oz and Charlie off to Uni – September is going to be an emotional month?'

'Yep. Losing both my girls at once.'

Abbey and Rachel coerced some of the restaurant staff to join in their drinking game and, having been force fed three shots of tequila, Jules took the opportunity to retreat. She excused herself to take Ziggy through the door into Newmans, thinking the level of intoxication and resultant noise was probably getting too much for the dog. As she settled him in his bed which she had dragged into the Newmans' living room earlier, she chatted to her animal about how pleased she was with the turnout.

She heard the kitchen door open.

'Why do you always have to show me up?'

'How have I shown you up?' Jules recognised James' voice. The couple had let themselves in to the Newmans kitchen to retrieve their coats from the counter. Jules hesitated, embarrassed at eaves dropping, but she was hidden from view on the floor with Ziggy so she decided to stay where she was until they had gone.

'You are drunk!' Lisa growled.

'We agreed you would drive and I am hardly falling over spewing on the floor.' James voice sounded dull and unemotional, so used to defending himself he barely put effort into it.

'I didn't even want to come to this fucking party.'

291

'Why did you then? I said I would come on my own.'

'Oh that's nice isn't it? You don't even want me here!'

'Not really. You spent all evening moaning about me to anyone who would listen.'

'If you were even half a man I wouldn't have to moan about you.' Lisa's voice was low and feral. Jules winced.

'Maybe if your heart wasn't as cold as the driven snow the other half of me would want to be here?' James immediately wished he had simply apologised like he usually did, but something about being at Jules', a woman who respected him for who he was, made him defend himself.

'You are the worst husband in the world! You fucking useless twat.' Lisa exploded, raising her voice so loud Ziggy barked.

The couple fell silent and Jules froze.

'What was that?' Lisa snapped.

'A dog. You were so shrill he thought you were communicating with him.' James said, irritating her more.

'Can we please fucking GO NOW!'

'Yes, just as soon as I find Jules to say goodbye.'

'She is probably helping herself to more cake somewhere, can't we just go?'

'Why are you such a bitch?' James sounded angry.

'Well you would think she would be thinner, having horses and riding. That blouse is barely covering her breasts.'

Jules looked down at her top. Yes she was buxom, she wasn't built like Lisa, she would never be a skinny woman, she had accepted that a long time ago. She still felt sick.

'At least she enjoys life.' James spat the words which were not enough, but he didn't dare get too defensive in case Lisa picked up on his affection for Jules.

'Yes and I would enjoy life if I had a brand new house

and a disposable income and didn't have to put up with you.'

Jules heard coats being dragged from the counter and waited until the door back through to her place had closed behind them before she exhaled. James wasn't joking when he said there was no love left between them.

Jules heard the door opening again and stiffened, Ziggy barked, giving their location away.

'There you are!'

She smiled to see Keith.

He walked over to sit on the floor with her. He petted Ziggy for a while without speaking. She glanced across at his handsome face and recklessly made eyes at him.

When he turned towards her and placed his hand on her cheek, told her she was beautiful and leaned in, she found herself kissing him back, desperate to remove James and Lisa from her head.

Jules stumbled towards the coffee machine. Bleary eyed she cleared the debris of half empty plastic glasses, paper plates and a half eaten piece of cake out of the way, to spoon beans into the machine.

She moved across the kitchen away from the grinding noise and noticed Charlie and Darran entwined and asleep on the sofa.

'Morning darling! The clean-up party has arrived!' Marianne burst in through the kitchen door, followed by Martin who was carrying black bin bags and a mop.

'Shhhhh....' Jules put her finger to her lips in an attempt to turn her mother down, not just because of the sleeping couple in the living area, but for the sake of her own pounding head.

'Few too many was it poppet?' Martin laughed, whispering to his dishevelled daughter.

Jules froze when she heard the toilet being flushed and saw the bathroom door opening through the hall. She wondered if she could make a dash to close the door but it was too late, Keith's lofty height towered in the door way. He was dressed, which was something, but he was carrying his shoes.

'Well good morning!' Marianne announced triumphantly, her words were aimed at Keith but her eyes darted at Jules.

Jules flushed to her core and was aware of her face burning red.

'Hey.' Keith looked mildly embarrassed. Clocking Jules' beetroot complexion deciding he had better scarper.

'Thanks for a lovely evening Jules, I'll call you?'

'Ok.' Jules muttered and turned back to the coffee machine. She heard the kitchen door open and her mother and father saying polite goodbyes. She poured herself a coffee but didn't turn around, sipping the hot liquid black so that she didn't have to pass her parents to get to the fridge.

'Have fun then did we darling?!' Her mother's voice oozing with anticipation.

'Leave her alone Marianne.' Martin chided gently, not wanting to embarrass Jules, or himself.

Jules sighed and turned around, deciding the coffee was too bitter anyway.

'Yes I screwed the builder. Yes, unfortunately you arrived before he left. Can we not talk about it?'

Jules witnessed her Dad's discomfort at her use of the adjective screwed and winced as she passed him.

'Ok darling, if that's what you want!' Marianne laughed, knowing she would extract the details at some point.

Rosie pulled her horsebox onto the hard standing at the gateway and jumped from the cab.

As she unclipped the ramp and lowered it, Peat let out a shrill whinny.

She untied Red, thinking she would let him go straight into the field and then lead Peat back to his paddock.

As she walked carefully beside her horse, allowing him to slowly make his way to solid ground, she noticed Matt stood at the gate.

'Can you shut that?' She called without making eye contact. She had said she would be back at midday, it was almost 6 pm. She had been unable to resist Jules' suggestion that they hack Romeo and Red out together. It had been a sedate ride due to their swollen heads, and it had taken them two hours to do the Shillerton estate block.

Matt obliged and she started to take Red's headcollar off. Sensing her tension, he flung himself away from her, eager to be released into his field. She struggled to unfasten the catch and the horse trotted off as soon as he was free.

'You are back late.' Matt said, a pointless statement, but for the effect of making her feel guilty.

'Rode out with Jules.' Rosie muttered as she re-mounted the ramp to fetch an impatient Peat.

'I might head back tonight.' Matt said as she reappeared with the pony. He had shut the gate with himself on the outside, meaning she had to lead Peat towards him in order to speak to him.

'Ok.' Rosie nodded.

'Makes sense not to have to get up at 4am.'

'Yes.'

Rosie nodded again and then turned to lead Peat back to his paddock.

'Rosie wait.' Matt called, obviously not thinking the

conversation was over.

'What.' She stopped without turning around.

'Are we ever going to talk about this?' Matt's voice softened slightly and hesitated.

'What is there to talk about?'

'You, me, Eve, when we are going to put this place on the market?'

'Do whatever you like.'

'But Rosie we need to tell Jimmy and Crystal what's going on before they buy a house here? We need to arrange livery for Red and...' Matt trailed off, sick of talking to her back.

She turned around, flabbergasted by his statement about Red.

'What do you mean find livery?'

'For when you and Eve come to Oxford!' Matt was irritated by her lack of interest in her own life.

'You still think I am moving to Oxford?'

'Well, yes, obviously. That's what we talked about.'

'And you didn't think to check that with me, while you have been busy avoiding me for the last month?'

'So you are not moving to Oxford?'

'No.'

'So you want to split up instead?'

'I thought we already had.' Rosie eyed her husband, dead pan.

'Well. Thanks for telling me.' Matt looked genuinely distraught. Rosie couldn't believe his reaction.

'What were you thinking then? All these weekends of sleeping on the sofa, ignoring me and taking Eve off by yourself?'

'I was giving you space to come to terms with it.'

'Well you gave me too much.' Rosie turned around and started leading Peat towards his paddock. She didn't look back.

By the time Rosie had finished cleaning out the horsebox and unpacking her tack, and had fed and settled the horses for the night, she expected Matt to have left.

'Oh god.' She muttered to herself as she saw his car still in the car port. She kicked off her boots and wrestled her overnight bag through the kitchen door.

Matt, Jimmy and Crystal were sat around the table. Crystal leapt up to make Rosie a cup of tea but Rosie waved her away from the kettle.

'What's going on?'

Matt leaned back, looking at his lap.

'Matt's just told us what's going on between you too.' Jimmy looked up at his daughter, disappointment clear in his eyes.

'Oh has he.' Rosie drew a chair back noisily and sat down next to Crystal who was trying to look supportive but was clearly uncomfortable.

'I think it's best if Crystal and I go back to London for a bit, give you two some space to sort things out.' Jimmy's expression remained stern.

'But what about Eve?' Rosie's jaw clenched tight as the adrenaline fired up inside her, her sweat glands opening in readiness.

'Well, you seem much better with her now Rosie, and you and Matt clearly need some time.'

'But what about during the week? What am I supposed to do?' Rosie's voice strained against the tension in her neck, she couldn't believe this was happening.

'I am sure you will be ok. I hadn't realised we were making things worse.' Jimmy softened slightly, but couldn't relent to his daughter, she had not been honest with him and there was a price for that.

'You aren't! You guys are the reason I haven't fallen apart.'

Jimmy stood up. Crystal looked hesitant but stayed sat, clearly not agreeing with his decision.

'We will head off tomorrow. Come on Crystal, we ought to start packing.'

'Dad no!' Rosie cried but her heavy heart locked her into the chair, the fear rooting her to the spot.

Jimmy and Crystal left the room and Matt looked up at her, his face a mixture of smug and guilty.

'I hate you.' Rosie spat at him.

'It had to happen.'

'No it didn't. You weren't getting your own way so you have given them their marching orders.'

'You have been getting your way for too long. It's time we faced up to this, just us, like it used to be.'

'Faced up to this? Have you forgotten you will be buggering off for five days in a minute?'

'No.' Matt stood up. 'I'm going to pack.'

Rosie watched him leave the room. The blackness shrouded her. She was back where she started, alone with a baby all week, no support, no freedom. Only this time it was worse because Jimmy was disappointed in her. It couldn't physically have got any worse.

Jules was pleased when everyone finally left.

She closed the door after her parents and sighed in relief. Abbey and Rachel had emerged from the spare room at lunchtime, when Marianne had successfully organised, over seen and completed the clean-up operation. The house now looked as though the party had never happened.

Charlie and Darran had mooched back through the door to Newmans soon after Marianne started hoovering around them. Abbey and Rachel accepted Marianne's offer of lunch and although it was lovely to spend some time catching up, she was anxious to get riding and was glad when Rosie had appeared.

Marianne and Martin had been asleep on the sofa when she returned.

Finally at 7pm when Juliette had suggested they make the journey back to Gloucestershire in daylight, her mother had taken the hint.

Jules ruffled Ziggy's head and the dog padded after her to her bedroom. She stood where James had stood the night before, trying to feel close to him, and trying not to look at the bed, where she had engaged in fumbling drunken sex with someone else.

She decided to change the sheets.

Keith had sent her two text messages since the morning. The first stated how much he had enjoyed the evening and asked what she was doing later. The second enquired as to whether she had received the first.

She felt bad for ignoring him.

It wasn't that she didn't like Keith, it was that she had given in and gone along with something her heart wasn't quite behind. She was an adult, she was single, she could sleep with whoever she liked, in theory.

She wondered how James would feel about it.

'This is ridiculous.' She told Ziggy and headed back to the kitchen counter to fetch her mobile.

She tapped out a reply.

Bit knackered (and still feeling a bit shit!), how about one night in the week?

299

There.

'Oh James.' she wailed and strode over to the sofa where she collapsed. Ziggy got up beside her and flopped onto her lap. The dog sighed as he relaxed.

'Oh Ziggy.'

Rosie left the cottage as quietly as she could. She put her holdall down on the doormat and eased the heavy wooden door closed behind her. She tiptoed barefoot around the outside of the house to the boot store by the kitchen door. The ground was still damp from Saturday's downpour and she eased her soggy feet thankfully into dry boots before setting off towards the field.

She called Red softly and gave him a small breakfast. She had to give Peat a handful of chaff to stop him whinnying. While the horses digested she ferried Red's things to the horsebox.

She bit her lip as she looked at Peat. He had dozed off in his paddock and had no idea his world was about to be turned upside down. She hated the idea of moving a horse, changing its routine. But she couldn't leave the pony on his own, he would scream the place down once she led Red away from him. She couldn't take him because he didn't belong to her.

She was relieved she had left the horsebox in the entrance of the field. The car port was right next to the bedroom where Jimmy and Crystal slept and starting the engine at 4am would surely have woken them.

She felt a pang of regret as she thought about Eve.

She had spent almost an hour of her sleepless night in the baby's room, sat beside the cot.

She had not been able to explain anything to her daughter, not because she wouldn't understand, but because Rosie didn't really have an explanation. She had simply gazed at her, hoping she would somehow sense the love that flowed quietly.

But love wasn't enough to stop her from packing.

Eve would be safe, she comforted herself in the knowledge that if she couldn't have been sure of that, she wouldn't have been going.

The horses loaded without incident and she kept the revs low, creeping the box along the lane past the house.

By the time she had travelled the few miles to Sue's it was properly light and the clock on the dash read 5:30. Still early, but not ridiculous for a horse person. She hoped Sue would already be up.

She pulled the box into Sue's small yard and called softly to the horses that she wouldn't be long.

She trotted up to the front door. When she knocked Sue's pack sounded the alarm with a chorus of barking. But there was no other movement. She looked over at the empty concrete area to the side of the house where Sue's land rover and trailer were usually parked.

'Shit.' She said out loud. Sue must have set off early to deliver a pony.

She stood on the doorstep, not sure what to do.

She noticed one of the stable doors in the yard was open and trotted over to look inside. There was a clean bed and she scooped out a handful of water from the automatic drinker to confirm it was working.

Red screamed as she unloaded Peat.

She led the pony to the stable and shut him in before running back to the box to grab a few sections of hay from the bale she had brought for Red, not wanting to leave him with nothing in case Sue was going to be gone for a while.

The pony called and Red answered as she ran back to the

301

box. Her last image of the small black pony was his little face peering over the stable door, eyes white, nostrils flared and ears pricked towards them, not understanding why he was being left.

She reversed out of the yard and set off on the road to Honiton. She could still hear Red's whinnies over the engine noise, could see him kicking out in frustration and fear in the small CCTV screen on the dashboard.

As she drove resolutely on, tears slid from her eyes.

She would need to call Sue later. Try and explain.

She knew when they woke up Jimmy and Crystal would be upset and perhaps even angry that she had left, but she also knew they would stay for Eve. She knew Jules and Gill would be miffed that she hadn't gone to Newmans.

In truth she was ashamed, too ashamed to admit what she was doing. She couldn't take Red to her Mother's anyway, although she had considered Selina as a bolt hole, given their recent closeness over the internet.

Instead she was heading for a complete stranger. One who had no investment in her.

She reached awkwardly into the back pocket of her jeans and slid out the card Kev had given her.

She hoped Dan the Horseman wouldn't mind an unexpected guest.

'Drink?'

Jules looked up to see James in the doorway of her office, his face a beacon to guide her back from the storm around her. It had been such a shitty day.

It had started with a case conference with the barrister she had regretfully instructed for a case which was going to the Court of Appeal next week. Her client had lost in the High court and she had managed to successfully apply to appeal on the basis that the judge had not interpreted the legislation correctly. The pressure was on. Having been granted the appeal, Jules had to make it count, not just for her client, who was undoubtedly losing sleep, but also for the firm, whose reputation could be at stake if she didn't pull it off.

She had hired a London barrister with a reputation for succeeding in complex copyright cases. What his reputation hadn't told her was that he was condescending, masochistic and ignored Jules repeatedly during their video call, preferring the sound of his own voice and his own ideas on winning the case. She had bothered to research and understand the intricate products her client was claiming had been unlawfully copied by another engineering firm, but the barrister didn't think it was relevant.

Frustrated and worried, Jules had spoken to David straight after the conference had ended. He had been of the opinion that, although the barrister might be difficult, he was the best at what he did, so Jules would have to keep him.

Then she had received a worrying telephone call from Jimmy. Her friend's father had not gone into much detail, but it sounded like Rosie had taken off with Red after she and Matt had an argument.

Jules wasn't surprised particularly, but she was concerned for her friend and hoped she would be in touch.

The afternoon had brought an angry call from an ex-client, one she terminated her relationship with in accordance with company policy for non-payment of bills. She also had three new cases on the go and another local county court case to prepare for, which had annoyingly fallen the day before the Court of Appeal case.

'Yes.' She nodded at James and his face lit up.

It was 7pm, she had probably lost her window to ride,

she had already called Maurice to let him know she would be late collecting Ziggy, and a few hours with James sounded like a good call.

She had tentatively agreed to a date with Keith on Wednesday evening, and apart from James' drunken comments at the party, their friendship had remained platonic for some months, so she didn't need to feel guilty. That was what she told herself anyway.

They drove in convoy to a small pub in a quiet village just outside of town, at James' suggestion. It was somewhere neither of them knew very well, and neither had friends who lived in the area, so it seemed like as good a place as any for some peace and quiet.

'Lemonade please.' Jules said as she slid her suited bottom carefully across the worn and slightly tatty looking bench seat by the window.

'Diet or normal.'

'Normal please. Technically of course I can't afford the calories but I will take calories over artificial sweeteners any day.'

James put his hands on his hips and shook his head.

'What are you on about? – Can't afford the calories, tut tut.'

'Get the drinks and I will explain.'

It was almost eleven by the time Jules collected Ziggy. After she had admitted to James she had overheard his argument with Lisa, he had been angry at his wife all over again. Jules insisted it was ok and really not a problem, what concerned her more was how awful things seemed for James.

He had been adamant that what she had heard was normal. The constant moaning about him to anyone who would listen was also normal. Jules had a snapshot into life as he knew it.

Jules expressed deep sympathy for James, genuinely sorry for him that his marriage had become so dire.

James had then requested a change of subject, saying he didn't want to waste his time with Jules. Jules had agreed at the time and they had chatted about anything and everything, in their usual easy way. After her crap day, it was like therapy.

It was only now, as she drove through darkening lanes towards home, that she thought again about Lisa.

She felt partly responsible, because she had insisted James try harder to make his marriage work. Unfortunately, it now seemed in not wanting to be responsible for his marriage ending, she had become responsible for his prolonged misery.

Jules let herself in through her kitchen door, wondering whether she should bother Gill. She would normally always have greeted her naturally after a late work finish, because they were in the same house, but now she wasn't sure whether to use the connecting door.

She need not have wondered.

Gill popped her head around the door and grinned at Jules.

'Hello in here!'

'Hello from in there!' Jules laughed.

'Good day?' Gill perched on the kitchen counter and agreed to Jules offer of tea.

'No, crap. Did Rosie's Dad call you?'

'Yeah.'

'Have you heard from her?'

'No. You?'

'Nope. I really hope she is ok?'

Jules waited for the kettle to boil and reached into her

jacket pocket to check her phone again in case Rosie had called or texted.

'I think she has probably just done what she felt she needed to do.' Gill crossed her legs and accidentally turned the dishwasher on. Jules switched the machine back off again, wishing Gill would get off her new worktop.

'You know what Rosie is like,' Gill continued, 'she was only going to put up with the situation with Matt for so long. She probably has a plan. She will get in touch when she is ready.'

'Hope you're right.' Jules handed Gill a mug and thankfully kicked off her high heels, which had been on since 8am. 'I hate to think of her dealing with this alone. She and Matt always seemed so solid.'

'They might be again.' Gill smiled encouragingly, wondering why it bothered Jules so much if Rosie stayed with Matt or not. 'I thought things were over between me and George and it all worked out.'

Jules sipped her tea and nodded.

She feared that for Lisa and James, the point of no return was long passed.

And where, she wondered, did that leave her? Whether it directly involved her or not, she sensed there was considerable discomfort to come for James.

Chapter Sixteen

'Look after her won't you?'

The man smiled as he eased himself into the driver's seat of the big black car, leaving George to count his cash.

Gill stood behind George and laid her hands around his waist.

'You didn't need to do this love. We haven't even heard from the woman since we sent the letter?'

'I know. But now the boiler has packed in at number 33 and I don't like the feeling of having nothing in the bank. It's not just the threat of being sued, I need to be prepared for things happening. If it means I have to use the Landover for a bit it's not the end of the world?'

Gill nodded into his back. He was so brave and sensible.

The house he let in the village was not a great source of income, but it was an investment. The rent he received from the couple who let it only just covered the mortgage, and in the week they had called to say the hot water had failed again. At least he could offset some tax for the new boiler.

That same evening he had a call about the Lexus and decided it was fate. After one test drive the man was prepared to pay the asking price.

Gill rarely used the Landover anyway, preferring the two horse box. Even if she was travelling without horses, it was usually to pick up something sizeable for the yard anyway. The Land Rover didn't get much use and as George had pointed out the evening before, when Gill had tried to persuade him not to sell the car he had worked so hard for and loved so much, he lived within a minute's walking distance of his business and the Lexus wasn't really getting used enough to justify sitting on the capital it represented.

'Right. Better get off to work.'

Gill smiled up at him as he turned around and kissed her forehead.

'Will I see you at 4?'

'Yep, will pop home for a snooze, tonight is going to be busy.'

'I will make sure I am here.'

George nodded and Gill watched him walk away down the lane, vowing that one day he would have a nice car again.

It was a Saturday with no races and although that meant a quiet day for Gill, it was still the busiest day of the week at the restaurant.

Gill kicked at the stones which ended up onto the tarmac of the drive when the feed merchant had misjudged the corner, scooting them back into the drainage valley.

'Do you want me to get you a shovel?' Kelly's laughter made Gill jump.

'What are you doing here, it's your day off!?' Gill ran at Kelly and pretended to aim a kick at her Jodhpur clad legs.

'Get off you mad person!' Kelly laughed as she ran away from her boss.

'Seriously – why are you here?' Gill demanded, terminally concerned that, even though she never asked Kelly to put in any extra hours, Kelly always seemed to.

'Actually – stroppy knickers – I am giving Carol a lesson and then I said I would hack out on Pickle with Leena because he's been spooky lately and she wants some help.'

'Oh...' Gill stood corrected. 'Alright then.'

It should have dawned on her that Kelly's plan for her

free day would still have involved horses.

'But that should only take until lunchtime and then I thought I would help you out by riding Monty!' Kelly cried as she ran madly away from Gill before her employer could throttle her.

The liveries had started to arrive for their Saturday morning hack. Now that the evenings were so much lighter, a few of them had taken to hacking out in the week after work as well and because their horses were fitter as a result, their Saturday rides were longer.

Gill wanted to do some gentle halter practice with Teddy and bring Amber in for a groom and a pamper, but she decided to wait until the bustle had died down. She preferred to leave the liveries to it when they arrived on mass.

Kelly caught up with Gill on her way to turn Zinee out in the stallion enclosure. The horse could have some paddock time and it would free up another stable.

'Any word from Rosie?'

'Not personally. Although apparently she did text Jimmy on Wednesday to say she was fine and not to worry.'

Kelly frowned sympathetically, easier said than done.

'Jimmy has been calling every day to see if she has been in touch. I don't think she wants to be found, she will only have text him to stop it becoming a missing person hunt.'

'I don't understand why she didn't come here? I mean, if things had got so bad with Matt she needed to get away, why go off alone?'

Gill released Zinee and he immediately started to graze. The horse had still not had his first run. After his enforced rest while she convalesced from her fall, the horse had lost muscle and condition quickly, becoming puffed out just from hacking and seeming unbalanced. She had agreed with Norah that they would build him back up to peak fitness gradually. Given his age and the changes his body was likely going through, Gill had been adamant they had to take it easy with him and thankfully, Norah had been in total agreement. During the same conversation she had congratulated Gill on managing to coax a win out of Pop, and seemed pleased with Monty's continued success, which helped take the pressure off the youngster.

'I think that if Rosie doesn't want to be found, it makes sense that she would go somewhere else.'

Kelly nodded.

'I mean, if she came here, Matt and Jimmy would know where she was. I wish she would get in touch – but I can't help thinking she knows what she is doing.'

'You mean you trust that because it's Rosie, she is probably ok?'

Gill nodded and sighed.

'I flipping hope so.'

Jules was less philosophical about her friend's disappearance.

She scoured the Facebook pages of various horsey establishments, knowing it was a long shot, but hoping that her friend would appear in a photo, heralded as a new arrival at a yard somewhere, Red standing proudly beside her.

But the pages brought forth only unfamiliar horses, memes and adverts.

It was her big Court case on Tuesday. She had very little to do now that the barrister had been briefed.

She sat back from her laptop, which she had on the dining table in front of her and decided she should probably ride Romeo. She had managed to ride at lunchtime on Wednesday because she had worked from home, so her date with Keith in the evening hadn't stopped her from getting her horse out. Then on

Thursday, a late finish due to a second case conference with the barrister had seen her agreeing to go back to the same strange little pub with James afterwards.

Yesterday, despite working at home again, she had not given herself enough of a window to ride. She knew Romeo's feet could become quickly less dynamic with a lack of work and getting him out had to take priority over scouring the internet for a friend that clearly didn't want to be found, or indeed, spending evenings with a married man. She could of course have taken the horse off grass to make up for her lack of a daily hack, but she hated to see him bored and picking at a haynet in the sandschool, much preferred to work him enough that she felt he could still live out. His paddock was pretty sparse now, but it didn't stop her feeling guilty.

Keith had offered to cook for her at his place that evening. She still hadn't confirmed.

She had a fairly nice time with him on Wednesday. They had eaten Mexican at a new place in Exeter and there was no shortage of conversation. They had talked about their travels, about Keith's new project to demolish a former farmhouse and erect a new state of the art eco-build. He had been working with the architect and seemed so animated when he talked about the plans, she couldn't help but be interested.

Thursday with James however, a snatched few hours huddled in a time warped pub, had been in a different league. Their conversation danced, words and ideas intertwining in harmony. His eyes saw into her, extracted the best of her, without leaving her short.

He had listened to her fears about Rosie, the frustration of not having heard from her friend, and understood.

If she gave in and agreed to go to Keith's, sex was inevitably on the cards. There was an assumption that she would be staying

311

over.

It wasn't that she didn't fancy him, it was just that against the force of the wanton desperation she felt for James, her feelings for Keith were not measurable. She would quite happily have spent an evening in his pleasant company and then gone home to her own bed for a family sized bar of chocolate and a good book, with Ziggy nestled in beside her.

She looked down at Ziggy who had stretched out on the kitchen floor tiles, positioned in the shade. If she left it much longer it would be too hot to go out, knowing how stifling it would become once the sun had reached its apex.

The dog looked up at her sharply, letting out a yelp of excitement. He always knew when a ride was coming, even before she had made any movement towards going.

'If I go tonight you will have to stay with Auntie Gillian?' She said to the dog, asking him if it was ok for her to stay away.

But Ziggy was already pacing by the door. Even if he could have understood her words, which she often felt he did, his concern was with the present, the imminent opportunity to run along sun bathed lanes and sniff and wee and find new sticks to carry proudly home.

She decided to take her lead from her animal and stop torturing herself with unanswerable questions about Rosie, Keith and James.

'Come on then dog.' She laughed as she shut her laptop and Ziggy barked at her to hurry up.

Jules pulled at her short skirt, wishing she had worn jeans.

She had blushed uncontrollably when Keith had shown her in to his modestly furnished but large apartment, and seen how much effort he had gone to. His small dining table was beautifully dressed, with fresh flowers and a white table cloth. He opened an expensive looking bottle of white wine and poured her a glass before placing it in the cooler he said he had bought especially for the occasion.

As she sat waiting for him to re-appear from the kitchen, she heard her mobile buzz from her handbag where he had placed it carefully for her on the sofa. She said a little prayer before she unlocked the screen that the text would be from Rosie.

It was from James.

I'm ironing. How is that for Saturday night living? Hope you are having a wholly more exciting evening..

Jules laughed and tapped out a hasty reply, feeling it would be rude to be caught texting when Keith came in with the food.

I'm on a date. Would rather be in slippers in front of the telly. Don't forget to starch those collars!

She stuffed her phone back into the ridiculously small clutch bag she had decided was more fitting for a date than her usual shoulder bag, but now regretted bringing, because it was so impractical. She managed to get herself sat back at the table before Keith came in with the plates.

'Afraid the table is more impressive than the meal. Hope you like slightly over done pasta.'

'It's my favourite!' Jules smiled generously and picked up her fork to show willing.

'So, Juliette, tell me about your day?'

By the time the meal was over and they had retired to the sofa Jules had drunk enough not to mind how the evening ended. She scowled at her bag, which had ended up on the floor. James had still not replied.

It shouldn't have bothered her that he hadn't texted her back, but it did. When Keith had been fetching the pudding, thankfully a shop bought chocolate gateaux, she had dashed over to check her phone but knew really, because it hadn't made a noise, that there was no text.

Keith sidled a little closer to her and she froze. The obviousness of his advance, coupled with her nerves at the prospect of things getting sexual, made her erupt in high pitched laughter.

Keith groaned and leaned back again.

'Give a bloke a chance!'

'Sorry, do it again.'

He leaned in towards her and she rose up from her slumped position to kiss him.

It felt nice.

Nice, Jules thought.

Just as she had started to genuinely get into Keith, feeling a warm surge through her as he firmly but gently caressed her large breasts, marvelling at their size in a flattering and not overly creepy way, her phone buzzed.

Great timing, she thought.

She wriggled apologetically away from Keith to read her text. James still hadn't replied, but finally, thank god, Rosie had.

'Oh lighten up Mother, it's only a car.'

Charlie rolled her eyes and demanded a subject change. Gill had been going on about the Lexus and how awful she felt for George ever since her daughter had arrived.

They sat at the kitchen counter eating pizza. It was Charlie's choice of takeaway but Gill was tucking into the fast food greedily. Ziggy sat patiently on the floor beside her stool hoping for a crust, but Gill guiltily ignored the dog's quiet persistence.

'Don't tell George how much I enjoyed this.'

'You have barbecue sauce on your chin.' Charlie shook her head, reaching for a piece of kitchen roll.

Darran's band had a gig in Plymouth and Charlie hadn't fancied squashing into the cab of the van with four men in order to stand around on her own all evening, so had called her Mother.

With George working and Jules out for the night, Gill invited her round without hesitation.

Gill had mentioned the boiler at George's rental house, and the sale of the Lexus, but decided not to tell Charlie about the problems at the restaurant. Gill had, however, confided in her daughter about Rosie having gone and about Kelly's imminent departure.

Charlie had brushed aside concerns about Rosie, even more resolute than Gill that if anyone needed a break and could be trusted not to get herself into trouble, it was Rosie. She had been in touch with Jimmy to confirm she was safe and not to worry, so maybe it was all right not to worry.

Kelly leaving however, was an altogether more serious issue.

'So she wasn't going to go, but then her Mum guilt tripped her into it?' Charlie summed up Gill's explanation and pushed her plate away from her, rubbing her stomach and letting out a loud belch.

'Lovely.' Gill tutted, reaching over to snatch up the half eaten piece of pizza which had beaten her daughter. 'Well, you have over simplified that a bit. There is more to it.'

'I don't think so. Kelly should be able to make her own decisions, not have to move half way around the world to hold her mother's hand.'

315

Gill was touched by Charlie's defence of Kelly, her concern for the loss Newmans would suffer. She had half expected Charlie to be pleased Kelly was going, because of how close Gill was to her, but she realised as they talked, she needed to give her daughter more credit for the adult she had become.

'I wouldn't have done it for you.'

'Oh thanks.' Gill cried and laughed.

'Seriously, if you wanted to move to another country now, I would support you and wish you well but I wouldn't give up my life to go with you.'

'And I wouldn't expect you to.' Gill nodded, knowing that she would always put Charlie first. 'But we mustn't judge, Charlie. It was not so long ago you would have been coming with me wherever I went because I was responsible for your wellbeing, I guess Kelly's Mum is having trouble letting Kelly go.'

'Speaking of letting go, has Dad called you?'

'No, why?'

'He keeps sending me texts, pretending they are from my bedroom, saying it's lonely. I figured it would only be a matter of time before he called you to whine about me not being there.'

'He's not been in touch. Why is your bedroom lonely?'

'I mostly stay at Darran's at the moment.' Charlie looked slightly sheepish, but had timed her announcement beautifully, having just encouraged her mother to talk about independence.

'You have moved in with him?' Gill wiped her mouth and tried to swallow quietly over the lump that had formed in her throat.

'Not like officially or anything...but I pretty much sleep there all the time.'

'Pretty much?'

'Yeah ok. I can't remember the last time I stayed at Dads.'

'How are you affording things?'

'I have been helping Darran to promote the band and organise their gigs, so I get a cut of whatever they make.'

Gill couldn't help but laugh, her daughter was nothing if not industrious.

'And what about Bristol?'

'What about Bristol?' Charlie teased, pretending to be confused.

'You know what about bloody Bristol Charlie.' Gill's tone changed, her daughter had been through a massive ordeal to ensure that she could follow her ambitions, if she was going to throw away that opportunity to live in a bedsit and make posters, Gill was certainly going to have something to say about it.

'Well actually, we have a new plan, and it's one I think you would...' Charlie trailed off as the kitchen door flew open and George stormed in, clearly furious, flushed and shaking.

'George what is it?' Gill slipped what remained of Charlie's slice of pizza as she stood up.

'That fucking woman.' George roared, uncharacteristically loud.

'What is it, what's happened?' Gill demanded, but George paced around the kitchen counter, clearly too wound up to explain himself.

'I had better be going, it's really late.' Charlie stood up, sensing George's silence was to do with her presence.

'Our conversation is not over.' Gill warned as Charlie gathered up her things.

'I know Mum.' Charlie kissed her mother's cheek and smiled reassuringly. 'Call me tomorrow.'

'I will.' Gill stated, wishing her daughter wasn't going, but George looked like a wild animal, ferocity like a poisonous gas, polluting the air around him.

Gill closed the door after Charlie and turned her

attention on George.

'Tell me what happened?'

'I am sorry I ruined your evening.'

'Never mind,' Gill said soothingly, 'what happened?'

George exhaled and sat on a stool. Gill stood in front of him and encouraged him to sink his head onto her shoulder. As she held him she felt the tension flow out of him, his muscles unknotting to her touch.

'She turned up during service tonight. Stood in the dining room looking for me or Rob.'

'She, as in the woman who made the complaint?'

'The same. She didn't mention the complaint in front of the guests but the implied threat was clear, she could have said anything and they were a captive audience. Rob's gone to see his sister for the weekend, thank god. I took her down to the office.' George stopped and sighed, he was as close to tears as she had ever seen him.

'And?'

'And I fucking paid her didn't I.' George exploded and stood up sharply, almost tipping Gill over backwards. He moved away from the woman he loved and stood with his hands on the kitchen sink, eyes fixed on his reflection in the window above.

'What?' Gill shook her head in disbelief.

'She said she would take eight grand, said if I paid up I would never have to see her again, and if I didn't she would be in every night to tell every one of my customers how I had poisoned her.'

George turned back to Gill, the frustration in his face gave way to weakness.

'I just wanted to make it go away. I have done nothing but worry about this for four months and I just want it to go away. The bitch was never going to let it go until she got her thirty pieces of silver and I couldn't let her threaten me, the business or us anymore. The money from the Lexus was in Rob's safe.'

'Oh George.'

Rosie shuffled uncomfortably, trying to get further away from the man behind her who seemed to think crowding her would make his turn come quicker. As she stood in the queue of the overpriced coffee shop, waiting to give her order, the pungent scent of horse wee emanated from her boots. She wished she had changed into her trainers.

Though small, the town of Melksham was fairly cosmopolitan and it hadn't taken her long to find a coffee shop that boasted free wifi. Well, it said free on the sign, but if the price of the coffee was anything to go by, she was paying for it.

She counted out the change in her pocket and decided on the cheapest thing on the menu.

She sat as far away from the other customers as she could, anxious to keep her smell to herself.

She waited until her phone had finished downloading Skype for mobile before taking her first sip of coffee, trying to pace herself.

There were seven messages from her mother, two from Jules and one from Matt.

Sighing, she opened Matt's first. Although her phone was deemed smart it was not prepared to do anything with any speed.

She waited for the message to appear on the screen. It simply said 'Please come home now'.

She scoffed and ignored the message, glad she had thought to set her visible status to offline.

She felt guilty that she hadn't been in touch with Jules or

Gill beyond the briefest of texts, they cared about her and clearly wanted to know she was ok, but how could she explain to them something which she wasn't yet sure of herself.

Her mother's messages ranged from 'have you gone mad' to 'what on earth are you playing at'.

She sighed and looked at her watch. It was 8pm, her mother would probably be online.

Horseyhall80:   Hi Mum

Rosie typed and then waited. Thankfully, she didn't have to wait long.

SHarding2013: Ah. The prodigal daughter. What have you got to say for yourself?
Horseyhall80:   I would have thought if anyone understood me needing to get away, it would be you, given   that it was your suggestion.
SHarding2013: Don't you lay this at my door.

Rosie stared at the screen in disbelief. The usual abdication of responsibility. She thought her relationship with her mother had moved on from blame apportioning.

SHarding2013: I suggested you plan a break away and have some time by yourself, not worry the shit out of   everyone who cares about you.
Horseyhall80:   Everyone who cares about me? They were all planning to leave me.
SHarding2013: What are you talking about?
Horseyhall80:   Matt told Jimmy and Crystal to leave, saying we needed to sort our issues out. Jimmy and Crystal were leaving in the morning, Matt left that evening.
SHarding2013: Jimmy did tell me Matt had suggested they leave.
Horseyhall80:   So you agree I should have been deserted?

SHarding2013: No.

There was a pause and Rosie read the conversation back to
herself. Should she have gone?

SHarding2013: Do you still love Matt?
Horseyhall80:　Not sure really.
He has been so cold and hard since I told him how I felt about
Eve. So disapproving and distant. The ironic thing was I had
started to feel better about Eve, having Jimmy and Crystal
there was working. But then he started demanding we sell the
cottage, that I give up my job and my home and my friends to
live in a flat, like it was no big deal, like he didn't know me.
Then when I wasn't playing ball he decided to punish me by
getting rid of Jimmy and leaving me alone all week again.
SHarding2013: If you were feeling better about Eve why
would being left alone with her have been such a big deal?
Horseyhall80:　I don't know whether it would have.
SHarding2013: But you had your choices been taken away?
Horseyhall80:　It was all so horrible. I didn't know what to do.
I didn't want Dad to leave. I knew Eve would be safe with
them and that they couldn't leave her so they would stay.

Rosie felt the tears well in her eyes too quickly to stop them. She
quickly swapped her seat for the one opposite so that she was
facing the wall of the cafe and hoped no one would notice her
public display.

SHarding2013: So you ran away?
Horseyhall80:　Pretty much.
SHarding2013: Do you miss Eve?
Horseyhall80:　Kind of.
SHarding2013: Do you miss Matt?
Horseyhall80:　I miss the old Matt.
SHarding2013: So basically, you left to punish him for trying
to force you to do something you didn't want to 　do?
Horseyhall80:　It wasn't like that.

SHarding2013: Yes it was. You were happy with the situation so you weren't prepared to have it changed.

Horseyhall80: I was trying to cope with postnatal depression, I was making progress. And it was in spite of him, he was totally rubbish, I was better off during the week when he wasn't there judging me and dedicating himself to Eve like she was in need of affection.

SHarding2013: Wasn't she?

Horseyhall80: No. For fuck's sake. I don't understand what everyone's problem is. Even when I was really struggling she was fed and changed and cared for. Then she had Crystal doting on her every need as well as Jimmy and Matt can't leave her alone.

SHarding2013: Because most people acknowledge that a baby needs a primary care giver, someone it recognises as being its protector, and that supplies it with unconditional love. Now it might well be that Eve is now looking at Crystal as that, but from Matt's point of view, you are her Mum and as much as you argue your point to him, he is not going to understand it. You made the baby together, you should care for it together.

Horseyhall80: But he left us! He went off to do this job because he wanted to be able to buy crap we could have done without anyway and was then surprised when I didn't cope very well.

SHarding2013: Of course he was surprised. You usually cope with everything. He is punishing you for not behaving like you, for upending everything he believed about himself, by virtue of your weakness. You are punishing him because he can't handle it.

Horseyhall80: I am not sure I want to be with him anymore.

SHarding2013: Well, you have certainly given yourself the opportunity to find out.

Horseyhall80: Is Dad really worried?

SHarding2013: Of course he is. He has been ringing every day. He feels like he is in Matt's house when he is not wanted but he can't, and doesn't' want, to leave Eve. He is worried about how much of a state you must have been in to have left in the middle of the night.

Horseyhall80: I have text him to let him know I am alright.

SHarding2013: I know, he told me, and that's why you are not on the missing persons register. Apparently Matt is completely traumatised, worried you have gone for good.

Horseyhall80:   Well he should have thought about that.

SHarding2013: There you go again! None of this is anyone's fault. No one is a bad person, you just aren't handling a tricky situation very well. You are much better at everyone else's problems Rosie, you have never been very good at your own. And before you say it yes that does sound familiar and yes you probably did get that from me.

Horseyhall80:   I don't know what to do.

SHarding2013: What do you want to do?

Horseyhall80:   I don't want to live in a flat in Oxford and keep Red at a livery yard miles away. I don't want to   live with a man who isn't sure whether he loves me anymore. I don't want to lose my home Mum. It's where Harry died, it's where I thought I would live forever.

SHarding2013: And yet you left it?

Horseyhall80:   Since Matt made it clear he had no ties there, and wants us to sell, I can't bear to be there, I can't look at the place without my heart breaking, I feel like I am betraying it.

SHarding2013: It's only a house Rosie.

Horseyhall80:   It's the first place that ever felt like home. It's where Harry's soul is.

SHarding2013: I firmly believe that isn't true.

Horseyhall80:   I should have known you wouldn't understand.

SHarding2013: No Rosie. I do understand. But I think Harry is with you. He is in your heart and he is beside   you wherever you are. You don't need to tie yourself to a place to be near him.

Rosie leaned back from her phone. The tears were really falling now and she no longer cared if anyone saw. It was all just too awful. This was why she had gone away. This was why she hadn't really thought about anything but Red all week, because dealing with reality was too big, too enormous to comprehend.

Of course she knew her mother was right. It wouldn't be

a betrayal to Harry to leave Orchard Cottage. It still didn't change the fact that she didn't want to.

If only she had not confided in Val that day. She could have gone on pretending everything was ok and Matt would still look at her like he loved her and Eve would still be the only one who knew how she really felt. Maybe she would have come to love Eve anyway, without Jimmy being there, without having space and freedom to bring her back around.

She sighed. She knew that wasn't true. Her relationship with Eve was only improving because she had help, even the counselling had played a part, despite her reluctance to give in properly during her sessions.

SHarding2013: Where are you?
Horseyhall80: At a natural horsemanship training yard in Wiltshire. They think I am just here to work with Red. I haven't told anyone about my situation. They have rented me a caravan. It's small - it's fine – and cheap. The biggest cost is Red's stable and the owner, Dan's time.
SHarding2013: How are you affording it?
Horseyhall80: I still had the cash from when I sold Red's western saddle. I didn't want to use the joint account, seemed wrong to use Matt's money and I don't want to benefit from his bloody job.
SHarding2013: Do you have a PayPal account?
Horseyhall80: Yes. Do you?!
Sharding2013: Yes, it's how the publisher pays me. Give me your email address, I will send you some money. Before you start protesting I have hardly given you much over the years. I am making pretty good money considering I don't spend it. The more I work the less I drink, it's quite good for the bank balance.
Horseyhall80: So you aren't going to persuade me to go home?
SHarding2013: No. I don't agree with the way you did it. But I do get it.
Horseyhall80: Thank you.

SHarding2013: Two conditions. You call Jimmy, now. And you give me Matt's number.

Rosie hesitated.

She had spent so many years not trusting her mother. She supposed though, as she drained now cold coffee, the issue had always been that her mother didn't appear to care, or that she was too intoxicated to be of any use. Faced with Selina's recent consistent contact and good advice, Rosie had to admit the only thing stopping her from allowing the relationship to change was the past. She had always felt like her Mother couldn't be bothered with her. She couldn't make that argument to herself any more. For all Selina's harshness and bravado, she knew Rosie better than anyone else on earth could have done.

Chapter Seventeen

Rosie arrived back at the yard just as the sun was setting.

A few of the permanent employees were doing final checks of the horses. The property was divided into paddocks with field shelters. Although there was an undercover area of concrete with hot and cold running water for bringing in and seeing to the horses, there were very few traditional stables. Dan believed, she had learnt, that horses were grazing, roaming animals and they should be allowed to graze and roam unless it was medically unavoidable. Even then there were precious few conditions he believed benefited from lack of movement. Horses were designed to move, healing is accelerated through movement, keeping them confined only led to problems, both mental and physical. Rosie liked his philosophy. She liked him too.

He didn't describe himself as being any particular method, nor did he brand what he did with a catchy or clever label, he was just Dan the Horseman, and his ideals were simple. Happy willing horses who were respected and offered choices. She could see why Kev thought they would get on.

He worked with people who were having issues with their horse, where riding had become difficult or dangerous. He only took on horses where the owner was prepared to work with him, believing there was no point in producing a horse, or indeed fixing an issue, if the owner was not part of the process. Horses who had come right under his hands could easily go home and have problems again, so in order to utilise his services, the owner had to get involved, analyse their own shortcomings, and work bloody hard too.

He was in demand.

Rosie now realised just how lucky she was not to have been turned away. Speaking to some of the other owners she heard how long they had been waiting for a place.

When Dan had agreed to Rosie and Red staying, and offered her a caravan to stay in, he had told her he was quite short on time. Rosie had agreed to pay a slightly reduced rate for being slotted in when he had a spare hour. She felt she could learn from the soft spoken and slight American. She had spent the week caring for Red, and watching Dan ride and work with horses whenever she could, learning so much just from being in his presence, from listening to the guidance he gave to the owners. She had busied herself helping out wherever she could, and Dan had not really acknowledged her beyond the occasional nod.

Then, he had found her first thing this morning and asked her to bring Red to the round pen.

He had watched her ride her horse in circles around him and asked her how she felt.

She said self-conscious and laughed.

Dan did not laugh and Rosie attempted a more serious answer.

'I feel ok. He is doing as I ask of him and he doesn't feel stressed or tense.'

'But?'

'But I don't feel connected to him like I used to. I am not sure he would listen to me if we were under pressure. When I have been dealing with or thinking about...stuff...he has wanted to get away from me.'

'And?'

'He used to be so connected to me, it was like we were

telepathic, but now he feels distant, like he is thinking about other things.'

'And that is why you are here?'

'Sort of.' Rosie had looked down at her hands. The minute she stopped focusing on where she and Red were going, the horse hesitated and tried to halt. She hadn't wanted to lie to Dan. But she didn't really want to admit the truth either.

'When you arrived Rosie, I almost told you to join the waiting the list and sent you away. The reason I didn't was not because I think there is anything much wrong with you and your horse, it was 'cause you looked so darn worried.'

'Thank you.' Rosie mumbled.

'Whatever you are running away from, is the same thing that is causing the distance between you and Red. Because you neither know nor trust yourself at the moment, you are giving your horse a reason to doubt you. He isn't sure, like he used to be, that you will protect him.'

Rosie looked across at Dan but his eyes were shielded from the sun by his cowboy hat. She had been wondering if the hat was permanently glued to his head because she hadn't seen him without it. Even when he rode it stayed firmly around his skull.

'I wouldn't let him down.' Rosie said, it was one of the few things she still believed in about herself.

'I believe you. But Red isn't looking for sincerity in your words, or courage in your convictions, he is acting on the chemicals you produce, the steadiness of your hand and the completeness of your attention.'

'I guess there is no fooling a horse.'

The lower half of Dan's face broke into a wide grin.

'Nope. No matter how normal you think your movements are, the fear and adrenaline your thoughts produce are like flashing warning lights to him.'

'I'm sorry Red.' Rosie placed a hand on the neck of her horse, realising how much her behaviour since Harry died and Eve had been born, in addition to losing Harry himself, must have affected her horse.

'He is a horse. He wants comfort and a carrot, not regret. Regret does not compute.'

Rosie drew Red to a halt and dismounted. She left him standing in the middle of the round pen and walked away, overcome with emotion, drowned in tears.

She heard Dan coming towards her, his footsteps light.

'When you are ready to talk about it, let me know.'

'But you just said Red doesn't want my regret?' Rosie choked out words through convulsing sobs, she felt like she was going to start hyperventilating and she didn't want Dan to see the snot which was running freely from her nose.

'No. Like I said. He is a horse. But I'm a human.'

So, Rosie had spent the rest of the afternoon pooh picking the many paddocks and helping one of the staff to sweep the vast concrete yard. Then as the day descended into early evening, without really thinking about it, she had said goodbye to Red, who was content with the equine companions he had either side of him and the grass under foot, and driven herself to the nearest town.

Rosie waved to the staff and asked if they needed any help. They shook their heads.

Rosie wondered if she was getting on their nerves. Most of the owners came for pre-arranged sessions with Dan and then left. Rosie was constantly hanging around.

She bid them goodnight and retreated to her caravan.

'Hi Dad.'

329

Rosie braced herself for the ear bashing she knew she deserved.

'Rosie thank god.' Jimmy's voice was pure relief. She felt instantly dreadful.

'I'm sorry Dad.'

'No I'm sorry.' She could hear Jimmy sigh and she was about to insist it was not he who should be apologising, but he continued and she let him speak. 'I shouldn't have been so pig headed. I knew how fragile you were, I shouldn't have given in to Matt's request so quickly.'

'Yes you should!' Rosie protested, 'you had your own life and your own needs and I am 33 – you shouldn't have to give everything up to look after me. And now I have made it worse because you can't leave.'

'God you are like your Mum sometimes.'

That was a new one on Rosie, it threw her. Jimmy explained himself, picking up on her stunned silence.

'Having help doesn't mean you are weak. At any age. It's ok to fall apart sometimes, and it's ok for the people who love you to want to see you back on your feet.'

'Having you and Crystal there, it saved me, or was saving me. I am sorry I didn't tell you about the way things were with Matt and me. Or that he wanted me to move. I thought maybe if you and Crystal bought a place nearby in the meantime it would mean Matt couldn't go through with it or I would at least have had an anchor in Devon for when we split up. I know I was being selfish. Then when he told you both to leave, I just didn't know what to do. I couldn't let what was going to happen happen. I'm so sorry for putting you in an awkward position and worrying you.' Rosie was sincere, it felt good to say she was sorry, even though it didn't nearly make up for it.

'My nose was put out of joint if I am honest. Matt was

quite rude about it.'

'It's my house too.'

'I know darling.'

'How is my little girl?'

'She is fine, I think she wonders where you are, and the teething is driving Crys and I a little nuts, but she is well and safe otherwise.'

'I knew she would be. I'm so sorry Dad.'

'Please stop apologising Rosie. I don't think we should spend too much time looking behind us.'

Rosie paused, her Dad had almost echoed what Dan had said – but part of the problem was, she didn't know where forwards would take her.

'I don't want to sell the house Dad. I love it there. I don't want to move to Oxford either. Matt is being so stubborn, he has made his mind up.'

'I can't make you any promises Rosie. I know what you mean about Matt.'

Rosie listened intently for her Dad to say more. But for once, he didn't have all the answers. He couldn't save her from her marriage.

Rosie told him where she was staying and promised to keep in touch. He didn't ask her to come home and she didn't offer up a timescale. He mentioned that he and Crystal were going to view a house a few villages away. She was comforted by the idea that her current lack of a plan had not changed his. Their intention to move to Devon regardless, showed unvoiced support for and belief in her conviction that she would not be moving to Oxford.

They ended the call with Rosie sending her love to Eve.

As she lit the tiny gas stove and set a pan of water to boil for her evening meal of noodles and ketchup, she felt a pang of longing. She cradled an imaginary baby in her empty arms, wishing things had not turned out the way they had, but quietly grateful for the pain of missing her daughter.

George sat quietly while Jules and Gill vented their mutual frustration at him.

He neither hung his head nor defended himself. He just wished they would shut up.

Gill had run out to greet Jules as soon as she had arrived home, barely letting her get out of her car before she began telling her what George had done, desperate for an expert opinion. It was done out of concern for George of course, but now he couldn't help feeling like a naughty child, as they discussed what a precarious position he was in.

'The problem is he gave her cash, and didn't get anything in writing, she could just deny the payment was ever made. Or potentially, she could deem it an interim payment to settle part of the claim and still pursue this in court.' Jules delivered the news and frowned.

George opened his mouth to speak but Gill got in first.

'I suppose the staff at the restaurant could act as witnesses that she was there?'

'But she could just say she visited in an attempt to settle, and deny any cash was handed over.'

'George, is there cctv in the restaurant?' Gill turned to George who looked completely switched off.

'Yes. But only outside. It's above the porch at the front to see who comes in and out, and at the back door as a security measure. We never wanted the staff to feel spied on or the customers to feel watched, so we didn't install anything inside.'

'Nice thought though Gill.' Jules sighed. She tried to formulate a plan to limit the damage.

'I still think I did the right thing. She was never going to let it go, and even if we had won, people never believe there is smoke without fire. We would have lost customers either way.'

Gill shook her head at George, wondering if he was failing to see the point.

Jules thought for a moment longer, appreciating the brief silence to allow her brain to process.

'Right. We need to get a letter off to her, enclosing a settlement agreement, asking her to sign it to formalise the agreement made and cash paid in person. I will help you draft it, it's not too tricky a thing to put together.'

'And if she doesn't sign?' Gill asked, nervous of the answer.

'Then George will have to instruct a solicitor to act on his behalf. As much as it's tempting,' Jules eyed George who focused on her at last, 'you can't just leave this and hope she goes away. You can't afford that cash to have been in vain. I appreciate you decided your best option was to settle this, even though I think you would have won in court, but we need to make the settlement stick. She can't just skip off with your money and potentially come back asking for more down the line.'

'Thanks Jules.' George stood up and excused himself.

'Thanks darling.' Gill reached forward and embraced Jules affectionately.

'It might not work Gill. You need to prepare George for the worst case scenario.'

'I will. Can I give you something for your time writing the settlement thingy?'

'Given the situation with my firm being involved, it's better that you don't.'

Gill nodded.

'Now then. Let's talk about the fact that you didn't come home last night!'

'Let's not...' Jules blushed and started to make her way towards the door to her home.

'Come on Madam – out with it!'

Jules sighed and laughed. Resigned, she reported on her pleasant evening with Keith, the pleasant sex and the pleasant company.

'Pleasant?' Gill picked up on Jules lack of enthusiasm. Her heart was clearly not skipping beats.

'As in it was nice.' Jules emphasised the word she was sick of using to herself.

'That doesn't sound like a very passionate description...'

'Everything he is, is ruined by what he isn't.'

'James?'

'James.'

'The grass isn't always greener. At least no one is getting hurt.'

Jules nodded and headed for her door to change for the ride they had planned. She paused and her shoulders drooped under the weight of the realisation she had already made during her drive home.

'Except perhaps Keith.'

Rosie huddled in the corner of the cafe. This time she had gone for tea instead of coffee, although she wasn't as keen on it, it seemed better value because she could string out the two cup pot for longer.

She logged into her email account and peered at the new messages on the insufficiently sized screen of her phone.

Three hundred pounds had appeared in her PayPal account. She gasped at Selina's generosity. She also felt like it was fate. What Selina had given her was almost the exact amount she needed for another week at Dan's. It made her decision to confirm the extension an easy one. She was desperate to log in to Skype and thank her mother, but given the length of time it had taken for her emails to appear, she supposed she should check the rest of the unread mail before exiting and waiting another age for the programme to load.

She selected a message entitled "You" from an email address she didn't recognise, half expecting it to be spam.

It wasn't spam.

Dear Rosie,
Your friend Juliette got in touch with me. She wondered if I had heard from you. I think she is worried about you. Are you ok? I know I probably don't have anything to offer you, but I want you to know I am here if you need me.
Eddie

Rosie scowled.

She was touched Jules had obviously been exploring all the avenues to find her before she had made contact with Jimmy, but she was irritated that her friend had given out her email address to a man who did not deserve it, and was not someone she would ever have turned to for help.

At least he had the decency to sign it Eddie.

Riled, but deciding she had enough to worry about without taking herself on yet another emotional deviation, she simply closed her emails and logged in to her skype account.

Her mother was off line, but had left Rosie a message. It started with a firm assertion that the money Rosie would find in her account was a gift, not a loan. Selina had then gone on to say that she had spoken to Matt. She described him as broken and scared. She suggested strongly that Rosie contact him, and urged her not to take his bull in a china shop approach to their situation at face value – there was more to it than Rosie realised.

335

She decided that as her mother had been so generous, she was obliged to honour the request.

She found and selected her husband's mobile number and waited for him to answer.

'Rosie...' The relief was evident in his voice.

'Hi.' she said, nothing evident in hers, she was too guarded.

'I miss you.'

'How's Eve?' She ignored his sentiment.

'She is fine, she is right here, do you want to talk to her?'

'No.' Rosie couldn't really see the point.

She was still so angry with him and it was hard to let go of, but even in her critical mind-set, she would have to admit he sounded softer and more Matt like than he had done for the last few months.

'I wish things weren't like they are.' He stated the obvious.

'Me too.'

Rosie waited. His silence was persistent.

'So...' She filled the gap, not sure what to say herself.

'I want you to know I don't want us to split up.'

'You have a funny way of showing it.'

'I am sorry I asked your Dad to leave. I just wanted things to go back to the way they were.'

'That's what I want too.'

'I am sorry.'

'Stop saying sorry. I am the one who should be sorry, I am the one who took off.'

Matt didn't say anything, so Rosie continued.

'I can understand things from your point of view. I do get where you are coming from, but I just feel like you are punishing me for my weaknesses. I know I am usually strong but when I wasn't, I needed you to be there, not get irritated with me.'

'I am irritated with myself. I know I haven't handled it very well.'

Rosie sighed. They were both making all the right noises, both admitting their faults and being gentle with each other, but what did it really achieve? The stalemate would remain.

'I am just not sure what to do for the best,' Matt continued, 'I am working such long hours and this job is so mentally draining, I am not even sure I would be around or much company during the week anyway. I just feel so far away from Eve. And even further from you.'

Rosie attached herself to the glimmer of hope he was providing.

'Maybe it's not worth the money Matt?'

'Maybe. But I want to give Eve everything she needs.'

'I am going to stay here another week.'

Rosie heard a sharp intake of breath and knew the tone of the conversation would change before Matt spoke.

'Don't you miss Eve?'

'Yes, but it's a good feeling.'

'I think you should come home now.'

'Sorry Matt, I need more time.'

'Yeah I could do with some time too. But I have to keep right on working at full speed. Some of us don't have the luxury of swanning off with a horse.'

Rosie's head became light and she felt the familiar dizziness, his hackles were rising again. All the times she had let things go, the way she had cradled him and been strong for him when he had needed her, made her feel angry. He couldn't just be nice, had to snap like a child instead of measuring his reaction. She felt suddenly very confident of her decision to stay away for another week.

'Mum has given me some money for this week, and I used my saddle money for last week.'

Matt ignored her.

'Can I come and see you? Jimmy told me where you were, I could come up tonight on my way back to Oxford?'

Rosie sighed, she wanted to agree so as not to hurt him, but instinct spoke louder within her.

'Sorry Matt, we both need time to think.'

'Yeah. So your Mum was saying.' Matt spat, annoyed that his strong willed and decisive wife was taking advice from anyone, let alone a woman she previously would not have given the time of day to.

'She seems genuinely concerned and wants to help.'

'Good for you.'

'Don't you think it is positive I am finally having a relationship with my Mum?'

'Is that the plan then? Wait until Eve is thirty to bond with her?'

'Like a broken record. Matt stop it.'

'You fucking stop it.'

'This is why I needed to get away.'

'Please let me come and see you?' His voice was desperate, animosity still evident.

'No.'

Before Rosie had time to add anything further, Matt hung up on her.

She closed her eyes and tried to breath. She hoped her decision that more time was the answer was the right one.

Jules walked past James' office for the third time since she had arrived at work, and for the third time, he dismissed her without so much as a glance in her direction.

She had arrived at 8am, having dropped Ziggy to the farm for a day with Maurice. Not because she had any real enthusiasm for Monday morning, but because she was desperate to see James. The weekend had continued with no further word from him and she hoped to catch him before the masses arrived at the usual start time of 9am, to find out whether he had just been busy, or his lack of reply was purposeful.

He hadn't arrived until half nine himself, and since, he had made it quite clear his failure to reply was meaningful.

Jules made conversation with his secretary in the hope he would venture out of his office and speak to her.

He walked past her on his way to the kitchen, carrying his mug.

'Is Claude still coming in at 12?' He asked his secretary as he passed her desk.

She nodded and he smiled at her before walking on.

Jules went back to her own office and Gregg offered her a coffee after bringing her a recorded delivery package from the barrister.

'No Gregg – let me makes us both one.'

'Oh ok Juliette – thank you!' Gregg excused himself to continue photocopying the documents Jules would need for the County Court hearing that afternoon.

James was standing in the kitchen, alone, waiting for the kettle to boil.

'Hello.' She said softly as she moved in close beside him to set her mugs on the counter.

'Hi.' He moved away from her.

'What is up?'

'Nothing.'

'James?'

James turned and faced her, his brown eyes full of hurt. His nonchalance with her had clearly been an act, she felt haunted by his sorrow.

'I didn't realise you were dating. I should have realised you would have been.'

'So we can't be friends anymore?'

'No of course not. I just...' James paused, perhaps realising he was being unreasonable, he leaned in close and whispered to her, conscious of movement in the corridor and the threat that anyone could walk in at any moment, 'I know I can't ask anything of you and I hate myself for this but the thought of you being with someone else just kills me.'

'Shall we go to the pub at 5?'

'Is there any point?'

'Yes.'

'Rosie, come and give me a hand?'

Rosie stopped grooming Red and looked up. Dan was stood at the fence of the paddock carrying a western saddle and two bridles.

Rosie set her brushes down on the ledge inside Red's field shelter and followed him.

She stood waiting while he tacked up his own horse, Charm, and then began tacking up one of the youngsters he was backing.

'Toad here needs a bit of trail experience. I thought you could ride Charm for me, she'll give Toad some confidence.'

Rosie knew from her former dabbles into western riding with Red, that trail meant a hack in American.

She departed to fetch her riding hat. She felt elated that Dan would trust her to ride his gorgeous bay roan mare, and honoured that she would be helping with Toad, a five year old gelding who Dan was producing to eventually sell on to the right person. She also felt incredibly nervous in case she did something wrong.

As they allowed their horses to pick their way up a stony track which led them away from the yard and onto open land, which formed a ridge of rock and sheep shorn grass above the levels, they remained silent.

Toad was slightly unbalanced, but eager, reassured by Dan's light hand on his rein and the trust they had built. It wasn't difficult to trust Dan, she decided, whether you were horse or human he had a way about him which induced ease. He was leader enough to instil a feeling of safety, but still responsive enough not to become overbearing.

As they reached the ridge, Charm settled into a long-strided walk, Rosie sat passively on the mare, feeling slightly awkward in the position the western saddle was making her sit, but Charm knew the way and her job inside out. Toad crabbed a little, overwhelmed by the wide open space beyond them, but settled with a soothing word from the man astride him.

'So Rosie. How are things?'

'I can stay another week, if that's ok?'

'Sure.'

'And I could talk to you about stuff, if that's still ok?'

'Sure.'

Rosie glanced across at Dan. His angular jaw, the way he sat so easy on the young horse, the breeze sweeping his dark hair out from under his cowboy hat. She bit her lip, thinking how fantastically sexy he was. He looked more like a Hollywood icon than a horse trainer. She sniggered to herself, thinking how inappropriate it was to be slightly aroused when they were about to have a serious conversation.

341

Dan's eyes remained fixed on the horizon, his patience was another thing which made him so good at communication. He would not have described himself as a horse whisperer because he was not arrogant enough to label himself. Neither would Rosie, when she thought about it - his virtues spanned beyond being good with horses, it was more than that. He could simply read a being, without making them feel judged, and help them by using that insight.

They rode on and Rosie eventually followed his gaze.

She exhaled so deeply, Charm almost halted. She clucked softly and the mare walked on. She opened with the thing that was hardest to admit, but easiest to start with.

'I came here because I had to get away from my marriage.'

'Please James.'

The barman clocked Jules anguish, before politely turning away.

'Please what? We don't actually have anything to give up.'

'But I would miss you.'

'I already miss you. I just think it would be less painful this way.'

Jules dropped her head in defeat. Since they had arrived at the bar, James had explained to Jules that he had done a lot of thinking over the weekend, not he insisted, just because of her text, and concluded that it would be easier if their friendship dissolved.

'Do you want me to stop seeing Keith?'

'I can't ask you to do that.' He snapped.

'No, you can't.' Jules said gently.

'I know why.' He acquiesced. 'It just feels like the more

time we spend together, the closer we become, the more I want you. I think if you were out of my life I would be able to cope better.'

'But what about me? What about the fact we work in the same office?'

It was James' turn to hang his head. He was effectively punishing her. They both knew it.

Jules sniffed and fished in her handbag for a tissue.

'Let's go out and sit in the car.' He softened, he couldn't just switch off caring about her, it broke his heart to see her cry.

In the quiet of James' people carrier, there was nothing to hold Jules back. She didn't wail as she would have if she were alone, instead her sobs came out in choking splutters every time she failed to hold her breath.

'Why are you so upset?'

'Because I don't want to lose you.'

'You don't have me.'

'We have a friendship that spans over ten years. I am not very good at friendships, but I was good at ours until it got all messed up.' Jules tried to steady her breathing, 'Now you are saying we can't be friends. Why do you assume this is only painful for you?' What Jules didn't add was that she felt rejected. She didn't want to cross the line, or encourage things to become even more intense, but she didn't want to lose the bright light of having his adoration either.

'I'm sorry.'

'I guess I had better go.' Jules hugged her handbag in towards her stomach, gathering herself to get out of his car. 'I guess I will see you next week?' Jules knew James was going away on a training course in London for the rest of the week, bitterly she supposed some cold turkey was probably not a bad way to begin their newly agreed relationship parameters.

'It's been cancelled.' James reached for Jules' hand, didn't want her to get out of the car.

'Oh?'

'Trainer is ill, it's being re-scheduled for next month.'

'Ah..' Jules kept her hand inert where his had covered it, not wanting to return the touch, but not wanting it to stop.

'I was going to stay in Northgate Hotel for the rest of the week. Lisa thinks I am away anyway and I need some space.'

Jules nodded.

'If you need to talk things through, you can always call me?'

James sighed and nodded.

'I probably will.' James sighed again and turned to face Jules, resigned, 'I am sorry Jules I don't really want to lose your friendship, I just feel so powerless and unhappy. I know it would be worse if we weren't friends. I guess I am just jealous that you can start a new exciting relationship and I have no right to ask you to wait for me.'

'It's not nearly as exciting as you think.'

Chapter Eighteen

Gill knocked nervously on the door marked 26b and hoped she was in the right place.

She took a step backwards, suddenly feeling foolish about the flowers she had brought. She had called in to a supermarket that morning and ended up buying a ripe bouquet of red tulips for her daughter.

Gill had suggested to Charlie that they visit her grandmother again. She had not been since her mother had been released from hospital and it felt like less of a chore with Charlie's brightness beside her. Gill had also, rather cunningly she thought, planned to quiz her daughter about Bristol.

But, Charlie had been one step ahead of her mother and suggested Gill come early to Darran's flat to collect her, so that they could talk.

'Hello Mum!' Charlie opened the door and beamed at her tulips.

Gill walked in to the small bedsit and almost laughed at Darran, who was dressed up in a pair of slacks and a shirt and tie and was standing awkwardly next to the double futon.

Charlie had clearly been to a lot of effort. The chipped work surface of the kitchenette had been scrubbed almost to breaking point, there were bright red and turquoise scatter cushions over the futon and the small two seater sofa beside it. A throw covered the sofa and Gill tried not to think about what it might look like underneath.

Overall the room was clean and although the carpet was threadbare in places, it was no worse than the average dorm room.

'Thank you for the flowers Mrs Newman.'

'Call me Gill.'

'Thank you for the flowers Gill.' Darran looked nervous and hurried over to Charlie who was frantically searching the cupboard in the kitchen area for something resembling a vase. She settled on a tallish coffee mug and Darran held the blooms steady while she cut them.

'Would you like a coffee Mum?'

'Ok.' Gill perched on the sofa and Darran loomed over her in the small space.

'How's the music career then Darran?' She asked politely.

'One of our members is moving away with his girlfriend, so we are going to be splitting up soon.'

'Oh dear.'

'Well actually,' Charlie handed Gill a mug and sat next to her, 'that's what we wanted to talk to you about.'

'Oh?' Gill failed to see how the fate of Darran's band affected Charlie.

'Well, we were thinking that as there isn't anything to keep him here now, Darran might come with me to Bristol.'

Gill pondered for endless seconds. She was torn between massive relief that her daughter was still planning to take up her place studying Law, and concern about her being tied to a boyfriend. Finding time to study, making new friends, larking about – playing house with Darran was bound to interfere.

'And how are you going to live?'

'I 've already got some auditions for bands up there – one of them is really established and doing loads of paid gigs, they need a new guitarist. Their stuff is awesome, I've already learned

346

most of it.' Darren came alive as he spoke. Gill couldn't help but be moved by the sudden passionate outburst from someone she had privately decided was quite vacant.

'And Dad has said he will pay for the deposit on the flat and half the rent. My loan pays for the tuition and I might get a Saturday job as well.'

'Haven't you got to live on campus for the first year?'

'I've spoken to the Dean already.'

'Ok.' Gill felt rather on the back foot, 'Sounds like you have it all sorted, why do you need me?'

Charlie looked up at Darran and rolled her eyes, as though Gill had just proven a point.

'Well dur.'

'Mrs...Gill, we wanted to make sure you were ok with it before we signed the tenancy.'

Later, as Gill drove home, she realised she didn't feel as concerned about Charlie as she had expected to. She still wished her daughter was going off on the adventure of her life, instead of dragging her first love along with her, but, she decided as she ascended the long winding climb out of Exeter towards Stoke Rewe, she was quietly confident that her daughter's future was safe in her daughter's hands.

Gill swung the Land Rover into the yard and saw Kelly was giving a lesson in the school. Her Tuesday client was a woman who had not ridden for some years. Gill could see the enormous improvement the woman had made under Kelly's gentle guidance even at a distance.

Gill felt a massive amount of pride as she locked eyes with the groom. Kelly smiled briefly before focusing her attention entirely on her pupil again.

The pride was followed swiftly by sorrow.

Without Kelly, her ship would be sailing in the absence its first mate.

Now that Charlie was renting a flat with Darran in Bristol, she would not be coming home between terms as originally planned. She might never see Kelly again.

Gill took a deep breath. She could neither stop nor begrudge either of them.

As she tacked up Monty and Zinee so that she and Kelly could make the first run up to the gallops with the two stallions as soon as the lesson was over, she tried to think positively.

It could, after all, always be worse.

The girl behind the counter smiled in faint recognition when Rosie ordered her tea.

Sitting at her usual table, Rosie logged in to skype.

She had not heard from her mother since she had thanked her for the money, which she was now using, and she fully expected to see a series of messages waiting for her.

Not one.

Strange. Where else would Selina be? Perhaps her laptop had broken?

Rosie sent her mother another message and then logged in to her emails. She scowled when she saw the one from Eddie again and sent it to the trash folder so that she wouldn't have to keep looking at it.

She glowered as she read a new email from Val. Jimmy had explained when Val had phoned, that Rosie was away. Val's phrasing was tentative, wanting to know the details but not wanting to push, like Rosie needed to be handled carefully.

She tapped out a quick reply. Pride made her breezy. She was having some quality time with Red and generally things were much better with Eve. Not a lie.

Her phone started ringing and made her jump.

Matt was trying to call her. Again. For the third time since their conversation at the weekend, Rosie hit the silent button and allowed the phone to go to voice mail. She knew he wouldn't leave a message.

During her ride with Dan she had talked about how she felt.

She was disappointed in Matt. For not seeing how she was feeling, for rejecting her when she needed him, but most of all for thinking he could fix the situation by trying to enforce a move that was tantamount to punishment.

She told him that she couldn't promise Red anything because she did not know where she would end up living, and spoke about how her love for the cottage was entwined with her love for Harry and for Red. She had expressed her understanding for Matt's stance, confirmed she didn't blame him and that neither of them had purposefully caused the rift between them, convincing herself as much as Dan. It didn't stop her from not wanting to speak to her husband now.

Dan had mostly remained quiet as they had ridden, simply letting her vent. He had said one thing though, one thing that was playing on her mind,

'Guilt - one heck of a good way to stop you being a friend to yourself.'

Jules walked wearily out of the office, looking forward to getting home and seeing her horse.

She spotted James, fetching his overnight bag from his car.

'I heard!' He beamed at her and reached out to squeeze her, 'The whole firm is talking about how awesome you are.'

Jules flushed but smiled back at James, basking in his

pride for a moment.

Her win at the appeal case that afternoon had certainly been triumphant. The barrister had used her argument in the end and even though he passed it off as his own, his arrogance did not reduce her glory.

'You off to the Northgate now then?'

'Yeah.' James smiled warmly, relishing the prospect of a few nights without the drama that had become his home life. His face fell slightly and Jules recognised guilt.

'Taking an opportunity to have some time for yourself is not a crime.'

'I know,' he smiled wryly, 'just feel rotten for lying to Lisa about the course.'

'You wouldn't be doing it unless you needed to.' Jules pointed out the thing that James' guilt had overlooked.

'Over the weekend she seemed almost as happy as I was about having a few days apart.'

'Then why are you worrying?'

James laughed. She knew him so well.

'Guess I had better go and get checked in and start considering the room service menu!'

'You do that.' Jules nodded and started to retreat towards her car, 'I am off for a celebratory ride!'

'Sure you don't want to come and check out my hotel room with me?'

'Hmmm...that doesn't sound quite the same as riding.'

'King size bed....you could always ride me!'

James chuckled playfully and scampered theatrically away before Jules had a chance to react to his lude comment.

'Behave yourself you!' Jules shouted after him.

She chuckled as she fastened her seatbelt.

If only he knew how much she wanted to join him.

'Gill!'

The tone of George's voice saw Gill running from the kitchen, where she had been eating toast and wondering which of the horses to ride first, to the office, where the sound had come from.

'What?' She surprised him by arriving so quickly.

He was sat at the desk, looking at the computer screen. The colour had drained from his face, he gestured at the screen before leaning back in the chair and covering his head with his hands.

She perched on his lap so she could see.

As she started to read, felt the same as her partner.

Dear Mr Bloom,
With reference to your letter, I have to say I am somewhat shocked. I have no record of having received the money you state you have given to me. I still await your settlement in the sum of £10,000. Look forward to hearing from you, promptly Mr Bloom, or you could find yourself in Court.
Mrs V Duckleton

'That bloody bitch.'

Gill called through the door to her friend's annexe. She was surprised to find she was not able to walk in, but vaguely remembered a text from Jules about being ill.

George had followed her into the kitchen.

'She must still be in bed.' Gill turned to her partner, frustrated at not being able to get an immediate answer from the solicitor. Anything to alleviate the tension in his chiselled jaw, to take the worry from his beautiful green eyes.

'We will get this sorted darling, she won't get away with this.' Gill put her arms around his waist and tried to draw him in to her, but he remained rigid. His brow knitted so tight it almost cast a shadow over his cheeks, he looked down at Gill and

351

reminded her they had no cards left to play.

'Actually, she might.'

Jules pulled her robe around her and trudged to the kitchen to answer the banging coming from the back door. She had been so pent up in anticipation of the Court case, she was not surprised that a cold had managed to take hold of her body once the adrenaline had subsided.

'Sorry darling, I know you are sick, I really need your help though.'

Gill looked distraught as she stepped inside and Jules tried to pull her head back into focus.

'It's ok, just one of these summer cold things, loads of people in the office have had it.' Jules croaked, knowing the only other person who had actually had a cold recently was, in fact, James.

'Do you have your laptop? George has sent you the email.'

'Email?'

'Best you just read it.'

As Jules flipped open her notebook, Gill leaned out of the kitchen door.

'Come on in Darling.'

George stepped into Jules' home reluctantly. Jules smiled sympathetically at the man, who looked as though he had been stepped on. George smiled politely back but then looked away from Jules, whose robe had shifted slightly and revealed some of her ample cleavage. She blushed and yanked at the garment. She shivered uncontrollably as she waited for the laptop to load.

Gill rubbed George's back gently as they waited for Jules to read the message. His muscles did not soften to her touch, but he did smile gratefully, if briefly, at her.

'Right.' Jules scowled at the screen. 'Duck face fights dirty then.'

'I have wasted all that money.' George crumpled towards the counter, his elbows catching him.

'Not necessarily George. It's not over yet.' Jules snapped the laptop shut. 'We will instruct my friend Radley, I have already told him about the case. Let's see if a slightly more strongly worded letter on some headed paper might make her think twice about her fraudulent behaviour.'

George looked up at Jules and nodded.

'Here is his card,' Jules fished in her work bag and handed Gill the business card she had obtained from the solicitor she had trained with at Hodges. 'His firm has got a fantastic reputation. I was his junior for two years and I know he will do his best for you.'

'Thanks Jules.' Gill took the card and linked her arm through George's. 'Come on darling, let's go and call him now?'

George nodded feebly and they started to leave.

'Do you want me to make you some soup?' He said to Jules.

'No thanks George. I just need to get back to bed.'

By the time the afternoon rolled around, George was feeling altogether better about his predicament.

Radley, or Mr Radley as his secretary had introduced him, had been upbeat and positive about the situation. George wasn't sure whether that was all part of the service, but he had been impressed at the speed at with which the older solicitor had grasped the situation.

A letter might not help, Radley had said, but if it didn't, he was confident that her conduct to date, including the claim itself, which was frivolous and had no firm evidence, would see her losing in court. They could issue an order to stop her badmouthing the restaurant.

Radley had strongly suggested George involve his business partner, or at least keep him up to speed, reminding George that it was not sensible to assume the liability personally.

He appreciated the solicitor had to advise him, but he had already decided in his head to continue to keep Rob in the dark unless and until, the need arose. His business partner was on top form again, and his brightness and enthusiasm at the restaurant was motivating the staff and ensuring a positive environment. Keeping the customers happy and the cash flow coming was, George determined, more important than honesty for honesty's sake.

Gill had been by George's side. He knew she was trying to spend every spare second she had with Kelly, but she had left her assistant to ride out the horses and carry on with the afternoon jobs in order to go with him. Her support, along with the confidence of Radley, made him feel stronger again. It was a nice feeling.

The only thing that still played on his mind was the obvious foolishness of his having kept no record of the cash payment. Although Radley had been confident they would win in court, he had not given any firm opinions on whether the money would ever be returned.

It was, George decided, as Gill drew the Land Rover up outside the restaurant, something he may have to chalk up to experience. It was a high price for a mistake, but it was certainly never one he would make again.

George kissed his partner, squeezed her hand where it rested on the worn steering wheel. He felt suddenly overcome by the safety of their togetherness.

He continued to gaze at her and she smiled, but she had already started thinking about the fact she still needed to ride Zinee and that one of the liveries needed his poultice boot changing, after a recent hoof abscess.

'Out you get then you dork.'

'I love you Gill.'

'I love you too.' She melted as she spoke. How silly he had thought the troubles at the restaurant would make her think any less of him, it would take more than being sued to cause her to jump ship, a lot more. He had been her rock when Amber was missing, her only solace when her relationship with Charlie had been bad and her own business was facing collapse. It was give and take, being able to trust completely, like a best friend but with benefits.

'Will you marry me?' George asked casually.

'Get out of the car.'

'Is that a yes?'

'Get out of the car and go to work you silly man.'

George frowned as he dropped to the kerb and shut the heavy door of the old vehicle.

Gill shook her head at him as he waved her off.

She chuckled as she made the short drive to Newmans, relieved he felt bright enough to have a joke with her.

Gill strode into the barn and was pleased to see Zinee had already been brought in and groomed. Good old Kelly.

As she swung the young black horse's saddle over his half door, she heard a snivel coming from Monty's stable.

Kelly was sat in the corner on the straw bank. Gill quickly let herself in and squeezed past Monty who had positioned himself across the corner, as though barricading out the rest of the world for Kelly.

'What's up?'

'She has bloody booked the flights. Bloody bitch.' Kelly was angry, red face crumpling into misery as she continued. 'Apparently her nursing job can start straight away and she found a cheaper deal for just over a week's time. She just announced it when I went home at lunchtime. Like it was no big deal.'

'Oh god.' Gill slid down the rough chipboard which clad the stable wall and sat beside Kelly. Monty continued to stand over them.

Gill had been trying not to make Kelly feel guilty by being too upset herself, but now it seemed pointless to fight it.

'I don't want you to go. I don't know what I will do without you.'

Kelly clasped Gill's hand, her attention instantly turned to comforting her boss, despite her world having collapsed around her.

'It's just too awful. Surely this can't be real?'

'Just over a week.' Gill shook her head in disbelief.

'I will still be here for Zinee's first race.'

'What about Newmarket the week after?' Gill thought about the large event, where the yard was due to have four runners.

Kelly shook her head sadly.

Rosie's mouth smiled, but her blue eyes would have matched her heart better in green.

As she watched the great horseman imperceptibly gather Red into a balanced lope, she wished she was half the rider he was. Western was what Red was bred for, and having agreed to let Dan work him in a stock saddle, she was also reminded of how she had woefully wasted the natural ease the horse found in the discipline.

'You can tell he's reining bred,' Dan chuckled at the horse, who, despite never having been asked before, changed legs across the centre of a figure eight. It was not a perfect flying change of the lead leg the horse cantered in, but considering it was the first it was pretty impressive. 'He is close coupled, works naturally off the hind, if this school had the right surface I would be asking for a sliding stop too!'

'He does that in the field!' Rosie called. She had the seen the horse playing with Harry, and more recently with Peat. He would gallop flat out, before coming to an almost instant stop with his front legs, causing his hinds to slide in under him to absorb the energy of his sudden braking.

'You should do western with him.'

Rosie nodded politely. She didn't want to make Dan feel awkward by admitting the money she had obtained from selling the western saddle some time ago, had funded her trip to his yard.

'I am not very good at it. I had a few lessons but he was young and green and I was a bit of a novice. It just didn't seem like a sensible way to train him.'

'Nothing stopping you now?' Dan drew Red to a gentle halt beside her. She reached out to smooth her horse's face but he turned away out of her reach. With Dan astride the horse was reassured, safe and understood.

Rosie was still, despite her resolve to be strong and her determination to solve the problems in her life, not communicating effectively. He meandered and crabbed when she rode him. Earlier that morning when she had tried to hack him out, he had been reluctant to leave the yard. He had always strode out confidently with Rosie astride him before, but he had clearly not determined her a worthy enough leader to go farther than a few steps from his new home and she had to dismount to

357

get him past the gateway at the end of the drive. His doubt in her confidence had laid the seed of her doubt, and she hadn't re-mounted until they had turned for home, even then his eagerness had only been to return to the yard, rather than a result of her riding.

'Why don't you borrow this saddle while you're here? Try again.'

'Thank you.' Rosie smiled at Dan and wished Red would turn his head back towards her, wished her horse had been more loyal than to simply accept and embrace Dan as though she hadn't existed.

'You did a nice job on this horse. He's calm as he is kind.'

'Yeah – with you on board.'

'All you gotta do is believe in yourself, and he will believe in you.'

'I know.' Rosie sighed. Somehow, since Dan had pointed out that Red was subtly questioning her leadership, no amount of trying to convince her horse would allow her to convince herself. Even her resolve to be better, to beat the anxiety, had a negative effect - now that she was consciously battling her demons, any failure apparent through Red weakened her again.

'You have four days left, make them count. You might not fix this right away, but you can be real for him, focus on him instead of letting your brain gallop off to places he can't follow– get consistent, a horse likes to know where it stands.'

Rosie nodded. She had no idea what the future held. If she and Matt compromised on a new location between Devon and Oxford, there would be upheaval and uncertainty and she was powerless to protect the horse from coming changes she wouldn't be able to explain or prepare him for.

It didn't matter how hard she worked at Dan's yard,

because she could not make Red any genuine promises beyond their time there. It was a human problem, but her anxiety flowed through to the horse so that her worry became his. She was so concerned about the horse's fate, what would happen to destroy his comfort zone, that when she asked him to trust her it was already a faulty premise.

'I don't think I will be able to give him what he needs until I know what is happening at home.'

'Then maybe instead of trying to fix every single thing, go for just enjoying him. Have a little try at western again. Leave the future where it is.'

'I have never been very good at living in the now.' Rosie smiled sarcastically, knowing mindfulness was not her strong point. She couldn't help but to project, if something was wrong in one area of her life, it infected all others.

'Now is all Red has. He don't believe in nuthin' else.'

'Mmmm baked vanilla cheesecake.'

'Donuts with hot chocolate sauce for dipping.'

'Oh god those fresh made ring donuts you get at fairgrounds...'

'Oh yeah...' Jules groaned longingly, 'Although right now I would settle for a slab of any kind of cake.'

'I could bring you some?' James waited on the other end of the phone, waiting for the inevitable knock back.

'No, you have only just got over this, you don't want me to re-infect you.'

'I just feel so awful though – here I am sat in a suite with room service at my finger tips and you are a snivelling mess in need of cake!'

'I might just go back to sleep.'

'Ok Jules, thanks for the chat.'

It was James' second stolen night away from home. He sounded so bright, so carefree without the looming certainty of having to see Lisa at the end of the day.

'Might see you tomorrow, depends on how much of a snivelling mess I am in the morning.'

'Sleep tight.'

'You too.'

Jules slid her mobile onto the bedside table and unpaused the film she had been watching on her recently installed bedroom flat screen. She blew her sore nose. She felt rather sorry for herself and invited Ziggy onto the bed for a cuddle. Where usually she liked her own company, and felt sure of her life as she had designed it, she wished she had a partner to look after her when she felt fragile. Like now, when she only had one tissue left and would inevitably have to get out of bed and fetch a toilet roll, along with something to eat.

She decided to watch a bit more of her film first.

Ziggy's heaving breathing, as the dog dozed off next to her, lulled her towards sleep.

Chapter Nineteen

Rosie's attempt to live in the now and focus on the time she had left at Dan's lasted only until the evening, when she found herself heading for the cafe.

As much as she tried to enjoy being with her horse, to think only of the world within her direct vision, her thoughts returned to her mother. In her last skype message she had given her mobile number, asking Selina to call when she saw it. There had been no call.

Rosie wondered if her mother had simply returned to her old ways. Perhaps the months of forged closeness would become past tense; it had all seemed too good to be true after all. Maybe her mother had hit a slump, old habits die hard. Either way Rosie had to know, maybe she could help.

She was probably romanticising as usual. When she did finally make contact with Selina, she might just reject her all over again.

Rosie decided to spoil herself with a Latte. Her time at Dan's was drawing to an end and she still had a fair bit of cash left.

As she slid into the booth, her phone had already launched Skype, she had learned that if she fired it up while she waited in the queue it was usually ready to use by the time she sat down.

No messages.

All that was visible in the chat window were Rosie's unanswered enquiries into whether her mother was ok.

She checked her emails just in case.

Nothing.

'Right.'

Rosie searched her phone contacts until she found her mother. The house in Sevenoaks kept the same phone line since Rosie was a child and as she stared at the number on the screen, she realised she would have known it by heart.

With trembling fingers she hit the call button. Their conversations and deepening relationship might not be replicated in real time. She held her breath, imagining the sound ringing out into the dusty dark living room which was her mother's lair.

No answer.

'Ok, that is weird.' Rosie spoke out loud and the woman at the table behind her said pardon. Rosie apologised without looking round.

She tried to think of who else she could contact. Her mother's solitude over the years must surely have rendered her fairly friendless. She couldn't remember the surname of Jean, the old magazine contact Selina had been working for. She had no other immediate family, at least none that Rosie knew for sure she was in contact with.

She sipped the latte which had lost its magic and stared down at her mobile.

She called again, maybe Selina was just in the bathroom.

Just as Rosie was about to give up and ring off, a breathless and unfamiliar voice answered.

'Hello.'

'Hi, who is this?'

'Annette.'

Rosie racked her brains. Who on earth was Annette and why was she answering her mother's phone?

'It's Rosie, Selina's daughter, is she there?'

'Rosie! Yes, hello. I live next door to your Mum.'

Of course, the female half of the couple she had seen over the fence when she had visited her mother a few years ago.

'Can I speak to her?'

'I am sorry Rosie, she isn't here, she has been taken into hospital.'

Rosie fell silent, the worry that had seen her repeatedly messaging Selina and now trying to call her was founded. She wished she had not been right.

'She called me from the hospital yesterday, asked if I could pick her up some things from home.'

'Oh god.' Rosie's voice wavered, but Annette did not offer words of comfort.

'I have to be honest with you Rosie, it's not looking good, if you can come, you probably should.'

Rosie got back to the yard and made a dash for Red.

She struggled to make a decision.

She had called the hospital after Annette had given her the ward details.

The ward sister had been vague about Selina's status, other than that she was comfortable, but echoed Annette's suggestion that Rosie get there if she could.

She had looked up the word the sister had used on her phone. Cirrhosis. Google provided the answers.

Permanent scarring of the liver, leading to liver failure, often caused by long term alcohol abuse.

Maybe her mother had known. Was that why she had been cutting down on drinking? Why she had at last made contact with Rosie?

As she stood with her horse she was torn. She knew Dan would look after him. She knew it would probably be kinder to leave the horse where he was.

She had no idea how long she would be gone, or what awaited her.

As she thought about moving in close to the horse to say goodbye to him, she knew she couldn't go through with it. Instead she started packing the horsebox.

'Thank you for everything.' Rosie reached out to touch Dan's arm as she said goodbye. He had been calm and accepting in his usual way when she had explained her mother had been taken ill and they would have to leave early.

'Do you have somewhere up there for Red here?' Dan smoothed the horse's neck and Red reached out to brush his muzzle against the lovely man.

'Yes.' Rosie lied, feeling uncomfortable. Their departure should have been more wholesome, she wanted to say more but she felt too sick.

'Well you are both always welcome here.' Dan nodded and walked away. She stared longingly after him, almost changing her mind, but he was out of sight before she could get any words out.

'Come on boy.' She smiled at her horse, who followed her into the box, with no idea of the ordeal ahead of them.

Jules stirred when her phone vibrated.

Her film had ended and the irritating enthusiasm of a game show host's voice blared from the telly. She fumbled for the remote and muted the sound.

Ziggy was on his bed on the floor again, he must have got too hot beside her. She was burning. She flung the covers back and almost instantly the sweat on her body caused a chill. She shivered and pulled the dampened covers back over herself, feeling wretched.

She reached for her phone and unlocked the screen. The vibration had been a text from James.

Go to your front door...

Jules donned her robe. Scared, but at the same time daring to hope, that James might be waiting outside.

She opened the kitchen door. There was no one there.

'James?' Jules peered into the darkness and croaked his name, which made her cough.

She shivered as a cool night breeze swirled around her ankles. Where was he?

She went to go outside to see if his car was parked on the drive, and almost stood on a box on the doorstep.

Crouching down she opened the box. Inside it was a slice of chocolate cake, two glazed donuts, some paracetamol and a pocket pack of soft tissues.

As she closed the door and set the box on the counter so she could pour herself some milk to go with her feast, her smile lit up her eyes.

Rosie leaned forward to switch the sat nav off. It had been of use in getting her from Wiltshire to Kent, but now that she was driving the familiar roads of her childhood, she found the curt female voice blaring from the dashboard annoying. She knew Red's legs would be travel weary, he would be craving company. As if to confirm her suspicion, the horse whinnied loudly as she drew up at a traffic light.

She knew the road to Harry's first yard like the back of her hand. She had cycled to the end of the housing estate and along the short lane so many times, filled with the glee only a girl with a horse waiting for her can know.

She prayed they would have space, prayed the owner, who had seemed old even when Rosie was a teenager, would still be there.

She drove carefully up the residential street, wishing they had not installed speedbumps, praying her horse would not be thrown around too much. She glanced at the cctv and winced as Red's chest hit the padded breast bar.

Her relief when they had finally negotiated the end of the sleeping policeman was followed swiftly by despair.

Where there should have been stables, there was an entire community. Newly built houses and their neat patches of symmetrical garden sprawled in every direction. Rosie stopped the horsebox and sat staring at the hideous reality.

'Oh fucking hell.' Rosie's face reddened dramatically in frustration and fear. Nightmares realised, she was stranded with her horse in an unnatural landscape which offered no comfort for a weary equine.

An impatient driver behind her beeped and she pulled the horsebox in towards the pavement.

She sat for a few minutes, no ideas.

The minutes felt like hours to Red who stamped his feet, making the box sway. He wanted, understandably, to get out.

She couldn't explain to him why he couldn't.

The light was gently fading, it was already 9pm and soon there would be darkness and the prospect of arriving at an unknown yard with no hope of anyone still being around, let alone willing to take Red.

She picked up her mobile from the benchseat beside her. Her handsfree calls to Jimmy and Gill to explain what was happening and where she was going had been filled with the reassurance that she did not need them, that they should not come to her. Now she longed for a familiar face, someone to suggest something. She could drive straight to the hospital, but how could she expect Red to stand inside the box in some busy carpark. He needed to move, to eat and to feel the ground solid under his feet again.

Her mobile had internet signal. The built up area at least offered that in way of convenience.

Her fumbling fingers accidentally opened her email account instead of the internet.

She stared at the screen. Desperation saw her navigate to the trash folder.

She remembered from the address at the bottom of his email that her father now lived in Kent again.

Having to ask him for help contradicted a year-long stand against having anything to do with him, but if anyone knew of a yard she could take Red to, it was him.

'Eddie?' She demanded, when the number she had found in the email was answered with a breathless hello.

'Yes! That's me!' His voice struck her like a torch in pitch darkness, the warmth of his tones in stark contrast to the monster she had created in her head.

'It's Rosie. I need your help.'

Rosie walked the long corridors of the hospital searching for Searne ward.

The hour had not mattered to her, she had simply been determined to find and see her mother. Now, as she walked through the deserted building, taking care to keep her footsteps soft, she felt like an intruder.

She finally found the ward, aided by a solitary porter who was wheeling an empty trolley.

'Hello, I am here to see Selina Harding.' She addressed the ward sister who was clicking away at her computer, looking as busy as if it had been mid-morning.

'Rosie isn't it? We spoke on the phone. Come on through, she might not wake up and you will have to be quiet, we have got her in a sectioned off area, but there are other patients trying to sleep.'

Rosie nodded, biting her lip and wishing her hands would stop shaking. She had travelled all this way, she had fought to come, but now the prospect of actually seeing her mother terrified her. Would she even recognise her?

'As you know Rosie, Selina has suffered from some quite catastrophic organ failure. When she is awake she is quite lucid, but she is mainly sleeping and for now we think that is best.'

'What's the prognosis?'

'When the doctor does her rounds in the morning she will be able to tell you more.'

'Ok.' Rosie nodded and followed the short immaculate woman as she padded along the corridor. Under different circumstances Rosie might have pushed for a more concise answer, but the atmosphere, the quiet and the shaking in her hands rendered her mute.

The sister showed Rosie to a brightly lit cubicle and smiled before departing.

Selina's body looked slight and lifeless beneath the thin white blanket. There was a chair next to the bed and as Rosie tentatively made her way towards it she caught sight of her mother's face.

Rasping breaths forced their way in and out of a slack mouth. Selina's eyes were closed and still, as though in a deeper place than where dreams might animate them. Her skin was grey and darkened pits had formed above her cheek bones.

Rosie perched on the edge of the high backed chair. She wanted to reach out to her sleeping mother, offer some comfort through her unconsciousness, but both of Selina's hands were underneath the blanket. She shuddered empathy when she noticed the catheter bag hanging from the bed.

Rosie's tears brimmed over as she watched her mother sleep. Selina's prostrate form and unknown fate now would probably only have resulted in an obligatory visit, during daylight hours, if it had not been for the past few months. If she lost her now, the very least, she would have known her better and drawn her in closer to her heart before it was too late.

She had spent so much of her life in fear of her mother. Then recently, found herself in awe of her.

The warmth of the ward was overwhelming, sweat beaded on her forehead. Her gaze drifted towards her own reflection in the window opposite the bed. She stared at herself, sobbing quietly.

'You look like Miss Piggy when you cry.' Came a rasping voice.

Rosie jumped and turned to see familiar eyes staring mischievously back at her. The lifeless form was replaced by her mother.

'You can't even be nice when you are about to snuff it.' Rosie choked through tears which flooded out harder in relief that her mother was awake and apparently as cantankerous as ever.

Selina sighed heavily, and smiled at Rosie.

'Did it to myself really didn't I. I knew something wasn't right, just thought I was old and knackered. More knackered than I thought.'

'Is that what they told you?'

'Doctors don't usually use the word knackered. But yes, in essence, I am fucked.'

Rosie nodded, feeling overwhelmed by the futility and

wondering why her mother appeared so calm and accepting.

'All the wasted hours and pointless days, but at least I got one thing right.'

Rosie waited for the pause to be over, for her to continue, but Selina's eyes had closed again.

'You, you dullard.' she said without opening them.

Rosie realised she had dozed off when a nurse spoke to her. She needed to attend to Selina.

She glanced at her mother, who was deep in sleep again.

Rosie ignored the aching in her shoulders from driving the horsebox and sleeping in an upright chair and tried to stand with dignity.

She told the nurse she would be back later and stiffly walked out of the ward.

It was 6am.

Get some sleep? Where?

Wait? For Selina to die?

Rosie decided to head back to Eddie's and at the very least comfort her horse, who must be confused by yet another set of new surroundings, and return in time to speak to the doctor as the ward sister had suggested.

'Jules!' Gill banged on the kitchen door of her friend's property. The internal door was still locked. She knew Jules was poorly and had simply wanted to rest, but the bombshell from Kelly, coupled with the phone call she had just had from Rosie made Gill more persistent.

Rosie had been firm, Gill did not need to join her. Knowing how little time Kelly now had left and what was going on with George, Gill had reluctantly agreed. She still needed to relay the situation to Jules though, so that she knew what Rosie was going through, and so they could discuss the Kelly-less Newmarket race.

Gill banged on the glass again and continued to wait. Jules' mobile remained switched off.

Gill swore under her breath in frustration and headed back to her own kitchen door, intending to make for the office and draft an advert for a groom.

Something she had no enthusiasm for and would rather have done with Jules.

As she closed the kitchen door behind her, she heard George coming down the stairs. He had been so late home the night before, arriving well after she had fallen asleep, that she had decided not to wake him when she had risen to see to the horses.

She dashed into the hall to greet him, now that he was awake, the words were forming in her head to relay the depressing news about Kelly.

His face, when she saw it, stopped her.

'Radley just called. Her response to his email was all sweetness and light. She is still denying I paid her anything.'

'Oh no...' Gill wrapped her arms around him, wishing bad news could come in ones, even twos, or just not at all for a while.

As Rosie finally pulled into the yard, having been stuck in the morning rush hour traffic, Eddie dashed outside to greet her.

'Well?' He looked worried, and had obviously not had any sleep either.

'She thinks she is dying, the people on the ward seem to think she is dying. I have to go back later this morning to find out what the doctor has to say. She woke up, briefly, but she is fast asleep again now so I wasn't sure whether to stay or not...' Rosie trailed off.

Eddie nodded.

He pointed to the stable which was closest to the house, Rosie walked towards it.

Red was tugging at a haynet and seemed completely relaxed. His straw bed was clean and thick, water pristine. He had no immediate horse company, but he could see the other horses in the fields opposite.

'If you had come from home I would have put him with the other horses, but as you have come from a big yard I thought it best to keep him away, at least for now.'

'That's fine.' Rosie mumbled wearily as she leant on the stable door, breathing in the scent of her horse and wondering how comfortable the straw bed was.

'I put him next to the house so he would be close to you.'

Rosie nodded vaguely.

'Are you going to come inside and go to bed for a few hours?'

Rosie hesitated. Under normal circumstances she wouldn't have entered her father's house if you had paid her. What dark secrets underlined the small but nicely presented cottage, the clean yard and the many comfortable horses? Had he fallen on his feet at the expense of his morality? Was Red at risk? She didn't want to believe it, but she hadn't wanted to believe it last time when her father turned out to be handling stolen goods.

She had unloaded Red and left him with Eddie after he had persuaded her his yard was the closest to the hospital and assured her that he would care for the horse like he was golden. It was Red's obvious immediate comfort in the man's hands that had seen her driving away, rather than the verbal assurances. Red responded to Eddie the same way he had responded to Dan. If Rosie had been asked the question just a few hours before - would you leave your horse with Eddie Gillant? - she would have laughed scornful at such a ridiculous idea, but the desire to get to her mother, and the look in Red's eyes had made the decision. Now, she wanted to know it was safe for sure.

'Just tell me this is all legit?'

She turned and looked into the familiar dark eyes.

Eddie looked almost excited, he nodded vigorously.

'The place belongs to a woman who used to run it herself. She has bought a new property for her and her own horses quite near here and concentrates on showing. I started out as a stable hand, there are lots of full liveries so it's quite a lot of work. When she decided she wanted to move, she offered me the manager's job and the cottage. I still have one of my youngsters, this is his stable when he comes in. I also do a bit of backing and training when people ask me, all just word of mouth stuff, but otherwise I run the yard. They trust me, I would not do anything to break that trust. Part of the reason I moved here after I got out...I wanted a fresh start where no one from that darker part of my life could reach me.'

'How long were you in?' Rosie almost didn't want to know, she shuddered when she thought about the last time she had seen Eddie, at a remand centre awaiting a judge who would determine his level of accountability.

'I got out the day I went to Court. They weren't really interested in me, I was a small player in a much bigger game. I didn't really know very much, and they said I had already served as much time as they would have given me anyway. So in a way it was just as well no one paid my bail.'

'So you were out quite soon after I visited you?'

'Three weeks.'

Rosie sighed heavily, although there would always be a part of her that hated her father for any involvement in horse theft at all, she had quietly admitted to herself in the months after the ordeal that she didn't really think he was an out and out crook.

'You didn't get in touch.'

'Thought I would give you some time, and try to make a decent honest life for myself. So that when we did meet again, I could be honest about what I did, and show you I had changed.'

'From what into what? How would I know?'

'I just wanted to prove to myself, and hopefully eventually you, that that period of my life was a blip. It wasn't who I am. I like waking up in the morning and knowing I don't have to listen out for a car arriving and wonder if the game is up. I hear a car and know it's an owner and it's time I should be getting the horse's breakfasts sorted.' Eddie paused and sighed, he didn't want to argue with Rosie, or play down his involvement because he knew all too well how she felt about it, but felt the need to explain himself one more time.

'All I did was agree to look after some horses I knew weren't legit, I never knew any details. I had previously bought and sold some dodgy tack, I will admit, but even then I was just a dealer. And look how it turned out? I lost you, got a record, spent three weeks locked up. I must be the most unlucky criminal going, I wasn't about to risk any more of my dignity or my sanity to make a few bucks – lesson learned.'

'Does the owner of this place know?'

'Most of it. I left out the part about you. Just said I had made some bad choices and paid the price. I was upfront and I think that was why she trusted me. That and I don't need much sleep.'

'Hard work here?'

'Incredibly. But no more than I deserve.'

'And being the best mucker-out is an improvement on being the worst criminal?' Rosie oozed contempt, but Eddie didn't bite.

'Exactly.'

Rosie smiled, not generously, but enough of her mouth creased upwards to make Eddie feel happier than he had done since the day he had met Rosie and betrayed her by hiding her friend's horses from her.

'I am so sorry, again, Rosie, if I had known about you my life would have been so different from the start.' Eddie reached out his hands to his daughter but she side stepped him and started to head towards the house.

'Show me this bed then.'

Jules stared out of the window again.

David had quickly agreed to her working from home, pleased to still be getting some billable hours out of her without infecting the office. In truth she felt much better. After her late night feast, she had slept deeply and woken late with the feeling that her body was winning against the virus.

She closed the case file in front of her and decided to take an early lunch. Leaving her mobile on the desk she clucked to Ziggy to wake him up and headed towards her horse and the comfort his broad back would offer. She decided in advance to use the mounting block to get on, knowing her weakened limbs probably couldn't support a scrabble into the saddle from the ground.

As she led Romeo towards the barn she spotted Gill and Kelly coming back from their ride on Pop and Zinee.

Gill's face was serious and she eyed Jules.

'Rosie's mum is dying.' Gill stopped Zinee just short of Romeo's rump so that the stallion couldn't touch the gelding.

'What?!'

'She has gone to Kent to be with her in Hospital. And

375

Mrs Duckleton has told Radley she had no money from George. And Kelly's Mum has booked their plane tickets for next week so we don't have a groom for Newmarket.'

Jules struggled to take it all in.

24 hours off the grid and everything had fallen apart.

'I'm sorry I haven't been around.'

'It's ok, you were ill, but now I could use your help.'

'Of course.'

'Kelly has a lesson now and I still need to ride Milly.'

'Come with me and Rome – fill me in properly? I was only going to take it steady though?'

'Fine.' Gill nodded and smiled, feeling thankful her problems would be shared and perhaps halved.

As Gill walked away, Jules started to brush Romeo's neck feebly, her arm tired immediately. The horse moved his head away from her to eye her, as though asking whether she was capable of the task. She sniffed noisily and agreed with her horse.

'I know, ok, I know.'

'How are you feeling?'

'Like crap.' Selina croaked. The nurses had propped her up into a sitting position and she looked a little brighter than the night before.

'Are you sure about what the doctor asked?' Rosie nervously re-visited the awkward conversation with Selina's consultant, which she had arrived on the ward just in time to witness.

'Yes. What would be the point?'

'But you seem ok, you are sat up talking to me, if your heart stopped now I would want them to try and bring you back?' Rosie's voice cracked into sobs and Selina got irritated.

'If my heart stops, and it will, I do not want to be

brought back so that I can feel like this for a bit longer. I have been slowly getting worse and worse over the last few years, I ignored all the signs because my brain still worked and I didn't need to do much more than think. My legs kept filling with fluid and it made walking a bit of a pain in the arse but I knew if I went to the doctor they would just tell me to stop drinking. Once I started doing my shopping online I didn't need to walk much anyway. I knew something was up but I chose to ignore it. The time to have done something about it was then. I didn't.'

'But can't you do something about it now?' Rosie pleaded, wailing. The "do not resuscitate" order seemed so final, so depressingly certain. The doctor had said there was no guarantee even if they tried to re-start her heart when it inevitably failed, but Rosie couldn't bear the thought of nothing being tried.

She had not contradicted her mother's resolute decision in front of the doctor, not wanting to go against her wishes, but it didn't stop her trying to persuade her mother to change her mind now that they were alone again. 'Please Mum?'

'Snap out of it child or you can sod off. I am in pain, I am losing my faculties and I am of no use to myself or you.' Even in her weak and vulnerable state Selina managed to sound stern enough to shut her daughter up.

'Why are you so ok with this?' Rosie's voice was level again, but she still needed to make peace.

'Because I just am. They have told me my liver is buggered and that I am not a good transplant candidate because my arteries are all buggered as well – I don't want them to do anything to save me, it would be a waste of NHS resources. I don't want to live in a nursing home, I don't want to be a burden. I have lived my life the way I wanted to and now it is coming to an end. Can you imagine me as some frail little old woman?

Living in some graveyard waiting room being told off for smoking?'

'No.'

'Well then, don't try and consign me to a living hell just because you feel bad that I am on my way out. You might be scared of death but I have been expecting it.'

'I should probably get back to Red.' Rosie knew her mother's tone, it was the one she dreaded, the scornful angry sound of her childhood. As much as she didn't want to leave Selina, hanging around and winding her up wasn't going to help either of them.

'You brought the horse?!' Selina laughed, which gave way to a coughing fit. Rosie waited until her mother had finished.

'I came straight from Wiltshire.'

'Have you got him at...MacKinnels?' Selina struggled to remember the name of the stables her young daughter had spent more time at than the family home.

'No. I tried to go there but it's a housing estate now.'

'Not surprised.'

'He is at the yard Eddie manages, he is looking after him.'

Selina's eyes widened and she struggled to sit herself more upright in the bed. Rosie took her mother's arm and tried to help her but Selina snatched it away.

'Don't fuss me child.'

Once more upright, Selina smiled.

'Bring him to see me.' Her eyes twinkled and she raised her eyebrows in excitement.

'You want to see Eddie?'

'Yes.'

'What if he doesn't want to come?'

Selina laughed and started to cough again. 'I am dying, you have to give me what I want!'

'You don't know everything.' Rosie sat back down. She was going to have to tell her mother the full story, the stolen horses, the court case, the fact that up until yesterday she hadn't spoken to him in over a year. She sighed heavily but didn't begin.

As she looked into her mother's expectant eyes, the joy that had warmed her cheeks from grey to pink, Rosie decided she never needed to know.

Instead, she told her about the very first conversation she had with her estranged father, when she had told him he had a daughter.

'He didn't get bored of you once he'd had enough of sleeping with you, like you thought. He saw you out shopping with Jimmy and realised there was another man. That was why he left town, why you never saw him again.'

Selina stared off into a distance beyond the sterile wall of her cubicle, reliving the pain when she thought she was written off as unimportant and easy. She smiled slowly as the past was re-written, the rejection she felt at the time undone.

'I don't know why you are smiling. You cheated on Jimmy and you hurt Eddie. You lied about me being Jimmy's child and you ruined two lives.'

'I know.' Selina said quietly and Rosie instantly regretted her harshness. 'Three lives.'

'Do you still want me to bring him?' Rosie enquired, softer.

'I think I owe him an apology don't you?' Selina continued to stare ahead, her tight lips and drawn expression defied the presence of a single tear which rolled from her right eye.

'Ok.' Rosie stood up to leave again and leaned in to kiss

379

her mother but Selina drew back, sharply, not wanting the contact.

'Bring him tomorrow, I need to sleep now.'

'Ok.' Rosie settled for squeezing Selina's arm where it sat limp on top of the bedclothes. Dark shadows cast over her eyes and she suddenly looked so ill and frail again Rosie didn't want to leave. She hesitated.

'Go away now.' Selina mumbled, becoming breathless with the effort it took to shuffle her way down the bed and turn her back on Rosie.

Rosie's shoulders dropped, deflated. She turned with a heavy heart to leave the cubicle.

'I love you.' Came a quiet but clear voice from under the bedclothes.

'I love you too.' Rosie whispered back and fled before the wave of emotion at hearing the words she had been waiting for all her life hit her.

Chapter Twenty

'So I will go and see George now and ask him about the races?' Gill finished untacking Milly and joined Jules back outside where she was leaning against Romeo's withers, looking exhausted.

'Yes. I will draft an advert for Kelly's job. We won't get anyone in time for Newmarket but at least we can start the process.' Jules was efficient despite her physical frailty and it was just what Gill needed. She always operated better when there was a plan.

'I'm sorry Radley's letter didn't work.' Jules added as Gill left the yard.

'Me too.'

'Best if George goes back to see him, firm up the next steps.'

Gill nodded and turned to trot away down the drive, leaving Jules to return her horse to his paddock and get herself back into bed, albeit with her laptop.

Gill was greeted, as always, like royalty.

Each of the restaurant staff took the time to ask her how she was, despite the fact that they were mid service and clearly very busy. Because she worried so much about the age difference, and about how the young female waiting staff might feel about her having snagged their gorgeous boss, it was a tremendous comfort that she was always made so welcome.

Alex's lack of respect for her had been apparent in his employees. She knew because of the way they spoke to her when she called, and the way they avoided her gaze when she had cause to visit his factory. Then he had left her for one of them.

She smiled as she headed to the office where she had been assured George was. He had probably told them all to make an effort with her, it was one of the things she loved about him.

As she made her way down the stairs and into the restaurant's office, she could hear Rob's voice. He did not sound happy. Apparently loyalty was the subject of the day.

'What the hell are you doing giving that bitch money?'

'How do you know I gave her money?' Gill could hear George was trying to stay calm.

'Does that matter? Really George?' She heard a chair legs scrape along the tiled floor and Rob's voice became even louder. 'I think what matters here is that you used our money to pay someone who didn't deserve a penny anyway.'

Gill didn't want to eavesdrop, she wanted to help. Grief over Kelly, worry for Rosie, even the situation with Charlie, the things she couldn't control, somehow gave her the balls to stride into the room and stop yet another problem from infecting their lives.

'He sold his car actually Rob. It wasn't your money.'

George's mouth fell open as the blonde vision swept into the room and corrected his business partner. Completely inappropriately his brain flashed an image of her pinned against the wall in the coat room as he slid down the fly of her tight riding jeans.

Rob on the other hand, not plagued by such fantasy over the enigma that was Gill, was outraged.

'What the... George?' Rob gestured angrily towards Gill.

'Gill and I are partners.'

'What happened to keeping it from her? Not wanting to hassle her with it?'

'That changed.' George smiled over at Gill, but her blue eyes were fixed on Rob.

'Look Rob, George has been so worried about this it has bordered on making him ill. I know you are angry he kept it from you, and I completely agree with you – this bitch of a woman has no claim – but George was trying to protect you – not pull the wool over your eyes.'

'I don't think..' Rob began, but Gill cut him off, unusually assertive and fiercely protective.

'Rob, regardless of whether you think George did the right thing, he was prepared to settle it without involving you, out of his own pocket. He sold his car – didn't you wonder why he's been walking to work?' Gill paused to let the message sink in. 'There is something bigger at stake here though Rob,' She sat on a chair and encouraged him to do the same. He sat, still annoyed. She reached her hands out towards him, 'That nasty woman is trying to say that she didn't get paid by George, that the eight grand he gave her doesn't exist, because he didn't get a receipt or ask her to sign anything,' Gill paused again so that Rob could follow her gaze towards George, who held up his hands and ducked his head.

'Not my finest moment.'

'So,' Gill continued, clasping one of Rob's hands in hers, further solidifying his essential role in solving the problem, and in doing so dispersing his anger, 'If you can tell us how you knew George had paid her, it could be what saves the day.'

Rob nodded enthusiastically at Gill and George made a mental note to enlist Gill's help with his business partner in future, such was her ability to engage him. She was soft and kind but had conviction in her words, infectious enthusiasm, dealing with Rob much in the same way she would have dealt with a horse.

Rob turned his chair around to face the computer and clicked on the CCTV icon.

'One of the customers thought they might have dropped some keys outside when they left on Monday night.' He clicked on the folder with Monday's date written next to it. 'When I looked through everything, the movement sensor had recorded for that evening, I found this...'

He double clicked on a file.

On the screen, colourless but clear, Mrs Duckleton paused on the path of the restaurant, to make a brief count of the wedge of notes in her hand.

'Rob you just saved my ass.' George clapped Rob on the back and grabbed Gill to reel her in for a celebratory kiss. 'Can you put that on a memory stick for me? I need to take it to my solicitor!'

Rob rummaged in the top drawer to find a suitable data conveyance.

'Come with me?' George beamed at Gill, wanting her to be part of it.

'I can't, I need to talk to you, that's why I am here.'

'I'm bloody well coming.' Rob turned around and folded his arms, defying George to deny him the right now that he was finally in on it and had unwittingly saved the day.

'Appointment is at three.' George confirmed and Rob nodded before departing to check on service.

Once they were alone, because the drama was over, Gill collapsed into George's arms.

'Kelly only has a week left.'

'What?' George steered Gill back onto the chair and knelt in front of her.

'Her Mum has booked their flights. Cheaper to go now apparently!' Gill threw her arms up in frustration. She hadn't been able to show her anger in front of Kelly but now the initial emotion at the news had run its course, she was wild. 'How could she do that to her? We thought she had another two months at least. She is in such a state.'

'I don't know what to say.' George sighed and shook his head sympathetically.

'You can say you will come and help out at Newmaket? Kelly will still be here for Lingfield this Saturday, but we have got four running the week after and it's Monty and Milly's big money race.' Gill rocked slightly in her chair, it was completely incomprehensible. It was an important enough race she would have been nervous anyway, but without Kelly? How on earth was she going to cope?

George gestured for her to wait in the office and headed up the stairs. He fetched the restaurant bookings diary and returned with it.

'We have got a big party in for lunch that day,' George pointed in the book and Gill's heart sunk further, 'but,' he continued 'they are pre-ordering so I can do all the prep the day before and it looks like Rob is definitely here. I will double check with him but it should be ok.'

Gill stood up and embraced him. He was no Kelly, but at least with him there she at least had a hope of getting the runners ready and two of the horses organised into the same race. His moral support would also be invaluable. She couldn't imagine the course without Kelly. Three people for four runners. It should have been ample, but because Gill felt Kelly was equivalent to two people, her brain was still producing panic toxins.

She shot up from the chair.

'I need to get back to Kelly.'

'I will let you know how it goes with Radley.' George caught her and cuddled her as she went to leave the office.

'At least one thing went right today.'

'Let's hope so.'

'I don't think that she can deny you paid her now?'

'Based on the way things have been going lately, I am not going to bank on it until the fat lady signs.'

The heavens opened on Gill as she walked back along the lane. They had predicted the baking hot July would be broken by rain at some point, and Gill thought how typical it was the downpour would happen when she was wearing a t-shirt and had no cover. It was still warm at least. She should really have paid more attention to the sky, it had been grey from sun up after all.

Gill trotted the rest of the way to the main street and ducked under the deserted bus stop to let the worst of the torrents come down around her.

She got her mobile out of her pocket, utilising her enforced standstill to check in with Rosie.

'Darling, how is she?'

'Not good. Not long.' Rosie sounded tired, as though she had been asleep.

'Did I wake you?'

'Yes and no. I was supposed to be napping but we have to go back to the hospital soon.'

'We?'

'She wants to see Eddie.'

'Blimey.'

'I know. Last wishes and all that.'

'How is it going with Eddie?' Gill's question was guarded, he was after all the man who had almost cost her Monty.

'I will explain in full when I return.'

'Ok. I hope you are ok?'

'Not really.'

'Sorry. Stupid question really.' Gill dried up. She so wanted to tell Rosie about Kelly, to listen to the voice that had always been reason, to give her the good news about the restaurant. She could tell from Rosie's tone that her friend had enough on her mind.

'How are you Gill?' Rosie asked absently, filling the silence.

'I will also explain in full when you return.'

'Touché.' Rosie chuckled, it was nice to hear her laugh.

'I guess you have no idea when you will be home?'

'None. I can't leave her like this. I feel like I am waiting for her to die by staying though.'

'Is it really that imminent?'

'She has refused all of the procedures they have tried to offer her. Not that they held out much hope anyway. They said she will probably slip into a coma at some point and then it's just a matter of time.'

'Rosie it sounds so awful for you. Are you sure you don't need someone with you?'

'Absolutely not.' Rosie was so abrupt she felt bad and clarified, 'You have races for the next two weekends, and you know what I am like anyway, I don't do being mothered.'

Rosie's slip of the tongue caused Gill's empathy to swell again, it was all so sad, she wished she could offer more support to her friend, especially given that Matt was no longer reliable.

'I will call again tomorrow?' Gill enquired tentatively, not wanting to overdo it, but wanting Rosie to know she cared.

'That would be nice, thanks Gill.'

'I love you darling.'

'And you.'

As Gill pushed her phone back into her pocket, she decided the rain was not going to ease and she might as well make a dash for it.

She was dripping by the time she reached the barn. The smell of damp dust filled the air and birdsong chattered from the hedgerows, as though the creatures were rejoicing in the bounty of fresh water.

She couldn't help but laugh at Amber who appeared to be swearing to herself by the gate of her pasture. Teddy kept shaking his little head, trying to get the droplets out of his oversized foal ears.

'Come on then.' Without bothering to get a headcollar, Gill ran to the gate and opened it for the mare, who trotted all the way to the barn and took the first open stable, Teddy at her side.

Gill followed them inside, closing the door behind them, and stood dripping onto the concrete floor. She wondered why she hadn't heard Monty greet his mare.

The black horse's stable was empty. That also explained where Kelly was.

She headed towards the bins to make Amber a small midday feed and saw the note that her employee needn't have left, saying she had taken the horse for a ride across the estate.

One of the last, Gill thought and the sadness filled her again.

Amber kicked at the door with an impatient fore hoof and whickered, reminding Gill of the important task she had failed to finish.

'Will you bugger off!'

Rosie heard her mother before she saw her and dashed towards the cubicle, trailing a nervous Eddie behind.

'Mum!' Rosie exclaimed, reprimanding Selina for swearing at the poor nurse who was hovering beside the bed with a small cup of pills and a small cup of water.

'There!' Selina croaked at the nurse, 'I told you she was coming.'

'Mum, will you please do as you are told?'

'Like I keep telling this madam,' Selina rolled her eyes towards the nurse who was becoming suitably irritated herself, 'the blue ones make me drowsy and I need to talk to you before they put me to sleep again. It's important.'

Rosie shook her head and turned apologetically to the nurse. 'I am so sorry, can you leave them with me and I will make sure she gets them once we have had a chat?'

'It's no trouble, I will come back.' The nurse smiled warmly at Rosie, before leaving the cubicle.

Rosie put her handbag down beside the bed, took the chair next to her mother. Selina was upright and wild eyed, but looked as though she would have been better off asleep.

Selina opened her mouth to speak but started coughing instead. Eddie hovered by the curtain.

'Rosie,' Selina sipped water from a beaker and lubricated her throat enough to speak again, 'I need to talk to you.'

'I know, you said, what is it Mum?'

'I want you to use my house.' Selina grasped at Rosie's hand but missed and banged her bony knuckle on the arm of the chair, 'Fuck!' she exclaimed as Rosie gently took her hand and rubbed where the chair had made contact.

'Use your house?' Rosie shook her head, wondering if her mother was asking her to move back to Sevenoaks, to live there again? Was she already that muddled?

'Yes. You said the problem with Matt and this job and the reason you might lose your cottage is money. Sell my house and use it to make things right.'

'But I can't sell your house?' Rosie decided it made

slightly more sense, but was still worried her mother was delirious.

'Yes you can, listen child for god's sake, when I am gone it will be your house. Don't you get all sentimental or think you have to wait a respectful time. Get the estate agents round. Today in fact!'

'Mum really?' Rosie felt tears prick her eyes and was conscious of Eddie staring at them. 'Can we not talk about this?'

'No.' Selina leant closer so that Rosie could smell the acid from her wasting stomach when she spoke. 'You need to make your life right. You know what to do.'

'Mum I am not going to start thinking about inheritance, you are not dead.'

'Don't care.' Selina leant back and folded her arms, her eyes mocked her daughter. 'That was all I wanted to say. You can get madam back.'

Rosie couldn't help but laugh at her mother.

'Don't you want to see your visitor first?'

'How much more of you do I need to see? Gave birth to you isn't that enough? I suppose if you are going to be here anyway you can get me a wheelchair and push me outside for a fag.'

'Not me you abhorrent woman – Eddie.'

Rosie gestured towards the terrified man who was all but shrinking into the curtain between him and escape.

As their eyes met, and Selina gasped, the connection between them brought him forwards. As he reached her side, his fears were replaced by the affection which, though brief in its duration, had apparently stood the test of 32 years.

Rosie found her feelings a hybrid of warmth, in knowing where she had come from, seeing the people who made her locked in one another's gaze, and also uncomfortable, like a gooseberry.

'Rosie move.' Selina ordered without taking her eyes off the man whose genes had stared back at her from a cot, had made her proud, and sad, and inevitably guilty.

Rosie got up and Eddie replaced her in the seat beside the bed. Selina reached out both hands to him and he took them.

'Look what we made.' She inclined her head towards Rosie and giggled like a teenager.

'I know. She is pretty awesome.'

Although the conversation appeared to be about her, Rosie had the sense to realise she was not part of it.

'I will leave you two to catch up.'

As she slid the curtain of the cubicle closed after herself, Rosie hovered a while, hearing Selina begin her apology to a man she had deceived and lost.

As she made her way towards the hospital cafeteria, intending to fetch a coffee for herself and to take one back for Eddie, she found herself grinning. As inappropriate as her joy was, given the circumstances, she felt the strongest sense of self, validated all at once in those few moments when her parents had reconnected and marvelled at her very existence.

Gill looked at the old clock on the wall of the barn.

It was 7pm, only two more hours of daylight. Gill wondered whether she should be starting to worry about Kelly. She also wondered if she should get Pop up to the gallops now, so that she had time to take Zinee up afterwards.

She counted back the hours, even the longest of the block rides couldn't have taken this long.

She wondered if George might have seen them going past Bloomswell. She picked up her phone to call him but then remembered how busy he would be, mid dinner service.

He and Rob had popped in on their way back from Radley's office.

Armed with the proof of payment, and having had time to think about it more, the solicitor had a new plan.

Rob had done a brilliant impression of the older lawyer when he had repeated the mantra which had sold them on the new idea, 'He who comes to the law, must come with clean hands'. Given that hers were now provably dirty, they had agreed to a letter which delicately mentioned fraudulent behaviour and pointed out the penalties of deceit. The letter gave her 14 days to return four thousand pounds and sign the new version of the settlement agreement, which included the proviso that she would be banned from dining at Bloomswell itself, as well as precluded from making any public statements about the food there. The letter attached a DVD of the CCTV footage, which Radley had asked his assistant to burn from the USB stick, before handing it back to George.

As Gill stood listening to their triumph, their mutual confidence, she couldn't help feel that at least one drama was over. Surely Duckleton would have to back down now, even if she didn't return any money, she would be foolish to attempt any further action. As the pair left the yard, already deep in discussion about the entrees for the table of 10 they had coming in that evening, she felt warmed by the clear bond between them, which was thankfully reinstated. It reminded her of the way she and Kelly talked.

Gill sighed as she fetched Zinee's saddle and let herself in to his stable. He immediately got in close to her and nudged her arm, hoping for a titbit. Just as she was about to gently back him away so that she could place his bridle over his pert ears, he stomped past her to put his head over the half door and stare out of the barn towards the drive. Gill dashed towards the yard in time to see Monty and Kelly at last returning.

Kelly dropped to the ground and stood beside the jet back Arabian, dipping her head and flushing an apology.

'I am so sorry Gill. I didn't mean to be gone this long...'

Gill raised her arm to stop Kelly's explanation midstream.

'Totally get it.' She smiled at the groom, who almost smiled back, but her face fell as she ran up Monty's stirrups and loosened his girth.

'Better get Pop and Zinee up to the track?' Kelly was composed by the time she looked back at her boss, focused as always on the next task at hand.

'Are you up to it?'

'I am not wasting a single ride.'

'Ok, sort Monty, I will get them ready.'

'Gill...' Kelly paused and Gill turned back towards her, hearing the catch in her voice.

'What is it sweetheart?'

'I only have three days left, then Zinee's race, then I will be gone.'

Gill stared at the floor. What could she say?

'Do you need some time off to pack?'

'No. I can sleep on the plane.'

Jules was waiting in the Newmans kitchen for Gill, when she finally got inside and took her boots off for the last time that day.

'I drafted the advert and printed off a copy for you to look at.'

'Ok thanks.' Gill tried to smile but her heart wasn't in it and she pulled herself onto a stool.

'Any word from Rosie?'

'Spoke to her at lunchtime. She's basically just waiting for her to die.'

'Tough. Just when she had finally started to get to know her again.'

'Least they had the chance.' Gill thought about her own mother, who she felt like she had lost years ago, but still lived on, cocooned in the prison of her own mind, and wondered which was kinder, a short sharp outage where you got to say what you needed to say and then depart, or years of decay, followed by oblivion, so that you were basically just a collection of organs.

'She and Red are staying at her Eddie's yard. She was taking him to see her mother this afternoon.'

Jules looked up sharply, feeling a coldness sweep over her at the mention of the man who had hidden her horse.

'I know. It's pretty messed up. We have to support her though.'

Jules bobbed her head in agreement.

'I might go and ring her.'

'She might not be very talkative, but I think that would be a good idea. I said I would call again tomorrow but give her my love.'

'Will do.' Jules turned to head for the door back to her own kitchen but Gill stopped her.

'Before I forget – we have finally sorted Truckleton!'

By the time Jules had finished hearing the good news, and the conversation had turned into one of the wrench they were facing with the loss of Kelly, it was well after eleven.

Jules had agreed to attending Saturday's outing. She briefly considered whether she ought to be trying to reduce her hours at Hodges in order to allow her more time and energy for Newmans. After the last Saturday of racing she had found the week at work hard. She did not normally attend the races or get very involved beyond helping out with riding to the gallops, which she viewed as an equivalent to time she might otherwise spend in a gym anyway. She liked her current level of involvement because it meant her career came first, but without Kelly, and unless the groom they hired was as good, which she doubted, she may have to make changes to her life to ensure the success of her investment.

She wondered if it was too late to call Rosie. She guessed things must be pretty irregular, but it would be typical if she rang at the one time Rosie had managed to sleep.

She texted her friend instead, asking if she was up and free for a chat.

'There is a nice short hack we can do if you fancy getting Red out before we head back to the hospital?' Eddie set a mug of coffee in front of his bleary eyed daughter. He said the 'we' tentatively, hoping she wouldn't baulk at his desire to go with her again.

Rosie slumped over the tiny kitchen table. Eddie's cottage was small, the furniture old, but it was clean and homely. He had given up his bed for her and she felt sure he must be suffering as a result of sleeping on the sofa, but he insisted he rarely slept the night through anyway and it was nice being near the telly.

Certainly this was true of the night before. He had spent over an hour with Selina before she had finally been unable to keep her eyes open, and her speech at become slurred. Despite her advancing years, the proud nose, and serious blue eyes still held fascination for him. Her sharp mind, despite a clearly blunt body, had captivated his brain to the exclusion of any other thoughts, just as it always had.

He looked across the table at the woman they had created. The circumstances which had brought Rosie to him were once again tragic, and he felt bad for being pleased she was there. He couldn't help it though. Not a single day had passed since he had found out she existed, when he didn't find himself thinking of her.

Despite their lack of contact, and knowing she hated him for what he had done, she had still become his inner voice. Every decision he made was measured against a benchmark of what he perceived might be her approval. He considered his life through her eyes - would it make her proud, would she think it was right?

She must think the yard and his job were ok or she surely wouldn't still be there with her stunning horse.

'I don't think I can ride Red.' Rosie said suddenly, having been vaguely considering his suggestion, despite appearing not to have heard it. She was too weary to bother to make an excuse so she was simply honest. 'We have been having trust issues. My life is a bit of a mess and while I am all over the place, it seems to make him anxious.'

'Perhaps you are a bit too close to him.' Eddie said thoughtfully. She looked up and eyed her father briefly. She still couldn't quite hold the gaze of the man she was still reluctant to trust, even in spite of the magical respite he had given Selina from her illness the day before.

'I can't hide anything from him. The more wrong I am, the more he sees me as a liability.'

'The more wrong you are?' Eddie didn't want to pry in case she told him to mind his own business, but he didn't understand.

'It hasn't been a very good year.'

Eddie nodded sympathetically, still not really any clearer on what the problem was.

Rosie reached into her pocket and took out her phone. She realised it was still on silent and alarmingly she had 15 unread text messages. Later. She scrolled through her photographs until she found a picture which made her heart ache like a foreign body in her chest.

'This,' She said as she handed him the phone, 'is your granddaughter.'

Chapter Twenty-one

By the time Gill had finished the morning rounds, she was exhausted.

This is what it will be like in future, she thought as she finally closed the last stable door, and the prospect of riding at all, let alone three times, made her feel even more tired.

Kelly had taken the morning off. Despite her determination to work each of her remaining days at Newmans in full, she had succumbed to packing and helping her mother. The storage truck which would be taking their furniture some ten thousand miles was arriving at lunchtime.

Jules was out on a date that evening, and was using her lunch break to ride Romeo, which left Gill with no help.

Despite her weariness she let herself in to Zinee's stable and began to brush the black horse. His eyes half closed in pleasure as the brush swept through his coat to remove the layer of barn dust which seemed to settle on all the stabled horses, no matter how hard she tried to keep the building as clean as possible.

She reached her arms around the horse's neck as he leaned towards her. He was such a soft and gentle animal. He was racing fit, a young stallion in his prime, and yet his focus always seemed to be on Gill. When they were in the stable he liked to be near her, when she was astride him, he listened to her intently.

Since her fall, she had eased him back into work gently, only riding when she felt strong enough to provide him with the reassurance he needed. She supposed she ought to have been nervous, but her primary concern was to ensure that the fall had not affected him and his confidence, rather than thinking of herself.

She was starting to worry about Saturday. The race was short, a 6 furlong sprint. He was doing easily double that at home, as well as work riding through the lanes.

She knew from experience though, that the travelling, the new environment at a racecourse, the pumping adrenaline of the other horses, and the overwhelming human noise from the milling crowds, could all serve to sap energy from a horse by the time it got to the start line.

'Well, at least I will be piloting,' she said to the horse, 'So if you do get tired, we can just go slower.'

Gill had already phoned Norah and told her she was planning to give the horse an easy first time out. Norah had seemed pre-occupied and simply agreed to Gills suggestions about the horse, which included that he should sit the Newbury race out. She made a mental note to find and speak to Norah after Zinee's race, just to satisfy herself there wasn't anything of concern behind the owner's unusual acquiescence.

By the time she and Zinee reached the gallops, she had put all thoughts of Norah and of Kelly firmly into the back of her mind.

All there was, was a woman and a horse.

She cantered him gently for the first half mile, allowing him to warm up and relax into a rhythm.

When they reached the marker, she stood up in the stirrups and drew in her breath. The horse rewarded her by running with a drive and impulsion she had not experienced before.

His gallop ate up the lengths at a speed which dried her mouth out, she felt like she was part of his energy. Although he carried her, they ran together.

His feet barely skirted the earth, the elastic in his tendons elevating them over ground, as effortless as it was beautiful.

At the end of the track she sat down again exhaled deeply. Zinee needed no pressure on his bit, slowing evenly in time with her cue.

'Do that on Saturday my boy, we might just make your owner smile.'

'Of course not!' Jules laughed indignantly, brushing off Keith's assertion that she had been avoiding him.

'I didn't hear anything from you for over a week! I couldn't be blamed for thinking you had gone off me.'

Keith's tone was jovial, his face smiling, but his eyes told a different story.

Jules wondered if she should just come clean. Tell him she was ridiculously in love with someone who was unobtainable, and that he was a tool she used to deny it.

She gazed at his handsome face across the table. He was such a nice man.

'I was ill, and it's all been a bit hectic really. Our groom is emigrating, my business partner's other half has been having some legal issues and my friend's mother is sick.'

The waitress arrived with their tapas and halted the conversation. After she had painstakingly laid out each little bowl and taken their orders for more drinks, Keith smiled properly again.

'So you are not going off me then?'

'No. I like you. I really do.' Jules reached for her wine and took a swig for courage. 'The thing is, I am a bit battle scarred, and my life is complicated. So I do need to take things slowly.'

Keith nodded and reached for his own drink.

'Let's just enjoy each other's company and see where it goes?'

'I really like you. Like, a hell of a lot.'

Jules looked around for the waitress, hoping she was coming back with more wine. Keith recognised he had made her uncomfortable.

'But I guess hearing that is exactly the kind of pressure you just told me you didn't want?'

'Kinda.'

'Tell me about your job? What does being a solicitor bring your way on an average day?'

Jules smiled and started to describe the way she made her living.

Her phone rang as they ate but she decided to ignore it, Keith deserved her undivided attention at least once.

'I am afraid she hasn't had a very good day today.' The nurse smiled warmly at Eddie and at Rosie, used to giving bad news, but clearly not hardened to it.

'What do you mean?' Rosie twisted her hands together anxiously.

'Well, she hasn't eaten very much and she has slept a lot. I can find a doctor to tell you more if you want to hang on here for a moment?'

Rosie nodded and Eddie resisted the urge to put his arms around her as they stood awkwardly at the entrance to the ward where the nurse had approached them.

As they waited, Rosie looked around for a chair, suddenly feeling light headed.

She resolved to compose herself as the doctor came

towards them.

'Hi, you must be Selina's daughter.' The doctor shook hands with Rosie and nodded politely at Eddie, before delivering the bad news.

'You can still go and sit with her, it is possible she might wake up for a bit, but her organs are starting to shut down because her liver cant dispose of the waste products in her body any more. There are things we could try and do, but she has made it quite clear she wants this part of the process to go quickly. She may remain asleep now until she passes, there is no way of knowing really.'

Rosie nodded. She felt isolated. No tears, no dramatic wailing, just a coldness which crept through her and rendered her silent.

'Thank you.' Eddie smiled grimly at the doctor, effectively releasing him.

As the doctor walked away, Rosie began to crumple, and Eddie moved in close to help her remain standing.

'It's too quick.' she whispered, 'she is too young.'

'I know.' Eddie said gently, wishing he could do something, anything, to stop her heart from breaking.

As Jules let herself in, she was surprised to see Ziggy skittering towards her. The dog would usually have been in with Gill when she was out for the evening. His desperation to greet Jules was overtaken by his need to pee and he wagged past her through the open door to relieve himself on a fence post.

'Good job I came home then.'

At the end of the meal with Keith she had started talking about the early start she had the next day and he had agreed to call it a night, he had to be up for an early meeting with an architect anyway. He had seemed slightly disappointed but she had cheered him by instigating a passionate good night snog and agreeing to him coming over to hers on Saturday night after the race.

As Jules waited for Ziggy to finish, she glanced up towards the horse barn and noticed the light was on.

She stepped into the kitchen and slipped off her high heels in favour of wellies and set off up the drive to investigate, concerned about why anyone would be up there so late.

As she walked she felt her phone vibrate and quickly got it out of her bag to answer it before the ringtone started to blare.

It was James.

'Hello?' Jules answered, concerned.

'Thank god.' James was hugely relieved to hear her voice. 'Where have you been all evening?'

'Out with Keith, sorry. What is it?'

'I went home this evening.'

'Oh, what happened to your last night at the hotel?' Jules was confused.

'I couldn't put it off any longer, I had to talk to her.'

'Oh my! And? What happened?' Jules stopped walking and leant on the fence which bordered the drive, her concentration redirected.

'I said we needed to talk and dropped the kids to her mums. She was sat in the lounge when I got back, it was almost like she knew, like she had been waiting for it.'

'And?'

'I said I didn't think things were working very well, and wondered how she felt about a trial separation.'

'Oh god James, you must have been in such a state – what did she say?'

'It was so weird Jules. I fully expected her to start bellowing at me and call me all the names under the sun until I gave in – but she didn't. She just looked at the floor for a few seconds, and then said she agreed.'

'Bloody hell.'

'I have spent so long being unhappy and not knowing how to get out. I guess I should have realised she felt the same. She didn't used to moan or shout. We were happy once, but we haven't been for a long time and I guess if I had to say what she was feeling, it was relief, the same as me.

'Then I started to cry. I haven't cried since Ben was born. I'm not really sure what set me off. Just suddenly felt so sad. Sad for the children, sad for us. I went into it thinking it would be forever you know?'

'Oh James, darling, of course you felt upset you were bound to.' Jules heart went out to him, picturing the tears sliding from his soulful and exquisite mahogany eyes. She wished she could hold him.

'Then she started to cry too. And we hugged. For the first time in ages. It wasn't like a passionate hug, it was just to comfort each other and she said she was sorry, and I said I was sorry.' James paused and snorted a dry laugh, 'It was the longest she's been without shouting at me in about two years.'

'You must be in shock. Where are you now?'

'I am a bit. Back at the hotel. We talked for a while about the kids and how it would work. She said she didn't want to lose the house and I said that was fine, I didn't intend to take it from her.'

'How will you afford to live?'

'Ben starts school in September, she said she will have more time for her business and plans to make more of a go of it, so she should be able to cope ok if I can help with the mortgage and the kids, which of course I will. I should just about be able to afford a little flat in Exeter. Unless she has suddenly developed a remarkable skill for thinking on her feet, I would say she had already got it all worked out.'

'You sound sad?'

'No not sad, just a bit bewildered. I was so geared up for a battle, I had steeled myself to cope with hurting her and I honestly don't think I did.'

'So you are waiting for the other shoe to drop?'

'A bit yeah. I feel relieved mostly.'

'I am very proud of you, even though she took it well, it still can't have been easy.'

'It really was.' James chuckled, 'almost think she must have someone else!'

'Really?'

'Nah. At least, I don't think so. Maybe just a logical supportive friend to turn to? Like I have.'

'You know I will be here for you.' Jules confirmed her intentions with sincerity, completely hiding her disappointment that she had not been categorised as more, because after all, it was what she had insisted on.

'I know. I don't think I could do it without you.'

'You kind of already did it.'

'I still feel like I am waiting for an explosion. I can't see her mending and making do. I have no doubt I will be able to see the kids as much as I want, but financially, I would anticipate I will be bled dry before this thing is over.'

"I need to go now James,' Jules suddenly felt cold and conscious that she was standing in the dark, her worry about the light in the barn returning. 'How about I join you for breakfast at the Northgate in the morning, after I have dropped Zig off at the farm?'

'Sounds lovely, thanks so much Jules.'

'I didn't really do anything.'

'You did, more than you will ever know.'

Jules shook her head as she put her phone back in her bag. Ziggy got up from where he had laid patiently at her feet. She walked quickly towards the barn, praying everything was ok and her delay had not worsened a problem.

'Ello Zig-dog.'

Ziggy ran ahead of her into the barn and she heard Kelly greet him before she stepped inside herself, and knew from the groom's tone all was well.

'Hey Jules, how was your date?' Gill smiled up at Jules from her plastic chair, Kelly sat opposite her, they were both red eyed.

'Yeah it was ok.' Jules dusted off a chair and sat tentatively on it, aware of her suit skirt, which she would not normally have gone near a horse in.

'You look...' Kelly giggled, 'very sexy.'

Gill noticed Jules' wellies which finished off her smart outfit in a manner fit for ridicule and started to laugh too.

'Yeah yeah.' Jules rolled her eyes at their giggles, 'My focus was on finding out why you are up here at almost midnight, not on ensuring the fashion police would be happy with my attire. Are all the horses ok?'

Gill nodded.

'After we finished up for the night we ended up sat here having a coffee, and we haven't moved since.'

'Speaking of which, I had better call mum quickly.' Kelly stood up from her chair and stretched, 'It's still ok to sleep here?'

'You can have Charlie's room.'

As Kelly left the barn to find a mobile signal, Jules leaned forward.

'Is she ok?'

'Yeah. I showed her the advert you wrote for the groom

to see if she thought there was anything we should add. I thought it might make her feel better to be involved. She got so upset, we ended up sat here talking until she calmed down.'

'Your heart was in the right place.'

'I feel like I should have done more to keep her.' Gill's head fell into her hands, despairing again, and Jules couldn't help but despair with her.

'I feel like it's my fault. When she was at loggerheads with her mum, I tried to put her Mum's point of view.' Jules paused and waited to see if Gill reacted to the admission of guilt that Jules hadn't really intended to make until that moment. 'I was trying to think of what Rosie might have said.'

Gill laughed sarcastically, but did not feel any anger towards her business partner.

'No one does Rosie quite like Rosie.'

'James left his wife tonight.'

'And?'

'And she didn't put up a fight. Think she was as relieved as he was that it was finally happening. They have both been unhappy it seems.'

'And what does that mean for you?'

Jules rolled her eyes and knotted her fingers together in frustration.

'It means I get to be his supportive friend and help him through his divorce.'

Gill got up from her chair to place a kiss on Jules forehead.

'Good girl.'

'Good girls don't have any fun, do they.'

'You are really only just working that out?' Gill chuckled as she donned the muck gloves, deciding to save some time in the morning by removing the dumps from the horse's stables.

407

'Even I know that.' Kelly said as she plodded back into the barn, overhearing the last part of the conversation. 'Better than bloody most.'

Rosie's eyes closed again, but her lolling head woke her as it fell forwards. The hospital chair offered little in the way of neck support.

'I think maybe we should go now?' Eddie murmured gently from his own chair beside Selina's bed. It was the third time he had said it, but Rosie seemed to be locked inside her own thoughts and he wondered if he should stop trying to engage her in conversation and start physically helping her up.

Selina had not woken up at all in the six hours that they had been there. Visiting times no longer applied it seemed, none of the nurses had asked them to leave. Eddie guessed when things reached this stage, rules were ignored in favour of respect.

'I don't get it.' Rosie spoke. It was the first time in what felt like an eternity and Eddie was relieved to hear her voice.

'That she was awake and talking to us yesterday and now this?'

'Yes.' Rosie stared at her mother's face. In her inert state, skin yellowing rapidly and becoming almost translucent, she stopped looking like Selina. She could have been any sleeping person on the verge of death. She snored loudly sometimes, sometimes she was so quiet Rosie had to check she was breathing. Rosie wished she would wake up, just to prove she was still in there, to see familiar eyes, to hear a familiar voice, ranting as usual.

Rosie had, at times, become so frustrated she had wanted to prod her mother. To shout into her ear and tap at her sagging cheek.

A nurse had tried to give her some tea but couldn't wake

her, despite being quite loud and persistent. Rosie guessed if the nurse couldn't do it, she couldn't either. She didn't want to leave, but, if Selina had even the smallest inkling that Rosie was there, she was not showing any sign of the awareness.

Rosie glanced at Eddie. She appreciated his patience. More so, appreciated having someone else who cared.

'I think I had better make some calls, people keep texting me to find out what is happening.'

'If you would like your husband to come to mine he is very welcome – where is it he works again?'

'Oxford, but no, thanks.'

Rosie continued to sit in the chair. She had managed to suggest they leave, but still couldn't bring herself to actually stand up. She wished she was at home. She wished she could smell and touch her daughter, it was more of a distant longing than a conscious thought.

She counted the days since she had last seen Eve. She felt the sadness, knowing the child would never meet her grandmother, as inappropriate and annoying as she was. Wished Red and Peat were in their paddock. Life had seemed so awful, she had been so desperate to escape from Matt and from herself. Now that she was experiencing truly awful, she realised how self-obsessed she had been.

Watching Selina, each breath laboured, each unknown minute, she couldn't help but think back to the moment when the seeds of her depression and anxiety had sprouted. She felt like she was going to explode with the emotion that filled her as she thought of that day, so she talked to the man sitting opposite her, giving up on keeping him at a distance, in favour of not screaming.

'Do you remember I told you about my horse Harry, when we met?'

Eddie pondered for a second, as though considering the question, but in truth he remembered every detail because he had played that amazing conversation they had shared, before things had turned sour, over and over in his head.

'Your older boy, welsh cob?'

'Yes. I lost him just before Christmas.'

'I am really sorry.' Eddie looked genuinely upset, as though he understood the pain. Not many did.

'I knew he was starting to fade really. He was 27 when he went. I think I had always expected him to be one of those record breaking horses who were still stomping about demanding their dinner at forty.'

'That's still a good age.'

Rosie ignored his reassurance and continued.

'I felt like he was getting more distant. He would sleep a lot, and stand gazing across the valley for hours on end, like he had forgotten to graze. But, he was still eating his dinner, he was still well conditioned and apart from a bit of arthritis in his hocks, he didn't seem in pain. I kept wondering when I would have to make the decision. I wondered if I should have already made it. I always thought I would know when he was ready to go.'

Rosie paused, the sadness around her catching. Eddie felt himself filling up, on the brink of tears, as he listened to her story.

'The decision got made for me.' Rosie steeled herself to hear the words coming out of her own mouth for the first time. 'I went up to the stables to give them their breakfast. He had been fine the night before, no sign of anything wrong, so I wasn't expecting anything out of the ordinary.

'Red was stood on the yard, waiting for his bucket I guess. I couldn't see Harry. I called him, and then carried on and mixed their feeds, expecting that he would amble down in his

410

own time as always. But he didn't come. I left Red eating and walked around the side of the yard and I couldn't see him. I started to panic and ran up the field.

'He was stood behind the stables. The ground is rough there and nothing much grows, so it wasn't a place I had been used to seeing either of them. I knew something was wrong. I knew I had to go to him, but for a split second I couldn't make my legs move. It was as if I knew, I knew I was going to have to watch him die.'

Rosie gulped in air and exhaled slowly, trying to calm herself down. In describing it, she was back there, stood in her field, in the drizzle, looking at her horse.

'He was sweated up so badly his rug was drenched. He had grazes on his face and his breathing was so loud and fast. I tried to ask him to move with me because I thought I ought to get him in to his stable, but when he tried to step forwards he fell.'

Eddie watched the tears streaming from her face, his own eyes wet, fuelled by a paternal instinct he had not felt before. Beyond the desire to impress and placate her - he suddenly felt like he would have cut his own leg off to have gone back in time and prevented her from going through it.

'I screamed for Matt. I knew he wouldn't be able to hear me inside the house. I didn't want to leave him on the ground but I needed help and a vet. I was heavily pregnant but somehow I managed to run back to the house, I don't think I could run that fast now even without a baby inside me. I got Matt up, I called my friend Nicola who lives across the valley, and I called the vet. It was a Sunday morning and I expected an on call vet to answer, but it was my own vet, Fred, who was on emergency duty.

'By the time we got back to Harry he was still on the ground. We kept trying to get him up but his hind legs just didn't seem to have any strength in them at all. Nic arrived and

411

we managed to get him off the stones to some longer grass so that at least it would be softer if he went down again. Matt practically carried his back end, every step took about ten minutes, but we got him there.

'Then Fred arrived and came up the field. He asked Nic to put a headcollar on Red and hold him away from Harry because by then he was trying to bite him. I don't think he was being mean, I think he was just saying, come on then, tell me off like you usually do, to prove to himself Harry was ok.

'But he wasn't ok. Fred listened to his heart and he was frowning. I knew it was bad. I said to him, if it's time, do it, I don't want him to suffer any longer than he has to.'

'Rosie that was so brave.'

'It tortures me sometimes, should I have asked for more tests, might he have lived. But I know deep down it was right, I just wish it hadn't been. Harry had fallen again so we didn't try to get him up. Fred said he had massive heart failure and he suspected he had a blood clot as well, which was why his back end was so cold and he couldn't walk.

'He warned me that after the injection Harry might gasp for breath and was trying to explain to me what he was going to do to him but I just told him to hurry. I couldn't look at Harry on the ground, suffering, panicking, I just wanted it to stop for him.

'I sat on the floor and held his head and he gave these two sharp breaths and then exhaled really loudly. And then he was gone.'

Rosie slumped back in her chair. Even after all this time she still couldn't believe it. Couldn't believe that the story she was telling was true, her Harry, her everything, it just didn't seem real. Nothing seemed real, even Eve, everything had a question mark by it because, how could a reality exist where Harry was not in the world?

'I am not surprised you found having a baby and your husband being away hard after going through that.' Eddie shook his head, to lose an animal you had for so long so quickly, just seems cruel. No matter how much his age should have prepared her for it, she was expecting to have to make a difficult decision at the end of a long battle, not to have him simply gone in one day.

As though she had picked up on his train of thought, Rosie started to speak again,

'It was better for him that his suffering was so brief. I have to be thankful for that.'

Rosie followed Eddie's gaze downwards to the bed between them, their eyes settling on the sleeping form, each realising the significance of what Rosie had just said. Maybe, quickly was the best way to go.

It was those you left behind who suffered the sentence of grief.

Chapter Twenty-two

Saturday came far too quickly for Gill and Kelly.

For Rosie, the three days had seemed like an eternity.

While Kelly had been desperately trying to eke out her remaining days at Newmans, making every minute count, Rosie had watched the hours slowly drag by. Sat at her sleeping mother's side, watching for any sign, waiting, but only for the inevitable. It was like knowing you had a root canal booked, part of you wanted it to be over and done with, part of you prayed it would never come.

Rosie stood up from the hospital chair, needing to stretch out her legs and wake her bottom back up. She noticed Eddie had dozed off again.

Despite how tired he must surely have been, he had come to the hospital straight after he had finished the morning routine. It was touching, really. She couldn't really show her appreciation because she still felt so conflicted, but he had taken the fact that he hadn't been asked to leave, to mean she wanted him there.

She had agreed to accompany him and his own horse for a short hack first thing that morning, but she had led Red beside her, reluctant to get on him. The horse had been well mannered. She could do little but walk passively along as he subtly showed his concern for his new surroundings and what dangers might lurk, but did not pick up the slack in the rope in her hand once, almost as though he did not want to upset her further. The love between them was visible, but a barrier around Rosie stopped the presence of her animal from being able to warm her from the inside the way he had always done.

She decided to leave Eddie to doze and go for a walk

across the hospital grounds, to clear her head and breathe fresh air for a few minutes.

As she exited the hospital, the sun beat through thick mid-morning haze, she breathed in the humid air deeply, relishing the freshness of it, in spite of the uncomfortable heat.

She decided to walk around the perimeter of the hospital complex. She switched her phone on and headed to the furthest corner of the hospital grounds. Texts which had been waiting to arrive beeped in quick succession and as she started reading she walked through an archway to the street. A collection of people were smoking. Ousted like lepers off hospital property they stood together, huddled in solidarity.

As she walked through the throng, the smell of rolling tobacco reached her like an old friend and before she had time to reason with herself, she was asking a man with a rollie in his hand if he could spare one.

The man raised his eyebrow, but something about Rosie, the obvious sleep deprivation and the slightly wild look on her face, made him hand her his tobacco tin.

With the deftness of a practised smoker she quickly rolled a modest fag and borrowed a lighter before handing the tin back to the man, thanking him, and continuing on her walk.

As she inhaled the smoke and the nicotine flooded through her system, she felt the muscles in her face relax.

She had missed calls from Sue and Jules, a text from Val, and as usual, a series of texts from Matt.

She sent the same text to Jules, Val and Gill to pre-empt them trying to call as well, saying there was no change. Then, instead of replying to Matt, she called Jimmy.

'Hey Dad,' her voice was strained with the lungful she had just taken of the roll-up and she exhaled the smoke quickly before she choked.

'Darling, how are you?'

'Tired. No change. She is still asleep, still in the same

state.'

'It's so good of you to be there darling. Is Red ok?'

'Yeah.'

There was an awkward silence. In order to fully answer that question, she had to mention Eddie. She wanted to tell him that he was still her Dad and Eddie was convenience at a difficult time and no more. But she couldn't quite provide him with the reassurance because she hadn't mentioned that Eddie was coming with her to the hospital, or the afternoon he had spent with Selina, and she felt guilty enough not to broach the subject.

The way she had felt seeing her biological parents together, and the knock on effect it had on the way she felt about Eve was progress, but the root of the progress would surely cause Jimmy to feel hurt. He had no place in the picture.

She felt with all her heart that Jimmy was her Dad, would always be, but the time to let him know there was no need for jealousy was not now.

'How is Eve?'

'She is fine. Missing her Mummy, but doing ok. The teething seems to have settled down a bit. She's been laughing so much today, Crystal made a pair of sock puppets and we pretended they were having an argument - we got tired of it long before she did!'

'Sounds like fun.' Rosie was pleased, but couldn't hide the sadness in her voice. 'I miss her so much. It has just kind of crept up on me.'

'She will be here waiting for you when all this is over.'

'I know.'

'When you come home, everything will be better.'

'I hope you are right, but I think that kinds of depends on my husband. Will you call him again?'

'Of course but, Rosie, yesterday he got ever so upset. He is finding it really hard that you are updating him through me.'

'If I call him and we get into another discussion about

the Cottage, I will lose the strength I have left, Dad, I am sorry to put you in this position but I can't risk falling apart right now.'

'I will call him in a minute. I do understand darling. I really don't think he would want to get into that conversation, he is just worried about you and wants to help you through this.'

'Why does he want to help me through this but he didn't want to help me through the last 7 months?'

Jimmy sighed. He could tell the conversation was winding her up and he didn't want to add to her considerable burden.

'It's ok, I have said I will call him and I will, but it wouldn't be right if I didn't tell you he is worried and wants to be there for you, would it?'

'No. Sorry Dad.' Rosie sucked on her roll up, savouring the last drag before stubbing it out.

'Call me tonight?'

'Of course. Kiss Eve from me?'

As Rosie walked along the path and back to the hospital entrance, she remembered Jules and Gill would be racing. Feeling bad for her self-centred text, she wrote another wishing them luck and telling Gill to take care on Zinee.

But Gill and Jules were not reading their texts.

They were trying not to panic, as they waited beside a failed horsebox.

Kelly squeezed between the partitions, trying to calm the horses, risking being squashed.

'Thank god it didn't happen on the motorway.' Jules tried to sound encouraging.

Gill ignored her friend. Quite aside from the growing panic in the back of the box, as the two horses grew anxious at the sudden hold up, Gill descended into thoughts of not making it to the course in time for Zinee's race. They had been waiting for the recovery service, who were trying to locate a secondary box to transfer the horses into.

The two horse box, which was usually so reliable, had spluttered and died just after they had exited the motorway and entered the B roads. Gill had managed to steer the powerless vehicle into a small layby.

Gill swore. It was Kelly's last day, Zinee's first race, and this was exactly the kind of drama she did not need.

They had only been waiting for ten minutes. Not exactly an eternity. But Zinee was not a seasoned traveller. The mare, Cleo, was a seasoned racer, but even she was starting to become restless. The horses didn't understand why they were not being unloaded, they couldn't comprehend that it was not safe to get out.

Gill put her head through the jockey door to ask Kelly how they were doing. As she called the groom's name Zinee let a blast of sound erupt from his nostrils, calling to see if any horse that might be nearby would shout back and give him a direction to focus on.

Gill could smell the sweat from Cleo, could feel the intense heat coming from the horses, in close quarters and confined together on an already muggy day.

'They aren't too bad.' Kelly answered when, at last, Gill could make herself heard.

'I don't know what to do for the best, it's...' Gill stopped talking when she heard Jules' excited voice.

'Yes please – oh thank you so much!'

Gill stepped back from the lorry to see Jules walking beside a young man. He had overalls on and was walking towards the lorry with a comforting smile on his oil stained face.

'Saw your bonnet up. I've got a garage up the road and I was just on my way home for my dinner – thought you might need some help?'

Gill could have hugged the stranger.

Kelly jumped down from the jockey door and the three

418

women followed him to the engine bay and stood around him as he leant over and peered at the feat of engineering which for all they knew, might as well have been rocket science.

'What happened then?' he asked, looking distinctly uncomfortable when he stood up and found himself surrounded. Gill stepped back to give him some space and pulled Jules backwards with her.

'It started spluttering a bit, then before I know what was happening it just died.'

'Turn it over for me, let me hear it.'

Gill nodded and jumped into the cab, as she turned the key the engine wretched and rattled loudly.

'Ok that's enough.' The man shouted over the din.

The man bent over again, leaning so far into the bay that his feet lifted from the ground, making Kelly snigger. Jules thwacked the groom's arm and shook her head.

'Yeah...' the man righted himself again, 'there's water in your fuel filter.'

'What does that mean?' Gill reappeared from the cab, praying for a positive answer.

'It means I need to get my wrench and loosen the drain plug to let it out.'

'And then?'

'And then you can probably be on your way.'

Gill didn't resist the urge a second time, she grabbed the young man and hugged him, ignoring his protest that he would get her oily.

When the man had finished his work he asked Gill to turn the engine over and keep turning it. After a tense moment when the engine tried over and over but showed no signs of life, it suddenly spluttered and caught.

Each of the women hugged the man in turn, he laughed and refused the cash Gill tried to give him. He told her to get it checked out properly once they were home and retreated, flushed from their gratitude.

Once they were safely on the road again, Gill handed her mobile to Jules and asked her to cancel the breakdown service.

Once she was off the phone Jules sighed and smiled.

'The kindness of strangers eh?'

'Who knew people like that still existed?' Gill smiled too and patted the dashboard of the box as if it were a horse.

'Did you see his arse?' Kelly sniggered, 'had to resist the urge to pinch it when he was bent over!'

'I had noticed yes.' said Jules in her best solicitor's voice.

Gill cackled, the laughter more from relief than anything else. As their giggles and elation subsided, the gloom settled back in to the cab. The panic was over, so the occasion resumed the sombre tone which had been set that morning, when Kelly had packed the race-day kit for the last time.

By the time Rosie sat back down opposite her father, he was wide awake, but Selina was not.

'No change?' Rosie asked expectantly, as though there should have been some great event in the fifteen minutes she had been gone, despite nothing having happened for the last twenty-four hours.

'A nurse came in again, to see if she needed pain relief.' Eddie sat as he stretched awkwardly within the confines of the chair. 'And the tea trolley lady came round, I got you a tea, it's on the side above you.'

Rosie reached up to the top of the cabinet and clutched the plastic mug of weak tea. She would have preferred coffee, but she didn't care at that moment, she was just glad of something to replace the horrid taste in her mouth.

'Shall we go and get some lunch before I head back?' Eddie asked brightly.

'Not hungry.' Rosie shook her head.

'I haven't seen you eat since you arrived at mine.'

'Don't.'

Eddie dropped his gaze to avoid her cold stare.

'I might come back to the yard with you.' Rosie stood up again having downed the awful tea.

'Ok.'

'Doesn't seem a lot of point being here.'

'We can come back together after the horses are done?'

Rosie nodded. Eddie stood up and for a moment they both looked at Selina. Did you say goodbye knowing you would not be heard?

Rosie bent over and kissed the gaunt cheek, but as she had expected, the touch evoked nothing. The rasping breaths continued, the slack jaw showed a painfully dry tongue which was turning white. She hoped beyond hope that the professionals were right and that Selina was indeed blissfully unaware of her predicament.

'I can't believe they just leave people like this and wait for everything to finally fail. It seems so barbaric.' Rosie said what they had both been thinking since she had told the story of losing Harry.

'Nobody wants to hang their hat on a decision that might be wrong.' Eddie followed Rosie's lead and leant over to gently stroke Selina's jaundiced forehead. 'I watched my Dad die. Took months. If he'd had his way he would have been out of here the minute they had decided it was curtains anyway. I looked into it, whether they can ever speed stuff when it's a done deal. But aside from not trying to fix a person who is at this stage, they can't actually do any to make it happen sooner.'

'Why is it ok to play god with an animal, but not even to prevent suffering in a person?'

'Blame? That one time in a thousand where someone is helped to go when they might have made it?'

'So we just wait, and watch her fade away.'

Rosie looked so forlorn and small, in that moment Eddie could no longer suppress his urge to comfort her. He walked quietly around the bed, eyes down and head ducked, as though he was approaching a nervous filly, and softly took her hand. She let him, despite everything in her head, her hand could not deny that human interaction was needed. She turned around towards him and put her arms around his neck. As they embraced, for the first time, Eddie felt slightly tense, but there was something so familiar about his smell, she lingered until he relaxed and properly held her. He was warm, strong and solid. Jimmy was tall, willowy and sharp featured, the smartest man she knew. They felt so different, yet so alike, because in both cases, when they held her, they meant it.

After a few minutes of simplistic wordless comfort, Eddie drew back and frowned.

'You had a fag.'

'Yep. And I could do with another.'

Cleo fluttered her delicate nostrils in greeting when she saw her humans walking down through the avenue of stables. The mare was back to her normal relaxed self now that they had finally arrived.

Thanks to the breakdown of the box, followed by some heavy traffic at the entrance of the course, they had arrived at Lingfield much later than Gill would have ordinarily aimed for. The main stables had been full and they had been shown towards an overflow block which was practically deserted. Although Gill was pleased it would be quieter, Jules was going to have to bring Cleo up to the stand with Zinee, where she would have to be walked in the pre-collecting ring during Zinee's race to avoid being left completely alone in a strange place.

As soon as they had unloaded the horses, Gill had to make a dash for the stewards' office to ensure she was declared for their races in time, and Jules and Kelly had both been busting for the loo.

Cleo called again, her pretty bay head craned in their direction, ears pricked and fixed on Gill. Gill trotted forwards as she realised Zinee's head was not over the stable door.

'Zinee!' she called, but still the black horse did not appear to greet them.

'Oh darling!' Gill fumbled with the catch to let herself in with the young horse, who was stood in the back corner of the box, meek, with worried eye and diminished status.

As Gill put her hands out towards him he brightened slightly, lifting his head to greet her, and she rubbed his neck comfortingly, vowing not to leave him again.

The sounds and smells, albeit more distant due to the location of the box, coupled with fatigue from the long and delayed journey, had rendered the horse somewhat shut down.

Gill asked Kelly to pass her a body brush over the half door and she spoke softly to the horse while she ran it over his downy coat, caressing his muscles with her free hand, feeling his tension decrease slightly as she worked.

'Little rest for an hour now poppet.'

As she continued to stand close to the horse, listening to Kelly outside explaining to Jules what would be needed when they headed up to the stands with the horses, she felt as though her staying with him was mutually necessary. Every time she made eye contact with Kelly she felt like shutting down herself.

'We'll look after each other eh?' she whispered, but Zinee, preoccupied with his own fate, continued to stare at the wooden wall of his box.

Eddie watched Rosie from the hall. She hadn't heard him coming back in from tending to a livery horse who had strained a tendon hunting. She had replaced the chair beside her mother's bed for the chair beside his kitchen table, she didn't really look like she was having a rest.

She had refused to go to bed, refused to eat a pasty when he had his lunch. He had managed to persuade her to eat a tiny piece of the cake one of the owners had brought for him as a thank for you for helping out with her horse while she had been away.

The frown lines in her forehead looked set, the gentle pout of her shapely but small bottom lip, so like her mother's, seemed to remain even when she smiled. He wished he could do more for her. Maybe he should call her husband, or even Jimmy, the man she called Dad. Having heard her on the phone insisting no one should come and that she was fine, he felt his intervention would not be well received, but he wondered how long she could continue to run on empty. He decided if there was no change by Monday, he would have to use the number he still had from when her friend Jules had called him, to try and enlist the support of people she might be more inclined to allow to support her.

For now, he decided to offer her the one thing he thought she might accept.

He walked into the kitchen, smiling a hello, and opened the drawer of the dresser. He pulled out a tobacco tin, and opened it to reveal his emergency stash.

He set the tin in front of her.

'You smoke?'

'Not much, and not often, but I always have some just in case I get the urge.'

'Something in common.' Rosie smiled as she reached out to make herself a rollie and Eddie took a small ashtray from the cupboard before he sat beside her and helped himself too.

'Thanks.'

Eddie laughed grimly.

'Not sure I should be thanked for encouraging you to poison yourself, but you looked like you could do with one.'

Rosie nodded vigorously as she lit up.

'Fancy coming out with me to do the afternoon jobs in a minute?'

Rosie looked blank for a moment, not sure if it was ok to engage in something she might enjoy while her mother was in such a horrible state.

'I could do with a hand, and I am sure Red would prefer it if you did his bed how he likes it?'

'Ok.'

Rosie sighed.

If nothing else she could do with the fresh air.

Gill stood awkwardly next to Norah, watching Zinee as he jogged around the parade ring. Kelly's arm would be aching, the horse pulled on his lead rein, begging her to allow him to move faster and satisfy his flight instinct.

He hadn't done anything silly though, like rear, and Gill was proud of the way he was coping with the crowds who watched him noisily from the other side of the rails. She wished she could feel as proud of herself. Her skin was white and inside she was jelly at the prospect of riding the horse down to the start.

She knew once the race started the direction and pace would be set, but as she envisaged herself losing a battle to keep Zinee under control on the way down, or worse not being able to make him move at all if he froze in fear, sweat started to form at the small of her back where her body protector was snugly encasing her torso.

Gill felt silly in her white breeches and silks. She was at least a foot taller than most of the other riders, she had been heavier too. Despite being svelte for her height, she had been almost a stone over and consequently Zinee had the worst odds of all the novice runners in his race.

She was weighed in, ready to mount and waiting for the signal.

'He looks fit enough Gill. Need to have a jockey on him for Exeter though please.'

'I have asked John to come and meet him and have a sit on him after Cleo's race, he doesn't have a runner in the third.'

Norah nodded, happy to indulge Gill this time, but not next.

'Good. All set for next week?'

'Yes. Monty is on his usual form and I think Pop might do well again, depending on the competition.'

'Good.'

Norah seemed in good spirits, dressed in her finery, beaming at her entourage who were waving to her from the rails.

'Was everything ok when I called in the week? You sounded a bit stressed?' Gill was just nervous enough about the prospect of mounting in a few moments to find her voice and ask the direct question.

'I won't be able to make Newbury next week. Got to have a little operation.'

'Oh Norah are you ok?'

'Oh yes. Just a little procedure, been waiting a while for it so they can't think it's that serious, but I will be off my feet for a few weeks.'

'If you need any help with anything do let me know?' Gill said politely, knowing Norah had an armoury of staff at the stud farm anyway.

'Good of you Gillian. It will all be fine though. I was just having a moment when you called.'

'No shame in being a bit scared. Natural.'

Norah smiled sarcastically, as if having a wobbler over anything was a completely ridiculous concept.

When the steward finally rang the bell and Kelly led a dancing Zinee towards them, Gill decided she could do it, for Zinee and for herself. She took a deep steady breath, letting her nerves out with it. If Norah could deal with the worry of a health problem and going under the knife, she could ride the horse she knew and trained without ruining his confidence with her own fear.

If only she hadn't fallen from him once already, it might not have been such a battle to keep the idea of falling from her mind.

As Kelly legged her up and she slid her feet into the tiny lightweight stirrups, she decided not to tell Norah about Kelly's departure until they had a replacement employed and trained. No point in adding to her worries.

Kelly led them out towards the soft ground of the brilliant green course.

'Good luck!' Kelly gave Zinee a final pat before unclipping his rope and retreating from the track.

'Let's hope we don't need it.' Gill muttered from beneath her hard hat.

The sun was high in the sky, bright enough to cause Gill to squint.

Zinee stood watching Kelly, confused because she had walked away from him. Gill gently patted his neck, knowing that his rigid frozen stance could be followed by an explosion if she pushed him with her legs too hard. Instead she fought her body's natural instincts in order to relax her legs and her seat, and to give Zinee confidence through her calm.

Gill waited until she saw another jockey being led onto the track. His mount appeared steady and Gill recognised him, not as someone she had used, but she had seen him around enough to know he knew what he was doing.

As the groom unclipped his horse, the jockey gathered up to begin the canter to the start. Just as the horse was about to pass Zinee, Gill squeezed positively with her legs, focusing on the horse and jockey, giving Zinee a direction and a friend in one.

To her utter relief Zinee followed the horse. The jockey kept his mount at a slow and steady canter and Zinee fell in stride with the small chestnut Arabian beside him.

'Going's quite soft today.' The jockey called to her, without looking up from his mount's twitching ears.

Gill looked down at Zinee's feet and was pleased to see the horse wasn't sinking too deeply into the rain soaked ground. His bare feet cut in just enough to give him traction without digging holes for him to climb out of.

'Yes, could be worse though.' Gill thought back to a few springs ago, when the courses had lakes on them, some of the races had been cancelled. The baking sun was drying the ground almost as quickly as the sky had wetted it.

The jockey looked across at Gill and laughed, recognising her.

'Thought you were a trainer?!'

'I am. This one is a bit of a worrier, wanted him to have a familiar voice first time out.'

The jockey nodded, she had expected him to ridicule her but he seemed quite impressed.

'I'm Ronnie.'

'Gill.' As they continued their mild descent to where the starter and his assistant were waiting, Zinee was ok. His ears circled around, trying to listen to his environment, but he was keeping a measured pace with Ronnie's mount and felt responsive beneath her. It gave her an opportunity to glance over at her companion.

His hands were light and gentle where they made contact with the mouth of the compact and fine mare he was riding. He looked, as many of the jockey's did, like he was a rider by design, no amount of lessons, no amount of training, could have bettered the natural seat he had and the way his body effortlessly balanced above the horse.

'Have you got a runner in the 4th next week?'

'Newbury? Don't quote me on it, but I think I am only in the first and fifth at present.'

'Do your yard mind you picking up rides?'

'Not at all.'

'I am waiting to hear back from my reserve but I might have a mare needs a rider.'

'Marilium's Immortal Mist?'

The jockey's eyes lit up at the prospect of riding the mare who, aside from Monty, was one of Newmans best known winners.

Gill laughed, impressed.

'No it's another mare I'm afraid, Cleo, the Lioness, second season out, she's in the second here today.'

'I could come and meet her after her race, I don't have anything in the third.'

Gill nodded, delighted he thought meeting the mare was important. John had double booked himself and she had been waiting to hear back from another jockey but he had yet to confirm whether he was prepared to make a long journey for the offer of a single ride and Gill didn't hold out much hope.

'Great, thank you.'

Zinee slowed his pace in line with Ronnie's mount and soon they were waiting for the starter to prepare the tape, which would ping back in front of them and signify the off.

Gill focused on keeping Zinee walking round, as the rest of the field joined them and the volume of horses increased, she kept the stallion's feet moving, riding him positively forward in wide circles, determined not to allow him to stop and freeze.

She and Kelly had practised with a piece of elastic tied to a post at home, Kelly holding the white strip taught and letting it go when Zinee had endured a few moments of standing. It hadn't fazed the horse, and she hoped they had done enough to avoid the starting tape being a problem now.

Once the tape was up, the starter called them forwards towards the line. Ronnie was at the other end of the row of horses and Gill wished she had been able to get Zinee closer to the chestnut. Too late now.

As she eased Zinee towards the line, a horse in close either side of them, she prayed all the other horses were walking towards it at the same pace so that the starter could let go.

'And their under starter's orders!' came the announcement from the tannoy.

And with that, the tape was released.

Zinee rose to the occasion. He knew this game, ping went the tape, off you went. Before Gill had time to ask him, the horse was galloping.

In a short race it was all push from the beginning, no pacing needed for the six furlong dash.

Gill, concentrating on keeping her weight up out of the stirrups and balanced so that she didn't interfere with Zinee's feet. The black horse's ears flicked back towards her and she said the magic word which had given Zinee his extraordinary burst of speed at home.

The horse responded. Without whip nor leg, Zinee engaged his fifth gear. Borne of their mutual trust, Gill's hours of training and working with the horse, it was partnership which saw the horse cross the finish line two lengths in front of the rest of the field, despite her additional weight.

Gill was crying by the time she reached the winner's enclosure. Ronnie had come in third and called his congratulations to her as they made their way back into the stands.

Her pride was overwhelming. She had thought he was too sensitive to ever perform, let alone perform like that.

She caught sight of Norah beaming beside the first place enclosure as Kelly trotted over. Together she and Kelly patted and cuddled, decorum forgotten, they were two girls delighted with a pony, for all their glee it could have been a gymkhana.

Gill posed for the photo which Norah had stepped forward to be in and heard the announcement, signalling that she could dismount.

As she dropped to the floor and immediately loosened Zinee's girth to make him more comfortable, noticing the horse had barely broken into a sweat, unable to keep her shaking hands away from his body, Norah threw an arm around her and pulled her in close.

'Alright, point proved. Change of heart. Exeter - you ride him.'

Gill slid the saddle from the horse's back and turned to Norah, expecting her to be joking.

'But for heaven's sake lose some weight!' Norah eyeballed Gill seriously for a second and then smiled before moving towards the official to receive her prize.

'Oh God.' Gill set the saddle on the ground by the rail and thought about sitting down herself.

'What?!' Kelly leaned over from where she was holding Zinee, who was stood rigid, transfixed by the bustle around him, but not disliking the attention.

'She said I have to ride him at Exeter!'

'Oh my!' Kelly shrieked, then noticed Gill's worried face, 'Do you not want to?'

'She said I have to lose some weight.'

Kelly clamped her hand over her mouth and giggled.

'No more chips for you!!'

'I am so glad you were here Kelly.'

Kelly handed the reins to Norah so that she could embrace Gill.

The photographer snapped a picture of Zinee and a beaming Norah which would end up on the cover of the Arabian Horse Herald. In the background of the picture, a trainer and her groom sobbed, their sadness at a time when they should have been celebrating immortalised.

Rosie's legs ached.

After an hour's manual labour helping Eddie out around the yard, she finally had to admit she had an appetite.

As she watched Red eating his chaff, she felt her mouth water.

Eddie appeared at the half door and leant over.

'Ok?'

'Starving.' Rosie said without turning around. She stood in close to her horse and put her arms over his back, leaning on the warm and perfect collection of bones and muscle. To her delight, he didn't shuffle away from her, simply allowed her to lean companionably on him.

'Glad to hear it.' Eddie beamed, 'We still have the pasture kept horses to check and feed, but we can pop in for a snack now?'

'Nope.' Rosie smoothed Red's back a final time before collecting up the licked clean feed bucket and trying not think about Kev's instruction not to feed the horse at all. 'Let's get it done.'

Eddie nodded and stepped back, opening the stable door for her.

'Do you have a paddock, something not too lush, we could turn Red out into?' Rosie asked as she rinsed the bucket out.

'I could shift some horses around so he could go out on his own for a few hours?'

'Yes please. Movement is important for his feet.'

'Ah yes you are one of these barefooters aren't you!' Eddie chuckled.

'One of these barefooters?' Rosie narrowed her eyes at Eddie.

'No in all seriousness, some of the liveries here work their horses without shoes and they seem to do alright.'

'It's personal choice really.' Rosie nodded, not wanting to get into a big discussion about something she knew horse owner's had the capacity to endlessly argue about.

'You can tell me all about it later. See if you can persuade me not to tease you about being a horse hippy.'

'A horse hippy?'

'I saw your bridle, no bit, no shoes, you are one of these new age horse hippies aren't you.'

'New age horse hippy?' Rosie growled at Eddie, but she was laughing as well, and so was he. She followed him back across the yard towards the feed room. He stopped when the bell above the door of the cottage started to chime.

'Phone.' He explained when Rosie looked towards the house, trying to figure out where the sound was coming from.

'Could be the hospital?' Rosie's eye whites reflected the afternoon sun as fear swept over her.

'You answer it.' Eddie gestured towards the house and walked after her.

As Rosie opened the door and dashed across the kitchen to where the old phone nestled in it's cradle, she tried not to think at all.

To hope for the end seemed wrong, but what else was there?

Chapter Twenty-three

'Two wins, no injuries. A good day for Newmans!' Jules smiled from her window seat in the cab of the box.

She looked across at Kelly and Gill, who both surely heard her, but remained stony faced, concentrating on the motorway.

She decided to check her phone and as she reached into her pocket, she elbowed Kelly and apologised. Kelly raised half a smile but did not speak. It was going to be a long journey.

She had a text from James, and one from Rosie. James asked how the race day had gone and said his first Saturday of freedom had been strange but nice, and mentioned a flat which one of the partners had for rent, which would be cheaper and hopefully more homely than the hotel room he was slowly going crazy in.

She replied, enthusing about the flat and telling him about the yard's winners, but not commenting on the miserable atmosphere in the horsebox, because she was sat so close to Kelly her screen would surely have been visible had Kelly thought to look down.

She suddenly remembered the jockey who had visited them at the race stables after Cleo's race, while she and Kelly had been packing up and getting Zinee ready to load.

'Who was the jockey?' She spoke clearly and loudly, addressing Gill firmly enough to snap her out of her sombre daze.

'Ronnie. He is going to ride Cleo next Saturday.'

'Seem alright did he?' Jules pushed, not wanting to allow her companions to settle any deeper into their silent misery.

'I liked the way he rode in Zinee's race, and the fact he bothered to come and meet her is a good sign. Just have to see how he goes, but it would be nice to have another alternative to use when John is booked up.'

'Sounds sensible Gill.' Jules smiled.

'I need to concentrate on the road now.' Gill effectively ended the conversation as they approached the intersection where the motorways split and she would need to get into the lane signed South West. In truth she knew the junction well, but she felt it was insensitive to continue a conversation about the next race, when Kelly would not be there, in front of the groom.

Jules sighed inwardly and went back to concentrating on her phone.

As she opened the text from Rosie, which was brief but provided all the update that was needed, she felt sick for her absent friend.

Hospital have asked us to go in, not long now.

Some three hours later, Gill summoned the last of the strength in her tired arms to heave the steering wheel and make the final corner of journey. As the box swung around into Newmans, Gill noticed an unfamiliar car on the drive.

'Keith.' Jules said, explaining the vehicle before Gill asked, 'I told him we were nearly back and he wanted to head over and wait.'

'Kelly and I can unload and finish up, you go on in.' Gill stopped the box when she was level with the cottage, gesturing for Jules to get out. Jules hesitated, not wanting to leave the last of the work to the obviously tired women, but realised from Gill's face in the dim light as she opened the box door, that she wanted her very last hour with Kelly alone.

'Thanks ladies, see you in the morning Kelly?'

Kelly nodded, tight lipped and unsmiling, trying not to think about her final visit to the yard to say her goodbyes before a taxi came to take her to the station, where a train would take her to the airport, where a 9 hour flight would put inconceivable distance between her and the things she loved.

Jules shut the door and made her way through the darkness towards Keith's car. He leapt out when he saw her, proffering the pizza he had brought for them.

'Oh Good, I am starved.' Jules smiled as he leant forward and planted a warm kiss on her dry lips.

'Good day?'

'Mixed.'

Rosie waited for her phone to start up and sucked on the end of her rollie. Eddie had stopped in at a garage to buy fuel on the way to the hospital and against her own better judgement, she had bought herself a pouch of baccy, papers and a lighter.

After an hour of sitting by Selina's bed, she had departed to open the fresh tobacco and make herself a fag. She leant on the boundary wall of the hospital's grounds and decided that if there was ever a time to smoke a little, it was now. The corners of her mouth lifted as the thought that Selina would probably have approved crossed her mind.

On the phone, the doctor had said Selina had taken a turn for the worst and the end was likely to be imminent. She and Eddie had arrived bracing themselves for what might await them, but after an hour of the usual bedside vigil, Rosie was struggling to see what the difference was.

Aside from her breathing being slightly more laboured, and the build-up of fluid which they had told her to expect anyway, which was filling out Selina's face and hands, Rosie wasn't sure how they could have determined the end was close, the changes seemed so small, the unconsciousness just as void, not visibly more.

She supposed they must have seen it all before and they were the experts.

Rosie had replies from almost everyone she had sent the same text to earlier. Jules and Gill offering support, Val once again offering to drive up and be with Rosie, Jimmy's usual supportive words in capitals because he hadn't figured out how to change his text settings. The only person who hadn't replied was the one which she had been in two minds about adding to the list of recipients.

He had been trying to engage with her all week, why when she had finally included him directly in an update, and one which would probably be the penultimate piece of news, had he not bothered to reply?

She chided herself for feeling angry with her husband, what was the point? He had proven his absence of love for her already, what had she expected?

She took a final long drag on her rollie before stubbing it out and putting the end into the bin next to the wall.

She wished she'd had the chance to eat before the hospital's call diminished her appetite again. She had been a healthy weight before, not too big or too small, but over the last week she had felt and ignored the pangs in her stomach, to the extent that her body had no choice but to start using its reserves. As she walked, leaded footed, back to the ward, she tried to discretely tug at her bra, which had become too big and was moving around her slighter frame uncomfortably as a result. At least she would be lighter for Red, she supposed.

As she walked towards the ward entrance, she noticed one of the doctors who had been talking next to the sister's desk looking at her. As she reached the desk the doctor stepped forwards, her face full of sympathy.

This is it, thought Rosie.

'Hello.'

'Hi.'

'We ran some tests earlier, and they showed that the toxicity in Selina's blood has reached a level that her body will probably not be able to fight for more than a few more hours, which is why we called you in.'

Rosie nodded.

'We have given her something to make sure she doesn't wake up during this stage.'

Rosie nodded again. 'Thank you.' she was genuinely grateful, but unable to smile.

'You can spend as long with her as you like.'

'It's ok. I have said my goodbyes.'

Rosie thought about what she had said, as the doctor stood patiently in front of her. She hadn't actually said the word goodbye. But Selina had said everything she had wanted to say to Rosie, and in saying that she loved her too, Rosie had also said the most important thing. Anything else would have been overly dramatic and probably false anyway.

'You know she probably has no awareness now. No one would think any less of you if you wanted to leave and let this last stage happen without having to watch.'

'It's ok.' Rosie had already decided she would stay until the end, as pointless as it probably was, but she was grateful to have been given permission to leave.

The doctor nodded and smiled warmly again before turning back around to speak to her colleague, leaving Rosie to head back to the cubicle, for the last time.

'I can't take this in!' Jules shook her head. 'I am really

438

pleased for you.'

Keith moved closer to her on the sofa and took the wine glass from her and set it on the coffee table. He clasped her hand in his and took a deep breath.

'Come with me?'

'What?!'

'I'm serious – come with me! You can rent this place out, let Gill run the business, so it's all still here when we get back.'

'I can't...' Jules began, releasing her hand so that she could reach out to caress his stubbled cheek.

He leant back away from her touch and stopped her from saying any more.

'I'm serious. What an adventure we could have!'

Jules shook her head and laughed.

'You are mad!'

'I know.' He nodded vigorously but then leaned back towards her and took her hands again, 'come and be mad with me?'

Jules looked into eyes, she could see he meant it.

After they had polished off the pizza and settled in on the sofa to relax with their wine, Keith had told her his big news.

He had been offered a contract to help build a new hotel in Dubai. It was expected to take a year and he would need to leave in a few weeks. He had been so excited he could barely sit still when he described the project, which would allow him to work with a world class architect in an exotic location, and no doubt elevate his career to a new level.

Jules had listened and been genuinely pleased for him, a little sad that their relationship would have to end in it's infancy, but relieved that her feelings for James would no longer cause her guilt in addition to frustration. Then he had offered her what would certainly be a wonderful opportunity, and indeed an

439

adventure, and put her in the awkward position of having to turn him down.

'I'm really sorry Keith, I am honestly tempted and very flattered...'

'But?' Keith slumped backwards into the sofa and away from her, knowing what was coming.

'But I am due to be made partner at my firm next April and Kelly is leaving so I am going to be needed here as well.' Jules looked down at her hands and felt bad for pointing out the most obvious issue, which Keith appeared to have overlooked. 'And, you must know I would never leave Romeo.'

'Not even for a year?'

'Not even for a week, if I could help it.'

Keith nodded. He hadn't really expected her to say yes, but in the face of losing her altogether he had to try.

'I suppose I can't really ask you to wait for me either?'

'You never know. I was hardly inundated with offers before you came along.' Jules laughed, but Keith clutched at the straw she had offered.

'I could try and come back for the weekend some times?'

Jules smiled and took the sweet man's hand.

'You will be busy, and you will need to concentrate on the project. I think we have to leave this up to fate. If in a year's time we are both available and up for it, we pick up where we left off?'

Keith sighed, dejected, but nodded.

'Let's go.' She stood up, finishing the contents of her wine glass in one gulp, and reaching for Keith's hand.

'Where are we going?' He asked, standing up reluctantly. She led him into the hallway, turning to face him as they reached her bedroom door, batting her eyelids and letting go of his hand so that she could wind her arms around him and press her breasts seductively into his chest.

'I am going to make the most of you while I still have you.'

'Does Monty need a top up?' Kelly called from the tap outside the barn as Gill walked past with haynets on both shoulders.

'I'll check when I put these in.'

Kelly set another bucket filling just in case and carried Pop's fresh water in behind Gill.

They let themselves in to adjacent stables and set about completing the final jobs, before they turned their attention to unloading the box and preparing evening feeds for Zinee and Cleo.

'Kelly!!' Came a shriek from outside. It startled all of the horses and even made Gill jumped.

Kelly muttered something which sounded like a series of swear words before addressing her mother.

'Hello Mum. What do you want?' Kelly opened Pop's stable door and stood waiting for her mother to enter the barn.

'I can't do it to you Kelly!' The short woman broke into a hurried shuffle and dashed into the barn towards her daughter. The woman stood, tears streaming, ample chest heaving from her ungainly run.

Gill closed Pop's stable door behind a bewildered Kelly, nodding a hello and making for the barn door to start unloading the lorry.

'No Gill stay.' Kelly's mum clutched at Gill's arm to stop her.

'Gill is busy Mum. We still have a lot to do – what do you want? Can't it wait until I get home?' Kelly's voice buzzed in irritation, surprising Gill.

'I needed to speak to you now.' Nervously the woman

gestured towards the seating area and Kelly sighed loudly as they sat down.

'I can't do it to you. It's not fair.'

'What are you on about Mum?'

'You have to stay here. I can't make you come with me.'

Kelly rolled her eyes, the penny dropping. She had endured her mother's guilt ridden twittering for the last few days, she was sick of telling her mother it was ok. It was bad enough she had to be so selfless in going with her, without having to constantly reassure her, and now having one of her last moments with Gill interrupted.

'What do you want me to say Mum?' Kelly wished her mother would leave, she was polluting the barn.

'I don't want you to say anything. I want you to stay here and live the life you planned for yourself. I am going to go to Brisbane on my own.'

Kelly frowned. Her mother was unusually assertive.

'Ever since you were born, my life, it's been about you. I wanted to make up for your Dad not being there and I wanted to be a good Mum. But for the last few years you haven't really needed me. Have you?'

Kelly shook her head.

'Not like I did when I was small, no.'

'You let me mother you to make me feel better. I made my life about you because you depended on me, but it changed didn't it? I make my life about you now because I am too frightened to do anything else and you are grown up now Kelly, I can't keep living through you can I?'

Kelly sighed and shook her head, staring into her mother's wet eyes, feeling a mixture of pity and relief.

'Gillian. Will you take care of my baby?'

Gill looked at the woman, not knowing what to say.

Kelly took care of her more aptly. She sensed Kelly stiffen in anticipation of her response and set aside the fears which flashed though her head, knowing she had to repay Kelly for her years of dedication by agreeing to this comparatively small request.

'I love her very much Mrs Bowham. I want the best for Kelly, and if you both decide that means she stays here, I will do my best to look out for her and be here if she needs me.'

Gratitude shone from Mrs Bowham's eyes.

Kelly cried hysterical tears of relief, sliding from the shiny plastic of the chair and bumping down onto the cold concrete of the barn floor, where she splayed her fingers and pressed her palms against the reality of the ground beneath her.

'Now then,' Mrs Bowham waited until Kelly had regained her composure a little, 'I got this advert off the noticeboard in the village. Two girls a bit older than you looking for a house mate to take a room. I called them this afternoon and you can go and meet them tomorrow.'

'But what about the flat? Can't I stay there?' Kelly snivelled, not really caring where she lived.

'I have already given the landlord our notice and I think it would be better if you lived with people your own age.'

'She could live here?' Gill offered, throwing another option into the mix, but Kelly's mother was adamant and shook her head firmly, causing her jowly chin to wobble.

'You need to have a bit more of a life Kelly. You are always either at college, or here or with me. I want you to make the most of being young.'

Kelly looked unsure, slightly nervous at the prospect of living with strangers, until her mother delivered the clincher.

'The one I spoke to said the other one rides, loans a horse at Folklands.'

Kelly laughed through her tears, elation took her breath

away, she just went on holding onto the floor of the barn, gazing at her mother with a new found pride.

'I'll miss you.'

'I'll miss you too. But you can visit, and I'll visit you, and I know that you will be fine.'

'What about you?'

'I'll be fine too. I need to stand up and be counted again.'

Gill, who had been struggling to comprehend that it was actually happening, that her Kelly was actually staying, decided that composure was not a necessary evil at that moment.

She got down on the floor beside the groom and wrapped her arms around the girl.

'I cannot even begin to describe how happy I feel right now.' She said into Kelly's ear as she clung to her so tightly.

'Makes two of us boss.'

'That's it then.'

Rosie stared through the windscreen of Eddie's old estate car and wondered how she was supposed to feel. She was sure it wasn't nothing. The numbness she had felt during the worst part of her post-natal depression had at least felt like an escape.

Her mother was dead, she wanted to feel something. And yet, since they had told her Selina had slipped away, while she and Eddie had dozed beside her unaware anything had changed, she couldn't muster even a solitary tear. It couldn't be shock – surely.

Eddie sat beside her in the driver's seat. They would have to come back in the morning for Rosie to collect the medical certificate which she would have to take to the Registrar of Birth's Deaths and Marriages. Then there would be a funeral to arrange. Then there would be nothing. No more Selina, and no more Rosie, because she would have no reason to come back. His sadness was selfish, but logical.

'I am so sorry Rosie.' Eddie twisted in his seat to face her and reached out to rub her arm.

'I wish I could cry.'

'There is no right way to feel sweetheart.'

Rosie nodded. She reached into her pocket and rolled a cigarette for herself, handing the pouch to Eddie who took it and made one for himself.

'Can we just sit here for a bit?'

'Of course.'

'I know she is gone, I didn't want to sit by her body. But it feels weird to just drive away.'

'I get it. As long as you need.'

They exhaled in unison. Eddie wound down his window to let some of the smoke out.

'Hope they don't tell us off, not supposed to smoke in the grounds.'

'I think it's acceptable in the circumstances.' Eddie took her hand and gave it a squeeze.

The steady drizzle outside made the air inside the car condense.

'Thank you.' Rosie squeezed his hand back before sliding hers away, implying that was enough.

'For what?'

'Everything. You don't know me at all and yet you have been so lovely, putting us up, coming with me...'

'I know it probably sounds morbid, given the circumstances, but it really has been my pleasure.' Eddie started to chuckle at his own statement but stopped, given how inappropriate the words themselves already were, 'Of course I would rather have had the opportunity to spend time with you under different circumstances, I am just glad I was able to be here

445

for you.'

'Well you were.'

The drizzle progressed to rain and Eddie had to wind his window up. A car pulled in to the visitors parking area. It was two a.m. They had been the only ones left.

'Bet that's bloody security come to tell us off for smoking.'

The car stopped in a space opposite them.

'No, don't think that's staff. Must be some other poor sod called in with bad news.'

'Or good. Could be a birth.'

As Eddie spoke, Rosie leaned forward suddenly, peering through the windscreen intently. As the occupant of the car started to get out, she flung her door open.

'Rosie?' Eddie called but she was running through the rain.

As arms wrapped around her and she collapsed into the chest of the man she had just a few hours before written off, the numbness around her evaporated and was replaced by flooding tears.

'You came? How did you know?'

'You,' Matt cupped her face and pressed his nose against hers, staring into her eyes with such proximity she couldn't focus on him, 'are everything to me.'

Jules groaned as she rolled over and reached across the sleeping man beside her to right the clock on the bedside table. Eight a.m.

Keith barely stirred as she slipped from the bed, intending on coffee and a nice gentle reintroduction to consciousness.

As she set the machine going she smiled. Keith had been more passionate than on previous occasions, perhaps because their time together now had a deadline, and had left her completely satisfied. She hoped it was something they could repeat during his remaining time left in the UK. Now that he couldn't put pressure on her to make the relationship more serious, she could simply enjoy him for what he was, a nice man, who was rather well endowed.

A sudden banging on the kitchen window behind her almost made her duck. She turned around to see Gill jumping up and down and punching the air. Jules scurried to the kitchen door and flung it open.

'Have you won the lottery?!'

'Nope. Better.'

'Better than the lottery..?'

'Kelly.'

'Kelly...' Jules had been about to say what, but the ear to ear grin on Gill answered the question, 'Not going?'

'Staying. STAYING!' Gill whooped and continued to jump up and down on the spot until Jules invited her in for a coffee and to hear the full story.

Gill left Jules' still giggling, because a sheepish Keith had appeared in the hall way, desperate for breakfast but not wanting to interrupt. As she walked back through to her side, intending to have brunch with George before he left for the restaurant, she noticed her phone was flashing where she had left it on the kitchen table.

Her smile faded when she read the message from Rosie, sent in the early hours of the morning.

Her reply, fuelled by a desire to make her friend feel better, and the residual elation due to the fact that Kelly was staying, contained a decision which would, although rushed, over time galvanise, and feel completely right.

I want to give you Teddy. Amber coming home safe and well was my special gift. As soon as he is weaned, I want Teddy to be yours.

'Until Wednesday?'

'See you then.' Jules kissed Keith goodbye and watched him get into his car.

As she waved him off, smiling at the thought of repeating the evening in a few days, and at the prospect of riding Romeo out with Gill and Monty. She was delighted about Kelly, she should have been bursting with joy. She wished the inevitable thoughts of James would decrease in their persistence. He was never gone from her mind for long.

Even when she thought she had successfully extradited him, he found his way in, running concurrent with her conscious thought, always part of her. All her triumphs in carrying on regardless, in enjoying a night with Keith, were empty, because he was so firmly engrained, that ignoring his existence simply did not work. If this was indeed love, it was the kind of love she had always dreamed of. Rather typically, when she had at last found something so powerful and instinctive, she had managed to find it with someone who she couldn't have. She wondered if it was, in fact, her destiny to be alone. Were all the failed relationships, the tendency to go for people it was clearly never actually going to work with all just hints of the bigger plan for her, which was that she was heading for eternal spinsterdom?

Still though, despite her depressing predictions about her capacity for relationships, James clung on, managed to force a smile from cold lips and a stir from cold hips. It was either, she decided, because in fact they were destined for one another, or because fate was being cruel to her. Perhaps it was just because, beyond the attraction which had grown between them, he was an old and true friend and it was the light of that connection she was mistaking for more?

In any event, he had bigger things to worry about, and she could do nothing beyond be supportive and passive. He had a stony road ahead of him, now that he had made the all important leap, and he needed her friendship more than ever. She had to steel herself to be strong, knowing that in the insecurity which followed the break up with Lisa he would be naturally inclined to try and accelerate his connection to her. She may yet have to fend him off again despite her own feelings. She had such a strong sense of how the aftermath of an ended relationship could skew judgement and knew, better than most, that the heart needed time to heal to avoid the next relationship being doomed from the start.

Breakups changed a person, you became a new version of yourself to cope with your new life, and sometimes you were better, and sometimes you were just broken for a while. Sometimes the people you thought held possibilities for your future were seen in a different light, after the metamorphosis.

She risked losing him altogether, it was a risk she could mitigate. She could not be a stepping stone. She had used others in the same way herself, only realising in hindsight how transparent she had been in needing a crutch to help her through the loneliness. She had done it with the vet she had started seeing after Tristan.

But, for all her sensible boundary placing, her understanding of how love could screw you over, James remained on her mind more than he was absent.

She wished she didn't find herself daydreaming about him, about what it would be like if they were together. Her imagination would slip into gear, slowly creating a fantasy world that she found herself in, whenever her conscious thought patterns were not demanding her full attention. Watching telly, walking along the high street. Anything autonomous seemed to lead to her to James. The James that lived in her mind had no wife, no complex entanglement, no children, no sorrow and no wounds which would turn inevitably to scars, awaiting him on the emotional horizon. He was just hers, and she his, and they laughed, and they ate donuts, and they shopped, and they walked Ziggy, sometimes she even taught him to ride. Whatever she was doing it seemed, an alternative version where he was her significant other, was waiting to play out in her head, if it saw the chance to occupy her.

Love was indeed akin to madness.

It was late afternoon by the time Rosie woke up. The vigil at the hospital now over, the trauma of the night before, her body's natural instinct had taken over and kept her away from thought for as long as it could.

As she stirred, she felt misplaced, for a second she didn't recognise Eddie's bedroom.

'Morning darling.' The warm reassurance of her husband's voice made her feel safe again.

She rolled over to see him sat up in the bed, where he had been patiently waiting for her to wake up.

He slid his arm around her and pulled her in, encouraging her to lay her head on his chest.

'How's Eve?'

'Fine. It's you I am worried about.'

'It's us I am worried about.'

'Look Rosie,' Matt caressed her head and pulled her in tighter, ' we really don't need to talk about anything. Moving, not moving, Eve, I just want to be here for you.'

Before Rosie had a chance to object, to tell him that the

450

uncertainty was destroying her and losing her mother had only made her feel more disjointed, there was a knock at the bedroom door.

The door handle turned a fraction, and then stopped. Matt got out of the bed and went to open it.

'Ah cheers Chap, not enough hands.' Eddie walked in with a precariously full tray and set it on the bedside table before sighing in relief at not having lost the contents.

The tray had mugs of coffee, sandwiches and slices of cake crammed onto it.

Rosie smiled in spite of herself. It was really very sweet.

'Thought you could do with something to eat. I put Red in the paddock like we talked about.'

'Bless you.' She smiled in thanks and made Eddie blush.

'I'll leave you to it.' Eddie retreated and closed the door behind him.

Matt looked across at Rosie who was eyeing up the tray.

'I'm quite hungry.'

'You look hungry.' Matt's hand ran disapprovingly down her bony arm.

'It didn't feel right to eat somehow, when she was lying there in that bed, not eating, not really doing anything.'

'I wish I had come sooner. You weren't replying to my texts and I didn't think you wanted to see me.'

'Let's not get into it now, I'll lose my appetite.'

Matt nodded and removed the mugs from the tray, so that he could set it on the bed between them.

As she tucked into a sandwich and chewed rapidly, savouring the sustenance at last, Matt couldn't take his eyes off her gaunt little face.

'I love you.'

'Stop it. Let me eat!' Rosie wailed, too close to tears to

stop them.

'I'm sorry, I don't mean to upset you, I just can't believe I have been so stupid.'

'We both have. And I have a plan. But before we talk I need to get some food inside me.'

'I'm sorry. Eat, I do love you though.'

'I love you too. Now shut up.'

Matt nodded, couldn't help but smile. In the wake of such tragedy, completely unexpectedly, she sounded like herself again, the woman he loved so much was there behind the dark eyes and hollow cheeks. And, she still loved him. He was convinced and re-born in that moment; nothing else mattered.

'How's work?' she said after the third sandwich. As the food started to hit her shrunken stomach, she felt full almost immediately and wished she had left room for some of the thickly iced carrot cake which Eddie had carefully cut into manageable pieces. She decided to have a little rest and promised herself a piece as soon as she could manage it.

'Not brilliant really.' Matt shook his head and rolled his eyes. After all his talk of the golden job, he was, even after everything that had happened, reluctant to admit it. 'Someone in my team left last week and the powers that be, in their wisdom, decided not to replace her, so it's only going to get worse. A lot of my job is trying to get things done, which could be straightforward, but because of change resistance and the fact nobody wants to take ownership of anything, are like wading through tar half the time. They could be so much more productive if they actually utilised the technology available. I like the people in my team, but beyond them I hit brick walls so frequently, the whole project is starting to just be a massive headache...' Matt sighed, shaking his head in obvious frustration.

Rosie tried not to get excited. The smugness that might have been there a week ago, the self-righteous response that might have led to yet another pointless argument, seemed so silly now in the aftermath of all they had been through.

Her excitement remained though, because to use her mother's plan, and act upon her wishes, might just fall into place. What better tribute to the woman who had only really made sense to Rosie in the last six months, than to absorb her wisdom, and stop waiting for things to come right, and mend her life. No knight in shining armour would gallop to her door, it was she and only she who could weave the foundations again.

Nonetheless, she couldn't help but feel guilty as she prepared to say the words, because a respectful time could hardly have been said to have passed.

'Get over yourself you stupid child, since when did respect matter to me?'

Selina's voice filled her head, telling her to get on with it.

'I'm glad.' She said.

'You are glad I am stressed and struggling?'

'I'm glad you are questioning it.'

Matt turned his body to face hers, awkwardly folding his legs beneath him so that he could remain on the bed with her whilst looking at her face.

'Selina wants, or I guess I should say wanted, me to sell her house. As quickly as possible, and use the money to make sure we will be ok.'

'She's leaving the house to you?'

'Yes.' Rosie smiled grimly, but again Selina was there,

'Spit it out you procrastinating fool.'

'Wow.'

'I want us to use the money to live on while you start your own business.'

453

Matt started to shake his head, eyes wide, unable to conceive of no monthly pay packet arriving on schedule.

'You have always said you would like to provide a complete IT package to smaller businesses whose productivity could be doubled with proper use of a network and software which is right for them. I don't just let you waffle on, I have been listening to you all these years, how frustrated you get and how differently you would do it. So here is your opportunity, your words and ideas in motion, instead of battling against management - put yourself out there with the support of this cushion, which Mum has given us, and have something which is yours.'

'But Selina...' Matt's mind was racing and unable to stop, but only at the prospect of an unobtainable dream, not because he thought it could actually happen, 'God knows your Mum made you suffer over the years, shouldn't this money be for you, to do something you really want with? You can't just use it to fund me – it seems so wrong?'

'Quite the opposite, it's completely selfish.'

'I don't understand what you mean? Maybe we need to get the funeral sorted, get back home and see how you feel in a couple of weeks, this is all so soon - you only lost her last night?'

'Yes, and one of the last things she said to me was, "don't mope about wasting time".'

Matt shook his head again, concerned about whether he should actually allow the conversation to happen, was his wife even thinking straight this soon?

'It's a selfish plan because, even though I would be giving the money to you, I get everything I want. You move home, you are based at home, you can help out with Eve when you are around, even if it's just being there while she sleeps so I can ride. No more long lonely weeks, no more feeling overwhelmed. I can

454

properly embrace my new life, and Eve, if I have you beside me. I think that's what's been missing all along. I can help out, invoices, marketing, we could be a partnership again.

'We don't work apart, we proved that. I want you back, the real you, but not to just be my rock, to have something you can take hold of and work hard at, knowing the rewards you reap are for us and Eve, not to further someone else's company.'

'I can't quite believe this. You are making it sound very easy!' Matt's eyebrows remained up, but his eyes beneath them told her everything she needed to know. He was, if still slightly terrified about his own ability, sold. Rosie's faith elevated him. It was a solution where one had been depressingly absent, and although it could be hard work, it was worth trying, now or never.

'It won't be easy, I do know that. Being self-employed is going to have its own drawbacks. But I don't see any other time in our lives when we will be presented with the opportunity to have a go? I am due back at work in January, I will only be part time, but at least it's a steady income and depending on what her house sells at, we can probably reduce our mortgage too.' Rosie finished her speech and waited, everything she needed could be at her door with a yes.

'When on earth, with everything that has gone on, have you had time to think about all this?' His admiration for her flooded through him. As much as he would hate to admit it, he needed her to be this way, to lead on the big decisions, to pull them forwards. When she had been lost and wallowing, his attempt at taking the reins had been clumsy and heavy handed. She needed his partnership and presence, he needed her natural arrogance free leadership, much in the same way Red did.

'I guess my mind must have been doing things without my knowledge. I just felt so numb and sad, but the real me was still in there. Losing Mum made me realise how short life is and her usual bulldozer approach, strangely, has given me strength. All my life I hated her for how opinionated and judgemental she was, in spite of all her own flaws, but she picked her own path, did only what she wanted to do and maybe, in a twisted kind of way given that it killed her, I needed to take a leaf out of her book. The turning point was probably having it pointed out to me how Red felt about my self-hatred, he was losing his faith in me.'

'As always, it all boils down to the horse?' Matt mocked her, but the intent was not recrimination, just further proof that she was her again, and he was, as a result, finding himself.

'Would you expect anything different? I think I was feeling that I couldn't have both, that embracing Eve was choosing her over Harry and then Red. But in truth I need you all equally, in different ways. Red to keep me sane, Eve to be a better person for, and you to be my partner.'

'You didn't really get chance to grieve for Harry did you?' Matt shook his head, in hindsight feeling he could have prevented so much of what had happened if he hadn't allowed his attention to first time fatherhood to become so exclusive.

'Funnily enough, Eddie kind of helped with that.'

'Lost your Mum, but found a second Dad?'

'Let's not go too far, it's still very early days.'

Matt nodded, respectful again, allowing his regret to darken him.

She slid her legs from the covers and stood up, stretching, and reaching for her jeans.

'I have to register the death and visit some funeral people in the morning. Not sure I will be feeling quite as strong for that. Will you take tomorrow off and come with me?'

'I already booked the week off so I can be around for

456

you. You have been through so much Rosie, I am so sorry I was so crap.'

Rosie pulled on her top and then climbed back onto the bed, kneeling in front of him. She ran her fingers through his hair and relished how good it was to love him again. It seemed so wrong to be energised and excited by the future, so soon after Selina's death, when she ought to have been mourning.

Selina, as always, had the last word,

'Mourning is for dumbasses, get on with it child.'

'Good. After that, let's go home, I miss my daughter.'

Chapter Twenty-four

'For god's sake Gill would you put the horse down and get in the car?!'

The solicitor bellowed at her friend, who had seen a window of opportunity in Jules having to dash back to the house for her car keys, and run up to Amber and Teddy's field to cuddle her mare.

'Coming!' She called in a singsong voice but carried on talking to the foal. 'We are going to visit your new human Mummy today, so I want a nice picture of you to show her.'

She stepped backwards away from the foal and tried to snap a photo of him with the camera on her mobile, but Teddy was too quick to follow her and get his mouth around the device, so she ended up with his nostril, one eye and half an ear. 'Well, I suppose Rosie better have an idea what she is in for, hey Mr Mouthy?' She saved the picture and chuckled, deciding not to try for a better one.

'Gill – I might as well have gone to work at this rate!' George shouted and she planted a final kiss on Teddy's nose, causing him to follow her, trying to nip her back.

They were already so late. They hadn't got back from Newbury until after midnight the night before, and they had all overslept.

It wasn't like Rosie would mind though, what was an hour between friends?

When she had invited Gill and Jules over they had both been determined to make it to their friend's cottage, knowing she had to head back to Kent for Selina's funeral in a few days, despite the fact that they knew in advance they would be knackered from racing. Then George had said he would take the Sunday off to come with them, which had reminded Jules she had promised James he could bring the children to Newmans for their Daddy day. At Rosie's agreement she had re-directed him to Orchard Cottage, and now instead of a girlie gathering, they had a bit of a do on their hands.

'Should we have offered to bring food?' Gill asked as she trotted towards the car, and finally they could set off.

'Definitely not!' Jules laughed, 'Rosie texted me this morning to say Crystal's gone way over the top – think we are in for quite a feast!'

Jules started the car and fastened her seatbelt, flushing as she turned around to reverse out of her space, because Gill and George were already snogging on the back seat.

'Will you please behave or one of you will have to sit in the front?'

As the pair giggled, she couldn't help laughing herself. With two winners, a second and a fourth, Newmans & Rogers Arabian Racehorse training had had a bloody good outing the day before, and now, albeit under the heading of friendship, she was going to get to spend time with James and introduce him to her friends.

She tried not to think about the connotations, the ache she felt for him all the time, and just enjoy getting to spend time with someone she cared about. She was terrified about meeting Ben and Erin. She had no experience, what were you supposed to say to a child?

As she settled the car into 5th gear and cruised along the A30 towards Rosie's, she cursed herself for her inability to make her brain step in line with her convictions. It was Keith's last day in the UK. She should have been taking him along to an afternoon with her friends. Instead she had taken Friday off work to say goodbye to him and satisfied her desire to see James as well.

'Shit!' Gill suddenly exclaimed from the back, 'Come off here!' Gill frantically pointed to the exit which they were coming upon rapidly.

'What??!' Jules flustered and managed to brake enough to make the exit without the car behind her getting too miffed.

'We forgot to pick up Kelly!!!'

'Shit.'

'Oh you should have seen Red when I unloaded him – dragged me into the field and did a lap of honour, just to check everything was as he left it, then came thundering back to the gate like 'right, where's my Shetland?', so my plan to keep him alone for a bit was foiled before it really started!'

'Where was his Shetland?!' Jules folded her legs up underneath her, settling in to the cushions which Crystal had scattered around the garden and on the benches, waiting for Rosie to continue.

'Well I had to go and see Sue didn't I? The things we do for our horses. She was not very happy, understandably, about the way I had left Peat back at hers. But, our conversation was being drowned out by Peat who was calling to me over the stable door. In the end she said, "well the bloody pony has clearly forgiven you for dumping him so I suppose I better had". To cut a long story short I bought him!'

'You bought a miniature Shetland?!' Jules giggled, and Gill finally managed to retrieve the picture she had taken of Teddy and displayed it on the screen of her phone.

'And this was your third horse this morning!' Gill handed the phone to Rosie, who expected some cutesy shot of

Teddy looking gorgeous and was met with an obvious blooper. She cackled and then shook her head.

'Between Peat and Teddy no object will remain without teeth marks. I can't believe I am going to have three horses.'

'Well the nice thing is, by the time Teddy is old enough for you to back, you will have had a nice long run with Red to concentrate on riding him and developing him, and by then Eve will be at school and...'

Gill noticed both her friends were raising their eyebrows. 'What?'

'You have really thought this through then, Rosie's life?' Jules mocked her friend, she would never fail to find it confounding that Gill was organisation personified when it came to horses, yet still couldn't organise herself or her accounts or even her wardrobe.

'Well yes, but I gave it a lot of thought, after I offered Teddy, it isn't just a whim you know?' Gill eyed Rosie, conveying her point and challenging Rosie to put up another argument.

'Let's not go there, in three months, he will be coming.' Rosie confirmed her intention to concede. Over the past week, Gill and Rosie had had a ridiculously long conversation via text, where Rosie kept trying to give Gill the opportunity to take back her amazing offer, and Gill had become more and more insistent that she was doing it and that was that.

'Sometimes things just feel right, and this does.' Gill raised her wine glass and Rosie leaned forward to clink with her.

'It really does.' Rosie smiled as she gazed around her. Matt and George were nursing beers and standing over the barbeque, men making fire.

Crystal and Jimmy were sat at the picnic table with Kelly, talking to her about her new housemates, making sure she didn't miss her mum too much, and generally providing a mature angle on Kelly's new life, making the girl feel secure and listened to, as was their combined nature. Blue skies above the cottage had defied the weather forecast, allowing their little gathering to be al fresco.

Eve slept in her push chair beside Crystal, delivering her usual and completely blissful ability to remain quiet when it was appropriate.

Rosie didn't want to wake her prematurely, but felt a wonderful anticipation, knowing that soon her little blue eyes would open, and cuddles would be in order.

When she and Matt had arrived home in convoy with Red, the grim tasks in Kent completed, Rosie had barely been able to contain her nerves at the prospect of seeing her daughter.

She had missed her so much, but felt so apprehensive, what if her heart had grown fonder with absence, but with proximity, the familiar emotional distance would resume?

After she had unloaded Red, and promised him she would fetch him Peat or another companion one way or another by the end of the day, she had crept into the house, wanting to save greeting Jimmy and Crystal until she had had the chance to see Eve. Luckily Matt was in the kitchen with them, filling them in on the events in Kent- which had allowed her to slip in through the front door and head to the nursery, where she found Eve having her afternoon nap.

Immediately she saw the change in Eve. Almost three weeks away and the difference was immeasurable to Rosie, the baby was bigger, her face more recognisable somehow, as though her development was reaching the stage where she was actually starting to resemble her parents.

As Eve opened her eyes and stared about her, as though focusing, Rosie saw herself.

She saw Selina. Saw Eddie.

She picked her child up and drew her in for the best cuddle she had ever had. Eve's little hands clung to Rosie's t-shirt, her face nestling into the crook of Rosie's neck.

Although Eve was probably just still sleepy, Rosie couldn't help but feel that her daughter was hugging her back.

'Let's go and find Daddy.' She whispered to her child, feeling a pride and a warmth which she had not felt before. Eve was not simply a burden, a limpet who represented the end of freedom, she was a part of Rosie, a part of their family. In time she would become a person in her own right, a voice to be counted, a future to unravel.

'Oh thank god...' Jimmy's relief was tangible. As Rosie walked in to the kitchen, carrying Eve so naturally, her head cocked so that her cheek could press gently on the soft downy crown of her baby, Jimmy could see everything was going to be better. She might still have ups and downs, things may yet be hard, parenthood was no picnic, as he knew, but he could see the Rosie in Rosie's eyes.

Matt moved towards his wife to kiss her and then kiss his daughter, but he didn't take Eve from her. None of them did, in fact, Rosie didn't put the baby down until she had to head up the lane to visit Sue.

'I'm so sorry about your Mum Rosie.' Crystal waited for Matt to move aside so that she could put her arms around both Rosie and Eve and hold her stepdaughter and grandchild.

Rosie nodded through tears and leaned in towards Crystal, signifying the embrace was welcome, allowing her emotions to spill out in the safety of her kitchen, surrounded by those she loved, and those to whom she had a lot of making up to do.

'*Stop blubbing, you silly arse.*'

'So, the funeral is Tuesday?' Jules hadn't wanted to spoil the atmosphere, her two favourite people either side of her, but having glanced at her watch she knew James and his children would be arriving soon and it wouldn't have felt natural not to ask, not to encourage Rosie to talk about her loss, while it was just the three of them.

'Yep. We are all going. Jimmy wanted to be there. We aren't having a wake, not even really sure who might turn up, it might just be us. In the afternoon I am taking Eve to meet Eddie, and Jimmy is going to the house to meet an estate agent, it's an old colleague from his real estate days.'

'Is Eddie not going to the funeral?' Gill was confused.

'No. I did ask him, but he said it would make things weird for Jimmy. Which is true. Maybe one day they will meet but it doesn't need to be now. Look, I know what he did was awful, and I wouldn't expect you guys to understand, especially given it was your horses, but he has dedicated himself to being a good person and let's face it, life is too short, if I don't let him meet Eve now I might regret it.'

'You don't have to explain yourself Rosie.' Gill smiled warmly, 'You are one of the best judges of character I know, if you think he deserves to be part of your life he does. Simple as.'

'Your faith in me is, if a little naïve, very touching.' Rosie glanced at Jules to make sure she was ok with it too, but her friend was looking at her watch again and trying to listen in case she could hear a car approach.

'Are you alright Jules?' Rosie enquired, hoping her obvious discomfort was not to do with Eddie.

'Tell Rosie the truth.' Gill demanded, eyeing Jules with a furrowed brow.

'What truth?' Rosie demanded to know what was going

on.

'Oh, for heaven's sake!' Jules rolled her eyes and screwed her hands together in frustration, part of her wishing not everything always had to be shared between them, part of her grateful that it did.

'This friend she has coming over this afternoon, the one she works with and is helping through his divorce?' Gill said the words for Jules, fed up with waiting.

'Yes?' Rosie's eyes twinkled making Jules sink further into her cushion, covering her eyes with her hands waiting for the inevitable.

'He's the one she's in love with.' Gill delivered the punchline and Rosie laughed, but then Jules squealed from behind her hands and Rosie shuffled up the bench to put her arms around her friend.

'Oh dear Juliette.'

'I can't even bloody tell him, keep having to fend him off because he is going through so much crap and I don't want to be his rebound fling. It's...properly shit!'

'Doing the right thing is never easy.' Rosie said comfortingly, drawing Jules in so that her friend could relax against Rosie's body.

'Stop mothering her!' Gill laughed as Jules surrendered into her friend's embrace and pouted up at Gill, 'I keep telling her not to be so ridiculous and there you are comforting her!'

'Love is not ridiculous. It's the point of life.' Rosie glanced over at Eve and Gill followed her gaze towards the pushchair, 'Sometimes, it just takes a little more time.'

'Oh Dear!' Crystal called to Rosie grinning, and Rosie laughed and knew it was her cue. She let Jules right herself and got up to collect her grizzling daughter, grateful Crystal had noticed her waking up before the full blown wail ensued.

As she reached into the pushchair and picked her daughter up, intending to take her inside, Crystal stood.

'I'll go and get her bottle, take her back over with you and sit with your friends?'

Rosie smiled and thanked Crystal, knowing how lucky she was.

Rosie sat with her daughter on her lap, and carried on quizzing Jules about James, in between blowing raspberries, which were making Eve cackle.

Crystal brought the milk at just the right time, when Eve's hunger threatened to replace her giggles with tears.

'Oh god!' Jules heard James' car coming down the lane and started to panic, she was delighted, but the prospect of meeting his children filled her with dread.

'Would you like Rosie to blow a raspberry on your neck?' Gill teased, making Jules laugh in spite of the butterflies in her stomach.

'I'm really quite good at them!' Rosie smiled up at Jules, who stood up to meet the two small children she prayed wouldn't immediately see through her complete lack of child knowledge and hate her.

Jules looked at Rosie, her child so naturally cradled in her arms, Eve's hand on the bottle beside Rosie's, as though they were sharing the task of feeding her. If Rosie could overcome all she had endured, she could overcome her own nerves.

'Take them up to see Peat?' Rosie gestured with her head towards the field. Jules nodded gratefully, the prospect of being able to present an incredibly cute pony as part of her opening line, hitching her confidence up slightly. 'But keep them away from his mouth.'

As she walked through the garden gate and strolled along the lane, she caught sight of a flash of long red hair as Erin ran from the back of the car to the boot to help James get Ben's pushchair out.

'Juliette!' James saw her coming and announced her so that Erin could thunder along the lane towards the woman she had been hearing all about in the car, sandals slapping on the tarmac.

Erin reached Jules and stared up at her, as though assessing her, before turning back to her father and shouting,

'You were right Dad, she does look like a princess.'

'So...' Rosie shuffled closer to Gill.

'So.' Gill smiled at her friend.

'George ok now?'

Gill glanced over to her partner, who was surreptitiously turning the gas down on the barbeque when Matt's back was turned, not wanting to interrupt their bonding over beer session by giving him sausage cooking tips, but not wanting to stand by and watch everything burn either.

'The woman isn't going to return any of the money. But she has signed the settlement agreement and confirmed in writing she isn't going to pursue things. So, but for a hole in his savings and a lack of car, things are back on an even keel.'

'It's a shame about his car. But at least you can all relax now.'

'We have been having such a good season, I have been saving my share of the winnings percentages, I almost have enough to buy a Lexus for him.' Gill bit her lip, sharing her secret with Rosie.

'Gill, that is so sweet of you.'

'I have to put most of it in the kitty, but Jules and I agreed we could each have a bonus out of any extras the owners give us. I want to do something special for him, he is such a good

467

man.'

Rosie nodded. She looked over at Matt just in time to see him staring, perplexed, at the barbeque, before wanging the gas back up to full power. Jimmy, who had joined the masculine group, leaving Crystal and Kelly to deeper conversations, handed more beer to the younger men and the three of them stood surveying the garden as they drank in stoic silence.

'Here's to good men.'

Later, as sun started to descend and the air grew cooler, Rosie was warmed from the inside. She could still hear the laughter coming from the garden, as she walked up the field to say goodnight to Red and Peat. Eve was in her cot, exhausted from her afternoon of attention. The people she loved were still picking at the cakes Crystal had made, and her horse was dozing in front of his stable, waiting for her.

She topped up Peat's water, the grass had grown a little in his paddock during his absence and she smiled, thinking he wouldn't look quite as pissed off for a few days, until he had eaten it back to a length fit for a bowling green.

As she moved towards Red, his ears pricked and his nostrils fluttered in a quiet soft greeting. She felt tears of happiness prick her eyes.

She reached for his soft muzzle and stroked his whiskered chin, meeting her lips to his cheek before staring into his huge brown eye, knowing from his body language that he trusted her implicitly.

As she stood with Red, she gazed up at the sky and noticed the North Star was already claiming its place, sparkling above them, even though the sun had not quite set.

As she watched the star, she felt a strong sense that Harry was with them, he was beside her, within her and all around her. Although she would never stop missing him, he was part of her heart, because he had helped to design it. He had helped her grow up, he had shown her the way to care for something else more than herself, he had made her who she was. In returning to her responsibilities, in finding herself, she was honouring his memory again, so that she could feel nostalgic and grateful for him without guilt at last. His influence was in Red too, the way he was so calm and gentle, the things the older horse had taught him were engrained in his personality.

She thought about a time in the future when she would be able to tell Eve about Harry, to show her his pictures and describe him to her.

She would describe her grandmother too, the brashness, the almost vulgar arrogance that allowed the matriarch to be both right and wrong at the same time. It was a long way in the future, but Rosie no longer felt the need to wish for a fast forward.

In two days she would bury her mother, in two weeks Crystal and Jimmy would be moving into their house in the next village. Matt's notice period would end and he would come home for good. By the end of August, his business would be starting to take shape. By Christmas, her hair would be down past her shoulders again. There were hard times to come, life would test her to her limit yet, she had no doubt, but, at last, she was comfortable in her skin.

The future was infinite in its possibilities, good and bad, but she was at the helm again -ready for storms, but quietly confident they would be balanced by blue skies.

'We should have time for little hack tomorrow morning.' She spoke softly to her Red horse, no trace of apprehension in her voice.

She didn't hate her new life.

'That's more like it, child.'

Indigo Dreams Publishing
24 Forest Houses
Cookworthy Moor
Halwill
Beaworthy
Devon
EX21 5UU

www.indigodreams.co.uk